Also by Katherine Dunn

FICTION
Geek Love
Truck
Attic

NONFICTION
On Cussing
One Ring Circus: Dispatches from the World of Boxing
The Slice: Information with an Attitude

TOAD

TOAD

KATHERINE DUNN

Foreword by Molly Crabapple

MCD | FARRAR, STRAUS AND GIROUX | NEW YORK

MCD
Farrar, Straus and Giroux
120 Broadway, New York 10271

Frontispiece photograph by Bob Peterson, used with permission
by the Estate of Katherine Dunn.

Library of Congress Cataloging-in-Publication Data
Names: Dunn, Katherine, 1945–2016, author.
Title: Toad / Katherine Dunn ; introduction by Molly Crabapple.
Description: First Edition. | New York : MCD / Farrar, Straus
    and Giroux, 2022.
Identifiers: LCCN 2022023658 | ISBN 9780374602321 (hardcover)
Subjects: LCGFT: Novels.
Classification: LCC PS3554.U47 T63 2022 | DDC 813/.54—dc23
LC record available at https://lccn.loc.gov/2022023658

Designed by Janet Evans-Scanlon

Our books may be purchased in bulk for promotional, educational,
or business use. Please contact your local bookseller or the Macmillan
Corporate and Premium Sales Department at 1-800-221-7945,
extension 5442, or by email at MacmillanSpecialMarkets@macmillan.com.

www.mcdbooks.com • www.fsgbooks.com
Follow us on Twitter, Facebook, and Instagram at @mcdbooks

10 9 8 7 6 5 4 3 2 1

FOREWORD

Molly Crabapple

Sally Gunnar is a hermit—by choice. She lives on an ill-gotten pension in a godforsaken town. Occasional visitors aside, her main companions are the goldfish who swim inside an old pickle jug upon her lovingly appointed breakfast table. Who needs humans when you have memories? Ugly, sensuous, and scathing, Sally Gunnar hides within her domestic fortress, content to bake her bread and luxuriate in her regrets, until, one day, her sister-in-law mentions two names that "slit [her] neatly from skull to crotch, and leave two halves gaping bloodily at the fish."

Sam. Carlotta.

From those two names unspools *Toad*, Katherine Dunn's harrowing novel of lust and death set among the hippie burnouts of 1960s Portland, Oregon, where the drugs flow, the pretense flies, the delusion soars, and where, thanks to the counterculture, young women have choices . . . but all of them are bad. Dunn wrote *Toad* during the seventies, when she was a single mom slinging drinks at a dive bar so rough that once a patron tried to slit her throat.* It was her third novel, and she

---

* Aaron Mesh, Matthew Korfhage, and Beth Slovic, "Master of the Sucker-Punch Sentence: Katherine Dunn '69," Obituaries, *Reed Magazine*, September 2016.

wrote it during a deep depression. She never published it. Despair, said her son, Eli Dapolonia, was not her style.*

Her fourth novel was *Geek Love*. Published in 1989, it smashed the best-seller list, and made Dunn into a bona fide countercultural goddess.

Geek Love is the story of the Binewskis, a family of itinerant carny freaks. Over thirty years after its publication, it is a totem for outcasts—born and made—the world over. It is the novel most likely to be referenced in a tattoo, an illegal mural, a strip club dressing room, or the smokers' parking lot outside a home for troubled girls. In my own misspent youth, I memorized *Geek Love* the way British schoolboys memorized *The Odyssey*. I also wanted to find my fictional forebears. The Binewski parents, Al and Crystal Lil, produced each of their children with love, hallucinogens, and radioactive waste, and taught them to hold themselves haughtily apart from the straight world. I too held myself haughtily apart from the good blond children who liked to throw Coke bottles at my head. For weird kids like me, *Geek Love* was both a respite and a weapon.

For all the freaks that Al and Crystal Lil created, they had their failures—the six dead babies who floated in jars in a special section of their carnival called The Chute. Until recently, *Toad* held a similar place. It sat unread and unknown, while *Geek Love*, Katherine Dunn's most famous child, splashed its way across the world.

At first, *Toad* would not seem to have much in common with its flashy older sister. *Geek Love* is razzle-dazzle. It's a fan-dance book, a sequined-garter book, a honky-tonk-piano, platinum-blonde-biting-the-head-off-a-chicken type of book,

* Douglas Perry, "Unpublished Katherine Dunn Novel Will Arrive This Fall," *The Oregonian*, January 31, 2020.

that you could use as an inspiration for a burlesque act, and which, in fact, several women did.* *Toad*, meanwhile, is based in Katherine Dunn's life—its pyrotechnic prose all in service of the shit and grit of lived experience.

꘎ ꘎ ꘎

Katherine Dunn was born in 1945, in Garden City, Kansas. Her father ran off when she was two. Working as itinerant fruit pickers, her mother and stepfather took her west, until at last they settled in Tigard, a small town near Portland. In 2021, it seems like most famous American authors are vat-bred in pricey MFA programs, but Dunn had the sort of background so often appropriated by artists looking for cred. She grew up broke. According to an obituary published by *Reed Magazine*, "Katherine would joke she didn't have money for booze or drugs as a young person, so she would float in Tigard's Fanno Creek like Ophelia, hoping to catch a bug that would give her a high."† Her mother beat her with any object at hand, and once threw a screwdriver at her so hard it punctured her calf. At age seventeen, she left the family home forever. In Missouri, she was arrested for passing a bad check and served a brief sentence in the Jackson County Jail; the jail cell horrors formed the basis of her first novel, *Attic*.

Like fellow Portland poor girl Sally Gunnar, Katherine Dunn was obsessed with the city's prestigious Reed College; it is the main backdrop for the first part of *Toad*. After her time in jail,

---

* Chris Griffin, "'The Glass House, a Sideshow, Variety, and Burlesque Tribute to Geek Love' August 9th at The Bier Baron," Theater Arts, *DC Metro*, July 31, 2015.

† Mesh, Korfhage, and Slovic, "Master of the Sucker-Punch Sentence."

Dunn returned to Portland, where she made her living hustling pool. Like Sally, Dunn cadged food in the Reed cafeteria and stowed away to sleep in the Reed dormitory stairwells. Dunn got a full scholarship to Reed in 1965. Unlike Dunn, Sally is not a student; she merely waits tables, while failing to write a play. "I would not be young again, not a day younger," she knows. This writer feels her reproach.

After her dirt-poor youth, Reed College must have been a revelation. Reed's current tuition runs $60,620 a year, and even back then, it was flush with enough trust fund bohemians to earn it the unofficial motto "Communism. Atheism. Free Love."*
Toad's Sam Rosen is one of these students. He is an aimless, impressionable, rapaciously curious manic pixie dream boy, and though they never sleep together, he becomes Sally's great love. Quickly, she falls into his orbit. Dunn mines her experience to create the characters that people Sam and Sally's world. They are pompous gits, who "flung etymological witticisms at . . . the staff, the faculty of college, Plato, Wittgenstein, Goethe, and various other defuncts with whom the whole group gave the distinct impression of having shared many a crust and chortle." They gobble drugs, live in cat-shit-encrusted squalor, cook up foul batches of horsemeat. They idolize their teachers (Dunn may have modeled Sam's beloved calligraphy instructor on her own Reed professor Lloyd Reynolds). They concoct fantasies of wise, exotic indigenous ways of being, to distance themselves from the prosaic suburbs where the parents who pay their tuitions live . . . and where their own futures more realistically point.

Fantasy is a hell of a drug, as the Binewskis knew, and the

---

* Carol Yost, "Communism, Atheism, Free Love: How a T-shirt Was Born," *Reed Magazine*, September 2015.

hangover is a motherfucker. At a party at Sam's flophouse, Sally meets his dream girl, a swoony hippie chick named Carlotta. With her slender waist and thick black braids, Carlotta has all the beauty Sally lacks. She wears suede. She dances barefoot. "She was all high arches and soft pink heels. Her toes were rosy and clean. She bent a knee and swayed, lifted one foot at a right angle to the other, and gently, precisely, set her glowing toes down on a tight little roll of dog shit . . . She continued to sway her arms, although now she writhed and twisted as she scraped her toes through the grass."

What does beauty get a girl? Dog shit, and the obligation not to notice.

*, *, *,

Fascination with feminine beauty and ugliness unites *Toad* and *Geek Love*. Dunn herself was a lank-haired hottie in her youth, with a mouth made to caress sarcasm like a sweet. Yet in her work, the ugly girls get the best lines. Even more important, they live to say them. *Geek Love*'s lissome conjoined twins, Elly and Iphy, may be tattooed on the biceps of countless alternative models, but their fate in the novel is to be raped and impregnated at the behest of their sociopathic brother. Their beauty brings their destruction. Oly, their sister, might be a bald, humpbacked, albino dwarf, but she's also the one telling the story. Sally Gunnar is a toad next to Carlotta's hippie goddess. She conforms to no womanly ideals—traditional or countercultural. But she fucks and loves and mutilates (figuratively and literally) as often as she is mutilated. Carlotta and Sam crash into the consequences of their delusions. Sally sees so clearly it hurts.

"We can imagine that they—that amorphous systemic 'they'—won't know we're equal until they know we're dangerous. More important, we won't know it either," Dunn wrote in a 1995 *Vogue* essay on the return of the Bad Girl.* This is one of Dunn's most dangerous suggestions. Conventional femininity may seem at first like an uncomfortable little dress, into which neither Sally nor Oly can cram their bodies, but in fact it is something worse—poisoned like Medea's wedding gown, it will consume its wearer in the end.

Katherine Dunn dropped out of Reed College in 1967. She had fallen in love with a New York drifter named Dante Dapolonia, and campus life made her antsy. The two hit the road. After three years in Europe, Dunn returned to Portland, having given birth to a son, Eli, and written two novels. *Attic* and *Truck* came and went. Still poor, she ditched Dapolonia; his next notable achievement was a string of bank robberies in the early aughts. Now a single mother, she did what she needed to survive. She squeezed herself and her son into a tiny studio. She painted houses and wrapped candy on factory assembly lines and posed nude for life-drawing classes. She waited tables at a diner and manned the taps at a bar frequented by biker gangs. "She always handled herself well and without fear," Eli said. "She took knives from men twice her size, stepped in between men bent on shedding blood, and never came home with a scratch. She was confident and fearless, and they respected her."† During this period she wrote *Toad*. It is many things, but it is above all a working-class woman's story, through and through.

---

* Katherine Dunn, "Bad Girl," *Vogue*, June 1995.

† Douglas Perry, "The Rise of Katherine Dunn: How the Late Portland Author Survived Hard Times and Became a Literary Legend," *The Oregonian*, December 3, 2017.

FOREWORD

,, ,, ,,

In 1989 *Geek Love* was a finalist for the National Book Award. For decades, Dunn wrote a celebrated boxing column for Portland's *PDXS*, and even trained as a boxer. In 2009, a sixty-four-year-old Dunn fought off a purse snatcher thirty-nine years her junior. "It was a helter-skelter affair," Dunn told *Oregon Live*. "Getting a tetanus shot, it made me feel young again."*

From Ernest Hemingway to Szczepan Twardoch, writers have long been fans of boxing. Boxing destroys the mind-body duality, makes the physical world as present as a fist smashing into a nose. Katherine Dunn never avoided the body—its excretions, its filth and longing. She writes about shit and blood and pus. Her stories rip off scabs. They revel in the beauty of wounds. In *Toad*, Sally is undone because she refuses to stay in the place allotted to her by her ugliness, and instead allows herself to lust. "It was never the cold hot dogs that drove me, not the sight of the picturesque sands. It was the muscles of your thighs, the warmth of your armpits, the thump of your blood in my ear. It was flesh, not philosophy," she says, to every object of her desire.

Toad was written at the moment just before Dunn and Sally Gunnar's paths irreconcilably diverged. After finishing her manuscript, Dunn left Sally in her hermit's house, like a stillborn in a jar, and then swaggered out to write her masterpiece. Katherine Dunn died in 2016. In this book, Sally gets her resurrection.

---

* Perry, "The Rise of Katherine Dunn."

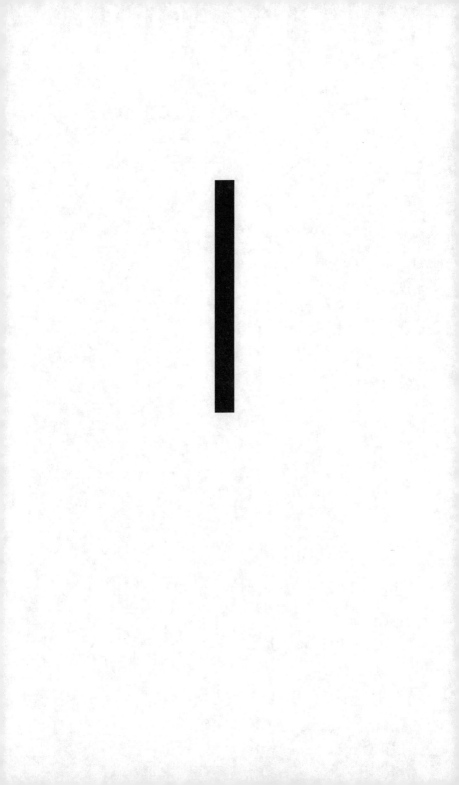

The goldfish, the pink chaise, the fly

I've been out in the kitchen watching the goldfish. They live in an old gallon pickle jug on the red breakfast table. There is a shaded lamp beside them that throws a soft yellow light over their movement. They dance. The light streams on their metallic bodies. I tap the glass sometimes to see them swerve and scutter into the weeds. They are stupid, of course, but still I imagine that they have built an intricate religion to account for me, for the unpredictability of the net that hauls them gasping into a dull saucepan and leaves them flicking nervously till they are poured back into the pickle jug, now miraculously free of slime. There may be an incantation to solicit food, a ritual to greet the lamp in the morning and the sudden darkness when I turn it off on my way to bed. It seems appropriate that I should be a godhead to goldfish. They have nothing to do but conjure reasons, and since the reasons are all outside of the jug what form could they take but religion? I am sure they are monotheistic. This may be my vanity, but the space between their eyes seems too narrow to accommodate more than one image. Inside the jug they are quite free. They turn and rise and sink to suit themselves. But when I feel like cleaning the bowl, out they come.

So I was sitting out there at the table watching the goldfish, waiting for my bread to rise, smoking, rubbing the furrows in my forehead with an index finger, when I remembered my old frying pan theory.

I was eleven probably, and had just been introduced to the idea of atoms and molecules. The illustrations in the elementary text struck me as identical to the schematics of the solar system. "The universe is infinite," someone had told me. I decided that the earth was a charged particle in the atom of the solar system and that our universe was a large, cast-iron skillet being heated by a giant for the purpose of cooking his supper. This giant's world was a particle in another universe comprising the skillet of a yet larger universe, and so on. I remember washing dishes, standing with my hands drooping into the steaming water and mulling over my theory. It was exciting. In fact, it made me nervous. I couldn't sleep. I asked my arithmetic teacher about the idea the next day. She listened and nodded and said it wasn't possible in a Euclidian geometry. I had no idea what that was. The frying pan theory went underground, became valuable to me, a mystique.

My acquaintance with physics went no further than that quick look at the picture on the page. It was too late, years afterward, when someone in conversation idly revealed to me that there are geometries other than the Euclidean. Still, when I think of it, the Great Skillet theory is accompanied by bland "why nots." I do not disbelieve it; I only do not believe it anymore. I call it my first religion. I am proud of it, not because I see it as original or ingenious, but because it is evidence of the patterns of my impulses. It was a convenient cult. It had no effect on my daily life. There was nothing to be done about it. It did not call on me to tell the truth when a lie was obviously in order, or to still my hand when I felt like giving my brother a smack. It was simply an idea, a smooth, round thing to be contemplated in idle moments. It was good for fending off other ideas, the headachy ones like time, space, the void, and the belly churners like death. It gave, you might say, a certain perspective.

I entertained less healthy cults after that. I was a great follower of persons. Flex a bicep, and I'd espouse your gospels. Lift an interesting brow and I'd follow you up mountains or sit on wet pavements swilling romance with my diet of river air. But the forms and fables of other people's minds were never more to me than the color of your hair or the length of your legs. They set a tone and gave a rhythm to your activities. Mine has always been a flesh worship, and now a time has come when I am allowed to admit it, when the purposes of my religion can surface. There are only two sins I recognize—venial discomfort and cardinal pain.

The glow of the goldfish above the kitchen table warms me, and the heat of bread whose flavor reaches my finger ends, and the cleanliness of my towels and toes and floors. Those who've known me on street corners or vomiting between profundities in the dark places behind taverns, those who have led me over rocks in blue dawns to sit shivering on picturesque beaches munching cold hot dogs in congealed fat may assume I've sold out. But it was never cold hot dogs that drove me, nor the sight of the picturesque sands. It was the muscles of your thighs, the warmth of your armpits, the thump of your blood in my ear. It was flesh, not philosophy.

Now there is no flesh left that supersedes my own, and so the truth comes out. I have bowed in every direction. I have followed whoever would lead me. In my time I have believed everything for the sake of particular veins in the forearms of particular people. But now the only blood that answers when I say, "What do you want?" is my own.

It's ridiculous to discover at this age that there is something left in me that wants, that needs, that prefers, and that would rather. I call the blood of all those others my loves, and I call this blood of mine my own religion. It is the cult of the warm room and the clean bed, a sect devoted to the smoothing of toenails in the bath and the inspection of the garlic shoots in the window pots.

If there is an ecclesiastical ferocity in the performance of my rituals it can be attributed to the zeal of the convert. I'm not at all evangelical. I don't want anybody else worshipping the shine of my doorknobs, or the act of shining, or the stiff old gray sock that does the polishing. The goldfish are a more appreciative audience anyway. I have put them in the pickle jug and placed them on the red table so the lamp shines through their water and lights them. I like the look of it. I like sitting there while the bread is baking to fantasize their fantasies.

This precious nest of mine is comparatively new. I didn't grow into it, I made it. Turned in my tracks one day and decided to go no further. Or was it that the track ended? I've forgotten a lot, though I pride myself on remembering. Sometimes someone sitting innocently across from me over cups will smile and say, "Remember . . . ?" Then something slits me neatly from skull to crotch and leaves my two spread halves gaping bloodily at the fish.

My brother's wife did that to me the other day. When I was a bohemian slob she despised me but now that I've got a clean spinsterish image we're friends. We were drinking weak coffee at the table next to the goldfish, absentmindedly devouring butter ball cookies while we dissected our friends in absentia. She paused with a cookie halfway to her mouth, her dainty pinky crooked—my brother's wife is a devout pinky crooker—and shook her fluffy head. "Remember Sam and Carlotta? Whatever became of them?"

It's hard. It's hard. It was not very nice. I wanted to crawl into the pickle jug and swim sinless with light sliding on my scales. But maybe the fish envy each other and are rude. Maybe they browbeat each other and float long hours with their faces to the glass, contemplating nasty retaliations.

My life is clean now. I wash myself and the house in the mornings. I pick at the garden and am ruthless to slugs and snails. People come to my door expecting warm rooms and a flow of food and the brown sympathy of my eyes. They tell me their life stories and I tell mine. I lie. But only to make the story better. I am polite, you see. Whatever I may think behind my big soft face I will never say anything to hurt their feelings. I gossip behind their backs but since my friends do not know each other it does me no harm. I allow no one to hurt me. I announce the worst of myself so we can proceed without discomfort, so they won't think they might discover any of my secrets, so they won't think me a fool. I am very careful. I offer no advice. I have withdrawn from the dangers of intercourse. I do not go to lunch or dinner at other people's houses. I allow no one to enter after nightfall. But still it's not safe. Still sometimes I am a fool.

♫ ♫ ♫

I was a fool more often in the old days. There was, in fact, another time when I was left alone and tried to fall back on my own flesh. But I was younger then and couldn't bear my own company. I lived in a small peaked room in the attic of a rooming house in Portland. There was a skylight, a streaky slit that I propped open with a coat hanger to show off a sooty gable and its chimney. A bare bulb hung from the white ceiling, and the white walls sloped to the floor. I had a narrow bed with one blanket, a small wooden table, a spotted kitchen chair. I kept a cardboard box beneath the bed to store my other pair of socks, my other shirt, my other pair of trousers. The bathroom was across the landing. There was no broom. I never swept. I had no towel. When I bathed I dried myself by jiggling up and down in the bathroom and standing on the toilet to examine my legs in the mirror above the basin. This was not poverty, it was ignorance. I enjoyed it.

I had intentions about the room. It was to be a cell. I promised myself to allow no old lovers to set foot inside. I had an unfortunate habit in those days of dragging things out. I didn't want to lie in this new place with the skylight propped open so I could hear familiar motors approaching from the street. I didn't want to wait for anyone in this room. I swore never to sleep with anyone I cared about in this room. It was to be kept pure, free of emotional associations. I paid twenty dollars a month for it.

I also wanted to buy a velvet chaise lounge and run a fin-de-siècle salon there. I pictured myself in a flowing dressing gown dispensing red wine to the literary substrata of Portland, Oregon, while they regaled me with wit and civilization and catered awestruck to my pontifications. I thought I would lie back in the chaise and dispense judgment on obsequious poets with my languid wrists and curling toes. The idea still appeals to me.

I kept an eye on the advertisements in the newspaper. Finally, I found the chaise. Peach-colored velvet, stuffed with goose down, and more comfortable than any bed I've known. A little grimy around the upholstery seams, a little dingy on the headrest. A pink-and-gray lady in a pink-and-gray apartment sold it to me. I decided she was a retired mistress casting off the old accoutrements.

The cabdriver complained that the chaise stuck out of his trunk. I gave him a quarter when he stopped in front of my house but he wouldn't help me carry it up the four flights of stairs. He helped me put the chaise on the sidewalk and drove off. I sat down on it and lit a cigarette and watched the people look at me as they passed, wondered how to get it up the stairs. The upholstery was very soft, but the frame was oak and heavy. A dirty little guy came out of the door of my house with a guitar case in his hand. Square grimy hands, thick greasy glasses. A spunky little character with an intellectual air. He stopped on the front steps and grinned at me. I grinned at him.

"That's quite a contraption," he said.

"You want to help me carry it up four flights of dark, twisting stairs?" I asked.

"Absolutely," he said.

These days I'm very careful to have no truck with guitar cases.

"It looks like it eats people," he said. It was as if his smile was built in. We lugged the chaise up to my room. I know now that Sam always stops to help. He helps ladies change tires. He picks up hitchhikers. He lifts the heads of drunks in alleys and takes the hand of the child screaming in the crowd. It's not from sympathy or charity, but curiosity, and a lust for the something interesting that can be milked from every brush with another person.

But I didn't know him then. I assumed he was interested in the possibility of being invited to bed. And I was lonely. I had been growing quite morbid up there under the eaves. I'd sit for hours beneath the skylight, tipped back in my wooden chair at an angle that let the cigarette smoke drift up and outside rather than smog the room.

There is something about small, compact men that has always fascinated me. I am a big woman and aware of the incongruity, but it's there despite me, a solid reality. Small faces hung around large noses, tense compact bodies, a woolly fuzz of the various hairs. I used to think it was simply the Hero's Friend

Syndrome, a cuddly quality. But now I think it has more to do with apparent energies: languid types tend to run big; little men are often either vivacious or fiercely restrained. Maybe this idea stems from the ant, whose disproportionate strength is attributed to the leverage of its short muscles. Or perhaps it's the sensation of mortality, the impression of fragility and the inevitable end that seeps from small bodies. Other monoliths like myself always make me feel completely indifferent to whether they'll actually survive through the eons, as they seem to intend.

Whatever the cause, I was saving my ass experimentally and displaying my cheerful fortitude all the way up to my room. We dropped the chaise beneath the skylight and fell giggling and puffing against it. His smile had only tightened a little on the stairs. He even talked through it.

"When you move," he was saying, "put an ad in the paper to sell it. Take the first offer you get but tell them they have to move it themselves." I was trying to appear sinuous while rummaging under the bed for the bottle of grape soda and the bag of chocolate cream cookies that were intended for my supper.

"It will be a new divorcée and her boyfriend who sells motorcycles. The moment they get it down to the sidewalk, I'll come out screaming, say I'm the manager of the rooming house and where are they going with *my* furniture." I took a slug of purple soda and passed the bottle to him. He brandished it at me.

"There'll be great protests! A lot of 'See here, misters,' a lot of 'The little lady only . . .' talk. I'll tell them you're behind on your rent and being tricky with my furniture and I'm going to have you thrown in jail. You come down and give them their money back and confess with tears and moans. They drive off in a rage. And, quite magically, the pink monster is safe on the sidewalk." He tips up the bottle and pours soda in through his smile.

I lay on the chaise and twisted my legs around each other seductively. Sam sat on the chair and talked. His totem animal was the fly, but a polite and hilarious fly. He was a second-year student at the local prestige college and was taking flamenco guitar lessons from the cough-syrup addict on the ground floor of my house. Sam was from New York.

"But why did you come to Portland?"

"To get away from my mother. Ninety percent of the students out here are from New York. New York mothers are really awful!" Our laughter exploded in the small room. Our cigarettes spewed toward the skylight. He played a one-handed chord on the guitar.

"My teacher is acknowledged as the best left hand in Oregon. He admits his right hand isn't so good so he's only showing me left-handed work. One at a time is plenty!"

He moved consciously, proudly, but not gracefully. A fly, on flower or dung heap, avid in the sweat-filled navel. He had me flummoxed. I couldn't yet sprawl comfortably, in case he was seducible after all, but I wanted to give up the effort and be friends. I didn't want to fail and have to look at myself all depressed later. He never stopped smiling.

I tilted my head back. The air moved out but not in through the skylight, and the peach velvet chaise was hot and I was sweating where it touched me, and I realized it took up too much room in the apartment, and seemed to take up some of the air as well and breathe out something useless, and yet I loved it. And I loved Sam, whose other names I did not yet know, and the crunch of the cookies and the fizzle of the grape soda, my unfashionable refreshments.

The fly lifted and buzzed, wavered between indistinguishable, alternative surfaces, touched lightly on my solid possessions, and moved over them, leaving his inevitable spore.

🦟 🦟 🦟

Now I own goldfish and am mean about flies. Yet our first encounter was on a real day such as these that still begin with the same glimmers, and there are no ends to the lengths that a scaled body might lead me to. Sam brought the clouds down and tickled them until they gave sarsaparilla. I drank it up and hated the hours when we were not together.

The sun was giving up and the skylight failing and he got up and brushed the crumbs from his knees and told me to come out to the college the next night and he'd feed me in Commons. It was obvious that he liked me, a distressing reaction to a woman with my intentions. But I would not give up entirely. I stood in the doorway with my hip tilted against the jamb and said goodbye with my smokiest laugh.

But we became friends, Sam and I. I gave up being sultry and lapsed into the norm. His way of liking someone was to glorify them past recognition. Mine was a maliciously cheerful phenomenology. I can't claim we were ever crucial to each other, no. But we each served the other's occasional purposes.

My life at that time was like this: I worked four nights a week at a coffeehouse as a waitress, the rest of the time I told myself I was writing a demonic play. "Souvenir," it was called. In fact, I dressed as soon as I woke in the morning, trekked across the hall to the bathroom, and sat in the chaise for a few hours doodling on a pad of paper and sending smoke up through the skylight, hoping for some deliverance, interruption. My creative energies were devoted to gross acts of nostalgia for wrongs I had inflicted or that had been inflicted upon me. I lay redoing them, living them over in the perpetual role of the afflicted, relishing my injuries, exalting myself with the guilt of having perpetrated even greater agony on my victims than any I had suffered. The pain I imagined for them writhed in me, and my own pain grew with each recounting. This all had a very literary bent to it, constant dramas played out in my peaked room. But it didn't get any plays written. It was all so depressing that every day at about noon I would feel the same great need to launch myself from the skylight and end the mood in the alley below me.

I would not be young again, not a day younger. All that silly misery.

Instead of killing myself I would go out. I slipped down the stairs, shedding that peculiar form of darkness, and emerged on the street electrified, prowling hungrily in parks hoping for dramatic encounters, or descending purposefully on acquaintances with exaggerated tales of my latest adventures. Usually by nightfall I was tired enough to be relatively sane, and hungry.

Once Sam revealed the ease with which a suitably disheveled young person could get a free meal at his college cafeteria, whether they were a student or not, I took advantage of it regularly on my nights off from work. Sam held court over the plastic trays and cheered on his team of balding scholastic diners. They flung etymological witticisms at the cuisine, the staff of the cafeteria, the faculty of the college, Plato, Wittgenstein, Goethe, and various other defuncts with whom the whole group gave the distinct impression of having shared many a crust and chortle. I would walk down the long, noisy room balancing a tray, and find a vacancy at Sam's table. Greetings, amenities, then I would work diligently at the food and listen. Sam's friends were all characters, if only in their enormous desire to be colorful. These sessions became a substitute for my dream of the literary salon in my attic room, the wit cascading at my demand. The pink chaise sat alone in the dark room across town. I confess that it all thrilled me: their strange accents, their irreverent familiarity with words I had read, could spell, and could write, but had never heard spoken aloud before.

On the nights when I worked, I ate sandwiches in the dark coffeehouse while the customers listened to local singers on the little stage.

Sam collected people. He never dropped anybody deliberately, but his cohorts were burned away by fatigue, or the satisfaction of their curiosity, or a distracting love affair. It didn't matter. Sam would discover a parking lot attendant who was building a computer into his record player, or a quiet girl in the back row of a statistics class with a sure method for betting on horses. He would question and prod them into a blaze of light, introduce them to his friends, admire and stimulate them, and then go on to his new discoveries. I was an intermittent member of the circus and felt no urge to abandon the show. I came whenever I could.

He also had a good friend named Rennel. A psychology major. I never liked him much, but he and Sam were together a lot. That winter Sam and Rennel moved off campus and shared an apartment, and I bought a skirt and a pair of black knee-high boots. In the cruelest heart of the winter, the furnace failed in my house, and I stalked late into the night for men to take me home with them.

Me: "Do you have heat in your room?"

Him: "Yes, a radiator or something."

Me: "Why don't we go there right away."

The answers were varied. Sometimes I slept behind the counter of the coffeehouse. It didn't occur to me to buy another blanket, or even a coat. It all still seems fairly innocent to me. It only makes me nervous when I think of the time that it led to.

During all this time Sam was celibate, and Rennel dallied with the bleach-blond drummer of a dormitory band who, it is said, later became a docile lesbian. This drummer I saw only once, a small, dark-browed creature with a square, soft face. Whether someone told me that she became a lesbian or I dreamed it and liked the idea, I do not remember. But it does seem a likely consequence of too many sessions with Rennel. For my part, as the weather got warmer, I brought odd folk home to my attic room and let it stink for brief periods of something other than stale cigarette smoke.

᛭ ᛭ ᛭

When summer came, Sam and Rennel went back to New York, and I went out to the college only to prospect at the swimming pool. My stomach churned at the sight of the other girls moving across the green campus. Their lives seemed so calm and ordered, directed and productive. I filled out an application to become a part-time student.

Sam and Rennel came back for the beginning of the school year but I didn't see them until October. It was my birthday, come to think of it, and it was really the beginning of everything that happened. It was my twentieth, worlds ago. I was attending two classes and writing lewd poems in response to some classical text I was reading. I remember I had actually gone down one night to a local spot that encouraged that sort of thing. I sat up on a stool under a spotlight and read my poems to the audience. I hid in my room for days after that, which shows that I had some sense after the fact at least. The poems were to be part of a long revelation of existence pro tem called

"The Fever City Series." These things don't make me wince anymore; I have the excuse of time, which allows me to despise my youth without being at all responsible for most of it.

Some guilt carries over, though. I heard, by some bit of eavesdropping, that there was another poet in town, a surprise to begin with, who was also dedicating himself to the production of a volume to be titled "The Fever City Series." At first this was infuriating, but through a further bending of the ear at this private conversation I discovered that the poet's name was Ram Deweese. I interrupted:

"Forgive me, but is his name really Ram, or did he make it up?"

"His name is Ramses, but his friends call him Ram."

A magical name. I had to find him. I thought of a golden nape of hair curling down his neck, a glass of wine, my eyes locked with his in the terrible struggle to communicate our affinities. I spent my twentieth birthday walking around the city, clutching a corner torn from an envelope with an address penciled on it. The backs of necks have been fatal to me at times; it was that imagined nape that drove me up one street and down another. The address, for some reason, was difficult to locate. Finally, as I passed a small dingy bungalow for the third time, the door opened and a pudgy, white-haired fellow came out with a saucer of cat food. He bent to put the saucer on the step and glanced up at me through his bleary spectacles.

"I'm looking for Ram Deweese," I said.

He straightened. "I'm Ram Deweese."

He had no neck. If he'd had one it would have been pink and covered with eczema. I mumbled something about having admired his poetry.

"Come in and have a drink."

"No," I said, and started walking back the way I'd come. "I

just wanted you to know." I waved the sheaf of my own poems at him. I'd brought them along thinking of praise and fulfillment and shortcuts to the realization of affinities. Instead I went home to feel glum in the chaise. I lay there with the weight of unspecified darkness, contemplating suicide, and hoping for an interruption.

Rennel came then. I heard his feet on the stairs. I jumped up before he could knock. He spoke his affected "Hullo," his klutzy imitation of the lowbrow romantic lead.

"How have you—? I'm so glad to see you." I was so surprised I could only offer clichés.

"Happy birthday! We're supposed to go over to Sam's for dinner."

Why was *this* the beginning? Because it was when we opened onto each other. Before that we were each enclosed and entertained each other without lasting effect. Just as my goldfish in their jug know of me only vaguely, and entertain me with movements they would have made without an audience. I could smash the jug. In the last gasp of a gill, they might finally see me, or my shoe, at least, descending upon them. And I in my small house, with my dressing gown and watering can, take in the milk when the bottles clink and invite inside the few who ring the bell. I will listen and regale as long as the coffee is hot and the cookies are being consumed at a steady rate, as long as the forms are preserved and enough is said to give the impression of saying everything.

Lance Sterling fires his cap guns, Omar takes a bath

The first problem was cat shit. The smell hit me on the sidewalk in front of Sam's house. By the time the door opened my eyes were watering. The shit lay in thin, stiff smears on the carpets. Sam had put down newspapers so he could walk, but the cats shat on them. He put fresh papers over the soiled ones. Walking was tricky. The papers shifted and were noisy under my feet. Nobody knew how many cats there were. Nobody claimed to own them. They came with the house. There were bowls on the floor with dusty puddles of milk in them, plates with crusts of moldy cat food. After a few hours the smell didn't hurt my nose anymore. It made me sleepy.

At first Sam lived on a sofa in the basement. Then somebody left and he moved upstairs. A bald philosophy major moved onto the sofa. There was a Puerto Rican physics major in the furnace room with his girlfriend, a linguist. An art major had the front bedroom. Moira Clancy lived in the little room off the main-floor kitchen. She was being analyzed and got her room and board for cooking for everyone. She played the violin and spoke with a phony German accent, the souvenir of an au pair position in Hamburg. She encouraged the cats.

They all gave Sam the rent and he mailed it to the landlady when he remembered. Sam lived in the attic. The door off the landing closed so the cats couldn't get up there. The attic had a cubbyhole kitchen and a closet bathroom, then one long room under the eaves. The ceiling sloped to the floor. You could stand up only in the middle of the room. There was only one little gray window.

Wherever Sam lived, it was always the same: piles of papers strewn everywhere, notes and outlines and unfinished letters and unfinished essays and unfinished chemical equations, dusty with cigarette ash. Books and pipes. Cartoon strips tacked onto the walls. Everything faded and flimsy from being talked about too much and touched too little.

Sam was in the little kitchen. I leaned in the doorway, watching. His square hands were grimy. I could see the top of his head; his brown, curly hair was gray with dust. He took a bloody paper bundle from the refrigerator.

"What stinks, Sam?"

"That's just memory. This refrigerator remembers everything that's ever been put into it throughout its history."

"Why's the meat green?"

He speared the hunks and held them up proudly. "Aging. Aged steaks. I read about it somewhere. Of course the main thing about horsemeat is that it's cheap." He slapped the smelly meat into the sink and scraped at the mold with a knife. "But if it's really true that you are what you eat, I'd rather be a horse than a cow. Also, it's very good for your teeth and gums, and has a lot of flavor. Beef doesn't taste like anything."

The knife sawed through the dark meat. Sam's hands moved slowly. He pretended to be precise in his movements, but I could tell he really didn't know what he was doing. He threw cubes of meat into the frying pan, poured oil over them. The pan was already caked with other charred hunks of horsemeat. The skillet smoked as the heat reached it.

"Go open the window, Sally."

The window was fogged with dust and grease, and stiff to open. Paint cracked as I slid it up. The air outside was wet, the sky dark. Inside the attic was gray with the smoke of singed flesh. Rennel sat under a forty-watt bulb reading one of Sam's essays.

"Are you helping him cook?" he asked.

"No, I'm just watching."

Rennel made a face and continued reading.

Sam was dumping rice from a twenty-five-pound sack into a big pot on the floor. California Pearl Brown Rice. He threw the sack into the corner and poured in water from the tap.

"I'm going to write a cookbook." He looked up to see if I was listening, plopped the pot onto the other gas ring, put a plate over it, and leaned back against the sink. "Call it *Zen and the Art of Cookery*! There'll only be one recipe but a lot of philosophy. Like you have to comprehend the essential nature of your ingredients. You look at the meat and say, 'This is a wild creature, a runner and kicker of heels, an eater of tall grass and a stealer of mares.' The same with the spices and vegetables. Precisely what *is* an onion's attitude toward life?"

His beady little eyes twinkled. The smoke drifted slowly from the frying pan, out the door, and moved weakly toward the window.

"Rice is very close to enlightenment in the Zen sense. It submerges its identity in a vast multitude. Of course, flour is even closer. In the act of making gravy you lift a thousand separate grains of wheat into Nirvana. Their eyes are lost and they drown and are reborn in the universal identity."

"Gravy."

"Sure. Or anything else really. See, first you have to understand your ingredients. Like, garlic watches TV in its undershirt and sweats at work. Cinnamon is a southern belle. Those two don't go together. Onions are hard-core romantics with a defensive cynicism. It's like a party. You bring all these characters together in such a way as to create a new, overall identity—a different taste than any one of them alone, but they all contribute to it. In things like stew you achieve a successful group therapy, but in sauces or gravy you get them right off to Nirvana."

"So what's the one recipe?" I asked.

"Oh, horsemeat and brown rice. That's just a friendly interaction, but I'm not up to any bodhisattva tricks yet. I just establish their egos solidly enough so that they can have a relationship without getting defensive."

The smoke coming from the stove was suddenly black. It stung my eyes. Sam coughed and laughed as he grabbed the skillet and rushed to the window. Rennel fanned the air with the essay to keep the smoke away. Sam held the pan out the window, sucking deeply at the night. The smoke paled against the black sky and moved off slowly. Sam looked back in at us, smiling.

Rennel snorted in disgust. "Any piece of meat that survives that treatment has a right to feel self-confident."

Sam showed me the pan as he came back into the kitchen: the meat was burned black, welded to the skillet.

"Those don't look like survivors to me," I said.

"Don't fret. This is horse, not a Muzak cow. There'll be something left under the crust. Do you want to sand the chopsticks?"

I stood at the sink and with rough sandpaper removed the previous night's rice and horsemeat off the chopsticks. Rennel stood in the doorway watching as Sam chipped the meat out of the pan and into the rice pot. He finished and shooed us out: "Sit on the floor so we can all reach."

He placed the pot on the floor. We crouched around it, dipped our chopsticks in, and passed a coffee can full of tea.

Rennel took all this in seriously. They sat waving their chopsticks at each other. Philosophy, psychology. Something big with words I didn't know. Sam was quick to smile and talked fast. Rennel was slow, ponderously performing sensitive pouts before speaking.

Sam shouted, "But you couldn't condition a dog to commit suicide! The response could only be elicited once! You couldn't reinforce it."

"But that's not the point . . ."

I couldn't listen to Rennel's points.

Downstairs, Clancy was playing the violin. She could earn her keep on a corner, I suppose. The attic reeked of cat shit, burned meat, Sam's sweat, all the accumulated dust and mold. I spied a pair of Sam's underwear going green in the corner of the room. Still, the dim pools of light were easy on my eyes. The talk continued. The smoke thickened. I got used to the stench; the dirt began to look familiar, less of a threat. I slept awhile.

I woke to the plunk of guitar. Rennel was asleep in the chair and Sam sat hunched over his guitar next to the record player.

"Hi," I murmured.

He stopped playing and lit a cigarette. "I met a pickpocket in an elevator this summer who is an authority on folk guitar music. I've given up the flamenco. Rennel says it is psychologically healthier."

We grinned and gossiped.

"Clancy likes to think of herself as the housekeeper, but she's not equipped to keep any kind of house. But her psychoanalysis is progressing. And she has a job now checking horse piss from the local track. It seems every time they run a race they take urine samples from the first three horses to make sure they haven't been doped. They also spot-check the losers at random. They run the stuff to Clancy's lab and she dunks litmus paper in it or something. She says it comes in gallon buckets, which she has to pour into test tubes for the technicians to work with. You should smell her when she gets home! Phenomenal. This is all because her psychiatrist insists on getting paid. The old fraud got her this job and told her it would straighten out her psychic this-and-that, give her more self-confidence. But I'll tell you, I'm not eating any more of her cooking. She doesn't bathe or change clothes when she comes home. The lady in the drug-store where Clancy buys her hairnets keeps asking me how her kidney trouble is."

Sam strummed a chord to dramatize the point. The guitar was scarred and stained at the neck. Sam's fingers were just beginning to grow calluses; his thumbs were still blistered, and the blisters broke and bled as he played. *Twelve Easy Lessons for Twelve-String Guitar* lay yellowing beside the record player. I wondered if he could read music.

"You're a fine one to talk about other people bathing and changing clothes."

"Oh no. That's a totally different proposition. I wash my hands, brush my teeth, and put on clean underpants once every week. Besides, I don't wallow in horse piss. I don't smell bad, do I?"

"Not bad. A little musty."

From under Rennel's feet, I fished out Sam's unfinished "Wittgenstein: The Effect of Swiss Cheese on Rye." There were a lot of big words. He didn't write like he talked.

"You seem more impressed with his diet than with his phi-losophy," I mused aloud.

"What?" His expression softened when he saw what I was

reading. "It's just that I'm impressed with his philosophy *because* of the diet."

He chuckled then began to strum again. I gave up. Time to go home.

Clancy was sitting in the living room when I went downstairs. She was playing with her chubby fingers. She had a thin face, a big nose, a sharp chin, then an abruptly enormous ass.

"Is he still playing the guitar?" she whined.

"Yeah. Does he do that a lot?"

"He does it all day. Every day. Or all night, I mean. I can't sleep and I'm working now. My analyst says it's good for me to get away from this house and have some human contact."

I didn't sit down because the cat shit smell was too much.

"He used to come down to dinner sometimes. We'd have strudel when the apples were cheap, and chicken. He'd come down for that. But I took him up a strudel last week and when I went back a couple of days later it was still there. He says he has to keep in shape so he's not eating at all except horsemeat and brown rice."

She put a "sh" in "strudel." Her accent and little-girl whine irritated me more than the cat shit.

*, *, *,

As the semester dragged on, the discussions no longer took place in the campus cafeteria at dinnertime. I ate in my room a lot but walked over to the campus three days a week to classes. One night I got a long-distance call from Sam's father on the phone in my hall. The next morning I went out to the college for breakfast.

Rennel was eating antacid tablets for breakfast. It was late, nearly time for lunch. The cafeteria was empty. Rennel sat in one far, dark corner, munching and belching sourly. I set my fried eggs down in front of him. His face went green. He scrabbled for another chalky tablet.

"Take that someplace else to eat it."

"I want to talk to you."

I rummaged my toast in the yolks, spread it around good, got the toast really runny with yolk, and then slid it into my mouth. I chewed voluptuously, never quite closed my lips. Rennel watched, fascinated, his fingers clenched on the roll of antacids. He just thought I was disgusting; it would never occur to him that I'd do it on purpose. I showed him a dripping bit of egg whites and poked my slimy tongue out of my mouth. Rennel pulled back, and his eyes bulged. His face was sweating, his cheeks swelled dangerously. He belched at length.

I lit a cigarette. Propped my muddy boots next to his little roll of Tums.

"Sam's father phoned me from New York last night," I said. "I guess Sam gave him my number and said he could be reached there. Anyway, Mr. Rosen was very upset. The school wrote to him to tell him Sam's flunking."

Rennel looked indignant. All his friends were crazy. The affront to his therapeutic powers gave him a sour stomach.

"I haven't seen him in a while," I continued. "Is he still playing the guitar?"

"Some. That was a healthy enough thing. Now he's really falling into something."

I could tell Rennel was carefully assembling a profound dissertation: his brows wrinkled, his eyelids drooped, his fat pink lips pouted.

"You know he spent his freshman year here faking mononucleosis. He didn't go to any classes. He just sat in the dormitory."

"Yeah."

"But don't you see? That was a massive withdrawal from academic competition. Sam got his scholarship because he was a minor prodigy at chemistry. So what does he major in? Philosophy. That bout of mono was actually a breakdown. He wasn't functioning relative to the real world."

"You wouldn't say that if you saw him haggling over the price of hashish. He was probably just having a good time. But what's got you so frothy all of a sudden?"

"He's changed his name to Lance Sterling."

"I don't believe it."

"Lance Sterling. He hasn't been to a psychology class all year. He came in yesterday wearing a cowboy hat and a pair of cap pistols in holsters on his belt. He told Mr. Leden he'd changed his name to Lance Sterling. He spent the whole class firing off caps whenever he approved of what somebody said. Really! Rebel yells and the whole business. I didn't get a chance to talk to him. It's not goddamn funny!"

Down the long cafeteria a small, bowlegged figure strolled toward us. Sam's guns clinked as they shifted in their holsters. His hat was red felt, from a dime store, tied beneath his chin by a white string. He smiled sweetly, and held a white coffee mug in one grubby hand. He walked gingerly, afraid of catching his invisible spurs in the carpet. He tipped his hat to me.

"Howdy, ma'am."

"Hi."

He settled the red Stetson on the back of his head and straddled a chair. He warmed his hands on the white mug; his eyes twinkled. Rennel glowered.

"Those are nice guns," I said. "Can I see?"

"Yeah. Got 'em at Woolworths for five dollars. Note the

revolving cylinder and filed sights. I've been practicing my fast draw."

"Show me."

Sam kicked the chair over as he leapt away from it. He whipped the gun out, fired three times, and then fell, twitching and moaning, onto the floor. The caps cracked loud in the deserted room. The gunpowder tang bit hard in my nose. His hand convulsed and the pistol rattled to the floor.

"Can you do that left-handed, too?"

"No. But you know, I figured out that two-gun slingers must have worn their guns with the butts facing forward so they could have a cross-armed draw."

He demonstrated and let me fire some caps. One of the cooks, the chubby little Russian who read *Anna Karenina* in the original, came out of the kitchen and stood with her hands folded into her apron. She looked at Sam fondly.

"Did you really change your name?" I asked.

"Well, I didn't go to court about it, but I'm not answering to Sam anymore. You can call me Lance."

"Could you tell me why?" Rennel asked, as though inquiring about Sam's bowel movements.

"A guy came to the door selling lightbulbs guaranteed to last a lifetime. Five dollars for a dozen, and you got a ten-day free trial. I signed up for them but I didn't want the bill following me around so I made up a name: Lance Sterling. It just popped into my head. Then I decided I liked it. What do you think of this gun? The belt? The bullets are made of real wood. I was sure they'd be plastic."

Rennel looked at the belt with exaggerated interest and said it was very nice.

"I want to go downtown and get a big leather belt with a

bucking bronco on the buckle. Wear it under the gun belt. Will you give me a lift when you get out of class?"

Rennel nodded resignedly. "Yeah. As a matter of fact, I'd like to talk to you. I'll pick you up in front of the library."

Sam eased his guns into their holsters, lifted his hat to me, said, "Adios," and strolled away.

Rennel rolled his eyes. "Oh, brother!" He took out his junior psychologist notebook and started jotting viciously. "He pretends he doesn't know that what he's doing is abnormal. He's got to be pretending. He's nuts!"

"You always say that, and he's always perfectly happy."

"He doesn't function. He's never adjusted to the competitive system."

"How can you say that? He's adjusted perfectly."

"Don't be stupid. He goes to a class about once a month and hasn't turned in any work since last year."

"But nothing worries him. It may not be normal, but—"

"He hasn't bathed or changed his clothes from September to July. Is that sane?"

"It's cold in that house of his," I said. "And how would you like to take off all your clothes and step into a tub full of decayed cat shit?"

"He locks himself in his room with his guitar and the record player for weeks at a time!"

"You just got through saying that was a healthy sublimation. You're just sore because he wasn't available for one of your bullshit sessions."

After that, Rennel didn't speak to me for a few weeks. Things slid back to normal. Rennel even started calling Sam Lance, but he was still bothered by the six-guns, the silver belt buckle, and the way Sam would crouch and fire whenever he wanted to add excitement to the conversation. He practiced his fast draw a lot.

Anything seems normal if you get used to it.

I once caught Rennel practicing his draw with his index finger in front of a mirror. He said he wanted to understand Sam's motivation. They argued for hours over the most efficient height for the holsters and how tight the leg strings should be. According to Rennel, Sam was fixated because he had no sex life. But the problem was that Rennel had no sense of humor.

*, *, *,

A rumor went around that Sam had found a tame junkie. He had made a pet of a heroin addict, took her in to live with him, and set up visiting hours for putting her on display. Weeks went by in which I did not see Sam but heard of him several times a day.

"Have you met Belle?" someone might ask. Or, "Have you seen Sam's junkie?" Or, more discreetly, "Have you been over to Sam's place recently?"

All this as a prelude to reverent descriptions of the way Belle ate brown sugar straight from the box with a spoon, or how she nodded into unconsciousness on the sofa immediately after playing her guitar and singing for a group of guests. It was one of her drawing cards, that she played and sang her own songs.

I took an immediate dislike to the whole business. There was a lot of pious awe going around in those days and it set me against whatever it was directed at. Even now, the word "Zen" triggers a reflexive sneer, and the most academic use of the word "enlightenment" blights my very digestion.

Drugs and folk music were two topics that always drew blathering mysticism from the dark heart of every student house and dormitory. There were dozens who found some pretext to visit Sam so they could sit worshipping their new ideas and get high. All of the students seemed to use hallucinogens, but heroin was holy by way of being fatal.

Still, I was jealous. Sam had hit upon something so much more colorful and gratifying than I could ever offer, and I despised him at last for being "taken in," as I fancied it. I didn't go to see him, and he, enveloped in the lively fascination he inspired, certainly did not seek me out.

He arranged a small performance at the college. Belle sang to as many students as could crowd into the main lounge. The reports were extravagant. She was "so wise," "so full of soul," "so beautiful." Sam must have loved it.

Finally, after weeks, he came to see me. He could not sit down. He was in a hurry. He needed fifty dollars for gas to drive Belle home to San Francisco.

"She needs to see her kids. She has two kids. They're with their father."

He expressed enormous admiration for her for having given birth, which he described as something mystical. He was sweating and gray. He could not talk well. I gave him fifty dollars, which left me with twelve. He promised to pay it back in a week. His red cowboy hat hung limply down his back from its string, forgotten.

I waited a while. The coffeehouse paid me once a month. After eleven days had passed without a word from Sam, I spent forty-five minutes in the corner grocery deciding what to spend my last half dollar on.

I bought chocolate and went back up to my room to eat it. It wasn't very filling, so I walked over to Sam's house to see if he was back.

The door had Xs on it, made with white chalk; they must have been visited by the gypsies. The stairs creaked beneath the ragged carpet. The kitchen radiated cold. Clancy seemed to have given up cooking. The cats were gaining ground. The whole house seemed like it looked, like it shouldn't have been standing.

Sam was glad to see me.

"I came back," he said. "We went to a party and Belle left with another guy. She always said she'd go her own way. I guess I'm supposed to be glad."

His shoulders were back, but he was standing like the weight of his own body was a little too much and he was giving out at the knees.

"Anyway I brought back some peyote. Have you ever tried it?"

At the same time, we both noticed smoke was coming from the little kitchen. Sam rushed in, flung the oven door open, and snatched out a pan.

"They're mushrooms, see? You dry them and crush them. I got a mortar and pestle from the chemistry lab. And here are the capsules."

He dumped the little buttons out of the pan to cool.

"I will keep the burned parts. They're probably still good. The Mexican Indians use them in religious rituals, but I hear they make you sick to the stomach if you take them straight."

We sat on the floor and traded off grinding the pestle. We delicately tapped the gray-green dust onto a page of notebook paper and guarded it from drafts.

"I really think I ought to start meditating seriously. Things have been happening that I can't account for. I'd like to just sit still for a while and let history catch up with me."

"Did you ever have a girl before Belle?" I asked. "Seems like you don't talk about it, but you don't go around with that frantic freshman gleam in your eye, either."

"There was a girl in high school. It was funny. We pretended we didn't know each other. I never spoke to her in school. It was pretty tricky, too, since we had a lot of classes together. But her bedroom was on the ground floor of her house. I used to climb in her window at night. She laughed when she had an orgasm. I always thought anything else would be a letdown after that."

"Is that all?"

"Well, there was a girl last year. She was working in a tobacco shop I used to go to. Heidi, her name was. She used to come over sometimes with a pan of lasagna. But nothing ever happened. We'd play records all night and she'd go off in the morning with the empty lasagna pan. After one of those nights she just never came back. I was never wild for lasagna."

"Does it bother you, not having a girl around? The rest of these freaks are always frothing about it."

"I get lonely."

"Yeah, but I mean . . . "

He dipped a capsule into the dust, took a careful scoop, then capped it.

I tried again. "Rennel says you're so maladjusted because you have an unsatisfactory sex life."

I could tell he smiled even with his head bent.

"Do you know who Rennel sleeps with?" I asked.

He smiled up at me. The peyote dust was stuck to the tips of his fingers. "Nobody I know of since Drummer Pillow." He grinned and continued putting caps on the filled capsules. "Well, I'll tell you a secret."

"Okay."

"Every once in a while, not very often, once every two weeks or so, he fucks Clancy."

"Agh," I groaned. "Oh, agh."

Sam nodded.

"She tells me all about it. Comes up here with her pissy strudel and explains that they have a lot in common because he's going to be a psychologist, and she's being analyzed."

"Agh!"

"Yes. But, you know, he's very bright. He's just not very perceptive about people."

"Dense, you mean."

"And he comes here late, when she's already in bed. He doesn't have anything to do with her in public, so he must realize that she's not presentable."

"But the smell and everything. She doesn't smoke, does she?"

"Look, if you needed to, and there was nothing else available, you'd piss in a dirty toilet, right? So don't be so snobbish."

"Jesus. Do you suppose he considers that a satisfactory sex life?"

"Survival rations."

I picked up a clear capsule, dipped it recklessly into the dust, capped it, and tossed it on the pile.

"How many of these things is a dose?"

"I thought we'd just divide whatever there is between us. It takes a lot to get an effect. You want to make some tea to take them with?"

I boiled water in the big pot and poured it over tea in two corrugated coffee cans. I rummaged in the refrigerator and found a bowl of cold rice. I salted it and brought it back with the tea.

"Does she like him at all?" I asked.

"Clancy? She says she always sleeps better after a fuck."

"She's hung up on you, ya know." I set the tea in front of him on the floor. The cans were hot.

"Yeah. There are twenty-one capsules for each of us."

We gulped the pills by the handful, washed them down with scorching tea. I ate some of the rice. We discussed the feasibility of assuming the classical lotus position while wearing six-guns. After a while we practiced, then fell asleep.

❦ ❦ ❦

When I knocked on Sam's door the next morning, Clancy opened it.

"He's still asleep," she said.

"What are you doing up here?" I asked. Sniffing his underpants, collecting belly button lint for a love philter. Something disgusting, I was sure.

"He invited me."

Clancy was smug. Her hair was loose from its bun, kinky. I could smell the horse piss sweating out of her. Behind her, Sam lay on the mattress. An old army blanket was pulled up to his hips so his big square hairy feet stuck out. There was no hair on his pale chest, just dirt. Clancy curled up on the chair, watched him. I noticed she was wearing his old blue-and-gray-striped pajamas, the ones his mother sent from New York.

"Is this what it looks like, Clancy?"

The story at any price. She looked dreamily at me, almost shyly. Her big horsey teeth stuck out of her bony face. Her piggy little eyes gleamed behind the thick lenses of her glasses.

"You knew how I felt about him, didn't you?" she asked.

"Did it just happen last night?" I asked. "I was here pretty late."

"It was the most amazing thing. I'd been sleeping for a while. Then I had a dream. I got up to write it down so I could tell Dr. Leiter. I felt so strange, lonely, and yet beautiful. I played the violin for a while. A little Mozart that my father always liked. And I really played so well . . . but you were making a lot of noise up here. Great thumps like you were falling down, and yelling a lot. Whatever were you doing?"

She was so prim, like Bo-Peep. What *had* we been doing?

"Kung fu, maybe," I said.

"And then, after a while," she continued, "I heard somebody kind of fall down the stairs and then go outside. That must have been you. And I heard Sam walking back and forth up there. I can recognize his steps, even when he's barefoot. I got back into bed and turned the light off. Tinker and Sambo, the cats, were there with me. I take them in to keep me warm. It's not very nice, sleeping alone. And I heard him come down the steps very slowly. I thought he was going out, but he knocked at my door and opened it. He looked very serious. Not smiling at all. I was a little afraid. He came and sat beside me and started petting my arm."

"What did he say?"

Sam lay two feet away. His mouth was open, he breathed softly. It would probably taste lousy when he woke up. He slept curled up, one hand beneath his head. He looked foreign. Unfamiliar. Had I ever seen him sleep before?

"He said you'd gone to get ice cream," Clancy answered.

"Yes."

"He wanted to come back up here. He made the cats stay out. It was wonderful."

She reached over to touch my hand. The button on the pajama fly popped. I could see her swelling belly through the gaping opening. Her great hips and thighs stretched the thin cloth.

"Aren't you supposed to work this morning?"

"I called in sick. I want to stay here with him."

"No. You'd better go to work. You can't afford to lose that job. And don't tell him I was here, will you? Don't tell him you saw me, okay?"

"But—"

"I have a surprise for him. I'll come back tonight. Can you loan me some money till I see you? I'm really broke."

She fished in Sam's discarded pants and pulled out a dirty dollar bill. I stood up too fast and jarred the kitchen chair that was at the foot of the mattress. Sam's guns were hanging from it, his red hat was on the seat. The guns clinked feebly. I went quickly to the door and out.

*, *, *,

I slept in my chaise until supper. I knew he must have been up by that time. I went to the corner grocery that sold frosted cakes in paper boxes. Thought I'd take him a little present. Cake and a quart of milk.

The broken houses on the block stirred in the half-light, that lavender glow you only find in damp, cool climates. Children screeched. I could hear the clatter of family suppers. Toys were strewn about in the patchy grass of front lawns. Sam's house was quiet. Dead. Nothing lively, it seemed, beyond the steps. But when I got closer, I heard a pan clatter. The smell of baking chocolate drifted out over the smell of cat shit. I could hear several people chatting in the kitchen, the others who lived there.

"Get out of my way if you want me to cook!" shrieked Clancy.

I sneaked up the stairs and entered without knocking. Clancy bustled by wearing a thick dirndl skirt. She slammed the oven door.

"Sam? Lance?" I called, walking past her without a word.

In Sam's room, all the trash had been shoved into one corner. I had never seen the bare floor. Thin layers of dust drifted in the room. Against the wall, his pillowcase was bursting, stuffed with moldy underpants.

"Sam?"

His voice, dimly: "I'm in the tub."

The bathroom door was closed. I pushed it open and poked my head in. Dank steam swirled, and there was Sam, up to his armpits in gray water, smiling. He held a kitchen pot above his head. He tipped the pot and water ran down. He grinned and spat and snorted. He dipped the pot to fill it again.

I shut the door and sat down on the toilet. Lit a cigarette. He rubbed a bar of green soap over his head, neck, and over the thick fuzz of his face. The water in the tub was dark. A thin film of dead skin floated on top.

He stopped with the soap smeared all over his face and grinned. "I'd forgotten how nice this is."

My cigarette burned noisily. "What's the occasion?"

"I decided to turn over a new leaf," Sam explained. "You want a slightly used set of cap pistols?"

"You mean you're Sam again?"

"No, the name is Omar." He soaped up his pits.

"Omar." I leaned back against the tank, took a last wet puff, handed the butt to Sam.

"No, thanks."

I dropped the butt between my legs into the brown-stained toilet bowl. Sam threw out his tea leaves in the toilet, I don't know why.

"Is there a blanket out there someplace?" Sam asked. "My clothes are out there."

I went out to get the old army blanket that hung out over

the sill. It felt like horse hair. Back in the bathroom, Sam stood in the tub, his back and knobby little ass facing me. He poured another pan of water over himself. I threw the blanket on the toilet.

"You'd better rinse with clear water," I said. "All your ick is sticking to you."

I left and lay down on the naked mattress. It had been flipped; the marks from the floorboards were still visible. Sam came out wrapped in the brown blanket. As he rubbed at his face and chest, dead skin came off his body in tiny rolls. He brushed at it and some of it floated throughout the room. He crouched beside me.

"Well, Omar, how long since you had a bath?"

He grinned. "Last summer sometime."

Water dripped down from his hair onto his face and neck.

"Something happened last night. That peyote was very good, wasn't it?" He looked to see if it was good for me. I nodded.

"Something happened. I flew off the track. You know the little guy running very fast down the track in front of the roaring train? And he finally jumps off? Well, I got a lift from the cowcatcher, but at least it knocked me safe out of the way! I can't tell you how relieved I feel! I was so close to getting run down." He was excited about this metaphor.

"So what happened?" I asked.

"It was after you'd gone. Remember you wanted mandarin chocolate ice cream? You said they only sell it in New York and you were going to hitch there to get it?"

"Yeah." I didn't.

"Well, I was walking around looking at things in the room, when all of a sudden I started thinking about Clancy. Remember we'd been talking about her and Rennel? I was walking around in my bare feet when it suddenly occurred to me that all there was between her and me were these thin boards and a few inches of plaster and rafters. I was her ceiling. I thought, She's not more than ten feet away! Rennel was there a couple of days ago and he wouldn't be there again so soon. She was alone down there in that big stinking bed that takes up the whole room. And then you'd reminded me of how she's always mooning around using her soft voice to me, but she hollers like a pig downstairs to everybody else. See, I was thinking there was no reason to be alone up here because she was right there. I just didn't want to be alone. I only thought of her because she was so close. But I gradually worked myself into the position of wanting *her* as opposed to any woman I'd ever seen. I felt sick with wanting her. Clancy. I came over here and lay down and started doing yogic breathing to get rid of the nausea. I thought I'd get up as soon as it went away and I'd go down and see her." He picked deliberately at his toenails. "Then I went to sleep."

"Oh. Well."

"But when I went to sleep I was in love with her."

A faint banging of pots and pans drifted up to us from the kitchen.

"What about when you woke up?"

"I wasn't anymore. You've got to understand, there's something basic about her that repels me."

"The smell, maybe?"

"About *her*. It's not the accent or her neuroses or her ugliness but something that they all add up to, or derive from. That's why when I realized how close I'd come to wanting that ugliness, I mean, I wanted her. Anyway I thought for a while I'd kill myself. For the first five or ten minutes after I woke up I felt really bad. It struck me as the sort of thing to kill yourself over. But I got out of the house. Got a ride over to the school. I was wandering around leaning against things. Not speaking to anybody. I leaned against the art lecture room. Dr. Duncan was talking. He's really such a fine old man. He's always stumping around with his pipe and his white hair. I could hear him talking about Zen Buddhism. He was explaining the still center, kind of the psychic center of gravity. He says most people are eccentric, and off-center, so they wobble crazily and are unhappy. But if you can orient yourself around your true center everything becomes cool. You sit quietly and the world is all comprehensible and slow. Like sitting in the middle of the merry-go-round at the playground. Your world becomes concentric. Mr. Duncan is a very bright man. It just hit me, standing against the window like that, on a misty morning shivering and hating myself. And out of the walls comes this friendly, old, cracked voice—like a sleepy god. He said, 'The thing about human beings is that they *hate* things. And if you're going to make something it might as well be beautiful.' Have you ever heard him talking?"

"But how did Omar happen?"

"Well, I decided I'd do two things: I have to meditate really seriously and straighten out my life. And I have to make things. I went into town right away and got some books and I enrolled in a Chinese painting class. Next term I'm going to take Duncan's course in calligraphy."

He was bustling around in his blanket, then hauled his backpack to the mattress and emptied it. Out came about a dozen paperback books on Oriental art and religion. He ran his hands over them excitedly.

"I came home and threw Clancy out. She was up here messing around. I couldn't even look at her. I started cleaning up. I'm going to take all this stuff to the laundry."

"But what about Omar?"

"Yeah. I decided I needed a new name. Mr. Sing is the teacher of the painting class. He's a weird little guy in a black wool suit. Very clean ears. He looks like a doctor. He kept saying, 'Oh my.' Every time he looked at me, he said, 'Oh my.' It seems like an omen. I just took the nearest sounding name."

"Omar Herschel Rosen?"

"No. I'll never use that name again. I'll think of the rest of the name and tell you later. Want to come to the laundromat? We can eat ice cream."

So we read haiku in the Siesta Time 24-Hour Laundromat, sitting on the washers to keep warm. Jiggled during the rinse and kicked our feet rhythmically during the wash. At the end of the night, Omar paid me the money Lance Sterling had borrowed.

Carlotta

I'm not invulnerable. I could be softened even now. Boiling and steeping me in thick syrup would do it. Though there's always the question of whether it would be worth anybody's while. It hasn't been for some time, I must admit. I am a dried fruit; my juices have evaporated, and I am tough and flexible. The old patterns of my life are wrinkled but they persist, and probably will until I fold them neatly around me in my grave, though that sounds too severe for any resting place of mine. One thing I can't help noticing, which I am even able to laugh about, is that all the men who've been my friends would not take me to bed, no matter how insistent I was, while all the men who've been my lovers I couldn't abide for long outside of bed. It's a terrible thing to be a natural-born buddy, a pal, a sympathetic face peering over the top of a glass, there to be wounded or cheered by others. An abomination to be loved by the despicable, a mystery to be liked by the enchanting.

But I love myself now better than anyone else ever could. My foibles amuse me, my stupidities are endearing to me, the overriding innocence and zeal of my crudest actions make them lovable. I am a dear and a darling, and it is quite unfair that there is no one to appreciate the full scope of my loveliness. No mother could be more solicitous of my moods.

Of course I have always felt that anyone who was truly familiar with all the facets of my character must have found me lovable, but it's only in this house and this time that I have come to love myself.

Simultaneously I have discovered for the first time that there are people who actually dislike me. It has only recently come to my attention that there are a number of people who, given as full a knowledge of me as it's possible to get on a casual basis, find me insufferable, disgusting, irritating—even actively boring. It's a shocking realization, nearly incomprehensible. Even people I myself have liked or admired, and have made overtures toward. If it were envy or jealousy, I could understand completely. Those are my own prejudices, often enough. But the clues are obvious: I'm often a fool but I'm not stupid. I can interpret a lifted eyebrow and a twisted mouth, or someone drifting away from my vicinity. Unappreciative dolts I am used to. The indifference of the masses doesn't bother me.

But that the shrewd, perceptive, and humorous might know me and turn away is something to think about. It is something to mull over in the bath and knead into the bread. So far my thinking on the subject allows two possibilities: Some of these people, by sheer form and inclination, are incapable of liking me. But some of these people must judge me by my own standards and find me wanting. Perhaps they think that laughing at the motivation for your own actions does not exculpate you from either motive or deed. I wonder sometimes myself. I tend my own vagaries with affection and cultivate a liking for those who like me.

❦ ❦ ❦

The great poet Jacob Figarty gave a reading on the college lawn. The sun shone for us. The grass was green. We'd have sat outdoors and listened to the poet as long as he'd go on. Figarty was known to us, his face and his friends, the outcasts of our fathers' youths. The crowd laughed and talked. We only pretended to be there to be impressed by the poet. Really, we were there to impress the poet. We tried to appear brilliantly analytical, or poetically sensitive, or hysterically enlightened, as it suited us. We waited for him to stop in front of us as he passed through the crowd. We hoped he would glimpse the soulful pain, beatific peace, or scintillated brilliance in our face and be struck with awe at the depth of our perception, sensitivity, or beauty of soul. Maybe he would reach out, take our hand, and lead us under the trees to talk with him. He might even turn his back on all the rest to be with one of us alone. He might ask us to fuck him, marry him, or be his traveling companion, all expenses paid, just so he could bask in our proximity. So went the fantasies.

This show among the students went on all the time, actually; the performance was just a little stiffer for Mr. Figarty. Even I had brushed my high black boots. I stretched them out in front of me on the grass, felt sure they had some significance.

Sam wandered through the crowd, smiling in his new gray-and-white-striped robe. Rennel stumped behind him, glowering in black leather motorcycle pants. They must always have been this way. Bare-faced when their fathers wore beards. Long gowns when their fathers wore tights and bloomers. I lifted a hand and they came toward me. Sam smelled sweaty, looked uncomfortable in all that wool. His hair was curlier in the humidity.

"It's all arranged," he said. "Figarty will come over at about four this afternoon. He has to go to a faculty reception after the reading. Wait till you meet him! He's very cheerful and wise. If he didn't laugh so much, I'd think he was enlightened."

Rennel stretched out on the grass, flexed his pectorals,

arranged the leather at his crotch to look more swollen. Out of the corner of his eye he looked to see if anyone was watching him.

"Are you trying to say that an enlightened man doesn't laugh?" he asked. "It's an instinctive reaction in many cases. He'd have to be very inhibited not to. That's a direct contradiction of the whole concept of enlightenment."

"But he'd only laugh genuinely, never in purely social contexts," Sam replied. "He'd never laugh to be polite or to cover up embarrassment."

They went at it. Above us the trees were in bloom. They swayed, flirted, vain in their own fashion.

The dean of students appeared wearing a well-cut suit, shining shoes, and a conservative frown.

"We're honored today . . . a man you all know . . . Somewhat unusual to welcome back a man expelled from this institution some seventeen years ago . . . Jacob Figarty!"

The poet approached from the trees. He was a paunchy little guy in work clothes and sandals, with a Benjamin Franklin hairdo. He clinked little bells, sang Hare Krishna, hopped up to the microphone, grinning. He released a roll of papers from an elastic band and flung them on the podium.

We all leaned forward, we mystics in Spartan rags and gypsy dresses.

Figarty began to read. The lines flipped and jumped. He stopped, giggled.

"Excuse me, I was just remembering—when I wrote this I was smashed out of my mind. Had to go puke between each line."

We roared. Sam rolled around, laughing. Rennel smirked his approval. I liked the poems, then. They were all about sitting on the railroad tracks in a condition of some kind, how wonderful the world is—Zap! It was lovely in the soft sun, watching the famous man who was standing there to be enjoyed. We waited for him to take off his clothes; he was known to do it.

The poems ended. Figarty told us how much he had enjoyed reading to us. He told us about the party at Omar's house, which we probably all knew about. He left the podium, jingled his bells, and sang Hare Krishna softly.

Sam jumped up. "Didn't I tell you? He's too polite to be enlightened."

"He's very nice," I said.

"He's a pervert and a psychopath. In any other era he'd be chained to a wall." So said Rennel, and then smacked his lips with satisfaction. We joined the stream of students leaving the lawn, and headed to Sam's.

␗ ␗ ␗

The sun slanted onto Sam's house. Clancy had already made the rice by the time we arrived. Sam rushed in to fix the horsemeat. The party was in the yard; the smell inside the house was too bad. A bongo and a banjo plinked Japanese music. The drummer rocked, tossed his hair with his eyes closed. I watched a pretty girl wearing a suede jerkin as she danced, barefoot. She lifted her arms and swayed, nodded her head to the music. She was all high arches and soft pink heels. Her toes were rosy and clean. She bent a knee and swayed, lifted one foot at a right angle to the other and gently, precisely, set her glowing toes down on a tight little roll of dog shit. She lifted the foot casually, danced out of the dirt and into the long grass. She continued to sway her arms, although now she writhed and twisted as she scraped her toes through the grass.

Rennel sat on the ground with his black leather jacket unzipped to show his naked chest. A group of meditators sat in a circle next to the porch, legs crossed in the lotus position. Their eyes were closed, aspiring to inner focus. They breathed deeply, and on each exhale they muttered the holy syllable, "Om."

Sam popped out the front door with a flaming skillet in each hand. He waved them slowly till the flames died down. I could smell the meat burning. He saw the growing crowd and grinned. He watched the dancing girl.

"Is that Carlotta? What's she doing?"

"I don't know what her name is, but she's scraping shit off her foot," I replied.

The droning "Om" drifted over the street and mingled with the ping of the banjo. Carlotta swayed dreamily and smiled at Sam. Everywhere there were colored scarves and beaded jackets, faded dungarees and army surplus clothes. Long, thin bodies bedded in jackboots. A fat intellectual argued macrobiotics. Sam watched it all, then ducked back into the house with his skillets.

I sat on the top step of the porch. Across the street another porch looked back. There was an old sofa leaning against the railing. A tired woman stood in the door, watching, wiping slowly at the glass with a striped towel. Her face was the color of my favorite chocolate. In front of the house, four boys and a girl in a long red dress flipped coins on the grass. The girl turned pages in a fat, yellow paperback and read out a line.

"Figarty's nuts!" Rennel was protesting. "He's flat fucking nuts! He's a paranoid schizophrenic with pronounced manic periods. He's a drug addict, he fucks his male students, and his brains are liable to start dribbling out his ears any minute!"

From far down the block people were still coming, wearing

their wild colors. The steady "Om" grew even louder over the din.

Sam sat down beside me on the step. "The food's all ready. I haven't got enough chopsticks to go around. I didn't know there'd be so many people."

He glanced around at the party until he found Carlotta, who was flirting with the bongo player. She tied a thin scarf around her hair. Her arms were long and strong, and I spied a thick black tuft of hair in her pits.

A fat black car stopped in the street. Figarty jumped out, shaking his bells, followed by four students in dungarees. His belly bounced; he'd finally taken off his shirt. The music was suddenly faster and louder. The "Om"-ing carried on, but deeper, more intense. Rennel stood up and faced a new group of people. Probably nobody ever fingered their crotch more ostentatiously.

Figarty grinned around at everyone and gave his bells a tentative tinkle. "Anybody home?"

Sam jumped up.

"Are you Omar? Aren't we all solemn today. Got any beer? I knew we should have stopped for some beer."

Figarty patted Sam's shoulder and moved past him toward the house. He flopped beside me on the step and looked around.

"Are you hungry?" Sam asked. "Supper's ready."

"That's great! All they had at the faculty do was sherry and pretzels." His laugh was big and silly. "I ask you, why are all those old soaks in the English department sipping and crossing their legs at me. At *me!*"

Sam went inside. I was afraid Figarty would say something to me directly, so I stood up and walked off. Soon Sam came out of the house with a steaming tin bucket and an empty tin can. Clancy stumbled behind him with an armload of chop-sticks and a pile of assorted plates: paper, pottery, tinfoil.

"Supper!"

The poet grabbed the top plate and motioned generously to the crowd. The "Om" died out completely as the meditators regained their connection with reality and came for their plates. Sam dipped into the bucket with the tin can and slopped out a steaming gray mess with dark chunks floating in it.

Clancy held out a trembling pair of chopsticks. Her glasses were fogged with her awe for Figarty, who took the sticks po-litely, then asked, "Have you got such a thing as a fork?"

Clancy went inside to fetch him one.

Hands reached for plates and sticks. Sam proudly splayed the food onto plates. Every now and then someone bravely said, "Oh, Mr. Figarty, your poems have meant so much," be-fore they drifted away, shyly, with their smoking food.

Music chimed from down the street.

Figarty put his plate down. "Ice cream!" I noticed he'd pushed the mess to one side to make an empty space, but he hadn't eaten. He stood up and raised his arms. "Wouldn't any-body like some ice cream? My treat?"

Nobody answered.

The truck stopped down the street and then continued. We watched Figarty approach the truck, which played its little tune, two bars over and over again. Figarty ordered from the old woman leaning out of the hatch; he held an ice cream bar in each hand and started eating them both.

Sam sat down on the doorsill and looked at me. "I sure would like an ice cream."

"Yeah. Me, too."

A frizzy-haired girl in the circle sniffed and clicked her

chopsticks into the rice can. "He's not a Buddhist! What a hypocrite!"

The ice cream truck drove off and took with it the sound of children shouting. The woman across the road stepped out onto her porch again, her hands wrapped in her apron. She looked up the street to where the ice cream truck had gone. She smiled. Then she glanced at Sam's lawn and went back inside.

The scarred old toad

Some of us despise our own youth with a vague and bitter nostalgia and fixate on our worst phrases and acts with miserable clarity. It's a relief for me, in a way, to remember these scenes, to re-create them, to breathe through them again with the cynicism I've gained since. I am glad they can never happen for me again.

It seems to me that everyone I knew in those days acted by a code chosen from books and films—or not even a code but a direct emulation of a specific character who was meant to be identified and attributed. No gesture was unselfconscious or undirected, all were modeled and formed with purpose. The alarming thing is that we were so obvious, that we all did it so badly, except Sam, who did it all too well. There was no cigarette lit, no itch scratched without a full awareness of the audience. If there was no audience, we rehearsed. If there was no prospect of an audience, we did nothing.

I have an insidious conviction that between the onset of puberty and the age of thirty, people, like the hypothetical painting in the desert, do not exist without someone looking at them. I didn't. After thirty, I suppose we become a corporeal composite of what all our viewers have witnessed, a kind of community gelatin.

All those hours, alone in my peaked room, were spent in the grave. If I wasn't asleep, I was miserable, lying in furious frustration beneath the skylight, not moving except to smoke. If I read it was to drown in somebody else's life, or with the bald intention of using the information in some future conversation. I could never take it for long, being alone, and I would be forced outside by the need to be somebody, which was only possible in the presence of other people.

But now the goldfish and the gleam of the clean sink, and the four people who come here once a month or so, are enough. I thought once of getting a cat, but decided it might interfere too much. It might make demands, need something at a moment when I wasn't in the mood to give it. Breakfast an hour early, maybe, or to be let out or in.

There is still for me a novel joy in the minor decisions that I make with no regard to any inclination but my own: What will I have for breakfast? Three cookies, two bananas, and a chocolate bar. What will I have for supper? If I don't feel like it, I won't eat. I may wait until bedtime and eat a bowl of laxative cereal and a peanut butter sandwich. Or maybe at three in the morning I'll get up without disturbing anyone except the goldfish, who can't complain. Even if they view my late-night visitation as a disturbance, they only move their mouths silently. I'll fry an egg and make toast and hot cocoa and cuddle myself, with a book propped up in front of me as I eat. I read at every meal. What will I wear? Something comfortable. Am I getting fat? I don't know, it doesn't matter, the goldfish won't complain.

I sprawl on the couch with unseemly comfort, prop my feet on the table, and wrap my legs around the chair. I do not tack a ladylike lilt on the end of my racking coughs, nor do I disguise my flatulence. When someone comes to call, I am discreet and polite. But usually I am alone. This solitude is like a child's dream of being a grown-up, that same delirium of eluding discipline that drives each college freshman to longer, later discussions in the dormitories: past fatigue, past pleasure, even, merely because she was not permitted to stay up so late in her father's house. The freedom is startling, exhilarating, addictive. It must be used and abused.

Perhaps it is different for others, but I came to this freedom suddenly, after long, if voluntary, subjugation. I am learning slowly what it is that I want. These trivial discoveries web my days with pleasure, and I am my own audience, and the audience of the goldfish, and of the scarred old toad in the garden.

*, *, *,

They were still in bed when I got there. I let myself inside the house and took the stairs to Sam's room. Rennel sat on the foot of the mattress, smoked his pipe, and stared at Carlotta while he discussed philosophy with Sam.

When I saw them, and when I got a whiff of Rennel's rank, expensive tobacco, I wanted to go back out right away. Carlotta was curled up next to Sam, one of her long, pale arms displayed on the blanket, holding a cigarette, looking bored. Sam sat up against the wall with the blanket pulled up around his belly, talking to Rennel. He looked uncomfortable.

Rennel puffed proudly at his pipe and offered it to Sam. "Try it now. This is a new lot. My mother sent it air mail so it's very fresh. Just try this."

Sam took the pipe, looked quickly at Carlotta, and then pulled obligingly at the pipe.

"It's very nice." He handed it back.

Rennel offered it to me. I shook my head.

"The thing is, Omar, that Wittgenstein was a homosexual. He was already outside the bounds of accepted society in so many other ways that it isn't at all surprising that he was free to approach philosophy with an unconventional, or even apocalyptic, perception."

Rennel glanced at Carlotta to see if she grasped his profundity. Her cigarette glowed in the dim light, her eyes were half-closed. She'd fall asleep soon. Sam wasn't listening; I noticed his arm touching Carlotta's beneath the blanket. They must have just gone to bed when Rennel arrived. Sam made a face at me, he wanted something. I understood.

"Uh, Rennel."

"Yeah?"

He looked irritated. I'd interrupted his train of thought.

"I'd like to talk to you. I've been looking for you. Can you come with me?"

A little mystery to lure him. He was interested but peeved. He wanted to stay and show off for Carlotta. "Is it important?"

"Yes. Very."

"Oh. Well." He tapped his pipe over an overflowing ashtray, picked up his tailored black leather jacket. "Well, maybe we'll be back a little later, Omar."

"I'm a little tired tonight. Maybe I'll see you tomorrow at school."

"Okay. Good night, Carlotta." He waved his hips as he walked, showing off his fine big ass.

Down through the stink and out into the night, cool and clean. Rennel was still waving his butt. For me, I suppose.

"Well, what's the problem?" he asked.

"What?"

"What did you want me for?"

"Not a damned thing, you great gawping booby!"

"For Christ's sake!"

"Yes, for Christ's hairy ass! Couldn't you see that they wanted you out of there?"

"They didn't say anything." He pouted. His feelings were hurt.

"They wanted to screw and you were in the way."

"Well, why in hell didn't they say so?"

"*You're* supposed to be the psychologist. You ought to be able to tell when you walk in on two people in bed that they more than likely aren't in the mood for intellectual conversation with a third party."

He leaned against a car parked at the curb and looked at his feet.

"You're really awfully dense about people, Rennel." I was beginning to feel sorry for him.

"I'm an only child. It's a common . . ."

"Shit."

We walked down the street. The other houses were dark. Working people already asleep. It was late. I'd come from the movies before I stopped at Sam's.

"If you'll give me a lift home, I'll give you a cup of coffee."

He perked up a little, started wagging his ass again, hesitantly. We slammed into his old Rambler. I hung on and said nothing as Rennel popped the clutch and tried to screech away from the curb. Performed his rumrunner's routing for me.

Up in my room, Rennel flopped on the bed and arranged the crotch of his pants. I went down the hall to the bathroom for water, put the can on my recently acquired hot plate, and flung the dregs from the cups out through the skylight. I sat down on the floor and waited for the water to boil.

"How long have they been together? Sam and Carlotta?" Rennel asked.

"It can't have been long. He hardly knew her at that god-awful party for Figarty."

"All I know is, after you left somebody brought some wine

and Omar took it upstairs. Carlotta was going around for a while asking everybody where he was. I guess she found him. I take mine black."

Poured hot water over the sticky instant coffee in two cups. Added a slosh of sugar from a paper sack and milk to mine. Rennel sipped loudly at the hot stuff, looked around for cake and cookies. I found him really disgusting. He wore his pants too tight. He lay on the beds in other people's houses. He slurped again and eyed me significantly.

"Do you know anything about her?" he asked.

"Just dormitory drivel. She's a freshman from someplace in California. Modeled bathing suits while she was still in high school. Somebody told me she'd 'screwed everybody there ever was,' whatever that means."

He smirked over the cup, nodded sagely. "I would have thought that she was out of Omar's class."

"Why? What's Sam's class? Clancy?" I said it just to be nasty. Sometimes I just feel like being nasty. But he didn't flinch or fumble. Didn't even notice, probably.

"I've seen her a few times with that big guy with the beard," he said. "He can press three hundred fifty pounds. And he's very good at handball."

"Yeah. I think she was kind of living with him. I've seen them drift through Commons together."

She always looked happy with her long braids swinging slowly and her eyes wide and bright. She had a big, slow smile on her face, like she was always stoned. She walked very slowly, following the big guy with the beard. She wore some kind of beaded black shawl.

"Why don't you open a window? You smoke too much," Rennel said. He waved a hand at my thick cloud of smoke.

"That's all right, you have to go now anyway."

"Oh? Oh, okay." He sat up and put the cup down on the floor, zipped his jacket. He smirked. "You're sure you're all right here, alone?"

"Oh, get the hell out of here. What an asshole."

He wagged aggressively toward the door and paused. "You're sure?"

I started to get up to slam the door but he backed out quickly and slammed it himself.

The restless creeping of the worm

Puff. The smoke from my cigarette is lovely, a flat, pale drift catching light in dark places. Harmlessness. I am in here trying to be harmless. That is, after all, the primary attraction of my seclusion: to move and sleep and fling my arms out no matter how the soft undersides swing, to mutter serious nonsense at the fish and flowers and walls and windows, to giggle and stamp with sensuality on the ghastly bodies of slugs and the grinding, clicking snails. In all this coiling self—this child's indulgence—I would like to injure no one, cause no discernible pain. (I turn my back, of course, on the pain of the gastropods.) I want to see no flinch or change of pulse as the result of my most flagrant acts. I never want to roil the bedsheets as I relive the embarrassment of some stupid moment where my vanity fell crooked on an unsuspecting head. Exuberance has always been a problem of mine. It mutes my judgment, or strangles it. Each blast of idiocy or malice snaps back and chips me till I am sadly maimed and disfigured.

Do not mistake: I have meant harm in my time.

Poor Moira Clancy. I certainly meant her harm.

And there have been others. But so many were accidents, misjudgments, the result of my carelessness and stupidity. How many million tumbling words I've let loose without first noticing their particular toxicity. Fortunately, I forget a lot, and what is left to remember is enough to keep me here. I seek out no one, and those who come to me, like visitors to an aging cobra, accept their hazards.

But I don't dwell on the impersonal wounds, those fated irritations caused by my moods glancing off some stranger like the weather. The countless frenzied sales clerks I have insulted, the thousand bums to whom I have not given a penny or my ear, the small children I have refused to push in swings, and the innumerable lies I've told for convenience or color and that have since been found out. They are all too vague and unintentional to harass me.

It is the memories of when my motives have been vicious that are difficult to tolerate. They hit me at vulnerable moments, at vacant periods when my brain is flaccid between manias. The loathing I feel for myself is tremendous. It overwhelms me while I lie in my bed, during my solitary supper, or in the midst of washing out my armpits. While acute, these fits of conscience are temporary; they pass with sympathetic doses of distraction and a diet of ice cream and murder mysteries.

What finally led to my self-quarantine was a chronic gnawing of the intestine, a steady and faithful worm of anxiety that questioned and weighed and twisted the most inoffensive words of my acquaintances. It considered my own comments, remeasured their trajectory, tested each phrase for every potential toxicity. No action or gesture was ever found completely innocent. But the worm always slept when I was speaking and came out when I was alone and quiet again. And every word I let fly, every idle snicker and coarse laugh, all the affected flopping of my ungainly body sprang forth once more, ungoverned, as my pulse raced and my indigestion flared and I failed to sleep.

I knew myself to be wild, essentially cut off from the eyes up. I was constantly terrified of the damage that I knew I was capable of. I was afraid of plate glass and the large windows of banks and department stores. I saw their vastness, their fragility, and my hand itched for a brick. On certain streets I forced myself to clasp my hands in front of me and hurry along, not looking. Among other people, I strove to maintain an aloofness to protect them, a perpetual mufti of language and demeanor to shield them from my harm. I would perform a smile or laugh, grow serious, force warmth or sympathy into my expression. All the while, inside me there was the restless creeping of the worm.

⁊ ⁊ ⁊

I was asleep when I heard a noise at the door. I turned over, and the rusty bedsprings made a racket. The door creaked open. They were angels grinning through the crack, they must have felt like that. They swooped in, stirring the dust with their wings. They smiled around, glowing with the power in their bellies. Silly as hell.

"Turnabout's fair play, as they say!"

Sam giggled and bounced, Carlotta floated over to the foot of my bed. She hopped in and crawled up toward me, planted her hands on my belly and smiled down at me, right in the face, like a message from heaven.

"We're going to be friends," she said.

"I thought you already were," I grunted.

Sam hopped onto the bed and tapped his head softly against the low slope of the ceiling. "She means her and you."

Carlotta smiled some more and dug her fingers into my belly to tickle.

"Let go or I'll piss on you."

She fell back and laughed, grabbed Sam's knees and pulled

him down on top of her. They rolled and wrestled, kicking me, pushing me off the mattress. I got up, pulled a blanket around me, and went down the hall.

They were cuddled in my bed when I came back, peeping out from under my blankets and giggling. Sam's work shoes poked out over the end of the bed. He sat up and pulled his cigarettes from his pocket.

"Do you always sleep with the light on?" she asked.

"I'm scared of the dark," I replied.

Carlotta smiled.

Sam admired her through his cigarette smoke. "You're really something, you know. I've known Sally for a year and never noticed that she slept with the light on." He smiled all over her. "And you know all about the American Indians."

They smiled at each other. I sat at the foot of my bed wrapped in the other blanket. Sam's footprints were all over the rucked sheet.

They carried on looking at each other. I fished a cigarette out from under my clothes on the floor. Sat puffing at them.

"You're in my bed."

They looked at me.

"That's just to remind you that I have some rights around here. What are you up to?"

They grinned. I noticed Sam wore a new shirt. A clean one, anyway.

"Carlotta's moving into my place. We want you to come and help. A kind of housewarming. We'll get Rennel to bring his car. Then I'll take us all out to dinner. We can go to Hung Far Low."

"Don't you have to live in the dormitory?" I asked Carlotta.

"I've been sharing a house with Beth."

"You know Beth, the Eurasian?" Sam asked. "Carlotta even has a red phone next to her bed."

"I have a dog, too. Angelina. I've had her since she was a puppy."

"But right now?" I asked. "What is it? Three in the morning?"

"We haven't paid the rent in a couple of months," Carlotta explained. "Beth moved out yesterday. I'm afraid I'll get stuck for all of it."

"Ah, well," I conceded. "Get out of here. Sit on the stairs or something while I get dressed."

When they were at the door I saw that Carlotta was taller than Sam by an inch or two. She stopped to tie a red scarf around her head in a tight band.

There'd been a frost overnight. White fuzz thickened on the grass. Sam walked in between us, Carlotta on one side, me on the other. We walked slowly, but her long legs moved slower than mine and Sam's. We chugged along, out of step.

"Is this it? I think so. Yes."

Rennel's place. Another dump. I suppose we all lived in houses like that, too run-down to rent to honest welfare cases. We liked it.

The door was unlocked, the bottom floor dark. I stepped on something hard. Sam ran into something ahead of me.

"Ow! Rennel's motorcycle. Watch out."

I could smell the oil. No cat shit here. Nothing living. We went up the dark stairs. A toilet and tub gleamed out of the dark bathroom. A square of night sky shone in through a window. A thin, yellow line of light from under Rennel's door. Sam tapped.

"Go away," Rennel grunted.

"It's Omar."

A thump. The door opened. Rennel wore pajama bottoms. A thin fine sweat stood out on his body. He glared and pouted until he saw Carlotta, and then he switched to a more seductive expression. "Well?"

"Carlotta's moving in with me and we wondered if you'd come with the car to carry the stuff," Sam said.

He raised his eyebrows. A speculative pout. He motioned us in. I ignored him and he ignored me. There was a mattress on the floor, a door across two sawhorses for a desk. On one wall a life-sized poster of a retouched world champion heavyweight lifter. The morning glory wallpaper was peeling.

Rennel picked up a barbell from the floor and sat on a bench in front of the full-length mirror. "I'm doing localized lifts. Build up my forearms. I've got a cousin who can do one-armed pull-ups." He posed with his elbow on his knee, curled his arm until the weight met his shoulder. He peeked slyly at himself in the mirror as he uncurled, glanced at Carlotta to see how she was taking it in.

Sam crouched in front of him, watched the whole operation. "How many do you do?"

"Twenty with each arm. The principle is light, repetitive exercise to develop optimum functional strength. The key word there is 'functional.'"

"How much does it weigh? Can I try?"

I sat in the chair at the desk and watched. Carlotta glanced at me. Her gray eyes were framed with black brows and lashes. Her skin was pale and pitted with pockmarks, acne scars. Still, a nice face, strong features elegantly assembled. She wore a long rawhide tunic and moccasins on her high, arched feet.

She glanced at Rennel, then back to me, then wrinkled her nose to see if I agreed. I grinned, not a little. Carlotta came over to me. Peered at the paper in Rennel's portable electric typewriter on the desk.

"'Dear Mother and Dad.'" She smiled and sat down on the floor. "Do you know Omar's parents?"

Her voice was low and pleasant. I hadn't heard it that much.

"I've talked to them on the phone. Never met them."

"What are they like?"

"Well, they only call me when they're upset. Sam gave them my number for messages, because he doesn't have a phone."

She waited patiently for the explanation.

"They're kosher, you know," I offered.

"Yes."

"Well, his mother's kind of hysterical. I always speak to Mr. Rosen. He's the one who calls."

"Is that his last name? Rosen?" She smiled as if she'd discovered a secret.

"Yes. He's in advertising, but I guess he's out of work most of the time. He seems nice, always trying to understand. It was funny, the first few times he called. The school was writing him nasty letters. He'd call and ask for Sam. I'd have him call back later and try to get hold of Sam in the meantime. Sometimes Sam wouldn't come. When he did, it wasn't very good. Sam's always pleasant to everybody, very polite. But not to his parents."

She stared at my face, listening, wanting to know everything about him.

"After a while Sam wouldn't come to the phone at all so I'd end up having long conversations with his father. He'd be like, 'How's my boy? Do you see him much? What's this I hear? He hasn't been to class in six months and they're getting ready to throw him out?' And I'd say, 'Oh, Mr. Rosen, he's fine. There's some kind of foul-up in communications between the central

office and the philosophy department. Sam's working on an
independent project, which is why he hasn't been attending
classes. As a matter of fact, I was talking to his professor the
other day and he says Sam's work may be revolutionary in its
contribution to the science of knowledge. Besides, the school
always exaggerates the seriousness of a situation.' On like that,
I'd go. And he'd be very patient and want to believe everything
was all right. But in the background I could always hear his
mother screaming and crying. Mr. Rosen had to stop every few
minutes to try and keep her quiet. Not very nice."

"They live in New York?"

"Long Island. Where are you from?"

"Palo Alto. My mother's a pill freak."

"What kind of pills?"

"Any kind. She's a pharmacist."

"That's handy."

We smiled at each other. She kept smiling when I was ready
to stop, so I looked at Sam and Rennel. She continued smiling
at me anyway.

"You look like an Indian."

"No," I said. "You do."

"Do you like real folk music?"

"Yes, very much."

"And you like Omar?"

"Yes. Very much."

"Did you ever sleep with him?"

I looked at her sharply, but I could tell she was only curious.
She must have felt safe with Sam if she could afford to wonder.

"No," I said.

I could tell she wanted to ask why, but Sam cut in. "What
are you two talking about?"

He'd been watching us. Carlotta smiled at him and he

smiled back and I was getting tired of their long-winded smiles, all that communing of souls.

In front of the mirror, Rennel rubbed his chest and belly with a soiled towel. He smirked at Carlotta while he rubbed lasciviously at his nipples, cupped one of his breasts in his hand. He dropped the towel and watched himself and Carlotta in the mirror as he untied his pajama cord. The pajamas fell to his ankles and he stood there in his underpants. He flexed his arms, rolled his belly a little while he watched it in the mirror. I smirked; Carlotta and Sam weren't paying any attention to him. They were still smiling at each other.

Rennel realized no one was watching him and scowled, snorted. He climbed into his leathers, slipped on his socks and heavy black boots.

"You people ready?"

The raised blade

There came a day I was in no way prepared for. Fifteen years had passed since I had seen Sam and Carlotta. I was thirty-six years old and living in Boston. Time had ripped me out of my holdings, out of my natural domain, and stranded me on my back looking at a horizon altogether too far away. I had blunted my mind beneath blossoming trees and written my little books in feeble defiance of mortality. I had spun exuberant lies and told crass truths, all to avoid pain and unpleasant incidents. I had dutifully loved and later settled for not loving. After years thick with colorful scenes and phantasmagoria, my life had gone gray, dull, and bereft of my own will, an abandonment of volition that carried me into the cold and out again, like a sand flea in the surf.

I had spent the past many months pursuing a young man. A poet. Jack. He was beautiful, and he despised me. First, I had given him money. When the money ran out I went to work again at odd jobs that seemed to separate me from him more than the hours accounted for. While I was away he took long walks or visited old girlfriends. He spoke well, too, and was a loyalist—novel after all my years with revolutionaries. He disliked my name and changed it. "Sally" he refused, and referred to me, when necessary, as "Miss Gunnar." For months I had tailed him. Eventually I moved in with him and ignored his talk of previous affairs and his sick, hungry staring at slim women.

I was fat by then. No longer just round, but thickening and clumsy.

We lived in a large room with high ceilings and an elegant blanked-out fireplace in one wall. We had moved the hot plate into the closet and dined at a small table in a corner. In another corner was the bed, narrow and too soft, where we smothered each other nightly. And two hunched, high-backed chairs stood near the table on which he wrote late into the night to avoid climbing into bed with me.

It was hot in the old house. The lady on the ground floor, bleary with glaucoma, watched four square inches of her television screen through a magnifying glass, and left her door open to hear us as we passed. She answered the phone in the hall when it rang, and shrieked the number up the stairwell: "Forty-one!" if it was for the pale cleric, "Seventeen!" if it was one of the countless faceless girls who called my phone for the pleasure of hearing his voice.

I told him once that I didn't care if he kept girls hanging on strings from the window ledge as long as I was one of them. It was not true, but it would have taken a lot of damage to mar him for me. I chose to accept his faults and keep him near.

I always thought of him as pacing, but in fact most of the time he sat very still. He was starkly beautiful with his feet up and the blank pain of boredom on his face. His jaws and lips and nose were so delicately cut that sometimes, as he slept, I would examine his face, marveling at its perfection. I was weakened by my love for him, and he was utterly miserable, stuck with me and by the small degree of comfort I could offer him with my money, my willingness to work for him, the cloying amiability of my devotion. He was not proud to be with me. I was too fat, my laugh too coarse. My occasional melodramatic weeping—"You can't love someone like me . . ."—all too easily explained what we both felt. He responded by dutifully patting my head. He was unable to say what I needed to hear, due to a lack of facility or his inclination toward lying, which only made him more appealing to me. Even as he patted and stroked my hair, he stared at the wall with a sick expression, yearning to be somewhere else.

Most nights, tired after working for hours at the small table with the lamp, when his poems had sucked him dry, he would slide in beside me. As he lay, breathing softly, looking up at the ceiling, I would be woken up by the pain plucking at him. So we both lay, unspeaking, until finally he would turn to me and work himself to sleep. I was grateful for this evidence of the strength of his will, if not affection.

Now, all those years I had never had an orgasm that was not self-induced. Fifty-seven men—I had counted, too many for comfort, and only a few of any interest—had come with my cooperation but made no dent on my pleasures. The exercise was necessary for my sanity. It reassured me and let me sleep. I sought it out with ravenous energy, but on just as many nights, when my desires were urgent and specific, I rubbed myself into quick peaks of relief.

But this fellow, the fifty-seventh—it is definitely unseemly to have kept count—had a quality of pride and a knowledge that the others had not. He was the first to rouse me, to make me run between the legs, even with only a look. One night he had been fooling with me for a while and stumbled upon the right place, *the* place, and set me off. I was surprised, and then I was wild with anticipation. I cried out, this time for real; I had pretended thousands of orgasms in my time, arched my back and trembled and rattled my heels, moaned, laughed, raked my nails—all to simulate the only models I had, from literature. But at last I was undone; my orgasm was real. I gave in. I grabbed his hand to keep him from losing his place. I gripped his hair, my hips stiffened. He went on for some time and my hands slid down to keep him there.

But he was insulted by my obvious enthusiasm; he must have realized I had been performing before. It disgusted him.

"Do it yourself, then!" he said, his bitter voice a bludgeon, and rolled away from me, furious.

I began to weep, my sobs puddling, coagulating, until snot and tears ran into my ear. I crept out of the bed, crawled over behind the chairs, choking and grunting with pain. The moon or some streetlight spared me nothing; my great white mounds of flesh spread out on the floor, in the periphery of his view. Though I might have bawled that he had never managed to bring me to orgasm, not once in all those months, that he was too ignorant of my anatomy to do so, that all that time I had been pretending, that all along *he* had been using *me* for masturbation—and likely any other woman he'd ever slept with as well, no matter what they may have said at the time—though I might have managed to screech this out through the snot, it would not do. It was not in my nature, not with him. He was my Beauty. To clearly explain myself, I would have also needed to describe the comfort that warmed and softened in my lungs and chest, the indescribable pleasure of his face above mine in the bed, sensations we have traditionally called love.

Instead I lay on the floor, hidden behind the chairs, snuffling, shaking, tears streaming. I did think of all these things to say, and also of the vanity and ignorance of a certain class of male. Since then, numerous books and articles have bombarded men with the truth—surely by now they must know. But in those days they all seemed to think that women needed some apparatus to masturbate. "Coke bottles!" "I couldn't figure out why she was so wild about zucchini. . . ." A thousand snickers, *jokus interruptus*, the despairing female entering the room just in time for the punch line and flushing red or going pale—not with embarrassment, but rage. Men fancied that, since we lack our own, women must require a mock substitute for their equipment. "Not true," we could have said. "We do it just like you do, by rubbing ourselves."

They would have responded, "Rubbing what?"

Or else, they'd ignorantly bluff about the clitoris: "Oh, well, it's just this little bump. Nothing much comes of it."

But I didn't say anything. To confess, admit, or announce seemed too dangerous, impossible, because I could see it would have given him an excuse to leave. It would have degraded me to tell the truth after all those months. And I see, from his perspective, how it would be disgusting to discover that this mooing, gyrating, strenuously passionate mammal on which you had been relieving yourself for some time had only been pretending to like it. Rather like emptying a very full bowel into an immaculate pot and discovering that it doesn't flush, it blows back on you. Truth must begin on the first night, or a woman must forever hold her peace and rub herself to orgasm in the bathroom afterward—while he's back in bed doing the same, probably.

⁂

One day I brought home two dozen donuts from the DoNut Shop, where I worked. He could not take one but watched, expressionless and still, as I ate them, ate them, and ate them. Soon after that I took to hiding them in waxy bags in the closet: in the suitcase, behind the laundry bag, beneath the sweaters piled on the shelf.

He never said hello when I came back from work but went

on reading or staring at the wall as the record spun out on its wheel of sound. I would come in as softly as my bulk permitted, kick off my broken shoes, and cavort cautiously to plant a kiss on his troubled brow. He would pat my head as polite as anything, and then I would seek out my hidden treasures while hanging up my coat. I'd rattle open the wax bag, take a bite, change my clothes, munching all the while. Then I'd flush the crumbs down the sink and rinse the sugar off my cheeks before going back to sit at his feet and ask what he'd like for supper. As often as not, he would say, "Nothing." He seemed to live on red wine, dried apricots, and the odd salt binge. Then I would tell him tall tales and resort to my caches repeatedly during the evening. In the morning I would wait until I got to work where the donuts would be hot and fresh.

One day when I returned home, the donuts were all gone. "You . . ." I began tentatively, "you haven't done anything with my donuts, have you?"

His swiveled his lovely head toward me with a chilly glitter in his eye: "They're out there." He nodded at the fire escape. "I pissed on them."

"Hee hee," I said, trotted to the window, and leaned out. He had always been amusing, perhaps he was joking. We kept an old five-gallon paint bucket on the fire escape as a garbage can. I pulled it toward me; it grated over the steel platform. Inside, melted sugar ran down, a shining syrup, and chocolate frosting was crushed into the donut mush. I also whiffed the stench of his urine.

I gasped, pushed the pail away, and whirled round on him, where he sat in my wing-backed chair. I was outraged. I unleashed the unadulterated anger I'd been holding in for months: "Why did you do that?"

"Because you must weigh two hundred pounds already. I pissed on them all day."

I was burnt by grief, rage, frustration—not, at that moment, by shame, not at all, but because the donuts were no longer edible.

I tried to stop eating them. The shame took hold and festered long after that particular hunger had evaporated. Shame was not new to me and had only been held off, like the remission of a terminal disease. Thinking about how he was shamed by me, brought low, as it were, by my very proximity, fills me even now with misery.

*, *, *,

There I lay, naked on the floor, snuffling in the moonlight, feeling already the pain of his inevitable departure, my tears running wetly. Dawn arrived; I could just make out the cheery contours of the furniture. My limbs ached; pain ripped my head slowly, jaggedly into two. Tears and mucus crusted my face and neck. All night he had been still and silent in the bed, while I, on the floor, made noise.

The sheets hissed as he stirred. I watched as he rose, strode to the closet, and took out the largest suitcase. His legs were all that were visible to me—his long, slender legs, graceful ankles, smooth hip, agonizing thigh. He emerged, all in view, but the dried mucus on my eyelids made it difficult to see. His face was, as usual, so still. He took his books from the table; his papers he laid on top of the clothes in the suitcase. He crossed the room in silence and leaned over me, looked directly at me for the first time since the night before. He so seldom looked at me.

"I have to go now." His face was as if built in some ecstatic vision. His fine, pale hair softened its planes slightly. "I have to go now. I cannot stay anymore."

I could have spoken, reached out, and grabbed his foot. Instead I listened to his soft footsteps, the door as it closed, his feet light and quick on the stairs.

I died without death at the end. No end for my pain. "Gone!" roared my blood. "Gone!" shrieked the air in my lungs. "Blank! Empty!" Each hollow cell of my brain echoed a tinny chorus.

I felt a cramp in my lower intestine and then a sudden gush as my bladder emptied over my thighs. I waited to collect myself to sufficiently to carry out my plan: get into the closet, stand up, turn on the light, and find a knife. I lay facedown in the mucus and dreamed of his laugh, rare and treasured, and the incredible length of his rib cage, how the bones sweetly bent toward the delicate beads of his spine. Then pain returned—memories of him buying gifts and taking taxis for his other girls, paying for it with my puny money all these months. I conjured images of my sagging plump body, the postures I assumed to seduce him but likely only repulsed him. He must be walking on air now, I thought. The relief he must feel! Had last night been engineered to trigger his escape? Or had he, too, experienced a sudden revelation: that not only was I not pleasing him, but that he was not pleasing me? All of his heroically polite efforts in vain, my devotion to him revealed to be impure. Or had it been my long, fluid honking throughout the night? He despised hysteria, was driven to nausea by the sight of weeping, and consigned to melodrama all professions of emotional discomfort. He only liked me when I was cheerful.

Then the manager of the DoNut Shop knocked on the door. I had forgotten she had promised to wake me up for an early shift. It was already five thirty.

I sat up. For fifteen seconds, I was sure he had come back to make peace, recover our life together . . . I scrabbled at my face, pulled on the door.

"Are you sick?" the manager asked when she saw me.

Yes, very sick, dead in fact. Especially now that she had killed me again simply by not being him. She was a small person, thin. I had managed to keep her from meeting him. The thought of them together had made me wary. She claimed to be intimately acquainted with the singers of the day, to have lived for years on the wit of her own songs and the stage name of Tiger Lily. She couldn't have been more than nineteen, and she was vastly ambitious for the salaried glory in the back room of the DoNut Shop.

I banged my face hard against the doorframe. I could feel my face hitting the wood, and I knew there should be pain, but I could not feel it. My nose felt wet again.

"What's wrong? Are you drugged?" She was worried. "Your nose is bleeding."

I didn't answer.

"Hey. Are you hungover, Sally? Can you come to work? I have to make deliveries and there's nobody else to work out front until after lunch. The bakers can't go out front and serve, you know. It's the union." Her soft, young face was grim with disapproval, the anxiety that I might inconvenience her, and the disgust at what seemed to be the aftermath of a problem with drink or drugs.

I let the door swing open and turned to find my yellow uniform. She leaned in the doorway, tapped her own elbows, and watched me. I was tousled, smeared—the alcoholic slut.

"Don't you want to . . . wash up?" Pat was her name, I think.

We walked down the grimy posterior of Beacon Hill toward

the corner. Prime location for a donut shop, directly across from Massachusetts General Hospital. I had managed to put on shoes, and by some miracle, my hair was out of my face.

"No more cheese rolls," I rasped to a customer from behind the counter. Tears rusted my vocal cords.

"I'm too tired to get you any more coffee. Go away," I snapped at a sassy intern.

"You are too fat," I muttered, glaring at a big-butted college girl holding a Rollo May book in a library binding under one upper arm.

"What?" she said. "I want a dozen maple bars."

"You are too fat!" I shouted, my throat aching. "Don't you know nobody will share your bed if you are too fat? Go away. Don't eat for six weeks and you'll be fine. Go away."

Mr. Chesbrough, the head baker, emerged through the swinging door from the kitchen. He'd been watching. I always called him sir. He liked me.

"What are you doing?" He spoke to me softly as I scraped the donuts from the display trays straight into the garbage. Sugar, glazed, chocolate, and butterscotch donuts slid into the big plastic garbage pail.

He stuck his arm out, blocked me from grabbing more. "Better lie down," he said as he led me along.

"You are an anti-fuck manufacturer," I said to him. "Too many donuts—no more flesh because there is too much flesh." I giggled. "You're a goddamn Nazi, handing out poisonous anti-fuck treats to innocent children."

He deposited me in the chair inside the office. Mr. Chesbrough asked for the name of my doctor. He was kindly, but worried.

"You seem to me like you've been smoking marijuana, but if you say not . . ." I hardly listened. "You were throwing my whole night's work into the garbage, and I am telling you that you are either stoned or drunk, drugged solid it looks like . . ."

There was a big office paper cutter on the desk. The long, machete-like blade was up, waiting. I hadn't noticed it before. Had no idea it was there.

I had calmed and was now slumped silently in the wooden chair. Dully, feebly, I was aware that I had just lost my job. I felt a certain relief.

"How could you get yourself in such a mess?" Mr. Chesbrough pleaded to understand. "I always thought you were such a lady." His face was dark with reproach. He was right. I had been so polite at the shop. I never laughed too loudly, I kept my head down, I sympathized with the poor quality of the equipment and the danger of walking to work at two o'clock in the morning. Hadn't I also admired photographs of his strange children? Wasn't there something about a diabetic wife? "Miss Gunnar," he always called me, and did not despise me or ignore me for my sweetness.

He leaned on the desk and peered closely at me. His sympathy melted me.

Tears—I didn't feel them until they hit my chin. The middle of my face felt shut off, shorted out.

"Gu-blug," I muttered, nonsense. My throat was full of mucus. I stood up, I tried to speak. "It wasn't—" I started to sob. The enormous ugliness of my face was distinctly tangible. I wanted to explain that it was a lost love that had made me behave so wildly, that of course I knew it was foolish for one such as I, hardly above slime, to presume to love. I wanted to tell him I had always been a sucker for a pretty face.

"It's not drugs! It's . . ." Pain, I was going to say, and to aid my credibility I employed a half-remembered tool of rhetoric, the downward swoop of the palms to the podium—in this case, the back office desk. But instead I fell onto the raised arm of the paper cutter blade. In fact, my not inconsiderable weight pressed the long knife straight down onto Mr. Chesbrough's right hand. It crunched.

"Yahhh!" Mr. Chesbrough screamed. His mouth opened so long I could see his quivering uvula.

I looked down at his hand, saw a flash of white bone, and jerked the knife up again. There was a sound in my ears that went on until I realized it was my own voice, squealing, "I'm sorry, I'm sorry, I'm sorry!"

Mr. Chesbrough's falsetto screaming continued. "You cow! You stupid cow!" And then he fainted to the floor. Blood pumped from the cut, gently and quietly, onto his white apron, and pooled in the folds of the cloth before slipping off to the floor.

I dropped down beside him and grabbed his wrist tight in my two hands, squeezing, trying to keep the blood from escaping. I whispered, "I'm sorry," as a kind of tourniquet for my conscience.

The office door opened.

"Christ!" said Pat. She swooped down beside me, reached for his hand, then stopped. "Is he dead? Or is it just his hand?"

"His hand," I said.

"Can we lift him? Between us?" she asked me, and we were tugging at his shoulders when he came to and began to cry. We helped him through the public serving area. Thankfully only a few tables and two stools at the counter were occupied.

"Idiot," Mr. Chesbrough said, nodding at me. "She did it. Miss Gunnar did it." It occurred to me he didn't know my first name.

"Call me Sally," I said.

It was slow that day at the emergency ward and they took him right away. I sat down in the green waiting room.

"Are you being helped?" asked a nurse.

"I'm waiting for someone else," I said.

"But it looks like you have a broken nose. You'd better have it treated," she said.

A little later, a doctor asked me to count backward from one hundred while he administered anesthetic. I relaxed on the paper-covered table and smiled at the white cone a nurse had slipped over my mouth and nose.

Sometime later I awoke and felt acutely nauseous. I managed to turn my head just in time so the gush of half-digested donuts arched out onto the tile floor rather than over me. Some reassuring activity began on that side of the table almost immediately, so I lay back and relaxed, calmly confident that I would never have to face that particular mess, no matter how much I deserved to. At first I was pleased that it had not been odiferous vomit, but then I remembered that my nose was not operating at full capacity, so it might well have been a very odorous puke, very disgusting for the aide or nurse or whoever did the cleaning to deal with. By the time I turned my head to look, he or she, and the vomit, were gone.

4 4 4

They were able to save Mr. Chesbrough's fingers. "Just a few stitches," a nurse told me when I was released the next day, and sent home with orders to rest. I wanted bed and a murder mystery. Doctor's orders.

The old woman downstairs was shelling peas into a bowl as I went by. The stairs and the door, the key itself, were such incomprehensible obstacles that I sat quietly for a moment on the bottom step. A final, enormous effort carried me up and into my room. My cheeks were beginning to itch from the bandage.

I leaned toward the mirror and smiled at my face and the big, white A-shaped bandage spread over my nose and cheeks.

I breathed deeply through my mouth. With an unusual deliberation, I rooted out my tobacco and cigarette papers, a saucer and matches. Carried them to the unmade bed and deposited them on the floor in reach of the pillow. As I smoothed the sheets and removed my uniform, a gentle fatigue began to sneak up the backs of my calves. It felt so good to lie down, to notice the small nagging pains of my body only as they were fading.

It seemed incredible that I should feel so empty and clean so short a time after I had been overcome with that lunatic misery; perhaps I was careful to edit my thoughts to only what I wanted to remember. As I lay in bed, I told myself time would begin again after some sleep. There were plenty of years left for bad thoughts, for replaying Mr. Chesbrough's bleeding hand, my indiscreet, self-indulgent maundering, and the events of the night before. Morning could bring the grief and shame again, but not before I had rested. I did not even smoke, but slid off wondering, with a grin, if everything had happened because I had so nearly managed an orgasm at some other hand than my own.

In that night of peace, those hours of necessary indifference, the possibility of solitude occurred to me. Lying sprawled there, unwatched, was so very comfortable. I did not feel mortified by the width of my thighs, the size of my buttocks, the thickness of my wrist, the flab beneath my arms and chin, the odor of my feet. If only, I thought, I could be sure of never going hunting again, of never being driven out into the night by my own desires. No more rooting and scavenging for listeners, no more posturing, no more clumsy experiments meant to attract. I mourned all the energy I'd spun away in my futile attempts to secure a back to hug for a night.

I thought of myself as a spider quivering in the center of a web while swearing off flies. I was harmless when I was only chasing and dreaming, but in those few terrible cases in which I had snared some poor prey, made them captives of my cross-eyed, ravenous devotion, the consequences had been strangely poisonous.

Now, on clear mornings, after coffee and an undisturbed hour with a book, I am able to confess that the injury I have produced has been mainly to myself, that those I have afflicted with my heedless acts or stupid talk have bled for longer in my reflections than they ever did in reality.

On other mornings I am visited by a prickling suspicion, haunting the periphery of my mind, that perhaps this self-harrowing is a distraction from some true, instinctive beast-liness. I vowed to form a structure for my retreat, fold my tents and creep into my ecumenical shelter, conjure up some idol powerful enough to hold me to it: silence, abstinence, and solitude. I hoped some gift of strength would enable me to remain there.

But even then, at that hour of epileptic misery, fifteen years after my last sight of them, if Sam or Carlotta had knocked, would I not have leapt up, told them my tale with humorous fugues, and then taken them out for a drink to hear their tale in return?

The Hung Far Low

Nobody had packed. There were rugs and shawls draped over the mattress. Long dresses hung in the closet. Strewn blue jeans and little boxes. A lot of carved wood boxes from Mexico with mother-of-pearl flowers enlaced on the lids. Indian blankets, a bottle with big feathers sticking out of it. And the dog. I'd seen her around campus. A tall, skinny, black dog.

"Half greyhound," Carlotta said. "Her name is Angelina."

When we came in, the house was dark and we could hear thumps and sharp yelps. Carlotta yelled, "Angelina!" The thumps got louder. The yelps turned into barking. Carlotta opened a door and the big stupid dog came out, slobbering and wagging and pissing all over. Carlotta shut her in the kitchen while we took armfuls of their stuff to the car.

I carried out a beaded curtain and a box of seashells, lots of clothes and rugs. Carlotta swept it all into fast piles. We dumped it all into the trunk of the car and the floor of the back seat. The dark street stayed dark. The light from the front door of the house shone down on the dented Rambler. Sam and Rennel conferred about the red telephone. They definitely wanted to take it but they argued whether to cut the cord or disconnect the wires from the outlet. Carlotta made a last trip out with a stack of records. When she came back the sky was lightening. We stood watching Rennel and Sam argue. Finally Rennel yanked the cord out of the wall; he clenched his jaw and stretched his neck, turning so we could see his hands and arms working. Sam carried the phone to the car. Carlotta got the dog out of the kitchen.

I sat in back with Angelina as we drove to Sam's house. The sun was just up, bright on the roofs. The street was still cold in shadow. Sam and Rennel went looking for a screwdriver while Carlotta and I carried things up. We dumped everything on the floor.

When we were finished, sunlight yellowed the front door and brightened the stairs up to Sam's place. Clancy came out and sat on the steps looking down at us. She wore her white lab coat. Half her hair had been brushed, the other half stuck out wildly. I could see little yellow crusts of sleep in the corners of her eyes. Her eyes were large and seemed almost liquid through her glasses.

"Is there a dog up there?" She nodded toward the faint yapping coming from the upper floor.

Carlotta nodded. "Yes. It's my dog."

"Did you know there are cats living in this house?"

Carlotta looked down at the newspaper on the floor.

"Does Lance know that you are bringing a dog in here?" Her voice trembled like she wanted to scream.

Carlotta backed down a step to look at her. "You mean Omar? He knows."

Clancy jumped up. Her whole body was shaking. Her nylons were bunched at the ankles.

"It's very inconsiderate! Very, very inconsiderate! I never would have thought he'd do such a thing!"

The bald philosophy student who lived in the basement popped his pink head out of the downstairs kitchen window. "Clancy, your oatmeal's burning."

"Oh!" She stopped in the doorway and screeched, "You

just better keep that dog away from us! My cats will kill it!" She pushed through the door, shrieking, "And I suppose you couldn't lift your intellectual hand to take your philosophical breakfast off the stove!"

Carlotta looked at me and raised her eyebrows. We went upstairs and shut the door behind us. Dropped the last of the junk onto the spreading pile. Carlotta opened the bathroom door and let out Angelina. Sam and Rennel were huddled over an old telephone jack in the woodwork. Carlotta and I sat on the floor. She wrestled Angelina down beside her and held her, twitching.

"That girl downstairs is mad about something."

Sam looked up anxiously. "What girl? Clancy?"

Rennel waved a screwdriver disgustedly. "Ah, she's nuts."

We headed to Hung Far Low, the twenty-four-hour Chinese restaurant, for a celebratory feast at 8:00 a.m.

"I met this guy the other day, Maury Lichtenstein," Sam started. "You know him? He's a philosophy major from the Bronx. He wants to be a farmer. He wants to set up a little place and raise one money crop and just what he needs to live. A little vegetable garden and a couple of pigs. A couple of calves for meat and a cow for milk and butter. Half a dozen chickens. It will make him independent. He's got it all figured out that he can work for four hours a day, and a little longer at harvest and planting time. He'd make a good living and have all the rest of the day for study and meditation—can I have the beef and bean sprouts, please? Doesn't that sound better than busting your ass for an insurance company all day, every day?"

Carlotta passed the platter. Sam pulled out thin morsels of meat with his chopsticks.

"You ought to tell him to read up on goats," I said, and brandished my chopsticks. "Goats are much easier to raise than cows or sheep. They're much smarter. They're like mules. They don't kill themselves by eating too much. They don't break their legs stepping into holes. They're resistant to diseases, and they're totally useful. You can drink the milk and make butter and cheese out of it. You can eat the meat and use the fur for rugs and the leather for clothes. They don't eat much and they can get by on rocks and moss. I think you can harness them to a cart, too. Besides they have a lot of personality. If you've got a goat around, you're not alone."

I didn't know what I was talking about, of course. I'd never had much to do with goats. But with Sam, it didn't matter what you said if you said it with authority.

Rennel shoveled in his rice and pork. He used his chopsticks surprisingly delicately.

"What a great idea!" Sam beamed. "I'll tell Lichtenstein that. Goats! I wish I'd known there were things like that when I was a kid. I went to regular camp. It was awful. Nobody liked me there. I was so unpopular that all the other kids started calling the toilet the Sam instead of the john. They went to the Sam all summer long."

Rennel smirked. "Well, save me some of that duck stuff for when I get back from the Omar." He stalked off to the bathroom, waving his ass proudly. Sam chuckled.

"Once in a while he does come up with something," I said.

"He's so bright. You ought to give him more of a chance," Sam said. "He's just not too good in social situations. When it's just two people talking he's sharp."

"Yeah."

Carlotta speared a piece of pineapple. She put it calmly into her mouth and said, "Rennel has a dirty mind."

"That's just from hanging around with laboratory rats.

Hazards of the psychology business. He needs to simplify his existence."

The restaurant owner stood stolid behind the till. Dragons were embroidered on scrolls hanging on the wall behind him. The food on our table sent up pleasant smells. Rennel returned from the bathroom and started poking at the plates.

Sam announced, "Carlotta and I are going to move out to the country as soon as we can manage it."

Rennel paused.

"Just a little house somewhere away from Clancy and the cats. We'll have a vegetable garden and a couple of chickens."

Rennel snorted. "What about school? Weren't you supposed to graduate this year? You're in a very bad way with the administration."

"We'll commute. Carlotta has a driver's license. We'll buy an old car. And out in the country with nothing to distract us we'll get a lot of studying done. We'll just come in for school, and for my Chinese painting class. We won't hang around at all."

I felt suddenly tired. They went on talking but I was not interested in their plan. I excused myself and left. Out the door, down the steps. The Hung Far Low sign flashed red. My belly was full. I walked straight back to my upstairs room and went to sleep.

A ten-dollar car for ten dollars

It was my father who brought me my first goldfish, long ago. He brought it in a clear bowl, along with a dark brown dress for my mother. My mother tore the dress and threw it on the floor. She was angry and hated my father and his gifts, which were meant to placate her anger.

I immediately loved the fish, its live beauty, how it dreamed in crystal water, yet I dared not turn my mother against me. I held the bowl in my hands and watched the fish swim inside the clear sphere I held with my fingers. The bowl was cool to the touch. I looked at my father, who was waiting to see whether I would accept the gift. But I also felt my mother watching, felt the heat of her anger beaming down. I stared at my father and let the bowl slide from my hands. It crashed at my feet. The fish heaved in the broken glass and spreading water.

"We could pick him up," he said softly. "You could still save it." But I felt my mother's hatred all around me, and I put out my foot in its red leather sandal and placed it atop the tiny flashing body. I crushed the fish, could feel it give beneath the sole of my shoe, and even turned my foot so that it ground against the floor. I was five years old.

My father went away. I could feel my mother's mood lift, could feel her pride at what I had done. She swept and mopped until the fish and its water were gone. She gave me cookies with frenzied cheer. But I would not take her warmth toward me; I was not too young to do evil, to kill, to cause great pain. The knowledge of my own evil and cowardice has never left me, it is with me even now, clear as the bowl and the water.

◢ ◢ ◢

The day is dead. One of my four friends, with whom I had a standing coffee date each third Monday of the month, is moving west to another county. Mr. Geddoes, my Fuller Brush man, was promoted to a more prestigious and profitable sales route. He came to my door today with the last order he'll ever deliver to me. My brooms and disinfectant will soon be delivered by some probably pink-cheeked local with ambitions to a district manager title.

Mr. Geddoes is Australian, a dried and withered man. He could make any cleaning product sound colorful and enticing: boxes of bug powder, tins of floor polish, toilet fresheners. But his sales depended on the compassion inspired by the sight of his emaciated frame keeling at a forty-five-degree angle in the effort to balance his enormous load. He used to say that if he ever gained ten pounds his business would be ruined. But there was no danger of that. The more he sold, the more he had to carry as he went about his deliveries; and the more he carried, the more guilty his customers felt.

I brought him in the first day he came. It was hot that day, and the wraith in the black suit at my door seemed so indifferent to the weight of his load that I was immediately convinced that he was laboring beneath some more personal burden. So I took him into my cool kitchen and told him I would never buy anything unless he accepted an iced coffee. He showed me the colorful catalogs, opened his strange sample case with its inexhaustible oddities.

My third Mondays with Mr. Geddoes became my keyhole to the wider world. He had spent his youth bludgeoning kangaroos for the bounty and had learned tolerance and a certain irony from the blood. His wife, he said, adored him—by which I assume he meant that she blasted and shriveled him with demands. The president of any country that came up was a grand fellow to Mr. Geddoes, just for getting away with such stuff. Mr. Geddoes liked to see a bit of larceny well done, with no crudeness about it, but a high polish, such as might be administered with one of his own waxes. Mr. Geddoes loved mystery, and he read murders and puzzles with the palate of the most erudite connoisseur. No glossing over the exact nature of a poisoner's tools could fool him. If it wasn't possible to kill a person in a particular way, Mr. Geddoes knew and could tell you why. We often spent the entire half hour of his monthly visits in furious disagreement over the acceptable subterfuges a composer of mysteries might inflict on his readers to conceal, till the last page, the solution. An iron code was the criterion for Mr. Geddoes. He claimed there were only three tales in the course of his long reading that had flummoxed him till the last.

"Page fifty-two," he would say upon returning some lurid paperback I'd loaned him on his last visit. After he left I would spend hours poring over page fifty-two to try to discover the precise detail that revealed the mystery's solution. Often it was neither a plot point or clue, but rather some revelation of the caliber of the writer's mind.

"I knew when he introduced that tawdry business of the red slippers," Mr. Geddoes might say, "that it's a mediocre mind this fellow has. He's no greater craft than an obvious twist at the end, and it'll be the one they suspected all along."

He knew strange things, Mr. Geddoes. And he was hyperobservant. He was a man who could appreciate that the covers were clean, that the milk and bread were fresh. He noted the specific reason for placing goldfish beneath a lamp and for deciding against cats.

It was Mr. Geddoes who introduced me to my toad last spring. When I asked him if he recognized the odd song that had been filling the garden in the morning he said, "That's a toad, that is. And a big one." He left his chair and went out into the garden, treading slowly, silently, listening. I followed. The song had bothered me. It had an eerie quality at first, when I didn't know what it was. Mr. Geddoes pointed. "There he is, by the compost heap. An old fellow." That's when I first saw the sulfurous yellow toad, hunched on the stones around the heap, his gnarled flesh bunched around him and an incongruous trilling coming from his pale throat. Well, the toad remains, and Mr. Geddoes is gone. He's moved over to the fancy housing development across the county line. Now the bright bottles and squat cans will have no more pleasant associations than the smells of the solutions they contain and their effect on my woodwork and tile. I am eaten by resentment, and whoever takes Mr. Geddoes's place will get no welcome from me. He will have to take his orders on the front step like the milkman and the paperboy.

❧ ❧ ❧

Weeks passed. A month, maybe. I didn't go to Sam's house. They wanted to be alone. I sometimes saw them from across a lawn at school, her long legs and her fringed leather tunic, Sam looking drab beside her in his robe. Angelina followed them everywhere. When she ran on the grass she wasn't so ugly. They picked up their mail and then sat for hours in the coffee shop. I don't think either of them went to class.

I was reading beneath the open skylight when I heard their

feet on the stairs. Carlotta entered first, smiling, then Angelina, then Sam.

Carlotta stared around the room. She smelled good and the beads on her fringed tunic tinkled as she moved. Angelina's nails scratched at the wood of the floor.

"Your room is so bare!" Carlotta exclaimed.

"Yes, I'm a monk, you know."

Carlotta sat on the floor and threw an arm around the dog. Sam crouched next to her. He began immediately.

"We've bought a ten-dollar car for ten dollars. I don't know what make it is because the chrome and the company name have all been ripped off. It's got almost no paint left. I believe it's a retired getaway car. But all I know for sure is that it gets about a mile and a half per gallon of gasoline and it won't go over twenty-five miles an hour. It takes two people to drive it because the ignition wires are loose. I hold them up against the contact terminals while Carlotta drives."

He paused, and Carlotta nudged him along. "And . . . ?"

"Yes, and the best news of all is that we found a little house in the country," Sam continued. "Wait till you see it! It's in the woods near the Tualatin River. It's next to a farm and is completely surrounded by trees. You can get down to the river through the woods. Really nice."

"When are you moving?" I asked.

"Tomorrow. Would you like to help?"

"Sure. I'd like to see it."

They came around noon. I'd been sitting on the front porch for a while and had almost forgotten about them. A dark car came silently down the street and jerked to a stop in front of me. The doors on one side had been closed with rope. Sam and Carlotta's pale faces flashed out at me through the dirty glass. I climbed in beside Sam.

"We had to coast in. I dropped the wires," he explained.

Carlotta peered stiffly at the street through the spokes of the steering wheel. Sam leaned his head back against the dusty upholstery.

He grinned and said, "We have to clean up the cat shit before we go."

My "What?" had three syllables.

"The landlady came by this morning and threw some kind of fit. We were still in bed, and she came right in and screamed at us."

Sam's eyes closed, reliving the pleasure of the memory. Carlotta glanced over and smiled at me.

"It was a truly remarkable scene. She was tiptoeing around, trying to pace without touching the dirty floor. She kept screaming, 'Filth! Filth!' She'd bend over and almost pick something up to demonstrate the filth, but at the last minute she'd realize it was *too* filthy and jerk her hand away. We were sitting up on the mattress by that time, with the blankets pulled up to our chins, and she was marching up and down being very careful not to look at us. Said she was going to have us charged with malicious property damage and she'd never rent to students again, and how her mother had warned her but she'd been deceived by my nice manners. She even said she's going to complain to the college and what would my mother think if she saw me in this kind of situation? Jabbering on and on, and all the time aching to sneak a peek at us, you know? At first we were a little scared, this crazy lady comes bursting into the room where we're sleeping, but it got funny very quickly. I started to grin and just couldn't stop. I winked at Lotta and she started to laugh. The lady really blew her top then. She just started screaming! Called Lotta a slut and a whore who had no respect for anything. Said she knew very well that we aren't married and that's a crime against the state and no woman would live in such a mess if she weren't sick, sick, sick. I got up and started walking toward her with my hands out like you do to a scared horse. I forgot I was naked. I was just trying to calm her down. In the middle of her big yarn about the cats and the smell and the dirt—well, I imagine she'd been working up her nerve to turn around and get a good look at me. But when she saw me standing there smiling at her, she flipped. She screamed, 'Help! Help!' and ran away yelling. We could hear her all the way down the block."

I leaned against the door, my belly aching from laughter.

"Clancy was running around yelling, 'Fire!' The phil major in the basement surfaced, everybody on the street poked their heads out to see what was going on. Anyway, she came back with a cop. By then we were dressed. He was embarrassed and didn't know what to say. But it ended up that if everybody moves out right away and we clean the stuff up we won't get arrested or whatever."

"But what about Clancy and all those others? They aren't your cats."

"Half the other people have already left, and if we leave it for them it won't get done. The landlady has only got my name. Right now you've got to drop me downtown. I have to see Mr. Sing. Pick me up on the way out with the first load. We ought to be able to do it in two trips."

Carlotta gripped the wheel. Sam reached to the wires and touched something beneath the dashboard. There was a stutter, a wheeze, a loud bang. The engine caught and gasped.

Carlotta grinned at me. "We named it Mr. Jones."

Sam hopped out in front of the Chinese painting studio, waved cheerfully as he went inside. Carlotta showed me how to touch the wires and then wrestled the car out into traffic. It was slow and loud. The dust from the upholstery coated my tongue, the inside of my mouth. The windows wouldn't roll down. Carlotta drove barefoot, her long legs fuzzy with hair. The leather of her dress was pale and soft and slid easily over her flesh. She killed the car in front of Sam's house. My hands were sticky from sweating on the wires.

Carlotta looked at me shyly. "You don't have to help with the cat shit. He just thought it was a funny story."

"It'd take you a week to do it alone."

The newspapers in the living room came up in stiff pieces. When we crumpled them they broke and tore. The bottom layer was sunk into the carpet. We got knives from the kitchen and scraped on our knees. Nobody else was home. Carlotta had shut Angelica in a bedroom, and she howled while we worked.

"I think it's the piss that smells so bad. The shit dries out and doesn't seem to smell."

"Ugh."

We carried the newspapers outside and laid them next to the piles of garbage at the back door. We scraped up the stony puddles beneath the bathtub and behind the kitchen stove. The smell didn't go away.

"Do you think we ought to move the sofa out and see what's behind it?" Carlotta asked.

"No."

I opened the door to the basement. It was pitch-black down there. The smell was the same, except it was also damp. I closed the door.

Carlotta was crouched under the kitchen table, scraping the linoleum. Her long haunches were up by her shoulders. She rocked back on her heels and smiled at me.

"I think I'm pregnant."

"Oh."

She stabbed absently at the floor. "I'm two weeks late. Anyway, I hope so."

"You want to be?"

"Yes. I stopped taking pills after the first time Omar and I fucked. After that, I wanted his baby."

"That's good. I was afraid you were going to ask me for the address of an abortionist."

"No."

"How does Sam feel?"

"I haven't been to a doctor yet. I want to wait to tell him till I'm sure."

"But he does know you stopped taking pills?"

"No. I don't want him to feel responsible at all," she said. "He can stay or go, whichever he wants. I don't want to tie him down, or make him do anything he doesn't want to do. I just want his baby. I'll support it and take care of it if he doesn't hang around. I just don't think that he ought to have to live with a thing I did on my own. Do you see?"

"Yeah."

"I never wanted a child before. I never thought of it at all, except as something I should try to prevent. Having a baby was always 'getting into trouble.' I've known a lot of men before Omar. But none of them ever brought it to my mind. After the first time, we were lying there, he was still on top of me with his face in my neck. The feeling just came to me, it started at my toes, that I wished something would come of it. You know? Like anything that beautiful and good should have consequences."

"So what will you do if he leaves?"

"I'll have my baby and keep it."

"Have you got any money?"

"My parents might let me have some. I can work."

"Have you ever worked?"

"I used to model swimsuits for a department store. Last summer I was a waitress at a place in Big Sur."

"Well, that's a reference, anyway."

"But my folks will keep sending me money until I don't come home in June. Will you not tell Omar? I want to wait to tell him when I'm sure."

"I won't."

᪲ ᪲ ᪲

I carried the heavy things to the car: the half-empty bag of rice, stacks of books, records, the record player. We crammed it all in. It was getting dark, too late for a second trip that day. Angelica sat in front and kept trying to jump into Carlotta's lap. I held her with one arm and the ignition wires with the other.

"She's excited," Carlotta said. "She's never been out in the country. She'll love it. There are lots of woods and fields around the house."

I curled my fingers in her fur to hold her down. Her bones beat against me, but she didn't bark.

"Do you know what a person's supposed to do when they're pregnant?" Carlotta asked.

"Well, you have to go to a doctor regularly. He'll tell you. Eat greens and all that."

"Doctors are such horseshit. Indian women didn't pay any attention until they knew it was about time, and then they just went off by themselves and had their baby."

"It can't hurt, going in to see a doctor," I said. "Just to make sure everything is all right. There's Sam."

Carlotta pulled the car up to the curb. The street was still, lit brightly by signs in the shops. Sam stood at the corner holding some bags in his arms. The dog tensed and I held her back while I opened the door. I dropped the wires and the car died painfully.

"Did everything go okay? Wow! How did you get all this stuff in one load? Wait till you see what I've got! First I had a good talk with Mr. Sing. He's really so clever. I asked him if he never made mistakes now that he's so good at painting. He said, 'Oh, my, yes.' He says even a master makes many mistakes, but he's a master because he knows to cover them up. See, he incorporates the mistake into the picture. If a stroke is a little wrong, he alters all the strokes that come after that just enough to restore the balance and make the original bad stroke right. You realize what this means? This is a case of a lot of wrongs making a right!"

He got in and was crushed against the door. The bags rattled. We got the car moving again.

"I got so excited talking to him about painting that I bought about a year's supply of rice paper and brushes and ink. He says I'm ready to use the good heavy ink now. And next week he's going to start me painting bamboo. It's technically the simplest thing to do but that's why it's such a challenge to do it really well. He says there are great masters who have spent their whole lives painting bamboo.

"Also! I found a feed and seed store while I was waiting for you. I've got tomatoes, lettuce, peanuts. Did you ever think you could walk into a store and buy peanut seeds? And I also have some seeds that are special for making bean sprouts. I guess they're beans. Come to think of it, peanuts' seeds must be peanuts. But you just wrap these beans in a wet towel and put them in a warm dark place and in a few days you've got crunchy bean sprouts with your rice. Magic."

Carlotta smiled. Street lights crept past in the windows.

"You want to drop me here, Carlotta?" I said.

"Aren't you coming out with us?"

"No, you won't want to make another trip in tonight, and I have to be here early in the morning."

The car pulled to the curb slowly, a halt so gradual I didn't notice it for seconds. Sam let me out and took Angelina and the wires from me. It was going to rain. The smells of the dog and the dust of the upholstery drifted out of the car.

"There aren't any lights on this car," I observed.

Sam laughed. "They're only so other people can see you coming, anyway. Maybe we ought to put a candle on the dashboard." He wrestled with the dog, his left arm rigidly holding the copper wires to the connection. The car rumbled dangerously. "Will you come tomorrow and see us?"

"Won't you be coming in?"

"No. There's a little town near us to get food in. I think we'll just spend a lot of time out there where it's quiet."

"I'll try to get a ride."

"And bring some horsemeat."

I slammed the door. The car moved off, shaking, and I watched them go until they turned at the corner.

I bathed strenuously, and then sat beneath the skylight making a careful sentence outline of a paper to be titled "Caliban: Scatological Imagery," for my Friday class. The image is not the thing, I told myself, the symbol is not the thing. Nothing is the thing but the thing. I kept sniffing at my fingers. It was hard to believe one bath could eliminate all traces of the cat odor. I slept with my hands under the pillow to prevent a finger from accidentally wandering into my mouth.

The country house

A good day for going to the country. I got two pounds of good sirloin tip at the horsemeat market and went over to Rennel's. He was working on his motorcycle in the living room. The front door was open. I could see him crouched over a pile of greasy black parts. His arms were black, his pale blue shirt smudged over the left breast. Been scratching his pits.

He grunted when I came in. I waited while he washed up and changed into his leather pants. Sat looking at the big green motorcycle. He'd had a wreck the day he bought it and had been working on it ever since. The engine hadn't spit once in over a year.

We climbed into the Rambler. Out past the natural gas plant. Across the Ross Island Bridge and onto the highway. We went through my old hometown and out past the new housing developments. The fields started coming up. Orchards and milk cows. We took a turnoff onto a narrow road. After a narrower road and a dirt road we turned onto a long twisting drive through thick firs. Dogs barked and a house showed through the trees on one side. We passed it, following the drive. More trees, more barking, and then Sam's new house.

It was small and white. A fine lawn spread away from it into the trees. The old car looked abandoned in the gravel. Angelina came charging hysterically around the house. The screen door creaked open. Sam came out to us smiling, walking slow, serene.

"Come and look. Oh, horsemeat, thanks."

There was a little kitchen, a smaller bathroom, a bedroom with enough space for a mattress. In the living room there was an old oil stove. Windows in nearly every wall. The rest of their possessions were in heaps on the floor. Someone, probably Carlotta, had tacked carpets and Indian blankets to the walls.

"What do you think?"

"It looks great. Looks just like somebody's house," I said.

Sam put on a record. He waved his hands and talked fast.

"We're going to divide the room into two parts. Move that big desk into the middle. Behind it, where the record player is, will be for relaxation and meditation. The other side is for work and study. We have good light for painting and reading. But the outdoors is the best part."

He opened a glass door and stepped through green vines onto grass. The music from the record player poured from the open windows. The woods, mostly dark firs, were silent, and brushed up to the edge of the lawn.

"I'm going to have little plots of vegetables all over. Angelina ran off this morning and I had to go to the farm next door to find her. They've got this big garden in back of the house. Long straight rows of everything. Very neat and tidy, but not very interesting. So I thought I'd plant things as though they were flowers. Say, 'Wouldn't a cabbage look nice under the tree?' and plant a cabbage. Just free in the grass, not with big dug-out plots around things. Maybe I'll dig little holes and plant a few seeds just any old place. All over the lawn and in the trees. I won't mark them or anything. The people at the farm have little sticks at the end of each row with the seed packages stuck on so they can tell what's planted there. But my way, it will always be a nice surprise. I'll be strolling along and see a plant and it will be a beet or a carrot. Be like an Indian brave going hunting. Come back from every walk with something good to eat. Maybe I'll open all the seed packages and dump them together in a bowl so I don't know which is what even when I plant them. That'd make it even more of a surprise when they come up."

He walked slowly in the sun. The air smelled clean. The sound of drums came from the windows. Sam's smile and the sun and the trees all mingled soft and easy together.

"You'd better not do that with your tomatoes," I said. "Tomatoes take a lot of babying."

I flinched at the word and looked at him to see if he knew yet.

"Is that so? What do you have to do?"

"Oh, you have to make sure that they get started strong. Most people plant the seeds in boxes indoors and keep them till they're fairly big before putting them outside. Then they run around at night covering them with glass jars and plastic bags so they don't get frosted."

"Well, they're worth the trouble, aren't they? Nothing nicer than a big, juicy tomato."

Rennel was doing chin-ups on a tree limb. Sam tried, but he was too short and had to jump to reach it. He hung easily; his strained forearms were broad; thick blue veins showed through his white skin. He pulled, but his chin didn't quite reach. He dropped lightly, bent at the knees.

"There's a little cabin back in the woods. It's got a wood-stove and a bed. We have the use of it, so if you ever want a place to stay, to go away and be quiet, you'd be welcome."

Rennel asked, "Can you show it to me?"

They went into the trees and out of sight. I walked back to the house to see Carlotta.

The record was over, the machine spun silently. I heard sizzling from the kitchen. Carlotta stood at the stove frying horsemeat. The rice pot steamed.

"How are you feeling?" I asked.

"All right." She turned the meat with a fork. "I made an appointment with a doctor to make sure I'm really pregnant."

"Have you been sick in the mornings at all?"

"No, but if you take pills, you usually don't get morning sickness."

"Is that so?"

"Somebody told me that. This girl." She leaned her hip on the stove. Her gray eyes twinkled as she smiled at me. There were faint dark spots on her suede dress.

"This is a nice place."

"Yes. I've decided to have my baby here."

"No traffic to wake it up."

"I'll get a doctor to come to the house. I want him to be born on the same mattress he was conceived on."

"Oh, you mean here?"

"I hate hospitals. They're sick, deadly machines. Nobody knows you or cares about you. They pop you in the slot and run you through, clanking and stinking. You come out alive or dead and the machine doesn't care which. The bill has to be paid either way." She frowned, then snatched at the leather thong tied around her forehead and tore one of her braids open. Her long black waves shone as they were freed.

"And all those women! Can you see it? In the maternity wards, all bragging about how many cars they have and what their husbands do. The filthy gossip." She picked up a brush from the counter and pulled it through her loose hair. The other braid swung, thick and stiff.

"And they don't let you keep your baby in those places. They keep them in a nursery and they're always mixing them up. Giving the wrong baby to people."

"Things can go wrong, you know."

"Women have been having babies for millions of years without paying a thousand dollars to have an audience while they do it. How do you think there got to be so many people in the world?" She flung the brush down and pulled the loose hair into three strands. Her fingers twined and yanked, braiding quickly.

"I was thinking I'd have one of those boards that the Indians carried their babies in. That way I could keep him with me all the time."

"You think it's going to be a boy?"

"Yes." She tied a piece of red yarn to the end of the braid. The rice had stopped steaming. She lifted the lid and with a fork added the meat chunks from the skillet.

"You ought to eat better," I said. "I don't think meat and tea and rice is all you need for making babies."

She frowned again. "What should I be eating?"

"Well, greens. You're always supposed to eat greens."

"Lettuce?"

"And spinach. It's all the iron or vitamin F or something. The darker green the vegetables the more it has."

"Broccoli is pretty dark."

"Yes. Also milk, I think, for bones."

Her fingers prodded deep into her belly. "My baby's bones."

"And you probably shouldn't take any drugs at all unless the doctor gives them to you."

"No. I know that. I haven't taken anything except marijuana since I stopped taking the pills."

The kitchen felt warm and close. A wind chime with dragons on the panes moved slowly near the window. I could hear Sam's excited voice outside, as he and Rennel returned from the woods. Carlotta reached for the leather thong and tied it tightly once more around her head.

The broken pencil question

My temper is getting worse. I don't notice it when I'm here alone. It only wants to hit out at those who can feel and understand pain. I fume a little, sit staring more than I used to, perhaps, but I don't really notice that I'm angry until someone comes to receive it. Poor Jean, my brother's wife, got it today. It was her mention of the faith healer that did it. I was only feeling depressed before that.

Jean, with her soft colors and discreet posture, and hard practical mind, set me screaming today, pounding tables. The water slopped over the lip of the jug. She went away with a tight mouth and a hateful glint in her eye. I may have lost another visitor. My brother's arthritis, it seems, has gone beyond pills and potions. A faith healer camped outside of town has done wonders for others, she said. "Maybe if we could convince Spike that it *could* work, it *would* work, if he believed." She said this with her hands tight on the steaming mug. The seam between her brows was deep, and I know she avoids frowning because of the wrinkles. She was serious, this told me. Why did it shock me? Because she usually drives a hard bargain? Because I've heard her express scorn for weak women who make scenes? Because she does what needs doing and doesn't moan about it until later, when it's convenient? And yet, in the rabid atheism of my youth, she poured a cup of coffee over my head because I said there was no God, at her table, in front of her children.

At that time I knew she was right to do it. Yet today, twenty years later, at my own red table, she asked me to convince my brother that he can be healed by prayer and I bridled in shock.

"But if there was a chance that it would relieve his pain, it would be worth it," she said. And I saw . . . what? My brother shaking, seated beneath the hands of a preacher, moans and shouts, and the pain of trying to believe on his face. My brother's face, my face—we're too alike. His jaws and brows, the boxer's nose, the lines and furrows of his frowns are only slightly larger, firmer reflections of my own. I do not doubt, I know, such things can heal. Nobody can know more thoroughly than I do the power of the mind to desire, to want, to create and destroy in the face of physical inclination or probability. It was that possibility, that it might work, that set me off. Because I know that if my brother could be cured in that way I could never look at him again. Never love him anymore. Never see his face in my own in the mirror without retching.

So I got mad and Jean left without finishing her coffee. My brother is still in pain. He walks and works and sits hunched over his plate in pain. There is no guarantee that it would have worked, or that he would be capable of believing. Yet I am ashamed. And my temper frightens me. I look back on all those years of equanimity. I could count the times that I have been really angry on one hand. Many times, of course, what might have been anger in someone stronger-willed was translated in me into hurt, pain, or humiliation by my subsidiary character, by my dependent spirit. But still, I might have been angry more often if I'd cared. Perhaps my indifference has fostered my sanguinity.

Even now, ashamed, I am still angry. I hate being made to look a fool. This is odd, I suppose, but actually being a fool doesn't bother me nearly so much as having someone, anyone, think I'm a fool when I'm not.

The possible consequences of Jean's walking out after my anti-spiritualist tantrum: (1) she'll never speak to me again; (2) after months or years, we'll reach a stiff reconciliation; (3) I'll apologize and gradually work back into her good graces; (4) a crisis will throw us together uninhibitedly; (5) she'll murder me in the night following my brother's agonizing death from deterioration of the duodenum.

Of course, there always seem to be more possibilities than there actually are. But the habit that has cost me companions, lovers, and sleep is the one that makes me fixate on and fetishize the most lurid alternative. I tell people it's so I won't be surprised if the worst happens. I'll have prepared for that by contemplating its ramifications beforehand. But secretly I believe that, if I dwell on the worst, it can't happen. It would be too absurdly coincidental for me to be studying the possibility of a safe falling on my head at the same moment that a safe actually falls on my head. So I spend a lot of time conjuring evil. It keeps my tail bushy. It keeps the tide flowing. It keeps me from feeling a fool if not seeming like one.

❦ ❦ ❦

"I have to tell you something."

Sam hurried through my door. The room was too small to hurry in. His face was pale, and there were red smears across his cheeks. He sat down in a kitchen chair, hooked his feet behind the legs. I could see him curling his toes inside his shoes.

"Carlotta's going to have a baby!" He wanted my reaction.

"Well, that's nice."

"Do you think so?"

"Don't you?"

"I don't know," he said. "Well, yes. I think it's nice. But she says I can go or stay, whichever I please. What kind of thing is that to say to me? She told me this morning. We were driving into town. I had to go to painting class and she said she wasn't going to come. She's taking the tea ceremony class at the same time from Mr. Sing's wife. She said she had an appointment with a doctor. When I asked her what for, she said, 'I'm going to have a baby.' I was thinking she had an ingrown toenail or a wart to be removed. Then she said this. Well. It's really strange. I had this feeling, right at that moment, that she wasn't actually saying it, but that I was remembering. It felt like remembering. As though it had actually happened, but a very long time ago. I know that I'll remember that moment when I'm an old man and remembering it will feel exactly the same as living through it did."

"But what did you say?"

"Well, you've got to understand, I was in no condition to be original. I said, 'Are you sure?' and she just smiled at me. We didn't say anything more then. I was just sitting there in a kind of stupor. We went into the Buttermilk Corner and drank buttermilk and she explained it all to me. She said she wanted to have my baby so she just stopped taking the pill. Months ago, right after we started living together. And she didn't tell me. I didn't know. It's not that I would have stopped her if I'd had the chance. But I've always wanted a son and I'd always thought I'd know when I was fertilizing a woman. I thought knowing that my woman was being made pregnant and that my son would come of what we were doing together would be the biggest thing that could ever happen to me. And Carlotta did know. She was aware that every time we were together we might be making a baby. I feel like I've been robbed."

"So, do you want the baby?"

"It doesn't matter much whether I do or not. I guess I've got it."

"She said you didn't have to stay around."

"What kind of thing is that to say to me? It wouldn't have occurred to me not to stay if she hadn't said that. Now I'll probably leave. I don't even want to. I like Carlotta. We have something very nice. If I'd thought of having a kid right now, I'd have wanted it with her. But saying she'll understand and it'll be all right if I run out is like those stupid true-false questions you get on quizzes. Or like, when you're a little kid and you break a pencil in two and then stick it back together and go waving it at people saying, 'Is this pencil broken?' You know very well nobody's going to ask you a stupid question like that unless the pencil is broken. But if you just hand a guy a pencil he doesn't look immediately to see if it's broken before he starts to write with it. Of course, there are people who've had broken pencils slipped to them so often that they've become very suspicious. You offer them a pencil and they give you a dirty look. You know right away that they've been through a lot in life!"

Sam grinned. "Or maybe it's really a multiple-choice question. Anthracite is: (a) hard coal; (b) soft coal; (c) the study of human culture. There always seem to be more choices than there actually are."

"Did you tell Carlotta all this? How you feel?"

"No. I just said I'd have to think. I don't really know how I feel. I'd like to be happy about it. She's happy. Maybe I am happy." He looked at me like I could tell him whether he was or not. His hands clutched each other in a big tangled fist. "A little boy of my own." He paused. "I don't know if I'm ready to set myself up as somebody's superego. Of course, there's a lot I could teach him."

"Would you like some coffee?"

The room was beginning to stink of us, thicken with our talk. I lifted the skylight and put the water on to boil.

Sam tilted the chair back against the wall. "I have decided one thing. I'm going to change my name. Whether I stay or go, there's going to be somebody in the world who thinks of me as his father. A father should have a good name. A fresh one with no bills and tickets following it. I don't feel like Omar anymore anyway. I feel like Omar Plus! Besides, I never did get a last name. Now it's going to be Aram Rommel."

He watched as I poured water over instant coffee. I handed him his cup.

"Did I tell you? We planted yesterday. We each went around with a bowl full of seeds and dug little holes with our fingers and tucked them in one by one."

꜅ ꜅ ꜅

When Carlotta arrived we could hear her for a long time before she got to the door. The stairs creaked as she came slowly up. We waited for her knock. The door opened instead. She wore a shawl around her face and pinned between her breasts. Cool air moved with her. Sam stood and took her hands. He looked up into her face.

"How are you?"

"I'm fine. Everything's fine. How are you?"

"I changed my name in honor of our son."

She smiled. "Who are you?"

"You can call me Aram."

"Aram."

I squirmed and ducked my head. Carlotta sat on the floor at Sam's feet and rummaged in a big bag.

"I got a mimeographed diet and some iron pills." She produced a sheet of blue paper. "I have to drink a quart of milk a day. I'm not going back to school anymore."

"Ah!" Sam leaned back, approving.

"You mean, not even to tell them that you won't be there anymore?" I asked.

"It's too late in the year to get any of the money back."

"That's true," I said. "Are you going to painting class?"

"I couldn't pay proper attention. If Mr. Sing asked me where my mind was, I'd be embarrassed to say, 'In my woman's belly.'"

They smiled at each other. Sam raised his eyebrows slightly. A signal. Carlotta nodded. They gathered their things.

"When you come out will you bring some horsemeat?" Sam asked.

I nodded and he left.

"And some oranges?" Carlotta asked. She listened to Sam's footsteps on the stairs and moved closer to me. "How is he?"

"He doesn't like your giving him a choice."

"He'll feel better about it later, I think." She moved out the door, pulled her shawl close under her chin.

The morning pill, bedtime pill, two o'clock in the afternoon pill

Disappointment. Bounce the word off the side of the fishbowl. Put my mouth close to the gray-green water, and mutter, "Disappointment," in a contrived basso, until the surface is frenzied with ripples and the shining denizens sink, quivering, to the bottom. Sing, "It was disappointment, I know!" while I slink torchily to the stove with four eggs, "and it might have ended right there at the staa-aarrt!" I drop them into boiling water. One cracks immediately and spreads a white foam.

"Disappointed by life" was the phrase I had just read in one of my paperbacks. The vicar's wife had been explaining the eccentric isolation of the no-longer-young but still beautiful widow (who is sure to be the murderer) to the inquisitive amateur detective.

Disappointment. I scrape the eggs into a blue bowl and smear them with margarine. The cover of the book is a smooth assemblage of red-spotted orchids looping over a skull, which sports a neat dark hole over one eye and a sad hand of poker—fine cards, faces exposed—gripped in its wealthy American teeth.

But not with life, this disappointment. Not me. The life around me, that I have noticed, has always been . . . sensational. Nor with love. Love has been precisely what I always suspected.

But there is deep and abiding disappointment in myself. I was led to expect better.

After catching Mr. Chesbrough's hand in the paper cutter, and the tumultuous sleep that followed the departure of the only completely beautiful creature that has ever fallen into my clutches (even his feet and elbows were nicely done), something in the sleep itself, some lost series of dreams that soothed and explained, made my waking hours calm. There was a little light in the earliest hours there in the summer. I stared at the wall and knew that I could rely on myself for nothing but survival. I could make no confident resolution about my own decency or good sense. That I might suddenly acquire dignity and self-reliance was as unlikely as my chances of becoming thin and graceful; all I had was resiliency, and that was merely depressing.

I spooned the eggs from my favorite bowl. The yolks were slightly runny, the same color as the goldfish. I often enjoy this snack at three in the morning with no thought of having to wake at a particular time. Sam has furnished his new apartment with balloons and combs the fuzz down from the crown of his head to display the shine of his bald spot. Carlotta smiles again. I go call on the creature in the garden. I spend many long afternoon teas over there beneath the bush. I stretch out there in the shade, surveying my own bulk, a broadcloth landscape of the swollen bits of my flesh. I prop my hand on the roots of the tree and peer over the roll of my belly to the beyond. I can see directly over my right big toe into the dark crevice where the toad hides. By the time the mug beside me is empty, he will have come to investigate the silence.

Here I am now, gross in my self-indulgence, maintaining the stock of the cookie jar, lying in bed until the crack of noon, dawdling over the bathtub knobs, meticulously arranging my well-dusted books—first by subject, and then by author, changing my mind every few months when an industrious mood coincides with gray, wet weather. I am free. No necessity dictates my waking or sleeping. No will but mine governs the shaping of my days. I do not work. I am not employed. My money, small and sufficient, comes in the mail on the fifteenth day of the month. I sign the check and put it into a new envelope addressed to the bank and my labors toward the cause of sustenance are ended for another four weeks or so. All those smooth faces on the streets that yearn for time, all those who would sacrifice meat and comfort, heat and fashion for the luxury in which to pursue their obsession or explore their preoccupations are right, if, in sighting me as I scrabble in the garden or polish the door, they condemn me for possessing a treasure that they long for and may never acquire.

I now have, by an accident of intention, been gifted with all a human could require for private life: food that I like, comfortable shelter, and the proximity of a large library with a mailing service. It is true that I cannot afford to dress in any fashion but secondhand, and a show is beyond my budget unless I save in preparation for a few weeks. But I am too large to care about clothes, my only concern with them is whether they will break when I bend, and I am too shy and snobbish to be tempted by shows. The joys I have can be relied upon. The magical independence is not fragile. My card is stuck irretrievably in the computer. My name and number are so deeply embedded in the fluid memory of the central machines of government that if the card itself is shredded to illegibility by some technological convulsion it will make no difference to me. The grooves of habit will remain and the checks will keep coming anyway, in much the same fashion as those magazine subscriptions which go on for eons despite nonpayment, or rejection, or the demise of the subscriber.

This glorious security, this gratefully acknowledged liberty, this beneficent cushion to my sensibilities, is due entirely to that far-off beauty of my last love, to that last, or perhaps sole, genuine wound, the result of having so ridiculously approached a penny-ante orgasm.

That day, awake and alone in the crucial bed, with the morning light of Boston seeping into the sad old room that had once known life lived as I thought it ought to be, I made my plan.

It was five o'clock in the morning. The sky was clear. I got up and danced around, slapping my arms and thighs and belly to warm up. Deliberately neglecting to put on any clothes, I opened my door. The musty hall was dark and warm. I stepped out and slammed the door. Clomped down the stairs with my thighs and buttocks clapping merrily together. The front door doused me with chill as I opened it. The shock made me reconsider, but, turning, ready to run back up to my room, I saw the old woman at her door peering out at me, lifting and dropping the water-thick lenses of her glasses, trying to get me in focus. Too late, I thought, and ran out.

A sudden exhilaration, the foreign feel of the cold air on my body, set me leaping, galloping, and leaping again. An old chuckle, the secret life of my lungs, started up once more. The light, so soft, lavender in the shadows and gold on the rooftops, was intoxicating. My legs, mottled and pale, moved beneath me. The pavement stung and burned. The grit bit my large, tender feet, caught in the pads of my toes. I had planned to run and it was fun. Running is one of the signs of aberration in adults. It connotes fear, urgency, guilt. Only in special shoes and coordinated exercise suits is running acceptable.

My plan was to throw a brick through the window of the DoNut Shop and get myself arrested. The shop was on the corner. There was no brick. In my experience, there is very rarely a brick when you need one. I ran on, keeping my eyes peeled. A huge double-trailered truck roared by. I had to pee.

There are no public restrooms in Boston. Restaurants offer a small sink in an open recess as a token washroom, but no toilets, never. Bostonians don't need toilets.

I was also out of breath. I slowed down, grinning now, because it didn't matter just this once that there are no toilets in Boston. I chose a large automobile, dark gray, fastidiously clean inside, with only one pearly silk cushion properly fluffed in a corner of the back seat. It was parked on the through street, but it belonged to one of the rich, quiet hill streets. I climbed nimbly (all my movements seemed supple that morning) up onto the hood, and stepped over to the point where the sloping glass of the windshield met the metal. I squatted and urinated, watching carefully so I could lift my feet or shift my toes if the vaporous stream came too near them. I stayed there until the drips had stopped. More trucks and cars passing. A few faces turned toward me and then disappeared. I was waiting for a particular car.

Down the block, a hole had been smashed into the sidewalk. The city workmen had left a yellow steel sawhorse over the crumpled cement. Black box letters read WORK IN PROGRESS over the yellow. It looked portable. I hopped off the car and trotted up to the hole. The sign was not heavy, but its narrow legs spread awkwardly and threatened to jab my shins as I walked. I was in front of a pawnshop. Its window was outlined with the silver tape that is supposed to reveal an alarm system. I hiked the sawhorse up to my chest and pushed it toward the window as hard as I could.

The sound was wonderful and the mess complete. Immediately, while the torn accordion and the geisha lamp and the rack of cameras were still falling, a feeble tinkling began at the back of the store. I admired my work. My whole lifetime of impish moments thwarted by the fantasy of consequences reached their long-awaited satisfaction. Delicious. I thought for a moment of taking something, a ring or a watch. But I had nowhere to hide it, and I did not want to confuse my situation. The yellow sawhorse lay on its side amid the glittering glass. I leaned in and pulled it out by one leg. With the sawhorse tucked under my arm, and being careful not to trip over it, I crossed the street again and took mincing steps toward the DoNut Shop.

There were more people. A woman in a white plastic uniform turned a corner, saw me, stopped, and reversed. A young man walking in my direction suddenly crossed the street, looking back over his shoulder at me. The police arrived in one car, then another. A tall young man in uniform hurried toward me, one hand unfastening his holster.

"All right, lady," he said. He was nervous all around the mouth and eyes. Another policeman strode past me to look at the pawnshop window.

"All right, lady," the young man said again. My lungs contracted, and I began to chortle. They always say, "All right." It's what you say when things are getting out of hand. Sometimes it is pronounced "Awwright." I put my yellow sawhorse down carefully.

"You are too early," I said, and this was in keeping with my plan. "I have not yet done what I set out to do. The pawnshop was only for practice. It would have been silly to lug this heavy sign all the way up to the DoNut Shop only to find that the glass was too thick for it." He listened. Someone approached with a blanket and threw it over my shoulders. I tugged it around me and held it close. The comfort of the warm blanket was so overwhelming that my eyes began to water. A police officer gently extracted my hands from the blanket and clipped the metal cuffs around my wrists. I giggled. Everyone was acting like we were caught in a low-budget film. Nobody else seemed to share my sense of humor. They persisted in their busy seriousness. Finally, I thought I might be spoiling the take with all my giggling, so I stopped.

Then began a time of exquisite luxury. Warm car, warm office, though too large. A green dress was found for me to wear. It was nearly large enough. I sat with one leg hooked over the other and didn't care that they, all those men, could see my immense hairy calves. I leaned back and breathed in and had a moment to imagine the tidy, clean life of the lovely creature who had left me just the day before. He would be moving easily in some street, crossing a room with economy, or lying back with his eyes closed, taking up no more space in any direction than Phidias would have dictated. He had always despised me, seen through to my crude interior. He might, if he had ever troubled to project a future for me, have foreseen precisely this. Even *I* had had a suspicion, although I had envisioned myself bulging out of a black dress and wearing too much makeup at the end of a neighborhood bar. My broken voice would croak along with the jukebox and the bartender would call me "Sal" as he ushered me out at closing time. But this starched green cotton was close enough, considering that I had no taste for liquor. Whenever one of the men asked a question, I talked until they turned their backs and walked away.

Then came a bunk in a cell. Clean. I slept. Woke to use the toilet and then crawled back in and slept more. Then another ride in the back of a car and a new, large room full of white beds.

TOAD

The observation ward. Whenever a painful idea came into my head I embraced it, rubbed against it until the tears came. That was part of the plan also—crying. Nurses in white jackets said "All right" to me whenever they wanted me to move, and each time I began to laugh.

But after two weeks of plentiful food and lots of sleep, I was suffocating with boredom. I went to the head nurse and explained myself. She thought my self-induced commitment very wise. She said the plan was a clever one, but she didn't let me go. A few days later, in the warm upholstery of the rear seat of another automobile, I rode to the state hospital, where I was admitted. The ward was crowded and noisy. I had no privacy. I explained and complained. I repudiated and elucidated. It was two months of grinding frustration. One day a social worker brought me into her office for an interview.

"Where will you go? What will you do? What if we could arrange a regular Social Security payment to support you?" she said.

I stared at her. I had assumed I would go out and sling hash in another fast food trough. I had thought of patrolling the parks and bars again, hoping to find some fresh meat to hide against while I slept. But this new idea was appealing.

"You are eligible for a stipend since you were still employed at the DoNut Shop when your breakdown occurred." She was proud at having read my file, at having all the facts in her grasp. Besides, she was specializing in Social Security payments that week. I signed papers and went back to the ward. Sat picking my lip all that afternoon, trying to think what would happen. Only later, as I was going to sleep, did I remember that she had said "breakdown." I felt my grin sliding as I fell into sleep. Of course, the blue bedtime pill helped, too.

There was the morning pill and the bedtime pill. There was

also the two o'clock in the afternoon pill. Between them, things were easy if not precisely pleasant.

"You will," said the social worker firmly, "be going back to Oregon." I promised to take the three pills faithfully and attend a twice-monthly therapy session.

My brother met me in the lobby. He was excited to have flown. He had never ventured onto a plane before. "They refuse to give you a parachute! Not a single one on the entire plane." His astonishment cheered me. We got drunk in the airport bar.

"What is this business about being crazy?" he asked over Nebraska.

"It was a plan to earn an undeserved vacation. After Jack left, I was in such a mood I knew I'd have gone whoring otherwise."

"I thought men went whoring," he muttered.

Instead of getting an apartment in the city, I took this little house in a town so small that it has no diversions. It is far enough from Portland to make going there an all-day project. It doesn't tempt me often.

After the first two years I stopped going to the group therapy sessions. After the twentieth explanation of the exercise and diet required to combat constipation induced by the pills, I did not go back and have never received any official discipline for my absence.

I have thought of saving my pills—I would never dream of taking them—for a rainy day. It seems the checks must stop coming at some point, and the pills would be salable. But I flush them down the toilet each month when they arrive from the pharmacy. Each month, I write the check to Ludlow's Rx on Water Avenue and put it in an envelope. The envelope, with pennies and nickels taped to it for the postage, goes into the box on my front door. Then the pills go into the toilet, and the little plastic bottles with their childproof lids go into the garbage.

I have contemplated dropping a blue bedtime pill into the fishbowl when I feel ready to die. The potential longevity of the goldfish annoys me, though their fragile realities draw my sympathy.

The red morning pill is small. I keep thinking of clipping minute feather bits from a leaking pillow and pasting them to the pill. Then I could attach a thread and dangle it in front of the toad in the garden. Presumably, it would make him hop, or dance. But each month I forget these malicious fancies and flush the pills down the toilet, not even saving one. This seems to fulfill my obligations to the federal government while also eliminating any fleeting temptations to do away with my sweet self.

This all happened so long ago that even my brother and his wife have forgotten now why they are supposed to keep an occasional eye on me. For a while, my case was reviewed every six months to approve the renewal of my stipend. But then some card tore or a typist skipped a line or a folder was lost in the mail, and the stipend check began to arrive with the declaration PERMANENT DISABILITY PENSION printed in calm, black uppercase.

My celebration involved a solitary but jubilant picnic in the rocks by the water, and the extravagant purchase of a leather-bound *Complete Sherlock Holmes*.

I offer this in my defense: it is expensive to be alone and still alive. The others do not like it, they make you pay. It is irritating to know of anyone who prefers his own company to ours. It casts an aspersive shadow over our labors as well as our pleasures. The hermit has an evil eye that chills the memory and upsets the digestion. But in other times, bread and milk were laid outside the caves as a token communication and no hermit would be maligned for choosing a hole near a generous village rather than in a complete desert. People are, reluctantly, able to concede a preference for God over their own society.

There are certain women, some with shopping carts, or paper bags, who pick through rubbish and arrange their goods around them on the pavement where they sleep. I am the last one who could glorify their position. I love my bed, and soft light, and being warm. Discomfort, I avoid. It makes me nasty. But I understand these aging libertarians, a little, and admire them, sneakily. If the price for my choosing silence were two sheets of newspaper in the dark behind a supermarket for my bed, why, I'd sing and chirrup and admire the roses fifteen hours each day. And if, to escape the burdens of early rising and dutiful arrivals, I had to dine on the scrapings from the ravioli tins and carrot stumps in the neighbors' garbage cans, you'd see me dressed in slick white nylon and sensible shoes at six in the morning, waiting for the bus in smug contentment. If the only restrictions on my capacity for mayhem were the offensive strength of my body odor and the obvious lack of hygiene marking my beloved person, then I would chew gum and spit out insults with every plate of hash slung, slightingly remark on every weakness or individuality that came inside my ken, and pinch babies in my spare time.

Of course, I'd feel terrible about it all. My dreams would haunt me into the day and the repercussions would cause my blood pressure to rise. So it is lucky that I can hide here with my generic malice in a comfortable "disability." But those women who disarm themselves by an act of will have always my surreptitious admiration.

Whether it has been ten years now or thirty-five since that

important night, I cannot be positive. A calendar and small subtraction could give me a clean and tidy number, but there is no corresponding knowledge in my peeling brain to refer to. The time has gone soft, blurred, taken on crimps and creases that prevent conforming to the standards of measurement. There are whole days when I am twenty once more and Sam and Carlotta may appear in the doorway at any moment.

A family of pastoral delinquents

It was days later when I went out to their place. I got a lift as far as their turnoff from the highway. Walked past the old folks' housing park. Two bedrooms each, with a garage and a two-hole golf course in everybody's backyard. There was a big strawberry field beside an old house. Turbot used to live there. I went to high school with his two sons. I heard they sold the place when he died.

It was late spring. Color bloomed out of all the green. The field across from Sam's driveway was planted with young wheat. It was green to the edge of the world, a barbed-wire fence where the field met the road. I saw the goat first. She bounced through the field, distant at the horizon. She stopped for a while and then rocked in another direction, her teats swinging from side to side. Sam appeared, a dark green figure in the young wheat, and chased the goat. I stopped to rest and watch. Put the bags of groceries in the ditch and leaned on the fence.

The goat stopped at the fence and chewed some green wheat. I leaned over the top wire and watched her shake her beard. Sam approached, his face flushed. His gray undershirt was dark in patches at his belly and at his pits.

"Hi. Just a minute." He held one end of a short white rope; the rest lagged in the dirt. He snapped it up and walked slowly toward the goat. The goat continued to eat. Sam jumped forward, grabbed a fistful of thin white hair, and swung one end of the rope around the goat's neck. The goat kept chewing, its long ears twitching, flicking.

Sam tied a knot in the rope and panted. He tilted his head and smiled. "I've just run about forty miles over this two-acre field." Behind him, the long rows of broken wheat shone silvery-green.

"How am I going to get her out of here? She jumped in."

"I'll hold the rope if you want to lift her," I said.

He passed me the rope. It was a clothesline. He grabbed the goat around the chest. It tittered hysterically as he heaved. The forelegs dangled, but the rear legs still touched the ground. Sam called from behind the goat's shoulder, "I can only get one end of her at a time!"

I scrambled over the fence. The goat's hair was longer around the hooves, which were yellow and curling. The goat kicked at me as we lifted her over the fence. Halfway over I dropped her legs. She got stuck, her rear legs sawing on the wire, twisted free, and dropped to the ground. One knee gave as she landed. She pulled up and trotted across the road, dragging the rope behind her. Sam straddled over the fence and we walked toward the house.

He grinned at me and wound the rope around his fist. "Her name is Kate." Apologetic shrug. "The guy who owned her before called her that."

"How's Carlotta?"

"Fine. She's drinking a lot of milk. Every time I look at her she's got a white lip. That's why we got the goat. But the milk tastes funny. As a matter of fact, it tastes bad. But Lotta likes it. We had the goat tied up for a couple of days. We'd bring her cabbage leaves and leftover rice. I thought she knew enough to stay around. Goats are very clever, you know. And she did just poke around when I first untied her. I went in for some tea and the next thing I knew there was this guy leaning in our front door, gawking around, saying, 'Excuse me. I'm sorry to bother you.' He was very red around the ears, embarrassed. But was it our goat in his spring wheat? There's another guy down the road who keeps bringing Angelina home in his pickup and telling me how she chases his cows. And we bought four chickens at a place up the road that sells eggs. They laid two eggs between them the morning after we got them, but now there's been nothing since. Two weeks without a single egg. We've got a whole family of pastoral delinquents."

"Is there a rooster?"

"No. These are laying hens. Fat white ones."

"I think you have to have a rooster to get eggs."

"Is that right? I never thought of that. Carlotta wanted to kill them for dinner. She said there was no use feeding them if they weren't good for anything."

We walked down a dirt and gravel drive. Sam led Kate on the rope. A hump of tough grass ran down the middle. It twisted through dark trees, over a muddy creek, past a silent house. It ended at the door to Sam's kitchen. The door was open and the room beyond it was dark. Carlotta sat on the sill. The top button of her blue jeans was open. A head of cabbage lay beside her in the doorway. She chewed serenely at a leaf. The grocery bags rustled in my arms.

Carlotta held out a cabbage leaf and Kate stepped up to take it.

"You know what 'mosey' means?" she asked. "That's what this goat does. Mosey."

"She wasn't moseying a while ago." Sam led Kate out to tie her to a tree. I dumped the bags on the counter. One finally ripped and oranges rolled out and into the sink, fell on dirty plates and spoons.

"Did Aram tell you he quit school?"

"No."

"Yes. Then they wrote a letter to his parents. We're expecting a nasty letter any time. And he got a job."

"Sam?"

"Yes. Aram." She smiled.

"Doing what?"

"Mending pipes for that big tobacco store on Broadway. It's part-time. Did you bring onions? I feel like onions."

She came over and rummaged in the bags, retrieved a yellow onion. She peeled it intently, poured some salt from a can and sprinkled it over the white flesh. Her eyes rolled and flashed as she chewed. Tears started to well in my eyes. I moved to the door.

"Got any peanut butter?" Sam asked as he reentered. "Any jam? Cookies? Got anything good to eat?"

"Candy bars in the bottom of the bag."

He emptied it onto the counter and took out a candy bar. Carlotta sat in the doorway again, her legs spread. One bare foot was in the dust and the other outside.

"I had to give up eating chocolate. It makes me sweat a lot and I get zits." She gnawed the onion.

"I hear you got a job."

Sam stripped the wrapper from the chocolate and nodded.

"I'm an apprentice pipe mender for five hours a day, three days a week at Dunhill's. It pays one hundred dollars a week and all I've done so far is get stuff off shelves and stir the glue pot. My boss is this very old man, Mr. Zendke, who is so clever, in his way. He's like Geppetto or somebody. He thinks pipes have personalities, like the people who smoke them. He says when they're sold they're innocent as babies, with a certain genetic potential. That's from what they're made of and how they're made. Then the way they are treated makes them grow up into good pipes or bad pipes. He doesn't say it quite that way, but that's what he means. He can tell all about people by looking at their pipes. Like, some people keep bringing in pipes with the bits snapped off. He says they have bad tempers, no self-control. The people who just gradually chew holes in the bits are tense, under a lot of pressure. He doesn't like people who smoke aromatic tobacco. He says they're fakes. The same sort who spend a thousand dollars on hunting equipment just so they can go drink in the woods away from their wives. Not really interested in the thing, you see, but using it as an excuse for some other thing they can't mention. Mr. Zendke is also very fond of banana malteds. Every day for lunch, I bring him one from a place down the street that knows how he likes it."

Carlotta threw the topknot of the onion into the long grass. The sun bounced white and hot off her black hair. She eased farther down on the doorjamb and the zipper of her pants slid open. She placed her hands over her belly. "I want to plant tomatoes today."

"That's right." Sam flicked the candy wrapper into the sink. To me, "You want to help?"

"I'll just watch. I have black thumbs."

Carlotta turned sharply toward me, scowling. "What's that?"

"You know how some people have green thumbs? They can get anything to grow. Well, some people have black thumbs. It's something about the chemical makeup of the body. Like the oil or acid in your sweat blights things," I explained, not knowing if this was true. "Why, if I ever run my hands through dirt that's been turned up, nothing will grow there for a full year."

"God! That's nothing to be proud of." She jumped up,

holding her belly, and glared at me. Then she disappeared through the door.

My mouth hung open.

Sam shrugged. "Don't feel bad. I'll tell her it's a joke. Lotta just feels very strongly right now about growing things and it gets in the way of her humor." He patted my arm. "Come on. I'll show you the chickens."

Outside was warm and green. Bright puddles and sheets of sunlight lazed across the shade. A chicken-wire fence drooped against some sticks poking up from the dirt. An old physics text held it down at the bottom. The chickens were balding; hysterical pink showed through stringy white feathers. They were harsh beasts. They scratched tiredly and aimlessly in the dust. Sam threw them a browning cabbage leaf; the chickens rushed for it and then turned away. Mechanical clucks. No telling what they thought it was.

At the far end of the lawn, Carlotta was bent over, digging with a broken shovel. She kicked it in with her bare heel and brought up black earth and weeds. We stopped a few yards away.

She moved a braid over her shoulder and glared again. "Just stay back there, Sally. Don't even walk on this dirt. Aram, will you get that old screen door off the junk pile?"

She resumed digging. The handle of the shovel was broken off two feet above the blade. Her shoulder blades slid and arched beneath her T-shirt.

Sam dragged the broken screen door across the grass and dropped it beside her. Carlotta kept digging. Sam sat down next to me and we watched. From his pocket, Sam took out a pipe and a green plaid pouch. I lit a cigarette.

"One thing about this job is that I get a big discount on tobacco."

I breathed in; the smoke tasted, strangely, like sunshine. Sam filled his pipe and lit it without taking his eyes off Carlotta.

"The thing that always bothered me about gardening is that it's such a discriminatory operation," Sam said. "You decide, 'Well, those weeds are no good. Down with the International Dandelion Conspiracy. We'll wipe them out and put in pure Aryan rutabagas.'"

He exhaled thick smoke. Carlotta stopped digging and tossed mounds of the shoveled dirt on top of the screen door.

"Even a little patch like that is a case of genocide. When we planted the other things we just looked for little bare spots in between the plants that were already there. That way you're just adding things without destroying anything. This formal patch business is against nature. Anti-evolution. If tomatoes were meant to survive they'd be able to compete in a less sheltered environment."

The dirt patch had become a three-foot-wide circle. All the loose dirt was piled on the screen. Carlotta threw down the shovel and picked up one end of the screen. She dragged it over the depression and shook it side to side. Fine, soft dirt sifted through the screen and down onto the open patch. Dark clods rolled and bounced along the screen. Sam stood up, laying his pipe carefully beside me. He picked up the shovel, retrieved lumps of dirt, tossed them back onto the screen, and broke them with the blade. Only sticks and rocks and weeds remained. Sam threw them to the edge of the trees. Carlotta's face softened as the dirt piled up beneath the screen.

"How deep are the seeds supposed to go?" She rubbed her arms over her face.

Sam leaned the spade on his shoulder. "Doesn't it say on the package?"

She fished out the envelope from her pants pocket and read it carefully. "It doesn't say."

Sam took the packet from her. "Well, the pumpkin seeds are big and we planted them deep. Those are real little so we'll just barely cover them, half an inch, say."

Carlotta ripped open the packet and crouched over the soft mound of earth. Sam retrieved his pipe and squatted, tamping the tobacco with his thick fingers.

"Aram, are you sure there isn't a top and a bottom to seeds? Shouldn't one end be up?"

Sam squinted and looked to me, turning Carlotta's question to me. I shrugged.

He stuck his pipe between his teeth.

"No. Just pretend you're the wind."

Rosen, Lance, Omar, Aram

I've been out in the garden all morning hunting slugs. I put out blue pellets of poison in a line around the beds. Every day there are new trails of mad, staggering, dying slugs. Once they pass the ring of pellets they begin to weave and ooze their shining slime; they fold back on themselves and writhe in strange formations till they are dead. In the morning, I crouch over the dark earth and trace the gleaming mucus paths they leave, in wilder and wilder swirls, that lead to the bodies. Gushy lumps of things. I hack at them with the trowel until they're part of the soil. The toad watches, sleepily, from the compost heap. He does nothing about slugs. His specialty is green flies, which I appreciate, but one slug can ravish a young lettuce in a single night. I've thought of getting a duck, but who's to say it wouldn't eat lettuce as well as slugs?

I phoned Jean's house a while back to ask for a recipe we'd discussed. Her eldest daughter said her mother wasn't home. It's true she's always busy, but she hasn't called back.

It amazes me that I ever knew more people, and even lived with them, sharing rooms and utensils and meals. I can remember going for months sometimes without a harsh word or an ugly look. Now I listen carefully to my niece's voice over the telephone trying to discern whether her mother has been saying nasty things about me in front of the children.

There are also the letter folk, the few people who I haven't seen in years who write to me as though I were a diary. And I write to them just as though I were writing here, this easy communication with a docile piece of paper. The envelope and the stamp and the fall of the letter into the slotted box are just the way to get rid of it. A ritual tidiness. There is no thought of the receivers, the reader at the other end. The letters that come from those people I read like a continuing tabloid serial. Sometimes I find myself analyzing the decision to write in a family illness as though it were a questionable turn of the plot rather than a fact for someone in a house with loves and curtains and spoons, like myself.

No. I cannot handle any more real people. Three is enough to embroil me. Four was too many, though it took me until now to realize it. Mr. Geddoes was the easiest, and I would rather have lost my sister-in-law than him. She has, I confess, always been a little tricky for me to handle. It was inevitable that I'd lose my temper with her. It is always so hard to be sure she approves of what I say. So hard to keep her from seeing through my tidiness to whatever it is that lies inside. I still feel myself in disguise around her. Even my tight hair bun and the fresh smell of my flesh seem to be a costume that could be penetrated.

But I do miss gossiping with Jean. She has a shrewd, cold view of her neighbors that is delicious to me. She has no humor, but I have enjoyed a hundred people through her eyes that I would never have approached with my own.

I have no patience with the bland righteousness that condemns gossip. What are literature and history but distilled and fermented gossip? Those who relish Zola and delight in Herodotus but turn up their snoots at a bit over the fence are the same crew who prefer not to know where the Sunday roast hung on the steer, and who would lose their appetites if introduced to the chicken before being offered its succulent, crackling flesh. But I won't defend it anymore. I am a snoop, an ear, a nose, an eye, but not a busybody. No more. I don't interfere. I only listen and question from a distance. I am comfortable now. I sit at my heavy desk before the fire and brood over petty annoyances, manufacture antique responsibilities, and am ever, always conscious of the warmth of the room, the luxury of the paper, the sanitary state of my crotch, and to this day I do not know whether the presence of a rooster is necessary for hens to lay eggs.

᙭ ᙭ ᙭

The long days came. The scaffolding of school was ready to give way to another summer. I stood in line to register for a class in the fall. Professor Casper marched up the dark hall to his mailbox. He seemed to practically twinkle for the girls in the line. He performed a theatrical skip-step to show he noticed me and had something to say. His pants were neatly tailored. His hair was wet. He'd been swimming. He smelled good.

"My dear Sally. I was just thinking of you."

I stood still. It was no use losing my place in line.

"Aren't you a particular friend of the extraordinary Mr. Rosen?"

"I suppose."

His Swiss accent didn't sound anything like Clancy's. His hand closed on my elbow and he elegantly led me out of line. I followed.

"Now, tell me. Is it true that the young man has definitely, irrevocably withdrawn from school?" His voice was deep but soft.

"Yes."

"And this is the same fellow who keeps changing his name?"
I nodded.

"What possible good does it do him? I was just sitting on the review committee. Of course, his name was still on the list. His names. Can you imagine—thirty-three blurry, blue, mimeographed copies, and on each one, 'Rosen, comma, Samuel, semicolon, Sterling, comma, Lance, semicolon, Omar, semicolon, Rommel, comma, Aram'? I tell you, it broke the committee. I saw men laugh today who haven't shown their teeth since Hiroshima. But can you tell me why he does it?"

"For fun, I guess."

"Oh, yes, definitely! But why is he dropping out? Though I must say the philosophy department seems ecstatic about it." His broad shoulders had practically been photographed into his tailored jacket. His shoes shone discreetly. A walk-on diplomat plucking his nose.

"His girlfriend is going to have a baby."

"Ah-ha! So now he must go and get the little job. How charming."

He faded down the hall, chuckling, and I went to the end of the line.

It was noon when I finished. I took the bus downtown. The fat little cook from the college cafeteria read Turgenev in the seat behind me. I thought I would treat myself to a sight of Sam at work. I walked fast and swung open the door of the tobacco shop so hard that it hit a display case. The man at the counter said the repair shop was around the corner.

It was a cubbyhole. No window. The door was left open for light. A workbench littered with little knives and pieces of pipes. Cardboard boxes piled under the wall shelves. The old man was big. A very large belly. He was tall. His pants were as wide and dirty at the bottom as they were at the waist. Stiff cuffs folded up to the elbow. His long, black hair fell in waves to the wrists.

"Need something?"

He pulled at the hairs bushing out from his ears. He looked at me and then went back to filling a pipe with what looked like dried worms.

"Does Aram Rommel work here?"

"Never heard of him. Nobody works here but me."

I flushed.

The old man tapped his pipe lightly on his palm and said, "There was a kid, Sam, who worked here for a while."

"Yes. That's him. A little guy?"

"Yes, but you know I had to let him go. You a friend of his? Well, he's a very nice kid, but he's not very smart. I gave him a fifty-dollar pipe to clean, just to get the rough stuff off the bit. He put it in the vise and smashed it. He didn't mean to, but it belonged to a good customer. I can't afford that. He's a good kid. My wife had a big nose like that. But you got to be sharp in this line of work. Pay attention, you know."

He took a coat off the wall and stuffed his pipe into a pocket. His hands were scarred. "I'm going to lunch now. You know a sharp young fella, send him around. It's not a bad job, and you learn a skill."

I left and walked quickly down the street. At a bus stop bench, I sat and waited to feel calm again. After a while I walked up the street and bought grapes and spinach and liver. Went off to get Rennel.

❧ ❧ ❧

The liver was softening in the bag. I put it on the floor of the Rambler and braced my feet on either side. As he drove, Rennel pumped the little automatic shift lever. His face was set in his Grand Prix glare. I caught him watching to see if I was watching. I looked away, down to the liver bleeding on my boots.

"A girl once told me that I drive just like I screw."

"Too fast, huh?"

We hated each other silently down the dusty road and up Sam's drive. Angelina jumped at the windows, yelping.

"She's as crazy as Sam."

Rennel jammed on the brakes. The Rambler reeled and shook to a stop in the gravel. Carlotta approached with a pan in one hand. Her belly was much bigger. Her legs were brown and fuzzy, stuck out beneath the skirt of a red flowered dress.

"You could have killed her!" she cried. She threw the pot down and pulled the black dog close. Rennel slouched out of the car.

"She ran right at the car. She's crazy."

I eased out of the car and lifted the bag of food. It was damp and smelly in my hands. Angelina wrenched out of Carlotta's arms and leapt at the liver. Her ragged claws caught in my thighs. I glimpsed down her long throat as her jaws closed on the wet bag. Carlotta reached for the dog's throat. Her long hands sank in the short fur. She lifted Angelina, legs flying, tail beating against her. The liver fell from the shredded paper. The dust darkened with thin blood. I dove for it. Snatched up the pieces and the split grapes and the spinach. I ran inside the house, clutching the stuff to my chest, and heaved it into the dishes in the sink. I splashed cold water over the dark meat. The dust ran off. The blood thinned and slipped down the drain.

I heard Rennel's voice asking for Sam. Angelina's idiotic yap. Carlotta entered with the pan. She stood beside me at the sink, shoved it under the cold water. I could smell her sweat as the pan filled. I slid the meat onto a used plate. Opened the groaning refrigerator. The light was out, but it was cold, and inside were two shriveled oranges and a bottle of ketchup.

"I'm watering the plants."

I followed her outside. She went to the tomato patch and poured out the water from the pan. There were some green sprouts sticking up.

"Are those tomatoes?"

"They're all alike, so I think so. When a different kind comes up, I take it out."

She sat down on the grass, leaned back on her elbows, and looked at the bulge in her dress.

"Aram told me that was a joke about your blighting things."

I sat down a short distance away and put a blade of grass between my teeth.

She frowned at her body. "But it wasn't a joke. It was a lie. So you wouldn't have to help plant. You could have just said you didn't feel like it. Aram does that all the time. Only he performs his lies instead of telling them. He'll get out of bed in the morning to make tea. I wake up an hour later with the pot burning on the stove and him listening to records and reading, not paying attention. I always end up getting the tea myself."

She lurched upright, stood, and grabbed the pan. "I don't mind making tea. I just mind him lying like that."

I got up, too.

"I never thought of Sam as lying, exactly. It's more like he just makes a game out of everything." She turned to look at me. Her face was tight. I could hear the chickens muttering softly. Carlotta leaned over the wire and emptied the rest of the water from the pan into their dish. Her black braids swung. The red dress climbed her thighs. We tossed them handfuls of leftover rice.

"They still don't lay eggs. We haven't gotten around to getting a rooster."

"So you're running a convent."

She smiled, finally, briefly. "You know, men don't feel the same about babies at all. Aram talks about it as though it's going to be born ten years old and ready to become his disciple. He talks about how he'll teach him calligraphy and painting and bring him up to be a Buddhist."

"Has he decided he's going to stay, then?"

"He never said. He's here. That must mean something." She kicked at the chicken wire. The hens puffed and scuttled. "But then, everybody else in the world is here, too, and that doesn't seem to mean much."

Somewhere behind the house Kate bleated. Carlotta shook back her braids and squinted at the sky. "He invites everybody to come and use the cabin whenever they want. There's always somebody there. They come in here to eat. Aram spends all his time out there talking. He doesn't care who it is. At night he tells me how brilliant they all are."

"I've never seen the cabin."

She looked down at herself. She smoothed the red cloth of the dress till it showed the round belly beneath her breasts. "There's a path through the trees. Lichtenstein is out there now. And Rennel."

She turned suddenly and walked toward the house. The pan banged against her thigh as she walked.

The brush was thick around the edge of the lawn. I pushed through. The path was almost invisible, but it widened. In the dark of the pines the underbrush was dead, leaving the bare red dirt and fallen long needles. The trees were close and the branches started high. I came to the beginning of a clearing and the sunlight broke through. A board cabin with pale, curling shingles. I could hear muffled voices coming from inside. There was a log on its side in front of the door. I stepped up on it and knocked.

A belly watcher I recognized from Figarty's party opened the door. The room beyond him was smoky.

"Is there a password or something?"

He glowered. I'd read about them, of course, and seen a few childish imitations, but this was the original article.

"It's Sally. Let her in." Sam's voice. I pushed the door open. A path of light fell into the room. Smoke rushed past me and escaped. The room was hot and stank sweetly. The belly watcher sat on the bed with his legs folded, the angle of his knee and the arch of his foot prescribed for ambitions to Buddha. He kept his fists clenched and his belly sucked in so we could see his muscles.

Sam crouched in front of a little woodstove. The hatch was open and glowed red, filled the room with heat. Rennel sprawled at the end of the bed, flexing. I slid onto a table next to the stove. Everyone was looking at me.

"Did I interrupt?"

Sam sucked on his pipe. "Well, it's kind of a secret."

"You're Captain Midnight and this is the Rangers' clubhouse?"

Sam looked hurt. "I'm applying to medical schools in India."

Rennel leered. The belly watcher nodded. I made a non-committal noise.

Sam waved his pipe. "Let me tell you about it before you say anything." He gestured to the belly watcher. "Oh, this is Lichtenstein."

He went on, "Well, Lichtenstein knows all about it. It seems you don't have to have any formal education, degrees, or anything. All you have to do is pass an examination. Well, exams are the same all over. A few tricks and a lot of bullshit and you're fine. All the classes are taught in English and it doesn't cost anything because the government is so desperate for doctors that they run the medical schools free. And you know how cheap it is to live in India!"

"Is it?" I asked Lichtenstein. He nodded.

Sam looked at me, triumphant. "Isn't that fantastic?"

"I didn't know you wanted to be a doctor."

"I do. Very much." He looked down at his hands. "See, Carlotta wants to have the baby at home. A child should come into the world in a place where everybody present cares about it, you know? We called a lot of doctors, but they all said no, they wouldn't deliver at home, and gave this big rigamarole about the glories of sanitary this-and-that. It's funny. As soon as you ask on the phone whether they deliver babies at home they get very cagey. They won't say one way or another. They want you to come down to the office and talk about it. You really have to get tough to make them come out and say no. After the first few times, when they started getting sneaky like that, we'd just hang up. But I'd really like to see my son being born. I think that's the kind of event that puts you so closely in touch with the nature of things that you could never be quite the same afterward. Anyway, if she goes into the hospital, I'd never get to see it. And I got to thinking that I can read as well as anybody and all the necessary knowledge is stashed in one book or another. So I decided I could deliver the baby myself. I've been going down to the medical school library. I wait till somebody with a pass comes along and then I follow him in very closely and nod and smile at the girl at the desk. They have this big room full of books on nothing but obstetrics. Hundreds and thousands. And no repeats! Every book is different.

It's an amazing thing, peeping into a forty-pound book full of pictures of human *insides*!"

Sam quivered with excitement. I nodded.

Rennel slipped his fingers into his crotch and lifted his hips slightly to clear a not-quite-silent fart. With the other hand, he adjusted the unlit pipe between his teeth. "What you said about a physical event bringing you in touch with reality and changing you . . ." He paused. "It can't actually change your mode of thought, but it can give you a lot of new information to work with. For example, a racing driver—"

"It can change you, totally and irrevocably."

The prophetic voice rolled from Lichtenstein, who stared into the flames. Rennel fell back, silenced. Sam and I leaned forward expectantly.

"Two years ago, I was a physics major," Lichtenstein continued, softly. "I wanted to build spaceships. That summer I got a job on a construction crew building a road."

He paused. The air was heavy and still. He started again, holding our attention.

"I'd wanted to discover new processes. I wanted to be rich. But on that job, I lifted hundred-pound bags of cement off trucks all day. Every time I hoisted a bag, I thought of money and medals. I practiced my acceptance speech for the Nobel Prize under my breath. It was hot. July. We worked without shirts. After a week on the job I stopped sweating. I thought I was getting good at the job."

He was silent again. He smiled faintly at the memory, his eyes fixed on the fire.

Carlotta popped in, braids flying. "Dinner's ready!"

The door swung into the table I was sitting on and she peeked around it, grinning. "Are you all stoned?"

Rennel groaned.

Sam smiled sadly and tapped out his pipe. "That's a broken pencil question."

Lichtenstein's eyes fell away from the fire. He looked disgruntled. His philosophic mood was gone. He'd wanted to tell us something that now we'd never know. We'd lost our chance.

We all filed out after Carlotta. Angelina ran on ahead of her. Lichtenstein came out last, slowly.

"What were you going to tell us?" Rennel asked anxiously.

There was a long pause in which the only sound was our feet padding over dead needles.

"How I decided to become a farmer." His voice was crude in the sunlight. It was a voice meant for small rooms in the dark.

I look behind me at Sam.

"I'm sorry you didn't get to hear that. He got enuresis and nearly died. In the coma, he had a revelation that changed his life. He really tells it well. Try to get him to talk about it again."

"Why's it a secret about medical school in India?"

My voice was low, but he grabbed my arm and nodded ahead at Carlotta.

Before we reached the lawn, we could hear the music. All the windows of the house were open. The sun dropped gold in the glass, and the music roared out to quiet the birds and disguise the wind that arrived as the sun went down.

The pan was placed in the middle of the floor. We sat around it with small wooden bowls and chopsticks and little gray bowls of thin tea. The horsemeat was tender. The rice was cooked well. Rennel explained the relationship between motorcycle riding and calligraphy and Zen. Lichtenstein explained how enlightenment can be achieved through physical labor.

Sam smiled and urged them on. "It's true. I'd like to go around picking fruit sometime. I met some migrant workers in town one day. One was an old man with white stubble all over his face. He looked frosted. He was telling me that all he does now is take care of kids. Everybody leaves their kids with him while they go out into the fields. He tells them stories and hands out cookies and apples or whatever. He was a wise old man. I sure would like to hear his stories. They were all fine people. Very full of life and their eyes very nice."

Lichtenstein lifted his head, agreeing with Sam. He stirred the rice bowl and tweezed out a piece of meat. "People who work with their hands and bodies are genuinely happier. What they do shows. Every move they make has an observable consequence that can be appreciated immediately."

"But you have to believe in what you're doing," Sam said.

"Yes. And be aware and in tune with the nature and rhythm of the work. That's where meditation comes in. The Native Americans had a custom when a boy came of age. First, he had to run twenty miles through the desert with his mouth full of water and spit it out at the end. Then he went alone into the wilderness and fasted until he had a vision. The vision became his totem and he took his name from it."

"That's something!" Sam cried. "That really is! But, you know, just doing something long enough and hard enough becomes unconscious meditation. That's the best kind."

Someone had shut the windows of the house. The bugs were coming in to the light. The music was softer. I had brought the liver special for Carlotta. She sat against the wall, took up pieces and chewed them from her fingers. The oil stove beside her sputtered and rumbled. Candles in bottles threw yellow light over us all. Angelina came in and slunk behind the stove, lay down and put her long black head in Carlotta's lap. Carlotta slipped a piece of liver between the dog's teeth. The throat convulsed as she swallowed.

"Angelina is a virgin."

Her voice was sleepy. Aimed at nobody. Her head was rested against the wall and her eyelids drooped.

Sam smiled. She smiled back. I didn't want that starting up again, so I asked, "Are you still working?"

Sam flashed a grin and lifted his eyebrows in horror. "You mean, I didn't tell you about that? What a scene. Listen, it seems that pipes are like diamonds. They're very tough, unless you hit them in a particular way. Then they go to smithereens. It's like dynamite. Nitroglycerin. You can drop it off the George Washington Bridge or run trains over it sometimes without anything happening, but if just the right combination of stresses and forces occur together, a fly landing on it will set it off.

"Well, I came into work one day last week. I put on my apron and put the glue on the hot plate to warm up. Mr. Zendke was very pleased that day. He was humming and bustling. He'd got a couple of really good pipes to work on. I told you before that he likes pipes better than people. His entire social life consists of playing with pipes and talking to them. If he gets a cheap pipe in he tsks and groans as though it were a criminal. If it's cheap and also smells of rum and maple, he snubs it completely. But this day we had two real aristocrats. Well-educated, high-principled, wise old pipes. He was fantastic. When he stuck the pipe cleaner in you could almost hear him say, 'Excuse me.' And he wiggles it around, intent on what he's doing, and then pulls out the cleaner and pats the pipe and actually says, 'There now, it's over. Isn't that better?' I was amazed. I'd never seen him with a really fine pipe before. But we'd been getting on very well. He told me all about his wife, who died twenty years ago, and I told him about going to college. He'd never studied and he has this superstitious reverence for anyone who has. He couldn't believe all the politics and talk that are really what counts in any school. So anyway, he's holding this pipe as though it were the Star of Kuala Lumpur or something, and he gives me a wink and says, 'Would you like to clean the bit?' He was giving me a treat, you know? So I say, 'I sure would,' and I take it from him and the phone rings and he says, 'Be very, very careful,' and off he goes to answer it. Well! By that time I was really nervous. I was scared I'd drop the thing, so I put it in a little vise on the workbench. Then I take this little tool for scraping the sludge out of the bit and I go at it very carefully. But my hands are shaking. It was like I was a brain surgeon working on Einstein. You can't help but wonder if you're up to it. Then there was a little snap. Just a faint little sound, but the pipe split in two, right up the stem. I don't know exactly what I did. And I don't know why it never occurred to me to take the bit out of the pipe. That's what you're supposed to do when you clean it. I wanted to hide it all, throw it in the garbage and tell Mr. Zendke that a masked man had taken it from me at gunpoint. But he came in and saw me standing there with the pieces in my hands. It wouldn't have bothered me so much if he'd yelled and jumped up and down. But he just came up to me and took the pieces out of my hands very tenderly. Then he kind of moaned. Then tears came out of his eyes. I felt really bad. We stood there for a while and I wished I could disappear. Then he says, in a very soft voice, 'Oh, boy, I guess you'd better go away. I'll send your check.' So I took off my apron and left. It's one of the worst things I ever did in my life. It was murder, as far as he was concerned."

Carlotta was asleep against the wall. Her mouth was open a little, a faint purr coming from her throat. Rennel sucked his chopsticks gravely and examined Carlotta's bare legs. Lichtenstein watched Sam with ponderous eyes. His lips parted in preparation for something profound.

"If you suffer for material losses you don't suffer in spirit."

Sam nodded. "But you see, to him it wasn't just a fine old Kapp and Peterson. It was a living thing that he loved."

They talked. I was tired. My legs were going numb. The record played softly. I picked up the bowls and the chopsticks and the pot and carried them out to the sink. When I came back for Carlotta's plate, her eyes were open but she hadn't moved. Angelina slept in her lap. I smiled and took the plate.

Carlotta whispered, "You look like a cat."

As I put the plate in the sink I remembered that Carlotta hated cats.

After that, more talk. A new stack of records. Lichtenstein rolled tiny marijuana cigarettes while we all watched. He lit one and the ritual passing began. Each of us with our distinctive suck, our individual methods of spending the time while we held in the smoke. Carlotta took one puff, passed the joint, and disappeared into the dark bedroom, holding her breath.

Lichtenstein left. Sam explained that he was living in the cabin to meditate for two weeks. We all meditated awhile. Angelina slept so still by the stove, she looked dead.

Rennel drove well on the way back to town. He didn't seem to be thinking about it at all. He began, with a string of belches, "You know Aram's taking a speed-reading course downtown so he'll be able to study medicine really well."

"Oh?"

"It's only fifty dollars for six classes, but it really works. I think he's beginning to take things more seriously."

"Yeah. That must be what's worrying me."

"It's the only thing that can save him from a descent into genuine psychosis."

I grunted.

"It's incredible that the human body can get so stretched out of shape."

"You mean Carlotta?"

"She had a good figure before this. What's she going to look like afterward?"

"Well, when the kid comes out, the belly flops down in a kind of bag. It's big, it can hang to the knees. That's why all women who have had babies wear girdles."

"Christ."

I leaned back and tried to sleep.

"Do you like Carlotta?" Rennel asked.

"No."

"Why?"

"Because she doesn't like me."

The toad's peculiar poison

I've been expecting my brother all week. I suppose now he won't come. It's my own fault for fuming at his wife. Stupidity. I used to pride myself on handling people. Another myth of myself expunged, and about time.

I wanted to reminisce. An orgy of nostalgia, a wave of fond compassion for the fascinating child I used to be and the heroic brother he used to be. No one is as good for talk of the old days as brothers, or, I suppose, sisters.

My brother, when he comes, brings a hammer and a couple of wrenches. He started that when I first moved back to Oregon. Checking up on me. Making sure. Of what? He goes around tightening the joints of pipes. He comes when my roof leaks at the peak, patches the holes and repaints the ceiling where it turns brown every winter from the seeping water. He fixed my locks, all of them. We don't know each other. What we have each become is strange to the other. But our child selves are friends, and when we are together there is the awkward adulthood between us only for a first few moments before we are crowing or scowling over some long-ago escapade.

We sit gobbling tuna sandwiches and raisins, our heels kicked up on my garden wall with the plate between us. He's been shoring up my chimney with cable and bolts. It seems natural to say, "If Ma saw you fooling around on the roof like that she'd have a fit." And he, with only the picture and no interfering thought, grins and remembers the grape arbor where we used to hang upside down, giggling and whispering over and over, "If you break your neck Ma will kill you." We'd go on giggling, gasping for air, for that was the ultimate joke, our mother's method of dealing with her own concerns for our welfare. If we did something dangerous, we were switched till we wished we were dead, briefly. Although there was never a mark that lasted past dinnertime. He knew my mother, and the houses and toys and the fears and freckles and vicious subterfuge, and I knew his. And when we are together that old time is new and rich again.

But it's only comfortable when there's no one else around. Because it's private. Because the things we can remember together nobody else could see, or could care about if they did.

I am getting old. I've longed for years to be old and now it's coming to me. My knees and hips have stiffened, and they ache if I sit without moving too long. I get up and trot around the kitchen, run in place and feel a satisfying swag of my rear with every jounce.

I know my brother will be back. There's no one else who remembers why he is called Spike. But I did want to ask him a question I can't seem to answer. Was I called "Toad" as a child? It seems to me there was some time when that was a name of mine, but I can't be sure. The thought occurred to me last week sometime, when I was sitting out in the garden easing my bunions on the grass and watching my bachelor friend. My brother will remember if it was ever true.

In first-year biology, I dissected a toad, a big brown one from a stinging vat of formaldehyde. I flinched and cringed getting the corpse to the worktable and then pegging him down. But then, with that first incision, that sly peeling of the skin flaps away from the abdomen, I saw the delicacy of the beast. How lovely his belly muscle, a solid disc, pink and round. And the strong casing of the pelvis and the powerful bone of the leg, its stem turning like some fine imagining out of the joint. It seemed beautiful to me. It seemed a desirable thing to die and be hooked out of a vat, all puffed and brown, so some young girl could slice and insinuate into me, and be moved to joy by the turning of my thigh bone.

Toad. Witches' brews, warts. The amazing Mr. Geddoes recommended an onion rubbed on the wart daily. It works. The thing just shrank up and tumbled off after a few weeks.

And once in another country, I rode in the back seat of a car at night, in the rain, and was stopped by a horde of toads, yellow, the size of plates, tidily winking as they crossed the streaming road. Dozens of them, there were, caught in the car lights, flopping in the sheeted water falling on the road, from one vineyard to the next.

My bachelor toad doesn't do much. I watch him. He hangs on the rock wall. If I tap too close he pulls himself into a dark crack where I can't see him. He sits in the sun waiting. When a fly wanders by he nonchalantly flips out his tongue, stubbier than I'd expected, and tips it in. When he swallows, his eyes convulse. That's all. At night and in the early morning he sings, his pale throat fluttering. Not exactly a parade, not precisely a circus, but he's entertaining enough when I'm sitting out there in the dirt with my skirt rucked up, the sun warming my thick veins, and my bunions cooling in the grass.

Mr. Geddoes once told me that toads secrete an odd variety of poisons from their skin in stressful situations. One South American tree toad oozes a curare-like toxin that the Indians use for tipping their arrows. It produces paralysis and death.

Mr. Geddoes said even common toads, if they are sick, turn

brown and secrete a mild poison which tastes very bitter and acts in a peculiar way on the human heart.

❧ ❧ ❧

Summer came. The chaise didn't absorb my sweat. It got slippery. I shoved it to the edge of the room, into the wedge between the sloped ceiling and the floor, and pulled the bed into the middle of the room. I lay on it in the heat. I read and looked straight up through the skylight. At night I served coffee in the strobe-lighted cave where long-haired musicians met pudgy high school girls wearing color-coordinated skirts and sweaters. They would have preferred orange soda pop. So would I.

Rennel worked with autistic children at a county clinic. He puttered by on his motorcycle whenever he could get somebody to watch him. He drove out to Sam's every few days.

Sam's ten-dollar car had broken down and wasn't worth fixing. Except when someone else drove out to see them, he and Carlotta stayed out there in the trees with the goat and Angelina. Sam went to a few of his speed-reading classes and came by my place afterward. He was excited about it and showed me how to move your fingers across the page in some special way to help you soft-focus your eyes. I kept threatening to test him. When the car broke down he stopped going to classes and didn't try to get his money back.

On the Fourth of July, Rennel stopped at my place on his way out to Sam's. He hadn't been there in a week, but he said they were probably all right. Some rich girl was using the cabin and she had a car. I was sick of my skylight and ready for a party, so I went along.

There were four cars on the grass around the house. The day was fine and the music screamed from the open windows. I hadn't seen Carlotta in a while. She stood wedged in the kitchen doorway as we came up. The red dress was tight on her belly now, and hung down shorter over her legs. Her long arms and legs poked out like candy apple sticks. She was the most pregnant woman I'd ever seen. She was alone in the kitchen and stood aside to let Rennel get by. She smiled a little to herself and leaned into a chair.

"It's pretty big, isn't it?" She stroked the top of her belly, her eyes half-closed.

"Is it twins?"

Her belly jumped and a protrusion developed, then disappeared.

"I think that's his foot."

"Have you been to a doctor?"

"No. We still phone when we go in to shop. But none of them will come to the house."

The music careened around the little house. Voices sang in the living room, out of tune.

"We're going to get married." She didn't smile as she said it.

"How come?"

She frowned slightly. "Sam's parents wrote asking us to. They want us to come to New York and be married in their house."

"I didn't know they'd heard about the kid."

"Sam wrote to them a while ago. They'd stopped sending money since he wasn't going to school. I wrote to my mother, too."

"So are they sending money now?"

"No. Just two plane tickets to New York."

"You don't look very happy. Do you dislike being pressured into it?"

"I just think getting married is a cheap thing to do."

"Sally! Come in and get stoned! I'm getting married!" Sam called cheerfully from the living room. The music stopped suddenly. I looked at Carlotta. She stared down at her belly.

The room was full of people in denim pants, nodding their heads. Rennel sat in a corner, puffing strenuously on a joint, trying to catch up. Sam got up from a large, black silk pillow and took my hand.

"Did Lotta tell you?"

"Yes. Congratulations." I hugged him and kissed his cheek.

"Isn't it a great idea?"

"Sure."

"Think of all the money you'll get," a man with curly hair contributed.

A round-faced girl in a mink pea jacket and torn Levi's nodded and winked. "I'll come to your wedding. We'll all come. We'll charter a plane."

Sam nodded. "It's true, we'll probably get a lot of money. When my sister got married she got ten thousand dollars in cash and a lot of pawnable goods."

Carlotta entered and crouched next to the cold stove. She had tied the leather thong around her head and slung a shawl over her head and shoulders. Our Lady of the White Wickiup.

"You know, Socrates was a very wise old man. He once said, 'By all means, marry. If you get a good wife, you'll be happy. If you get a bad one, you'll become a philosopher.'"

The rustling cushions and the smell of sweet smoke. Carlotta lunged up, her belly swaying. She went into the kitchen and I heard the outside door slam. I got up and went after her.

She lay flat on her back in the tall grass at the edge of the trees, her hands on her belly. Her eyes were closed, her face passive.

"Are you all right?" I sat down near her head and chewed blades of grass. When she spoke, her voice was nasty and sharp.

"I get so fucking sick of cool old men. Every time he goes to town he comes back with another 'cool old man' story. An old crock he gives a nickel to on the street. The fat fart who pumps the gas. If he doesn't meet a new one he reminisces about an old one, Wittgenstein, or the art teacher in his junior high school. Every old turd in the milk is a wise man." She sneered. Her eyes were dark and cold. It frightened me, until she started to cry.

"It used to be so good with us. Sometimes when we make love it's still beautiful. But sometimes it's horrible."

She blinked and more tears slid down her cheeks into her hair.

"That Laura. With the mink. Aram really thinks she's something. She's staying at the cabin, but one night there were a lot of people here, her friends. They were all stoned, except me. I went to bed and when I woke up, Aram was beside me and there was Laura and some guy on the other side of me and a couple of people on the floor. They were saying, 'Come on, Aram, show us how you fuck a pregnant woman!' and he was trying, and Laura was doing it with this guy next to me, and I just couldn't. Aram couldn't, either, but he kept trying. Rubbing against me, all soft, till he was sweating. Then he jumped up and went outdoors and didn't come back all night. I think he slept in the cabin. But all the others were passed out by then anyway. I went out and slept by the stove."

She stared at the sky and calmly blinked out her tears. I put my face down on my knees so I didn't have to watch for a while.

"The next morning Laura and all of them woke up really hungry and ate up everything in the house without even asking," she went on. "Aram came in talking about how he was going to make a lot of money going around the woods gathering rare herbs. I don't know what he wants. I just want to be happy and think about my baby."

Her hands climbed the mound of her belly and kneaded it gently. The grass in the lawn was yellowed and stiff. It stuck up between our legs and cracked faintly beneath us. The sweetness was gone, but I pulled the grass slowly from its husk and chewed.

"The Indians sometimes had two or three wives," she said. "The women always did whatever the men said, but they didn't really have to pay any attention to them. You know what I mean? They'd cook and sew and take care of the babies, but they could really ignore the men except when they were actually screwing. The men were off hunting or having debates. They didn't have much to do with the women."

She sat up quickly and jerked the shawl around her face. It was a gray shawl of soft wool. Her mouth was firm. "What's New York like? I've never been there."

I told her about New York. Got lyrical. We walked around the house. We weren't touching, but it seemed as though she was leaning on me.

"It doesn't sound so bad."

"Well, everybody sees it differently."

Kate was tied as far from the house as possible. Small black balls of shit were piled beneath other trees, and showed where she'd been. The music reached her and her ears flopped and twitched.

"Do you like goat milk?"

"No. It's too strong for me," I said.

"I do."

Somebody inside the house laughed.

"Do you know how to make acorn flour? Some Indians used to live on that. Nothing else at all. They were near Palo Alto, I think." She rubbed the side of her face where her tears were drying. "I'd like to do that. Just wander around in the sunshine naked and eat acorn cake for supper with a drink of water."

"Your baby couldn't do that."

"The Indian babies did."

"My mother used to make a good, cheap bread out of oatmeal. That was nice. You pound it around a lot and then let it sit in a warm place by the stove with a wet dish towel over it till it rises. The whole house smells good. It's supposed to be better for you than regular bread."

Her face brightened. "Really? Could you live on it?"

"We used to put peanut butter and jelly on it and drink milk."

She untied Kate's rope and untangled it from the brush. The goat paid no attention at all. Angelina came loping across the lawn and sniffed excitedly at the goat's pale udders.

"Can you get me the recipe? I'd like to make bread."

We led the goat toward the house, around to the kitchen door. Carlotta handed me the rope and darted into the dark kitchen. She came out with a clean coffee can and crouched at the goat's rear.

"Hold the head up close. Her tits are tender for some reason."

Carlotta put the can below the left tit and squeezed spasmodically. The goat's pale eyes rolled and her ears flapped. I could hear the thin drill of the milk into the metal.

"I always thought goat milk tasted like greens. Weed greens," I said.

Carlotta lifted her head and smiled at me over Kate's bony back. "It's really good once you get used to it."

The sound of the milk pinging against metal changed to a soft splash as the bucket filled. Carlotta moved around the goat, squatted with her knees far apart and her belly hanging between them. She reached under the goat and gave a little twist of her wrist. Kate bleated loudly, her mouth opened a little around the cud, and green saliva flowed out onto my hands. I almost dropped the rope. Kate's body buckled and doubled. Carlotta held one kicking leg with one hand and pulled quickly at the teat with the other.

"I was wondering when the goat got relieved."

My head jerked up involuntarily at the new voice. Laura stood naked in the doorway. Her breasts were all right, but her legs were heavy. No ankles.

"What are you all got up for?" Carlotta asked.

I stepped back holding Kate's rope. Angelina lolloped against the milk can and bluish-white fluid sloshed up over the lip and down Carlotta's leg.

Laura raised her eyebrows mildly. "We're all going skinny-dipping in the river. Aram says you're to come."

She smiled pityingly and receded into the gloom of the house. Her ass was apple-shaped. I have always preferred pear-shaped asses, myself.

Carlotta was suddenly pale and tired-looking. The flesh around her eyes was dark purple. She folded to the ground, her whole body clenched around the great ball of her belly.

"Hey."

I touched her head. It was hot from the sun. Kate was

following me too closely. I threw down the rope and crouched, tried to embrace Carlotta. She was too big to take in my arms. Instead I sat close and slung an arm over her shoulders, tried to lift her face out of her arms.

"Hey. Hey."

Her body spasmed rhythmically and her heels jittered against the hard earth. It occurred to me that I could leave, go down the road to the highway. Put out my thumb and go to the beach. I wasn't of any use there. I was good only as an eye and an ear and a mouth, emptying out beneath a skylight.

"Hey."

That time I said it right, soft but rough. She continued to shake but I pulled her head up out from her arms. Her eyes were open wide and dry, but she breathed harshly, in and out. I pulled her onto the ground, on her back. She didn't try to stop me, didn't do anything. Her belly looked like a Halloween joke. I held her hand. It lay still in my paw. Her breathing quieted, slowed. She blinked slowly up at the sky. I realized I'd lost track of Angelina. Kate was off browsing a spilled bag of garbage.

"What's that river called?" she asked.

"The Tualatin. It's some Indian name. I don't know what it means."

"Were there Indians here?"

"Sure. They fished, mostly, I think. Lived in big, crowded bark houses with a hole for the smoke. They made dugout canoes to eat out of at parties. They threw a lot of parties."

"We've been going down there a lot. There's an old boat I row in just about every day."

"I think we ought to go skinny-dipping. It's the Fourth of July."

She sat up slowly, stiffly. She looked tired. "I can't take off my dress."

"No. I won't take off my clothes, either. I'm too ugly. But I think we ought to go. You'd just wonder for twenty years what went on down there if you didn't."

"Aram doesn't swim well." She engineered her way to her feet, walked like a newborn thing. I found the goat's rope and tied it to the knob of the kitchen door.

The river was strange there, near Sam's house. A half mile away on either side it was just a pleasant river. Deep and slow, maybe fifty feet across most of the time. The water was dark and the trees leaned over. Near Sam's house the water was gray and the trees on the bank were all dead. Down by the water, the bark paled and the leaves thinned. Moss hung down into the water. The banks were black and muddy. At the top of the hill, the trees were normal. We could hear splashing as we neared. The paths to the water were slippery and steep. I went ahead and Carlotta followed, balancing her belly. Her bare feet left big, splaying prints in the mud.

We couldn't see the water till we were almost in it. There was a line of thick gray brush and then the short bank. There had once been a dock, but it had sunk into the mud. The bank was full of naked people sitting, lounging. I didn't know any of them. I hesitated, but Carlotta moved past me. She waded up to Sam's pale body, waist deep in the water. She crouched and they spoke.

Laura approached me. "What are you smiling at?"

"I'm not used to seeing a lot of people undressed. They all look alike."

She smiled. "Take off your clothes. It'll sharpen your discrimination."

"I'm keeping Carlotta company."

She shrugged, her tits lifted and fell. Her body was pale and hairless except for a thin, curly triangle at her crotch. She turned away and went to the water. She moved as though she were beautiful, and everyone looked at her as though she were. I sat in a pile of sticks and removed my boots and socks. Stretched out my damp, smelly feet in the sun.

There was ferocious splashing. Gray water lifted in great white fans. Rennel stood up and walked up the bank, snorted and puffed, flexed his muscles. He flung his hair out of his eyes and posed on the bank, ran his hands over his body and strolled over to Laura. A thin gray film covered his body. It dripped from his hair.

There weren't any other women. A few people talked in groups, but the rest sprawled, looking feeble in the sun. The bodies were thin and soft. Scholars' asses flattened and pinched by the sticks.

Carlotta was like a red balloon floating in the water. I couldn't see her face. Sam spoke to her with a serious expression. He reached out and touched her. She leaned into his hand, held it against her. She sat down on the bank and stretched her legs out. Sam patted Carlotta's head in its shawl and climbed onto the bank. He came toward me, spoke to other people on the way. He stopped in front of me and sat down, smiling. His prick was big and soft. The matted mud in his pubic hair was beginning to stiffen.

"This is nice, isn't it?"

I watched as Laura and Rennel stepped into the water and then dove at the same time. They surfaced and swam noisily toward the far bank. A race.

"When are you leaving for New York?"

"Day after tomorrow. I've been thinking when we come back we'll have some money. I don't know how much. It would be nice to go together with some real friends and buy a farm. With a big house that we could all live in and work together.

With enough people we could be practically self-sufficient. Like Rennel could keep a car running and Laura knows about animals. That guy with the glasses near Carlotta is a fantastic electrician. He can set up a little generator with just a trickle of water. As long as we could get a place with a stream on it, he could manage it. He's a history major."

Sam's eyes were bright. He looked anxiously at me.

"What about medical school?"

"Oh, well, I applied and they refused me. It was amazing. I got this three-page letter that was so polite! They talked about how their school were meant to supply India with the doctors they need and an American would naturally be drawn back to his fatherland. It really made me want to go there." He nodded enthusiastically.

A thin man talking to the man in glasses yelled over his shoulder at Sam, "Was the theory of natural catastrophe Bentham or Malthus?"

Sam looked surprised. "I don't remember!" He trotted over to them.

There was a splash across the river. Rennel and Laura had found a low branch to jump from. Laura came up with gray water streaming from her hair. She strolled up onto the bank and lay down on her back with her arms above her head.

Carlotta wandered over. "Do you want to go rowing with me?"

"No, thanks. I think I'm going now."

She picked up a dead stick and peeled the bark. "All right."

"Will you come and see me before you go to New York?"

"If there's time. Laura's driving us to the airport. She'll be staying here to take care of the animals. You can come out and stay, too, if you want."

She looked out to the water, then headed off toward the

brush at the far side of the clearing. She pulled an old blue rowboat out of the brush and slid it down the bank. She climbed in awkwardly and took up an oar from the bottom of the boat.

I jumped up and headed toward her. "Hey! Can you swim?"

She cocked her head. "I was on the school team in Palo Alto."

I waved at her. She lifted the oars stiffly, spread her legs, and leaned forward with her belly hanging. The oars lifted, her red dress rode up around her thighs, and I could see her cunt and the patch of black hair above it. She steered the boat out into the stream. The boat staggered sideways down the river. She disappeared around the bend.

I hobbled over the sharp rubble, brushed off my feet, and put my boots back on. If the boat went over she would come up belly-first.

Rennel came up out of the water and stalked past Laura, scowling. Laura rolled over onto her belly and murmured intimately to a guy with a big mustache and slender ribs arching in his chest. Rennel ripped up handfuls of dry grass dying near me and rubbed at his flesh. He scraped fiercely at the clinging scum. I assumed he'd seen this work in the movies. He sat down to rub at his feet and looked at me.

"What are you looking so depressed about?"

I suppose I had a lot of nerve to look depressed when he was mad.

"Laura give you a bad time?"

Rennel looked over at her and the mustache guy. He shook his head. "I could break him in two."

"I doubt that would interest her."

"Haven't you heard of evolution? A female naturally wants a strong mate. Not that you'd know anything about it."

"What a creep you are."

"What a bitch you are!" He threw down the grass and jogged over to Sam.

I went up to the house then. There were clothes piled in the living room. I looked at Laura's mink coat, tossed beneath a chair. It was pretty ratty. I drank from the tap in the kitchen and went outside. Kate was jumping around on her rope. She'd eaten what was interesting from the garbage and couldn't reach any grass. I tied her to a tree at the edge of the lawn on my way out.

The fewmet of the bully

In the old days it was considered crass, ill-bred, and potentially criminal to ram the lady in front of you with your shopping cart simply because she had slipped into the checkout line out of turn. One was encouraged simply to accept the proffered offense. The myth of the Golden Rule was so widely respected that the most avaricious landlord could be made to squirm if accused of violating it. It was a feeble weapon, ineffective for prevention and, for most of us, only titillating as a punishment. Still, one knew where one stood. The bitching, the insults, the studious or random malice flourished, but it was quite clearly not nice. Now if a cup of weak coffee should be tossed into the face of the waitress, if an old man is obstructing the path of a more vigorous one and is kicked aside, if a wedded couple shares no holy province in their vows, if your neighbor tells you precisely what she thinks of you while munching your cake, it is all right. The waitress will retaliate with a ketchup bottle, the old man will lash out with his cane, the marrieds will sue for simultaneous divorce, and you may feel free to elucidate your own opinion of your neighbor. We all express our needs as individuals, defend ourselves, and prevent the buildup of unhealthy frustration and silent resentments.

Personally, I have always found it safer to eat shit. This phrase, peculiarly apt in its redolence of the ignoble canine, refers to the policy of accepting whatever is offered and displaying sweet gratitude or regret, or total self-abnegation in apology, whichever may seem most likely to succeed in placating the enemy. The principles of this approach are twofold: try desperately, no matter how degrading it might be, to make everyone, even the most despicable, fond of you; and avoid trouble at any price. I had nearly forgotten flattery, as rudimentary a tool to the ardent shit eater as a jimmy to a burglar.

It is certainly true that in my many years as a dung gobbler I have felt a great deal of frustration and considerable resentment, but I have suffered no ulcers, no migraines, and no hemorrhoids. This exemplary health I attribute to my practice of keeping someone in reserve to whom I can confide what I actually felt, what I should have said, and what I might have done. When my confidant himself mortifies me, I have recourse to thoughts of murder or suicide.

Of course, I never attack the well-equipped. The bemused and innocent are plumper. The prospect of a blow in retaliation terrifies me. All my assaults use guerrilla tactics and reveal the putrescent core of the secret bully.

But I am old-fashioned. The years of kowtowing, the million false smiles, the bibles and snacks and banquets and smorgasbords of reeking feces are a source of pride to me. It seems a major accomplishment to have deceived so thoroughly and often. The failures rankle. Those who saw through me or were too subtle or simple for my techniques are a lasting embarrassment. But to have manufactured peace and even liking in a relationship whose true elements, if revealed, would be completely explosive, makes me smug.

My meanness, on the other hand, horrifies me, makes sleep a precarious state in which my dreams are agonizing, and remind me of my own venom. I would like to be able to accept the Catholic religion. Formal penance seems clean and enviable.

Maybe the new eclectic absolution could free me of this little scene:

Dusty, my object of adoration at the time, was in the hospital recovering from minor injuries suffered during an automobile accident. My feelings toward him had always been mixed, but were, nonetheless, passionate. It had come to my attention that the urine queen, Moira Clancy, had taken him to bed with her on several occasions during my occupancy. I had always maintained distantly cordial relations with Moira in much the same manner that a well-fed and relatively wise mutt is on good terms with a stink bug. My jealous fury, combined with a need to use my muscles on somebody, encouraged me in hatching a plot. I invited Moira to drink wine in my room. I also invited Raymond. The audience was crucial, a silent ally, a goad. When they arrived separately I furnished equally warm welcomes for them both. The wine passed. We grew jovial, though I detected in Ray's eye a consciousness of the disparity in our trio, a surprise at finding himself in a small party that included Clancy. The peanuts were going around. I stared into the glass while drumming up my zest for what followed.

"Moira, you may have been wondering why I asked you to come here . . ."

She blinked flatly; the light glanced off the lenses of her spectacles.

"I have something in particular to ask you about."

She gathered her big knees close, lifted her chin, attentive.

"But first I'd like to ask you how regularly you sleep with Dusty."

"Ah!" said Moira Clancy. "But . . . not regularly . . ."

She fidgeted her hands. Ray moved to get up.

"I'll be going if you ladies are going to be personal." His voice was nervous and a little disgusted.

"No, please." I gestured him back to his place on the floor. "I have a reason for wanting you to hear this."

A certain curiosity, a misplaced trust. He settled back on his haunches and sipped his wine.

Then I carefully, systematically, lovingly, elicited Moira's tale of romance. Dusty, too, had gone to her because she was there.

"He didn't mind about the cats. He let them stay," she said.

She was easily lured. Perhaps because she so rarely found herself with a willing audience, she forgot who I was, or felt glorified by it, as though we sat with our chipped glasses on some Olympian plane of civilization in which there was no rivalry or jealousy. Or maybe she felt a cruel pride herself in dealing out her memories to the supposed official owner of the burgled property. We found it hilarious to discuss his capacities.

"He always ejaculates too soon," she lisped.

"Yes!" I laughed. "And he has never heard of the clitoris!"

"Couldn't you have told him?" Ray asked.

"Could you?" I answered, and we both laughed at his complacence.

"I told him he was the best ever," she smiled.

"Naturally. So did I."

Finally I had played enough. She had gushed every detail of their four meetings in her big bed. She had renounced his skills and confessed that it was the friendly exercise that soothed her and insured her a good night's sleep. In this I concurred whole-heartedly. We refilled our glasses. I raised mine and looked at Moira over the rim.

"You really are," I said, "just like the toilet in the house. Everybody knows where to find you when they need you."

She giggled, but a nervous crease formed between her eyebrows.

"And, like the toilet in that house of yours," I continued solemnly, "you are too dirty to use except in an emergency."

She frowned at me, her eyebrows forming an anxious peak.

"Did you really imagine that I liked you?" I inquired ironically. "Did you suppose I could find anything about you even tolerable?"

Her lips opened as if to answer; some quick word came up as far as her teeth and then stopped. I waited, coolly, offering her the chance to defend herself. I let my hands dangle between my knees, on call for specific emphasis.

"Have you never realized that these feelings of inferiority that you are swamped with are legitimate? Why is it that your odd, slimy romp is always initiated with a knock at the door of your room in the middle of the night? Hasn't it occurred to you that the men who take you to bed never take you anywhere else? Never let anyone know about it? Never, ever, allow themselves to be seen with you? Don't you think it possible that they would be ashamed to have it known that they were forced to stoop to the likes of you as much as if they had used a sheep or a dog that way?"

The gently insistent inquiry of my voice still deceived her. I was very proud of that control over my voice. It allowed her to feel, even then, that she dealt with something familiar and might yet prevent any major damage, circumvent my intentions somehow. The words that had clotted in her teeth spilled out in the second that my interrogation voice ceased.

"I always thought it was because they were living with someone who didn't satisfy their sexual needs, but whose feelings they didn't want to hurt," she said. Her gall enraged me. My blood surged through my head. I glared at her and felt a small stirring from the place where Ray was sitting. He thinks she's right. I knew it and felt the fear of shame scoring my face. I sipped at the wine, rolled it against the top of my mouth.

"No," I began calmly, "it is something else, you know. To begin with, there is your phony accent. Three months of speaking another language does not account for five years of polluted English. Then there is your personal hygiene. I had always heard that there was nothing dirtier than a dirty woman, but I never realized what that meant until I met you. Have you ever washed your sheets? Or are you lying in two years' accumulation of crusty semen and mucus and sweat? And how many times a month do you take a bath? Or is it *that* often? In all the dozens of times I have seen you on every day of the week at any time of the day I have never once been near you when you didn't smell like an overloaded outhouse. That's why no one wants to eat your cooking. They're all afraid of food poisoning."

She was feeling it by then. She drew her pudgy feet beneath her skirt to hide their grime. She clenched her hands in her lap and then slid them beneath her armpits to conceal her stained fingertips and the gray dirt beneath the nails. She even folded in her lips to protect her teeth from view. She trembled.

As I recall this night again—it has had so many midnight performances in my sleep—I always wonder why she did not just get up and leave. She must have been very curious about it, all my vile talk, directly and specifically aimed at her and derived from her. She couldn't often have been the subject of such intense disdain. Whether she only felt it or could identify it, she had produced in me a powerful effect. I had always condescended, chuckled, and sympathized, and nodded distantly, but at that moment I was filled with hatred for her, glutting my eyes on every detail of her person. I would find that degree of attention flattering, myself.

"And then again, people do not care to hear what you told your psychiatrist. No one wants to know what he told you. But you complain and moan and confide your internal irregularities. When someone treats you rudely you produce a tantrum and harrow everyone else in reach with it, including those people whose parents brought them up to be kind to freaks. There's only one solution. You are stupid."

Tears streamed down her face, dripped onto her forearms. She didn't sob or moan. Her nose did not run.

"I know I'm not as intelligent as you . . ." she said. Her accent was still heavy, still fluttering the cadence of her high, thin voice. I took it then as an admission, as a vindication of all I said. Now it sounds in my skull like a plea, and the beginning of some small self-defense.

"I don't blame you, really, for taking whatever comes to your door at night. You don't have any choice. I wouldn't blame a starving man for stealing bread. But in a way I have to be grateful to you. I could never allow anybody who has screwed you to touch me. Once a prick has been dipped into that rotting meat of yours, it's permanently defiled as far as I'm concerned. So, in a way, that is a loss. But I'm glad to know that Dusty isn't worth a damn before I spend any more time or effort on him. Any man who would even consider baring himself to a woman like you, any man who could manage to get it up over you, even in the dark, is too desperate for notches on his cock to have any character at all. The syndrome, I believe, is known as pig fucking."

I couldn't tell her how fat she was, how grotesque her hips and legs were, pegged onto her merely plump top. Any mention of her fat would lead to comparisons to me and redound to my sorrow. Any reference to rudimentary ugliness would do the same. I sat watching her cry. She didn't look at me anymore. She seemed to know I was finished. I drained off my wine and refilled the glass. I turned and poured more wine for Ray without looking at him. I sipped. A delicious fatigue was leaking through me. I had done precisely as I had planned.

"Go, now," I said. "I'm through with you."

She scrambled about her for her coat and purse before getting onto her knees and then onto her feet. She closed the door softly and I listened to her heavy clogs on the stairs all the way down. When the quiet came I turned to Ray. He lit a cigarette. I waited until he'd exhaled.

"What did you think of that?"

"A bit like hitting a fly with a two-ton truck," he said.

From the moment he spoke the vile sensation in my chest began. He had been curious enough to stay for the show, but indifferent to whatever reason I had for wanting him there to witness it. The reason has been lost to me now, too. It was forgotten the precise moment that Ray spoke. The unpleasantness in my innards was the conviction, born full-grown, that I had been behaving despicably and that, given the slightest encouragement, I would have continued to do so. If he had only sat reviewing the scene with me, if he had only been impressed by my leonine ferocity and restrained delivery, that harangue, so magnificently purging, might have stood as one of the great pleasures of my life. As it is, the incident, even after many years, remains bitterly humiliating and is the true cause of my lack of correspondence with Ray.

It is not Moira Clancy that bothers me. She was a groveling, glutinous beast and any wound she picked up that day was at least genuine rather than imagined. It certainly did not drive her anywhere near suicide. If I had gone to her room and said those things, I would regret none of it. I could sit over coffee in the morning light and click my tongue proudly at having once in my life said what I thought to the person involved.

But I had to have an audience. And not just an audience, but an ally as well. Without his presence would I have dared to do it at all?

There is something basically disgusting about needing an audience. The finest performers give us the impression that they would be behaving just the same if they were alone. The charm of a child is strongest when it prattles, unselfconscious, unaware of being observed. But the same child at the same game seems sly, unpleasantly precocious, and self-serving when we see that it knows we are watching. The ancient suspicion of actors, the denigration of their morals and the general disdain for their psychic makeup (insecure, suffering from massive inferiority complexes, no personality of their own, egotistical) all derive from that dependence on the audience, despite the specifying of their intentions by the formal act of stepping onto a stage. It is, I propose, the basic wariness of all those things that smack of duplicity. Doing something not for its own sake but for the sake of attention or approval is dishonest and considered showing off. Then, too, we despise that which is dependent, weak, cowardly.

Ray, in his tidiness, in his ingrained decency, left after the debacle. His retreat dispelled my fantasies of a righteous attack and left me alone with the drip of my own slime. If he had not been there, I would have conceived of saying, wished to say, and perhaps bragged to friends of having said, all the same cruel phrases without ever muttering a syllable in actuality. The thought and the deed bearing totally dissimilar consequences in real life, these ephemerals would have distracted not an iota from my self-esteem. Faced with Clancy alone I might have elicited the same account of her relations with my friend Dusty in precisely the same way, ushered her out with the warm sentiments of alliance and avoided her and the man forever after. That smarmy bit of grande dame behavior would have been a satisfaction. Instead I have this fewmet of the craven bully to carry, tucked inside my helmet, melting down my neck in the sun, and cascading chills in the rain.

*, *, *,

I didn't see them before they left. I drank grape soda under the skylight and read trash. After a week or so I thought they'd be back so I went out there. I walked up from the highway. I could hear the music from half a mile away. There were cars in the drive all the way out to the dirt road. I must have rubbed bellies with twenty-five car bumpers getting up to the house. As I came closer to the house, the music had the same effect on my ears as a jet engine. The hens in the wire outside the living room crouched, petrified, their yellow eyes frantically staring. Angelina was running crazy between the dancers on the lawn, her barking grown hoarse as she was chased by a nipping, noisy, ragged ball of white fur half her size. I recognized most of the people from the school, but mingled with the leotards and beards were a few pairs of sheer stockings in low-heeled pumps, a few deliberate hairstyles.

I may have imagined a white shirt and tie.

It was late afternoon. There were bedrolls piled by the kitchen step. I recognized Liz Fink, a woman from school, presiding over the rice pot. Two girls in fluffy sweaters and matching skirts sat on the one kitchen chair clenching the knees of their blank legs. On their faces were identical expressions of shock. Liz carefully munched rice off a crusted fork.

"Hello, Sally. A little more thyme."

She pinched green dust from a paper box and sprinkled it over the rice. She bent down to smell the mixture. She wore a black sweatshirt and a tent skirt. She turned from the pot, snorted, and scratched idly between her huge flattened tits with the fork.

"Sally, you can testify for these innocents. Is it or is it not true that I blow Charlie every night of the week?"

"Jesus Christ."

"He's ruptured, you know. I think of it as Heloise consoling Abelard."

The two girls looked at me. It was not the act they doubted, it was the actress. Liz combed her black fetlock with the fork and smirked.

"They don't even know such things exist." She took a sudden lunge at the little window and pointed through it.

"See him? Right out there with that bitch poetess Lerner. The tall guy with the Nazi boots. That's the one."

The girls obediently gandered at old Charlie Bigelow hee-hawing out on the lawn. Liz struck a professional pose and waved the fork.

"It's not at all unpleasant for the woman. Very exciting, actually. You start by murmuring into the hollow of his shoulder and kiss and nuzzle on your way down."

I opened the door to the living room and breathed in the noise with relief. It was dim. The incense was thick in the hot air and made me feel sick. I pushed through a mass of bodies dancing or clumped together talking. I bumped up against Rennel, who was leaning his head out the window and breathing. I tried to speak to him, but it was impossible. He motioned toward the door. Then I spied Moira Clancy in Carlotta's leather tunic. She followed us out through the crowd.

We had to go down the drive a little way to keep from being stepped on. Clancy leaned against Rennel.

"Where are Sam and Carlotta?"

Rennel smirked. I smirked back.

"They're not here. They haven't got back from New York yet."

"I thought this must be their wedding party." Clancy swayed her hips to the music and gazed adoringly up at Rennel. The hem of the tunic dragged on the gravel. The rest rolled and creased over her flesh. The seams were spreading and opening in little puffs down the sides.

Rennel watched the moving figures on the lawn. "I don't know exactly what it is. Sam called me from the airport the day they left. He said Laura had decided to come with them and would I come here every night and feed the animals. I came out to stay because I'd finished work and have two months off."

Clancy gave me an anxious smile. I ignored her.

"But what's all this?"

"I don't know. They all started coming in yesterday saying Laura invited them weeks ago. They brought their own drugs and food. It's like an Italian movie, isn't it?"

"Or a dormitory beer brawl."

"But don't you think it's good for people to release their inhibitions and seek a lifestyle in harmony with the rhythms of their existence?" Clancy said, with her most winsome accent.

I smirked gleefully at Rennel.

He glowered and shivered theatrically. "Oh, shut up."

Clancy winced and jerked her hand away from his back. Her lips parted and her glasses started to mist over. She hobbled away, pulled awkwardly at the skirt of the tunic to keep from tripping. Rennel stood, making his most ferocious face. I waved distractedly, shook my head. My own nastiness made me sick; it was time to go home.

It's nice shitting in the woods

I sit here all snug and smug in my bungalow. Look down my nose at whatever doesn't please me. Bigotry is a comfortable state well-suited for recluses, hermits, and trolls. I was in the attic putting my flannels in mothballs the other day and got to reading the old newspaper lining the bottom of the trunk. Found I have hard opinions on all sorts of things I've never thought about. What the town council should have done in June four years ago. Who of that year's court *should* have been elected Miss Crawdad of 19—. That's the ingrained skill of the experienced bigot, to have a prejudice ready-made for any and all occasions. "I don't like her face, I tell you. Mouths like that give me the flux."

I've been sitting here being prejudiced about the house. It isn't mine. I rent it. Mail the check to a box number every month and nobody comes to throw me out. Nobody changes the locks on me. But these things inside are mine. I chose them. This place reminds me of my grandmother's widowhood house. I saw it once when I was ten or so. It had the same summer camp look, clapboards and a low porch. Living room, kitchen, one bedroom, and an afterthought bathroom. Even the furniture is the same. Overstuffed vintage with a Salvation Army or Goodwill veneer. My walls are deep colors, but hers were all pastel. She had a lot of starched doilies and antimacassars. She had a lot of little glass junk. Nothing was worth much, no crystal or china. Just the little variety store cats and mushrooms and pink, sequined ballet dancers that old ladies of a certain sort seem to exhale. There were also fancy cologne decanters sitting empty on the windowsills, a green glass locomotive with three plastic carnations coming out of the smokestack. I never knew her very well, but I remember her house.

My place has a similar fussy feel to it. Lots of souvenirs. No lace doilies, but a lot of signed books and empty envelopes with significant postmarks. But even the souvenirs seem to have failed me. Like this old clock I purchased for myself one Christmas when I was twenty-odd. It ticks. I time my bread with it. I have to work myself up, concentrate, and say out loud, "Why, that is the clock I bought with so-and-so in the snow with the bells of the charity Santa Claus outside. I couldn't afford the one I wanted, which had dragons on the dial, and had to settle for this one with the flowers. I hated those flowers for years before I got to like them," etc. And still it doesn't set me off. The words themselves have become things associated with the clock now and not with me in these old days. It's the same with the coal scuttle and the salt shaker, and my womb-shaped sugar bowl. When the phallic cream pitcher broke a few years ago I was depressed for days—but that was just loss, not nostalgia. But I go through the motions. I've put Mr. Geddoes's last order form in the Death and Taxes drawer of my desk, so I'll have a spur to think of him every spring or so when I get to clearing things away. But the spurs and hooks I assemble are no help to me yet. For now, at least, I don't need them. I cling to them for the future. I wouldn't throw the clock away even if it didn't tick. I'd put it away in case someday I can't remember the so-and-so who stood beside me in the snow that day. In case the sight and shape of him manage to slip by me as my brain slows, I might need the touch or look of the clock to bring it back.

The rest of the furnishings are accidents of liking, temporary or lasting, and availability. The bathroom is painted Sinbad Blue, which looked good at the store, and the name appealed to me, but it is wretched. It's been wretched for five years now. I suppose it might be expected that I'd become accustomed to it, but I haven't.

The living room is maroon. A color I chose because my brother's first car was that color and seemed well-omened. The bedroom is a dead place. I can't remember, when I'm not actually in there, what color it is. It stinks of me and there's no room for anything except the bed and the opening of the closet door. I think, occasionally, of having a huge ant farm installed against the far wall to liven the place up, but I can never convince myself that the ants wouldn't manage somehow to get out. As it is, I lie in there reading with the lamp next to me and go to sleep with the light on and wake with the light still on and the book collapsed against my chest. When it seems necessary to comment on that habit I declare blandly that I'm afraid of the dark. People always take something that denigrating as the truth. But I have no concern about the dark, one way or another. The reason I sleep with the light on is that I fall asleep while reading, so that if I wake in the night I only need to lift the book and focus my eyes. The thing I am afraid of is the weakness of my mind in that period of half-sleep, the vulnerability I feel in the process of sliding into unconsciousness. There are thoughts and events and people that would encroach on me then if I allowed them to. There are the shivers and quivers of my little sins lurking about the edge of my mind, you see. They are always waiting for

TOAD

me to slow down, and when I do, when the current relaxes for only a minute, they snatch me up and gobble away.

Sam's joke: When is a failure not a failure? When it makes a good story.

*, *, *,

It was a fine day a week or so after the party at Sam's place. I'd been down to Karafotia's Grocery for purple soda pop and a package of cookies. As I came back up the street I saw Sam sitting on my ragged porch talking to one of the other roomers. As I came up the steps the man went into the house and Sam gave me a big grin.

"That's an interesting guy. He's a teacher down on the coast and comes up here every summer to take courses in marine biology."

"I know. When did you get back? Where's Carlotta?"

"She's shopping. We're out of everything. We just got back last night."

"Well?"

"You mean, how did it go?" He took a cookie and munched on it. "We're married."

"Not very nice, huh?"

"It's not that. I'm just trying to think how to explain what an incredible situation the whole business was. First my folks picked us up at the airport and my mother ran up and kissed Laura, thinking she was Carlotta. When that got straightened out my mother started rushing around trying to get a wheelchair because she didn't think anybody so pregnant ought to walk as far as the parking lot."

He chuckled and took another cookie. I passed him the

soda. He was clean and his clothes were clean. His old dungarees looked thin and soft without their usual tinge of dirt.

"Maybe you've heard, my mother is a little hysterical. If
she's out of bread twenty minutes before suppertime she cries.
Well, we dropped Laura at a hotel and went home. My sister was
there and all these neighbors started dropping in. Carlotta was
tired so she went upstairs to sleep. It was funny seeing her in my
old bed with its bucking bronco bedspread. I sat up late and ate
bagels. Why is it that you can't get bagels out here?"

"I don't know?"

"Well, the first thing, we had to go see the rabbi. He is a very
nice guy who's been my parents' rabbi since I can remember.
They wanted him to marry us. My folks are kosher. We called him
up and he invited us over for tea. He had a nice study. All dark
wood and millions of books and an old brown globe and maps
of the world three thousand years ago. So we sat in these leather
chairs and drank tea with milk and sugar in it from these fine
old cups that were made in Dresden before the war. He had a
lot of beautiful things. I don't know when the last time was that
I had a saucer under my cup. You get away from things like that
and they really seem strange when you run into them. The
whole business of a saucer is so clever. It allows for human fal-
libility. It acknowledges that even a grown-up can spill his tea.
Drinking from mugs is symptomatic of a whole different view
of life, 'I don't care if I do spill my tea.' Of course, the Orientals
drink from little bowls and naturally assume that no civilized
human being would be so careless as to spill a drop. They don't,
either."

"So, the rabbi?"

"Yes. He wanted us to bring the baby up to be kosher.
Wanted him circumcised and for Carlotta to study and convert.

Carlotta got mad. She said she didn't want the baby cut and she was going to bring him up to worship Manitou. There was kind of a row. He said he wouldn't marry us. He practically threw us out. My folks were really upset. They had this idea that unless the rabbi approved and married us the whole thing was doomed. My mother thought that.

"Then we went around and saw all my old friends. We invited them all to the wedding. They're all very cool now. My friend Jim, who I think I've told you about, is the drug king at Haverford. The word got around somehow, but he's such a brilliant student that the philosophy department wouldn't let them expel him so the president of the college called him in and forbade him to set foot on campus. Jim really liked that. He does all his work at home and just mails it to the professors. He says he gets a lot more work done that way."

Sam smiled and I leaned back against the porch post. I took a drink of soda and handed the bottle to Sam. He tilted it up and the sun shone through purple onto his face and throat.

"Laura came, too, and brought some *very* interesting people. There was this saxophone player who's been living for years in Tangiers. Then one day he heard a Rolling Stones album and decided to give up jazz and take up hard rock. He was very big and dark with an Afro haircut that stood out from his head about a foot. When my mother saw him she dived into the kitchen and spent the whole day of the wedding making chopped liver. Once in a while she'd stick her head through the door with a tray of drinks and things. But he's a very loving, gentle guy. He noticed he was making her nervous so he went into the kitchen and sat talking to her. I looked in and she was feeding liver into the grinder while he turned the crank. He was saying, 'You got too much syrup in the 7 Up in this country. It's a real drag on your scene.' And she was nodding away. His name was King Tut, and by the end of the party she was passing him things, saying, 'Now, Tut, you try some of this.'"

Sam laughed and bounced his heels on the step below him.

"The wedding itself was hilarious. We were all stoned by then. My father was drunk and my mother was crying. They'd got this rent-a-rabbi who came running in on his way to something else and was in a big hurry. We were all barefoot and Carlotta had been eating licorice. She read somewhere that it prevents infections. It made her mouth black. The rabbi stood in front of the fireplace and we stood in front of him. He didn't have the right glasses and he stepped back to try to see what he was reading and knocked over this potted plant my mother keeps there in the summer. We all started to giggle and he had to start all over. Then he ran through it so fast we didn't know what was happening, and then he was popping into his coat, grabbed the money from my father, and ran out the door. Every time I looked at somebody I had to laugh. It was one of those days." Sam sighed cheerfully and ate another cookie. I sighed, too.

"It sounds pretty strange."

"It was strange all right. I was sure glad to get back to my little house in the trees. I've definitely decided I don't want to have anything more to do with New York. I want to live very simply and quietly in the woods and just have my friends around me. My father gave me a thousand dollars and Carlotta's mother sent a thousand. We ought to be able to do something with that. Did you see that article in the paper about the hermit up in the Siskiyou Mountains? It seems he has six kids and he lives up there with them and his wife on nothing but their garden and a few animals. The school board keeps trying to give them trouble because the kids don't go to school. But when they gave them tests to measure their educational level, they were so far ahead of the normal grade level for their age. He and his wife both have a couple of college degrees and teach the kids themselves."

I could feel how happy it made him, thinking of it.

"There was a picture of the whole family in the paper. They really looked fine. They delivered all their babies themselves and none of them have birth certificates."

There was a rattling down the block. Carlotta came into sight pushing a shopping cart full of paper bags. She walked slowly, leaned back a little, and stretched her arms out past her belly to reach the handle of the cart. She wore the same red dress and the same gray shawl over her dark hair, which fell loose around her shoulders. Her legs spread wide as she walked. She held no expression. Sam watched her curiously.

"Do you think she's ugly, pregnant?"

"No. Not at all."

She parked the cart at the bottom of the steps and smiled at us. She scratched an ankle with a bare toe.

"Hello, Mrs. Rosen."

"Rommel," she replied with a grin.

Sam slapped his knee. "That's another thing my parents had a fit about."

Carlotta climbed up to us and snatched the bottle of grape soda. She drained the last three inches in the bottle. She rolled her tongue around her lips and wiped her mouth on her arm. She sat down and stretched her legs out to either side of her belly.

"I asked them to give me the money instead of the green stamps. They wouldn't so I took the cart."

Sam grinned. I handed her the cookie bag.

"It might make a good baby bed while he's little," I volunteered. "It would be handy to be able to roll him around."

"Aram's going to build a cradle."

"That's right. I have to practice being my own carpenter and plumber. I'm going to build a house for the goat, too."

Carlotta said, "There's something wrong with Kate. And the toilet has stopped working. There was some kind of big party at the house while we were gone. Some of my dresses are gone, and a few of them are ripped. There's garbage all over." She shook her head.

Sam peered down the street. "There's Rennel now. Do you think we can get the cart into his trunk?"

"Just a minute, Carlotta, I've got my mother's oatmeal bread recipe."

I went into the house as Rennel's dented Rambler screeched up to the curb. She was still sitting on the steps, smiling, when I came back out. The bags of food leaned against each other on the sidewalk as Sam and Rennel tried to tie the grocery cart into the trunk of the car. I handed Carlotta my mother's neat filing card with the doodle daisies printed along the top edge. I sat beside her.

"How did you like New York?"

Her smile disappeared. "It was horrible. Aram's mother is a fanatic. She has a double kitchen—two identical halves with two of everything: stoves, sinks, tables, everything. Half is white and the other half is red. Even the floor. There are even two doors. On the days she serves meat she locks the white door so you can only go on the red side. It's all about not boiling a calf in its mother's milk. I didn't go in there the whole time. Not through either door. I was afraid of profaning something. And I had these terrible dreams about seeing my baby boiling in my milk. His skin turned red and started to swell up and separate from his flesh and his eyes looked up at me through the bubbling milk and his hands were reaching for me. Ugh."

She stared at the sidewalk, seeing it again. Rennel grunted as he shoved the shopping cart farther into the trunk of the Rambler. Sam encouraged him. Carlotta pulled idly at the hem of the red dress.

"I was wearing this all the time. We just took the clothes we were wearing. Aram's mother went out and bought me this *thing*. A real thing. She wanted me to wear it to the wedding. It had a little white collar and pale little bears all over it. When I came down in this instead, she burst out crying. And the rabbi came in on his way to a funeral and rushed through it and kept staring at my belly with his nose in the air. Afterward Aram's mother spent all her time in the kitchen and would only talk to some black guy there. She wouldn't even look at me. She'd get suddenly very busy and say, 'That's nice, dear,' if I said something to her. And then Laura came in with a lot of people none of us had even seen before. And all Aram's friends from high school were sitting around making stupid jokes."

She twisted at a thin gold ring on her left hand. She watched them fooling with the cart.

"Did you get to see much of the city?"

"We didn't go in at all. We sat in Aram's room the entire time we were there, or went to see his old friends and sat in their bedrooms in their parents' houses. This place was just the suburbs, just houses and shopping centers. I never got within twenty miles of New York City. Once they took us out to dinner, Aram's folks, and we went to a restaurant in a motel up on the highway. I ordered pork chops."

"You want to go?" Rennel hollered from the car. Carlotta pulled the shawl close and stood.

"Did Laura come back with you?"

"She went to Athens. She wanted to go to a party there, or something." She descended the stairs slowly. Sam's grinning face flattened briefly against the car window. I waved. The shopping cart shone in the open trunk as the car disappeared down the street.

At the other end of the block a fire engine tinkled discreetly beneath a tree. The little lesbian who lived a few doors down stood with her legs spread and her arms crossed over her breasts. A square man with huge bare forearms talked to her while another lifted a ladder against the tree. An empty birdcage was on the sidewalk. In the shifting greenery of the tree, a tiny speck of blue and yellow appeared and disappeared with the lift of the wind.

* * *

It got very hot that summer. The color went out of the grass and the streets dried out. There were two sorts of people in the town, those who went to the beach and those who went to the mountains. The few who stayed home were too poor or too old for anyone to think about. In the Sunday heat the streets were dead and everyone was cranky about it.

I'd lost my job at the coffee shop. They'd hired me for my black boots and fired me the night I came in barefoot. I lay under the skylight, sweating, and listened for feet on the stairs. Rennel came once and took me to see a movie he wanted to argue about. He came again the next day and told me he was going to California to surf until school started. He drove me out to see Sam and Carlotta one last time before he left.

She was scything the long grass. It waved in the wind up to her knees and she waded slowly through it, swinging an old gray scythe. The long curved blade hissed and hacked at the dry yellow stalks. It fell, shaking, clumped behind her in a stubbly path. She stopped when she saw us. She lifted her heavy braids off her neck, laid the scythe down carefully, and headed toward us. The sweat was even and shiny on her face.

"I've been scything."

"Do you think you ought to be doing that?" I asked.

"It makes me feel good." She smiled and sweat dripped clean from her jaw.

There was a rapping in the trees. She gestured toward the sound. "Aram's building the goat house."

We'd brought strawberries and ice cream, celery and onions and lettuce, steaks. Rennel waded off toward the noise in the trees and I carried the food into the kitchen. It was dim and cool, the air heavy with the smell of yeast bread. Carlotta followed me. She drank water from the tap and splashed it over her face. She went into the living room and put a record on while I washed the live stuff in the sink. There was a new picture hanging over the stove. Cut from a calendar. A flat-faced woman holding a pale-eyed baby. Their clothes looked soft and comfortable. Gold plates were balanced behind their heads. A blue shawl covered the woman's hair and a small cross hung on her breast. The ceramic bells shivered beside the picture.

A long roll of Chinese script lay browning on the refrigerator. She must have taken it down to hang the Madonna. The music came up, not loud. Carlotta came back in and sank into a chair.

"What a lot of food!"

"It's Rennel's farewell dinner," I explained. "He's going to California to surf."

"I like strawberries."

My hands hurt in the cold water. I pulled the green stems

from the berries and dropped them into a bowl. Carlotta stared at the floor and listened to the music. She couldn't lean forward anymore, so she either sat up very straight or leaned back. The belly took up all the space between her breasts and her knees.

"I want that to be playing while my baby's being born. I want that to be the first thing he hears."

I slid the strawberries into the refrigerator. I looked around for the rising bread, but I didn't see it anyplace.

"Have you found a doctor? You could afford a hospital now with all your marriage money."

She wrinkled her nose. "Nobody will come out here. And I'm not going into any hospital." She caressed the ledge of her belly, then asked suddenly, "Will you be able to get out here without Rennel to drive you? I thought you'd be here."

"When's it due?"

"The middle of August. Aram will deliver him, but afterward I thought you'd be able to come out."

"I'll come if you want me. I'll be glad to see the little shit after all this."

The bread smell seemed stronger from the living room. I leaned in the doorway and saw the three fat loaves on the old stove, swelling beneath a dish towel. The pilot flame muttered.

"Is this the first time you've tried the bread recipe?"

"No, I've made it twice now. It's really good. Mrs. Strong brought us some fresh butter. She's the landlady. She lives in that big house in the drive. I pick dandelion greens and boil them and put butter and salt and pepper on them. I think it's going to be a very easy birth. I haven't had any pains or sickness or anything all the way through."

"Have you got everything you'll need for the baby?"

"My mother sent a little sweater. That's all so far. What will I need?"

"Diapers. Dozens, I think. You'd better make a list."

"I'll remember. What else?"

"Shirts. Undershirts, like. There's this funny kind that has two little strings to close it in front. Or maybe they're on the side. And blankets. What did you ever do with that book I brought? Didn't it have a list in it?"

"What, *You and Your Baby*? Listen, I threw that right out. It had all these stinking pictures of what the fetus looks like."

"That's lovely. That's very clever of you."

"Do you think the Indian women knew or cared what their babies looked like while they were growing inside them?"

"What are you two arguing about? Have we got a sharp knife?" Sam bounced in and I turned away from Carlotta's fierce glare. He rummaged in the kitchen drawers.

"What are you doing out there?"

"Come and see."

He bounced back out the door and I followed him, Carlotta's eyes burning my back.

Sam wore a torn T-shirt and carried a paring knife in one hand. The rip of a saw drifted through the trees. "There's this great guy helping me. He's a welder. He lives over in Sherwood and works in Portland. He gave me a ride out from town one day and we got to talking. He built his own house."

Sam pushed through the brush to a clearing and I followed. Rennel sat on a thin log to steady it while my brother sawed one end. They both looked up as we approached.

"Hello, brother," I said.

"Sally, Christ, don't you have any shoes?" Spike asked. "Every time I see you, you're running around with your mud hooks flapping."

We grinned at each other and Sam and Rennel stared, confused.

"You two know each other?" Sam asked.

"That's my big brother."

"But your names . . ."

"We had different fathers."

Spike wiped his face with his forearm and went back to sawing. Sam placed the knife down near him and sat in the pine needles beside me. A pile of thin logs was stacked beside Spike. The branches had been stripped and sap oozed out where they'd been cut. The ground was littered with needles and yellow sawdust, and the warm air reeked of sweat and pine. Spike's work shirt was dark in patches and he'd rolled his sleeves high over his strong freckled forearms. Rennel held the log they were sawing, flexed his arms, and watched Spike curiously.

Sam leaned in close to me and spoke softly. "He's really a fantastic guy. He knows all about carpentry and machines. He's got a lot of kids and they're all pretty nice. He didn't even graduate from high school, but he's really sharp!"

I looked sideways at Sam, but he seemed only excited and interested. He was not making fun of me or my brother. "I know."

"Oh, yeah. What a small place this is. Imagine running into your brother!"

Spike lined the log and measured it against the others. He took up a light ax and stripped off the bark quickly, using the knife around the knots where the branches had been.

Sam whispered, "It's really exciting watching somebody who knows what they're doing."

I nodded gravely. "Yes."

"It's like Mr. Sing and his painting. He just goes right in and does it without any palaver."

"Yeah."

Spike stacked the stripped logs in a neat pile. They were each six feet long and four or five inches thick. He stood back and looked at the stack, then bent to pick up the saw and the ax.

"That's got to dry awhile. I'll come back in a few weeks and show you how to knock it together."

Sam stood up and moved forward, smiling. "That's great! Should I cover them in case it rains?"

Spike frowned a little. "It's not that kind of dry."

He looked at Sam to see if he understood. Sam smiled, eager.

"Rain won't hurt it. You sure you don't want that toilet fixed? I can't do that, but I know a guy who can."

Sam waved his arms. "Thanks very much, but we really like it the way it is. It's nice shitting in the woods. Come back to the house and have a drink."

Rennel went to one of the stacked logs and lifted it like a barbell, balanced it, and curled it up to his chin with his hands spaced carefully along its length. When he put it back he looked relieved.

It was strange to see Sam walking with Spike. My brother's old dungarees and work boots and Sam's old dungarees and heavy shoes. Spike said they could put the goat shed on a sledge so it could be dragged to wherever the goat was grazing. Sam thought that was wonderful.

Music came from the house. Sam went in to get Carlotta to make lemonade. Spike stopped at the door to leave his tools.

"You want to come over to the house with me, Sally? We haven't seen you in a while."

I could see my face mirrored in the freckles and creases of his. "I'm supposed to stay for dinner here."

"Well, come over and see Jean when you can. We always figure you're up to no good if we don't see you for a couple of months."

"I'm glad you're helping Sam. He can use it."

Spike looked through the door into the dark house. "Sam Aram? Is that his name? He's a nice kid."

"Yeah."

Rennel walked up chewing a grass stem and trying to look competent. We went inside and I could hear dishes clinking in the kitchen. Spike took in the piles of cushions, the little inlaid boxes of dark wood, the strewn records and books, and the gaudy rugs. A poster of screaming women hung next to a Navajo blanket on the wall. There was an aftertaste of incense in the air, and all the ashtrays were full of butts. The music was not too loud today. Spike looked at me and I grinned. Sam entered carrying a tray of ceramic tea bowls and a coffee can full of lemonade. He slowly set it down on the floor. The ice in the lemonade chimed against the sides of the can.

"Sit down anywhere."

Spike looked around, embarrassed. I flopped onto a pillow to show him. He eased down carefully and stretched out his stiff knee. Sam noticed.

"Is your leg sore?"

"No. There's a metal plate in there instead of a kneecap. I wore the old one out kneeling on concrete while I weld."

Sam stared in wonder and tipped lemonade into the tea bowls. "Is that a good job, welding?"

He passed us each a bowl, and one to Rennel, who hunched beside the record player. Spike explained that it makes a living, but he'd like to be a fireman.

Carlotta came and sat next to me.

"Is he really your brother?"

"Yeah. Listen. He's got four healthy kids. Why don't you ask his wife what you'll need? She knows all about that stuff."

"That's a good idea. He's nice."

"Why don't you let him get your toilet fixed?"

"It's so nice shitting in the woods. Aram's face gets this beautiful expression when he's done it. Very still and strong and peaceful."

"You go out together?"

"We hold hands. Sometimes it's hard for me." She leaned back against the pillows and closed her eyes.

Spike was explaining how he used to smoke grass with some Mexicans he knew when he was a kid in California.

"I don't see anything wrong with it. But I don't run across it anymore. I drink beer now in the summer and red wine in the winter." He lifted the tiny tea bowl in one scarred brown hand and sipped politely at the lemonade. Sam was delighted.

"If you ever want to try some again just come on over."

"I'd like to see Jean stoned once. She's pretty funny when she's had something to drink. That's my wife." He put down the tea bowl and got up gingerly, bending his good leg and keeping the other stretched out in front of him. "Well, I'm going to take my kids swimming. Why don't you all come along?"

Sam jumped up. "Thanks, we'd like to, but we've got dinner all set up here. But we'll come over. And you come here whenever you're passing by, okay?"

My brother nodded. He looked down at me, crouched and barefoot. "You'd better come over sometime."

The Volcano Bar diet

The great Volcano Bar diet is the only one that has ever worked for me, and I remember it with enormous affection. Still, it must be admitted that an intricate concatenation of factors are necessary for its success, and the exact circumstances would be difficult to reproduce for the benefit of the generally obese public.

I should explain that the Volcano Bar diet has always been an object of intense and luxurious adoration for me. Since the latter stages of infancy I have yearned for this particular sweet above all others. It is smallish, just one and three-quarters of an ounce, a hump in the rounded spreading form of an aging monadnock. The appearance is not inspiring and has, even by devotees, been described as reminiscent of varying forms and states of excrement. There is a lack of glint in the chocolate surface that, to the aficionado of chocolates, denotes an absence of paraffin and a corresponding increase of the crucial cocoa itself. The color of the chocolate is mellow, warm, and smooth. I have always imagined that by the syncretic quirk of some elderly Swiss gentleman (pink-cheeked he would be, and in the habit of walking everywhere clothed in long white tweeds), a fine standard of quality was pursued at the expense of profit: yellow cream must have been stirred into the milk chocolate rather than dried skim crystals, and perhaps the slightly granular filling suspended between the rich and mellifluous chocolate is a miracle of confection.

The nature of this crunch, as it were, has been the subject of close speculation to no definite conclusion. Once, I was convinced that it was crushed walnuts. A Philistine salad lover has proposed that it is merely sugar crystals, or toasted cereal crumbs. I reject both theories. The underlying tenor of flavor, that series of subtle, possibly wholly imaginary chemical effects which are sensed on the roof of the mouth and beneath the tongue, convinces me that there is some genuine source of strength in these particles. The problem in analyzing them is that they are so small, and so totally integrated with the chocolate, that it is very difficult to separate one so as to get a look at it. I have many times managed to extract one from some crevice in my teeth only to have it disappear in an involuntary convulsion of my tongue. The few instances in which I have removed it from my mouth, delicately licked the chocolate from it, and held it up on the tip of a finger for scrutiny have convinced me that it is indeed a form of nut. It does not dissolve, so it is not sugar. It does not grow soggy, so it is not cereal. It is a pale, indeterminate shade between white and yellow, which coincides with nut nature, but it does lack the acidity which points to the walnut. It is not coconut, for not even dried and desiccated coconut can be so totally stripped of its potent taste. My conclusion for today is that the crunch is pulverized filberts, which, I have discovered, are grown in the vicinity of the Volcano Bar factory. Though Brazil nuts cannot be eliminated as a possibility, I reject them on the principle that they would require expensive importation. I must emphasize at this point that what I have labeled "crunch" is not a strenuous exercise for the jaw. It is nowhere coarse enough to introduce a noise to the chewing process, and could never irritate even totally naked gums in mastication. This crunch is a subtle fibrillation to the tongue, a delicate contrast to the smooth chocolate, one of the revelations of genius displayed in the bar as a whole.

Now, this textured milk chocolate is not a fragile surface ornament, as is the case with so many of the crasser candies, but instead constitutes the greater portion of the bar. Begin where you will—the top, sides, or the base—and proceed, nibbling cautiously, through a full half-inch of this delectable concoction. Gentle inquiry with the tongue at this point is rewarded by the magnified sensitivity of anticipation. As you approach the center, the mysterious heart, the final, minute crust of the chocolate breaks away and is absorbed slowly in your saliva. Now is the time: lift the bar to eye level for examination. There, among the chiseled excavations, a tiny break has appeared, about half an incisor in width. There, instead of the predictable darkness of the ordinary crack or fault, is a tiny leak of white, gleaming coolly in the surrounding chocolate. In the next delicious moments, carefully remove still more of the dark wall encasing this bright secret, this snowy core, this glacial mystery. It is smooth, balanced in its nature on the brink of flowing, but never yielding. The first touch of the very tip of the tongue to this pale miracle induces a moment of surprise, a reorienting of the senses after the relative roughness of the surrounding case. The texture of the white center is silky, not as resilient as young flesh. If the first ice cream, sweetened with honey and loaded with eggs, were somehow transformed from its basic nature and could retain its prime firmness at room temperature, the effect would be not unlike this delectable magma at the core of the Volcano Bar. But the texture is augmented by a flavor of such sweetness, concentrating such intense sensation on those small areas of the tongue that respond to that stimulus alone, that it borders on pain. And inextricable from this sweetness is the redolence of pure vanilla. There is no confusion of tangs, no multiplicity of artificial fruits or distillations of bitter purple flowers to clutter the response and mangle the attentive nerve endings with irrelevant messages. This one clear note, sounded in the subtle passages of the sinus, reverberates a devastating joy.

There are, I know, cannibals still at large, and small children who eat the frosting and leave the cake. There are mammalian females of many species that, in pressured circumstances, will devour their own young. These and other violent extremes I can comprehend and can, in some deep crack of my inner self, find some sympathy for. But that class of insensate savages that take the center of their Volcano Bar in one bite, separate from the enveloping chocolate, sets the small hairs of my body stiff and vibrating, causes waves of shock to traverse my entire nervous system, and sends venomous serpentine convolutions into my very dreams. These grotesque and impious humans may include in their number some small portion of nearly suicidal aesthetes intent on blotting out every drab complexity of their prosaic existence by repeated, massive, petrifying jolts of ecstatic sensation, much as a violent psychopath is relieved of his symptoms by the passage of insupportable forces of electricity through his body. For these devotees, if indeed they exist, I can summon a horrified pity and a niggling drip of understanding. But there is that majority of the Big Bite perpetrators, many thousands strong, whose act is unconscious, unresponsive, motivated only by animal hunger or most ignorant habit. When that mellow nugget passes their lips nearly whole, its nature is relegated to the mechanical atrocities of the molars. No concept of the chemical processes of appreciation is present. The lump, smeared, chomped, and mixed only crudely with saliva, passes the uvula, is gripped by the uncaring esophagus, and is shuttled without thought into that senseless chamber of destruction—the stomach. The prospect of such waste is devastation.

My own way is slower. It is really useless to begin a Volcano Bar with less than an assured half hour of undisturbed leisure before me. Every glittering soupçon of the center must be nibbled off simultaneously with the exact balance of chocolate wall. Too little of one or the other, too large a bite, an interruption that forces me to swallow before the dark and light have completed their warm amalgamation in the hollow of my tongue and been circulated through the areas of my mouth like newlyweds at a reception—any of these accidents precludes the full enjoyment of the strange combination. They produce a certain willful bitterness, as in "Jeez!" (short, I have always supposed, for "Jesus!"), and they require a resettling, a beginning again, a moment of contemplation, a composed and reverent spirit, before resuming my affectionate consumption. It seems to me there is more pleasure inherent in a properly approached Volcano Bar than in the average five-course meal. And in those old days it still cost a dime.

The price was crucial. I had fifty dollars, with which I had planned to redecorate my boyfriend Joe's little house. I had gone back to him despite him (evidently Leda Van Hoerderbroeck had found him unsatisfactory). But a few months later, Joe had to go east, to Florida, in fact, to visit his mother. His plans were always meticulous. He would drive, taking six days for the trip each way. He would be gone precisely forty days, spending Christmas in the bosom.

Meanwhile, the rent was paid and I was to mind the house. I had fifty dollars left of my life savings. I had dripped the rest away in the months since my attempted suicide. Finding a new job had seemed too much for each day as it dawned. But I wanted to commit some massive act of love, to create some in-eradicable mark that would tie Joe to me in an external way, some clip and chain independent of my awkward body. I thought of the decorating because Joe admired the house of a local effete of our acquaintance, a man whose personal incapac-ities were in direct proportion to his undeservedly large income. Joe had never so much as tacked up a calendar, and a certain deference prevented me from attempting my usual weeds-in-jar approach to ornament. But now he would be gone, this was my chance. The noise, smells, and mess would not disturb his ritu-als. Besides, I knew I had to keep busy or I'd very soon be raving, caught once more in my old ailment. Not knowing what he was up to for such a long time would be a rich agar for my imagination.

I asked him if I could paint the bedroom while he was gone. He said it was very nice of me. His pleasure at the idea puffed me up, to the extent that I abandoned my original plan to spend twenty-five dollars on the house and to live on the rest. I could go around to the college cafeteria and wait for an acquain-tance to walk through the line with me. I could go to dinner at my mother's. I could steal.

He left. I wept. Bawled actually. That night I ate all the food in the house: potatoes, fried; six eggs, fried; half a loaf of bread, toasted, with butter and jam; two bananas; and the last of the coffee cake that remained from his farewell breakfast. I slept all right.

The next day began a frenzy that nipped me, tore me, and drove me through the next thirty-nine days. I began with a glass of water in my gut, to walk about Boston visiting paint and hardware stores. There was a particular color I had in mind, a Victorian mustard tone, and lush velvet flocked paper in gold for the bedroom. I'd seen something similar in an ice cream parlor. I visited a dozen places to compare prices. That night I scrubbed the kitchen walls and ceiling. The revelation of the fine state of its paint, which seemed to have been preserved beneath a layer of grease, made me decide that it didn't need a new coat. One less can to buy. I slept with the light on and a book open beside me in case I woke and needed rescue from my dreams.

By the end of the week, an inflexible regimen had developed. I walked around each day to check on sales and develop a plan. I carried home my finds and worked until late into the night, steadily, methodically, with an energy totally foreign to me. No argument of health or duty could have pressed me to such labor. I did it to drive out jealousy, idle imaginings, and that febrile revving of my anxieties caused by the emptiness of the bed. I was always nervous.

At the point of pain each night, when my arms would no longer lift without protest, I would put the brush or mop away and climb into a hot bath. I sat in it, staring at my own grimy feet in stupefaction until they were cleaned by the process of erosion and the water was chilled enough to force me out. Then, with the lamp and the book and the single Volcano Bar, I would climb into bed.

There wasn't really enough time to scrounge for food. I had calculated and come to the conclusion that I could spare four dollars for food for forty days. At ten cents, only one Volcano Bar a day would fit my budget. I bought them one at a time, always at the same drugstore four blocks from the house and in my direct path when returning from my daily ramble.

I put the bar on the pillow the moment I entered the house, and kept it in the back of my mind, a sort of consolation as I painted and papered and scrubbed. Toward the last, when I was sewing covers for some cushions I had stolen from the dormitory lounge of the local college, I would listen to the burr of the coarse thread moving through the cloth and dream of the white filling concealed in its chocolate casing.

Only once during this time did I eat a meal: Christmas at my mother's house. I hardly knew I was there. I noticed nothing, felt fatigued by the dull taste and weight of the food, was harassed by the movement of bodies other than my own.

There were two other interludes when people visited my house, Joe's house: a man and woman came asking to see the guitars in the workshop. I let them in. They were eating from a large bag of pastries, soft with red filling.

"Won't you have one?" the man said. I could tell he would have liked it if I had taken one, but I said, "No, thank you." But they were not through with me.

There was a sheet of paper in Joe's typewriter, the first page of one of my laborious little tales. It was a sentimental accident. He used the machine for business letters and I had decided to compose a story on it while he was away so that our finger oils would blend in the tiny depression of each key. Normally I did not use a typewriter at all. The woman leaned over the machine and lifted the paper. My hands jerked up, trying to find some prohibition drastic enough to retrieve the page even as she read it. She laughed. I sat down. "Look at this!" she said to the man, and they leaned over the page.

The unaccustomed assault flattened me for the day. As soon as they were gone I crept into bed and slept through the afternoon and night and well into the new morning. The sight of the pristine blue-and-white paper that wrapped the Volcano Bar was the first image I saw that day, and allowed me to plan around it. No need to go out at all that day since the night's supply was already at hand.

Once, also, Ray came to visit. I met him on the street and

he came that night bringing a bag of oranges. He thought I looked ill. There were ten oranges in the bag. It touched me terribly that he should do this. He sat beside me and talked quietly of books. I peeled an orange for him and one for me. We sat in such friendliness that I felt safe and calm enough to eat. No fruit ever tasted better.

For eight days I ate an orange every day just before the Volcano Bar. It lengthened the anticipation, it cut my hunger so that the ritual of the chocolate could be prolonged. I could actually put the bar down beside me after the white filling had been breached and sit, reading, with the luxury of the knowledge that there was still more whenever I stretched out a hand.

My clothes were more baggy than usual, looser. This seemed the natural effect of constant wear. I could see no change in my naked body.

The curtains were deep blue against the yellow walls. Dried grasses, seeded stalks, the woody pods of winter I had walked miles out of the town to find, stood up in jugs in the corners of the rooms. On the day Joe was due, all my work seemed equally dry and dead, wasted, and ugly after all. I bathed, dressed in my only soft garment, and waited for hours. There was no money for a welcome-home supper and my grief over that was mild but constant. The waiting then continues in me now, when I have resolved to wait no more for anything. He came at last, the tones of his motor as familiar as his step or voice. I ran out of the house to the door of the car, pulled it open before he could disengage the key.

"I was afraid you would do that, I wanted to sneak up on you!" he said. And he was pleased. He loved the house. He brought wine and told tales. He initiated the bed in its new bordello walls, but he saw no change in me.

TOAD

A week later Rennel came calling and walked past me without speaking. "Where's Sally?" he asked Joe. Joe, amazed, pointed silently to where I stood across the room. "Can that be her?" asked Rennel. He stared. "Maybe, if she's lost a lot of weight." Then Joe saw, too. But my pleasure was one of shock as well. My awareness of my fatness was so integrated to my sense of self that I felt it still. I had not even considered I would lose it. The chocolate regimen had been one of self-indulgent economy. The blind preoccupation of my solitude had eliminated any awareness of its effects on my physique. On that last day, trying to pretty myself in the old futile ways, I had despaired over the purple bags under my eyes and the scrofulous look of my beaten hands. Nothing else seemed changed. Still, pouches of flesh hung behind my knees and rolled out from under my thighs when I sat down. Rennel's observation excited me. A beat of light pulsed in my head. Early the next morning, I wheedled Joe into taking a walk to the drugstore. I could not abide leaving him long enough to go by myself. He looked at magazines and I stood surreptitiously on the scale. One hundred and forty pounds, it read. Glad. Wept sweetly. Sashayed hopefully. Since my thirteenth birthday I had weighed one hundred and eighty pounds.

It's funny to think of Joe not noticing that his bed partner had shed forty pounds while his back was turned. Now I have only five teeth left in my jaw, just enough to anchor my bridges. That colors my thinking about the chocolate bar diet. Now I am again spread and heavy and indifferent, but I remember the mysterious pleasure of walking down the street in human form. To meet the eyes of strangers and find them holding no laughter or disgust—amazing. It was not a sense of beauty that thrilled me so; I was not beautiful. It was the simple fact of no longer being grotesque, of being at least inconspicuous in my ugliness.

The depth of gratitude I still feel, as it is undiminished even presently, to have known for a few years the innocence of the unselfconscious, I owe to that unique and voluptuous convection, the Volcano Bar, and its price, ten cents.

The first tomato

10:00 a.m.

There is some kind of mold between the tiles in the bathroom. A soft gray fuzz in the cracks. It's ironic. I've always been suspicious of the kitchen tiles and have scrubbed them every week with ammonia and the wire brush. But the bathroom got by me. The tiles there are set closer together than the ones on the kitchen floor, and it's too tempting to just sprinkle disinfectant while I damp mop. I wouldn't have noticed, but I put a stronger lightbulb in there this morning just before I got down to cleaning. I felt sick when I saw it. All these years I've been going in there barefoot. I soaked it with the last of Mr. Geddoes's solvent and put my rain boots outside the door so I can put them on before I go in. I can step right out of them into the tub and directly back into them when I get out of the tub. I'll let it steep until morning and then scrub. If that doesn't work, I don't know what I'll do. Jean would have some idea but I can't call her.

I have to go down to the rocks this afternoon for a load of seaweed. And some periwinkles would be nice, in case Rennel actually comes on his appointed day. No one else comes anymore.

That seaweed has to go on the compost heap this month or it won't be any good to me in the spring. Maybe the sand flies will follow it up again this year and titillate the toad. He seems sleepier lately.

I keep reminding myself that I have done what I could see to do. The light wasn't strong enough before and the smoky blue walls seemed to suck it in and reflect none back.

I'll get new rubber gloves on the way down to the rocks. This last pair has holes in both thumbs. I usually only wear through the right one. I'll want them for the seaweed. This way they'll be strong for the morning, too. A human can do filthy things with rubber gloves on. I myself have wrung chicken necks and stripped the feathers from the flopping corpse and shoved half my arm into the hot cavity to rip out the lights without flinching or blinking. Without a shudder, because of the gloves. Because when I run the yellow rubber under the tap the mess streams away and I peel away the act with the glove and put my clean hand directly to my face without thinking. I wear the gloves to kill slugs and smash snails. If I ever murder a human being it will be because they've enraged me while I'm wearing gloves.

6:00 p.m.

Now I'm tired. Got a wheelbarrow full of red weed, a plastic sack of periwinkles, and a bloody gash in my left calf. I used to love the rocks. Last year I was still good at walking over them. They were slippery today. Things aren't going right lately. Maybe it's part of getting older.

I was nervous today. There's that story in all the shops about the new nun at Stella Maris slipping on those rocks and being dragged out to sea. Made me nervous for my life. Ha. I suppose the milkman would notice after a couple of days. They'd find the wheelbarrow and I'd probably wash up beneath Tower Hill in a week or so. There I'd be with my skirt pinned up to my belt like a diaper and my bun undone. At least the goldfish would have starved to death by that time.

TOAD

*, *, *,

The sun tried to get in through the windows. The lush orna-
ments of the room looked sad in the dim daylight. Rennel
looked at the piles of books, Carlotta lay with her eyes closed. I
stepped out. The goat made noises somewhere, but I couldn't
see her. The chickens had scratched away all the grass inside the
wire and sat blinking stupidly in the dust. I went looking for
Kate. Found her snagged to a tree, her head twisted in the rope,
tangled and knotted in the bushes. I untied it and spent a while
walking around disentangling it while Kate jerked and riffled
and twitched her ears. Her bags were swollen and mottled, pur-
plish. They hung very low. As she moved, the right teat dragged
a little and one of her yellow hooves kicked it accidentally. I
held the rope short and bent to look. The teat was cracked;
there were long, gaudy fissures in the strange flesh. A thin fluid
seeped from them, shiny in the sunlight. I reached out to touch
the bag and Kate trembled. When I felt the rough shiny scab,
Kate screamed and jumped away from me. I wrapped the rope
around my fist. Kate's eyes were dark and bright. Sam came up
the drive whistling softly.

"Your brother is a fine man!"

"Did he look at this goat?"

Sam frowned and crouched by the goat. "It's worse."

"I think you ought to get a veterinarian. And Carlotta better not drink any more of this milk."

"That teat was tender when we got her. It got a little red.
But I don't think Rennel milked her while we were in New
York. It was a lot worse when we got back. Poor Katie."

"Well, tie her up someplace where she won't get all hung up.
I'll get her some water." I headed to the kitchen to find a pot.

There was bread in the oven. The smell was rich and fine.

Rennel leaned in the doorway explaining the semantic delicacy of the Hopi language to Carlotta. She sat in the stiff chair with the shawl draped over her face.

"Carlotta, have you got any milk beside the goat's?"

"No. Why? What are you doing?"

"I'm just getting some water for Katie. But her tits look pretty ugly and I don't think you ought to drink the milk until a vet looks at her."

"She won't let me milk her anymore. She yells and kicks. I thought if I just left her alone she'd be all right. It's because they took her baby away from her, I think."

"Maybe Rennel can drive into town and get some milk."

Rennel rolled his eyes.

"And look, how about while you're gone? How are you fixed for supplies?"

"I did a lot of shopping a week or so ago. We've got plenty of rice and some horsemeat in the freezer. It's only a couple of miles over to Sherwood."

I took the water out to the goat. She buried her nose in the dented pot and didn't come up till it was almost gone. Sam lay under the trees, staring up, smiling. I took the pot back for more water.

Carlotta took the bread out and set it up beside the Madonna to cool. Then she disappeared, said she was going out in the boat. I went into the little bathroom to piss but there was a rug over the toilet and a smell, so I took a quick walk in the woods.

Rennel went into town for fresh milk and salad dressing, which I'd forgotten when we drove out. He also brought a big cardboard box of canned milk. Sam came in and sat beneath the kitchen table. He'd decided to buy a Jeep station wagon with the marriage money and go homesteading. Rennel leaned his chair back against the Arabic Zodiac calendar and said there wasn't any more land available for homesteading.

Sam shook his head. "There was some just a while ago in Nevada. There still is in Alaska, and the Yukon. Lichtenstein knows all about it."

"Whatever became of him?"

"He's out in the cabin right now. He's honeymooning with his wife. He went back to New York just before we did and married this girl he went to high school with. She's very pretty. Looks like a Byzantine princess. What I wanted to say is that I really long to live far away from cities and people. A very simple life in which I need no more than I can provide for myself. This goat house is perfect practice for building a cabin. It could just be one room the first year. Chink the walls with mud and plant a big garden. Set out a trap line and maybe shoot birds and things. A place with a little stream nearby. See, this is what the day would be like: I wake up before light and put on the kerosene lamp that sits on the table I made for myself. I start a fire in an old woodstove like the one in the cabin here. I brew up coffee and sit watching the sun come up through the windows. When it's light I put out the lamp, go outdoors and chop wood, weed in the garden, and go look in my traps to see what's for dinner. I come back for lunch and spend the afternoon painting and writing poetry. Go for a swim just before supper. Read late into the night by the kerosene lamp."

His eye shone. Rennel nodded, and I could tell he, too, was dreaming of his own muscles stretched beautifully in clear sunlight. And I had an ache, too, and a different solution every other Tuesday. A tiredness crept into my bones. It weighed in my marrow and turned my joints into a sorry liquid. Carlotta's voice floated clear and soft, calling Angelina.

Sam asked me, "Don't you think it's a good idea?"

"Oh, I don't know. I suppose it's possible. What about the baby?"

"As long as he's warm and gets love and enough to eat, isn't that what babies need?"

"You're the one reading obstetrics."

"That's just while they're inside. Doesn't say anything about afterward."

Rennel looked down at his greasy fingernails. "The thing is, Aram, you don't know anything about living in the woods."

And I? I smirked. Only because Rennel said it instead of me.

Sam took up his arguing pose. "The only way you learn is by experience. Spike was telling me he got to be a welder by being an apprentice from the time he was seventeen. He found out how to build houses by helping his friends build theirs, and then building his own. I can't help it that my mother's a refrigerator and my father's an electric can opener, but I have to accept that. I can learn to do things. Think of all those trappers and pioneers coming out from the East. Most of them weren't even very bright. They learned as they went along . . ."

He went on. Rennel crouched in the doorway to argue better.

I opened the refrigerator and took out the steaks. Four, red and triangular. The meat was soft in my fingers and I laid the steaks beside the sink to warm a little. Scratched a match to the little hole on the floor of the oven. The blue light of the flames flickered to life in rows. Took another match to the naked broiler jets. I cut chunks of celery and wads of lettuce, ragged slices of onion. Dumped them into a shallow pot and sprinkled it with the dressing. Carlotta's laugh wrinkled the air sweet and Angelina crashed into the kitchen, breathing loud, her nails clicking on the torn linoleum. She careened off the low walls and occu-

pied the room. Carlotta stepped through the door, smiling. She
held up a little yellow tomato.

"Our first tomato! All the rest are knobby and green yet!"

Angelina got up on her hind legs to snatch at the meat on
the counter. I grabbed a handful of hairy flesh, loose at the back
of her neck, and marched her out the door. She ran around the
house and I heard the chickens squawking feebly.

Rennel held the tomato reverently. He ran a finger over the
firm skin. "You actually grew something! I never thought you'd
do it."

Sam grinned and squeezed Carlotta's arm.

"Would you like it in the salad?" Sam asked.

"Yes! Won't that be great?"

Carlotta took the tomato from Rennel and handed it to me.
It was small and hard, but probably edible.

"Slice it thin so we can all have some."

I rinsed it and removed the green at the top. The slices fell
cleanly from the knife. The seeds inside were still green. It didn't
matter. I sliced the pieces into the salad pot. Carlotta bent and
licked the juice from the counter.

"It's so good."

It was good. We smoked a little grass to make us hungry.
We listened to the steaks crackling in the broiler. There was hot
bread with real butter and the meat fell apart on our tongues.
The celery crunched and the tomato melted. Later we filled our
mouths with strawberries and white ice cream.

We lay on the floor with the remains of our dinner around us
and talked profoundly. Rennel complimented Sam on his serious approach to life. I said I dreamed of a window that looked
out on nothing.

Sam said, "If my boy ever asks me why he doesn't go to

school like the other kids, I'll say 'School is a place where you walk in, are assigned to a desk, and made to sit there quietly for twelve years.' That ought to solve the problem."

Carlotta drank long swallows from a carton of milk. She licked her white mustache and didn't listen to any of us.

They played their favorite song. I cried a little and wiped my nose on my knee.

Carlotta went to bed. Rennel showed Sam a judo hold, but Sam couldn't go through it for fear he'd throw his back out. I fell asleep next to the stove.

When I woke it was dawn. Pink light crept in. Rennel sat cross-legged in the middle of the floor. His shirt lay beside him and he watched me gravely as he rolled stomach muscles for me.

"Om," he said softly. "Om."

He ignored me when I got up and stretched. I went out the back and crouched to piss in the grass. Not bad, really, with the dew falling pink on my ass. Went into the kitchen and sozzled under the tap. Put water on for tea. Rennel was doing push-ups between the dishes on the floor of the living room.

"How about toast and jam with your tea?" I asked.

He snarled at me and continued his push-ups. Sam came out in his pajamas and took a walk outside. Carlotta followed him out, smiling, puffy in her red dress. I buttered toast and watched the light coming in through the kitchen door.

Sam and Carlotta came back holding hands. I set the tea and toast out on the kitchen table. Carlotta went for her shawl. Rennel sat with us, growling, and chewing antacids.

"If you wouldn't do all those exercises on an empty stomach you could have something to eat in the morning," I said.

"Shit."

"Sure is a pretty day."

"Sure is good bread."

"Sure is."

I washed the dishes from the night before. Carlotta wrote down her parents' address in Palo Alto so we could stop by for the surfboard. Rennel burped around his last Tums.

"Oh. I almost forgot." He went out to the car and came back with a new red paperback book.

"I brought this for you to read. *Ishi*. It's about the last wild Indian. They found him wandering around California in the 1910s. He'd been up in the hills all his life and never seen a road or a white man or a telegraph pole. He was the last of a tribe that had been starved out."

He handed the book to Sam. Carlotta looked hungrily over Sam's shoulder as he turned the pages.

"Pictures!" she exclaimed. "What a fine-looking man!"

"Yeah. Look at his chest," Rennel said. "They took him to the Natural History Museum and taught him how to use a toilet and stuff. He died a while later of tuberculosis."

The pictures showed a broad muscular man with a flat bewildered face. He was naked except for a strip of hide between his legs. A wiry man in a mustache and a tight-waisted coat, a style of the early 1900s, stood smiling beside him. The curator of the museum. There were pictures of Ishi with a bow and arrow, crouched beside a bush in demonstration. Ishi building a fire with two rocks and a pile of grass. Ishi spearing fish. In each picture the little man in the tight suit stood nearby, smiling. The last picture was of Ishi in a tight suit. His hair was short and a bowler hat was perched high on his head. He looked pained.

"He lived in the museum after they found him?"

"Yeah. There wasn't a reservation for him. His tribe had

been thought extinct for years. There weren't even any other Indians who could speak his language."

Sam's eyes glowed. Carlotta reached over his arm to turn the pages.

"What a good book. I'll read this right away."

The goddamn baby

There was a refugee bus in front of Sam's house. The paint was dark and smooth but it had the feel of war surplus. There were three seats and then the rest of the bus was empty. It was hot. Angelina lay on her side beneath the bus. She didn't even lift her head when I looked at her. The kitchen door was open. All the windows hung away from the house on their hinges. It was cool and dark inside. I dropped a bag of oranges into the sink and put a package of spinach into the freezer compartment. There was a strong, unfriendly smell inside the place. I heard a rubbing and scratching sound from somewhere. A mattress took up half the living room. It humped over the cushions and the piles of books. A mound of clothes was piled at one end. The noise and the smell came from the bedroom. I went to the door.

Carlotta was crouched in the bare little room scrubbing with a wad of wet rags. Next to her, the big saucepan was full of suds. An open bottle of green fluid sat beside it on the old boards of the floor. She rocked back and forth, rubbing at the wood until it was dark and wet and the stench of the disinfectant was stinging.

"Hello."

She rocked back on her heels and looked at me. Her eyes were red and streaming. Clear snot ran from her nose down over her lips. Her smile was shiny with snot and tears.

"Why are you crying?" I asked.

"It's just the disinfectant."

"When's our friend due?"

"Anytime."

She brushed her arm across her face. There was a hole in the armpit of her sleeve. The seams of the red dress were split in places, and long ovals of her white flesh showed through. Her belly was wider than any other part of her.

"Spike's wife is really nice. We've gone over there and they've come over here a few times. She told me all about what to do and what to get. She gave me some things, too. I went to her doctor. His name is Bump."

"Will he come here?"

"No. But he looked and said everything seemed all right. He thinks I'm planning to go to a nearby clinic for the birth."

"How do you feel?"

"Fine. I feel finer all the time. Any time now, my little boy will be here and everything will be all right."

She continued scrubbing. Her belly jolted and swayed, it scared me. I took the rags from her. Her long white hands were sore and red and her knuckles bore deep cracks.

"The walls and ceilings are already done. The smell kind of bothers me."

She went out and I took over. Wrung the rags out in the suds and scrubbed again. Moved over to where the floor was dry and scrubbed more. I noticed the small window had been cleaned. The ceiling, made of painted board, was still wet from her scrubbing. It dripped a little near the lightbulb. I scrubbed my way out the door and hauled the pan of disinfectant with me. I shut the bedroom door to trap the smell.

In the living room, Carlotta was kneeling on the mattress, stuffing folded sheets in a grocery bag.

"Spike's wife gave me these sheets. She's boiled them, but I had them hanging out in the sun this morning. The sun purifies things."

I sat beside her on the mattress and rubbed at my running eyes and nose with my arms.

"What are you going to name the baby?"

"I don't know." She closed the bag carefully and laid it on top of the piled clothes.

"Aram says we ought to wait awhile and see what he's like. He says a name can influence your life so it ought to be appropriate to a child's nature. Not picked to please some great-uncle or something."

"Where is Sam?"

"Out in the cabin talking to Lichtenstein. His wife left him."

"Already?"

"She didn't like the life. She wanted a toilet and a washing machine. She was a real phony. Six inches of mascara. He only married her because he caught Laura going around with Professor Lynch."

"Oh."

She stretched out on the mattress and put her hands on her belly.

"Where's the kid going to sleep?"

"In there."

She waved an arm and I went to a corner with a cardboard box full of diapers and shirts. The size of my hand, the shirts. They made me nervous, giggly. Next to the clothes box was an apple box. It reeked of disinfectant. A woven blanket padded the bottom. Another blanket cushioned the sides.

"That'll do for a while."

"I thought of that shopping cart, but I don't like all that shiny chrome. And I can move this around anywhere. Babies aren't supposed to use a pillow—did you know that?"

She went into the kitchen. I heard water running into a pot. Angelina entered the living room and sniffed. The disinfectant seemed to please her, and she snorted about with her long nose. Carlotta walked by with a plate of cold rice. She leaned out the door and scattered the rice for the chickens. Their chuckling sped up and became cheerful.

"Ugh. Come look at this."

I joined her at the door and looked out. There were three white hens with beady yellow eyes and pale pink combs. The fourth hen huddled in the corner. One of its wings dragged limp on the ground. The wing point was torn. The feathers were gone, the flesh red and seeping blood. I glimpsed a flash of bone. The chicken was barely alive. Her head bobbed on her neck.

"Christ."

"Something got at her the other night. We heard the noise and Aram came out. It was gone, whatever it was. But now the other ones won't let her get near the food and they peck at her all the time. They're horrible, stupid animals."

"You ought to kill her. There's nothing you can do about that big gash."

"We ought to kill them all. There's something about them . . . And they don't give eggs, anyway." She drew back into the kitchen. The water was boiling on the stove.

"How's the goat?"

"Kate's a lot better!"

Carlotta entered with tea and a couple of little bowls. We squatted on the mattress and drank.

"Spike brought a veterinarian he knows. He gave her something. A lot of stuff. He says she won't give any more milk, now, until she has another kid, but the sores are healing up. It was some kind of infection."

"You got any tea for us? How did you get here, Sally?"

Sam and Lichtenstein came in the living room door. Their hair was wet. They carried their shirts. Lichtenstein was tan to where his underpants showed above his dungarees.

"What happened to your face? What's that stuff on your arm?"

Carlotta paused in the door on her way for more bowls. "I was too polite to ask," she said.

"It's leftover poison oak," I answered.

Lichtenstein sank down onto a corner of the mattress in his stock meditation pose. Sam sat in front of me examining my shrinking rash.

"That's very interesting," Sam said. "I was just reading that the West Coast Indians never got poison oak. They'd start out very early in the spring when the leaves were small and tender and eat one every day. They'd keep it up for a month until the leaves started to toughen up. Then they were immune. They had immunity figured out five hundred years ago, while white men were still talking about evil humors and bleeding each other to death. That *Ishi* book was full of things like that."

Carlotta brought more bowls and poured pale tea into them carefully. She sat with her legs bent on either side of her belly. She nodded at Sam, smiled.

"'Ishi' means 'The Man.' It's like being called Adam. I think that might be a good name."

Sam grinned and sipped from his bowl. "Maybe. You ought to go swimming, Lotta. It's really nice today."

I hadn't thought the rash showed much in my freckles.

"Did you see our new car?" Sam asked.

"That bus?"

"It's more like a jeep. Four-wheel drive and everything. It's made by a tractor company and it's supposed to be very tough. That's what we're going to use to escape into the wilderness."

"Are you going to buy a place?"

"There's no money left. But Lichtenstein's uncle has a cabin in the mountains in Montana. He's going to loan it to us for the winter. He only uses it in the summer for fishing."

"What are you going to live on?"

"My mother's sending us fifty dollars a week."

Carlotta sat up and smoothed the red dress over her bulk. "She also sends vitamins and iron pills."

"For you, Ram-Tam Buddha Belly!" chuckled Sam.

We went for a slow walk. Carlotta ambled with her hands on her belly, feeling it shift, I suppose, and listening to what was going on inside of her.

We passed the goat house in the clearing. The back wall was up, supported on the sides by poles that ran into the ground. The chips and sawdust and the logs themselves had gone gray in the humid heat.

"He's just waiting to finish it until Spike comes again," Carlotta explained. I noticed the dark circles under her eyes, almost like bruises.

"I wish you'd go to a hospital."

She stopped short. "I don't want to hear any more about that."

She pulled up a switch from an aging bush. It whistled through the air as she swiped at the trunks of the trees.

"They all have such fine reasons—doctors, you, and even Spike's wife. My mother, too. But what it comes down to is that I'm alive and the baby is alive and you want to put us through a machine. You want a tidy cellophane package with a brand name and an address to complain to. They'd knock me out as soon as I got there and I'd wake up with a bloody bed and some nurse in an ironed brassiere peddling me a kid whose face I didn't see when it was born. That's the worst kind of robbery. Stealing hunks of people's lives."

She wouldn't look at me. She stood still and beat at the trees with her switch. Sliced through ferns, caught her own leg. When she spoke again her voice was soft and steady.

"I want my son to live touching things that are alive or have been alive. Leather and wood and dishes that grew up between somebody's fingers. Plastic shrivels your soul, and people who don't care kill what they touch.

"You don't care. You sit up in that naked attic drinking purple syrup and feel smug because nothing ever quite reaches you. You talk and laugh and bring presents, but you're not fooling anybody. You leave the lights on when you go to sleep and you spend too much time with people you don't like. So don't you tell me what I ought to do. Because you don't really give a shit about me or whether my baby is alive or dead. It's just gossip to you one way or another. And gossip's all you want. That's all you can handle."

She strolled away, her back straight. I watched her long black braids tap softly at the small of her back. The trees were tall here, and bare for thirty or forty feet before the first branches began. Nothing moved but the flicker of Carlotta in her red dress walking between the trees. Without deciding to, I sat down.

After a while I got up again. I walked back through the trees and brush, and crossed the lawn away from the house. Kate was making noises somewhere out of sight. Hung up again, probably. My boots crunched in the gravel of the drive. I walked down the dirt road, up the paved road, past the old folks' housing development to the highway.

Exactly four days later I had just finished my weekly shopping. I had a six-pack of grape soda, four paperback mysteries, and a few packages of cookies. The white Rambler was sitting in front of my house when I came up the street. Rennel leaned out of the driver's side, watching till I got up to him. He wasn't putting on any faces that morning. I don't think I'd ever seen him with a relaxed face before. He even pouted in his sleep.

"The baby came yesterday."

I stopped and put the six-pack on the fender.

"No shit."

"Sam called me this morning. He's been trying to get you. He wants you to come out."

"Are they all right?"

"I guess so."

"I don't know if Carlotta's going to want me around."

"Will you get in? I've been sitting here for an hour."

My fine black boots were falling apart. Bent up at the pointed toe. My legs were clammy inside. Didn't put my socks on when I went out. I threw the stuff into the back and climbed in beside Rennel. He started off toward the highway.

Sam was standing at the foot of the drive when we got there. His face was white. There were shadows in his cheeks. His eyes were rimmed red. Rennel pulled up beside him and he grabbed at my window as I rolled it down.

"Boy, am I glad to see somebody!"

"What's wrong?"

"Nothing. I just don't know what to do." He climbed into the back seat to ride up to the house.

"I'll tell you, I was really scared yesterday, but it turned out all right. I thought she was dying."

Angelina snoozed on the kitchen step. It was one of the only times the door to the house was closed. Rennel stopped the car quietly. We eased out and looked at Sam. He nodded toward the closed door.

"They're asleep, I think," he said.

"Did she have a hard time?" I asked.

"Well . . ." He looked at the ground. "You would have thought so if you'd seen her. But we went around to Doc Bump afterward and he said she was fine. Didn't even need a stitch. And the baby's fine. All he does is sleep."

We all stood awkwardly looking at the kitchen door.

"Well." Sam reached for the doorknob. We stepped over Angelina's body as quietly as possible. The cords in Rennel's neck flexed. Once we were inside, Sam stopped and ran his hand over his hair. The smell of disinfectant was faint but still detectable. It had sunk into everything.

"Aram?" Carlotta's voice. She sounded normal. Sam disappeared and came back smiling.

"She wants some tea."

He put the teapot on. I could tell he was delighted to do these things. He beamed at the pop of the gas igniting.

"Shall I go see her?" I asked.

"Please, yeah."

I tiptoed into the living room. There was no sign of a baby. Three cushions lay in a line with a blanket crumpled across them. She must have been sleeping there. The door to the bedroom was open. It was dim.

"Carlotta." I stepped inside.

"Hi. I was just taking a nap." She sat against the wall on the mattress. Her dress was blue. The gray shawl fell from her hair, rested softly on her shoulders.

"Where is he?"

"Here."

Our soft voices fell lightly in the room. I bent clumsily in the doorway to take my boots off. Walked on the mattress and crouched beside her, where the baby lay in a box. Looked in at the little boy. His tiny face was like a clenched fist, and he was tied up in a cone-shaped bundle. Black, wet threads of hair on his head. I looked at Carlotta as she stared into the box. The muscles of her face were slack. Her eyes were dark, fixed on the small thing breathing. When she finally looked at me, I tried to smile, but it felt strange. Sam came in with a bowl of tea in each hand. He bent tenderly to Carlotta.

"There's milk and sugar in it."

She glanced at him, took the bowl, and then looked back at her baby. Sam handed the other bowl to me and crouched at the edge of the mattress.

"Well, what do you think?"

The baby's small ear looked mangled, and there was blood crusted in the folds. There was blood matting the hair. Sam and Carlotta were looking at me, waiting for an answer.

"I guess you really did it this time," I said finally.

Sam bounced a little on his heels. His grin lit up the dim room.

Carlotta dragged deeply at the tea. "You don't know how to bathe a baby, do you?"

I shook my head.

She turned to Sam. "Maybe Rennel will take you over to Spike's. Ask Jean if she'll come and show me how."

Sam leapt out the door. I heard him hustling Rennel. The kitchen door clicked, the Rambler rumbled and moved off over the gravel. They waited till they were far down the drive before slamming shut the doors. Carlotta watched the box. I watched her.

"So what's it like to have a baby?"

Her hands tremored faintly as she answered. "It's like taking a big shit. That's really what it feels like."

She looked tired. The bruised color beneath her eyes was

deeper. She smelled of sweat, through the tang of the disinfectant. A fine, electric frizz stood up from her braids.

"Were you scared?"

"Yes." She cupped the bowl. The puce-colored tea dregs rocked lazily. Her jaws tightened and the soft look disappeared from her face. "Not at first. I wasn't afraid at all for nine months."

She put the bowl down on the mattress and leaned back against the wall. There were streaks in the paint from her scrubbing. She kept one limp hand on the edge of the box.

"Everything was ready. I put the sheets on with a bunch of newspapers underneath to catch the blood. I made a double batch of bread so I wouldn't have to think about that for a while. We took all the clothes into the laundromat in town. But I couldn't be sure exactly when he was coming. Aram was getting pissed off waiting. He kept saying, 'Do you feel anything? Do you feel anything?' and then a couple of days ago he said he didn't think I was trying. With this ugly look on his face."

She sat up and peered intently into the box. The baby slept. His breath moved the blanket. He didn't seem to have any eyelashes. I tittered a little nervously.

"He was just joking," I said. "It must be hard waiting for something that could happen any time but doesn't."

She reached for the baby like she might pick him up, and then put her hand back to the edge of the box. Her eyes, when she turned to me again, were hard and glittering.

"Don't tell me anything about Aram. He was scared. And he's a liar! When I started having pains, he was surprised! He was shocked! I was just getting into bed and I felt a little twinge. I lay here for a while and felt a few more. He was reading beside me with that candle lit. It was the first time we'd ever slept on sheets together except at his mother's house. I said, 'I think it's starting,' and he put his finger in the book and said, 'What?' It was maybe three in the morning. When I told him it was the baby, his face went yellow, like he was sick. He looked ugly. He started sweating. It looked like chicken grease on his face. At first he pretended he didn't believe me. He kept smiling, looking really sick, and saying, 'Oh, sure.' I was happy, you know? I was a little sleepy and I wished I'd gone to bed before, so I'd feel stronger, but I felt warm and good and I thought he'd be happy, but he was just scared."

"They're supposed to be nervous. Fathers. That's what all the cartoons are about."

She waved me away like a fly. She leaned forward, gripped her knees, and rolled her neck on her shoulders.

"He was wearing an undershirt and he jumped out of bed and started running around. It was too short, this shirt, his belly button showed, and he looked really strange with his short legs and hairy ass and naked prick. I can't explain it. He looked feeble, running around like that. And you know what he did? He put some water on to boil. At first I thought it was just funny. Boiling water. I sat here and laughed. He kept running in here with tea and asking how I felt. The pains weren't coming very often. They weren't bad at all. Then he started talking about a clock. He said he'd forgot to get a clock and you had to time the pains. He wanted to rush out right then and get one. As though the baby wouldn't come out if you didn't know how many minutes passed between each contraction. I still thought it was funny. He can't drive. He hasn't got a license, and he has trouble with all the gears anyway. I told him I thought it would take a while. Somebody told me that. Spike's wife. She said first babies take longer. Can I have a cigarette?"

The baby slept. The room was quiet. I fumbled around for cigarettes and handed her one. She closed her eyes and breathed in deeply as I lit it. She exploded in coughs. Her face reddened, her eyes leaked tears. She patted her chest as she rocked, coughing.

"That's not . . . !"

She coughed and fell back to breathe and coughed again.

"That's stronger than marijuana!"

She wiped her eyes and face with her forearm. The cigarette was still pinched between her thumb and forefinger. She took a discreet puff, blew it out slowly, and looked at the baby. He slept.

"Well. I got up to go out and piss and my water broke all over the floor. I thought at the time I'd pissed myself. It didn't feel like piss, and I still pissed when I got outside, but I didn't think of the water bag until later. I really felt fine. Excited, but good. The pains didn't really hurt. They were just squeezings. I felt like walking around and talking to people. I came back in and made some tuna salad so Aram wouldn't have to cook for a while. I did it all right, dicing the onions very fine and covering the bowl with paper before I put it in the refrigerator. There was some water boiling on the stove so I turned it off. When I came out, Aram was sitting over on the cushions waiting for me. He seemed very calm and cheerful then. He pulled out this little box and gave it to me. It had all kinds of charms in it. Holy water and a clove of garlic and a little swastika and a star and a cross and a piece of wood he'd pulled off that Indian canoe in the museum downtown while nobody was looking. All sorts of things like that. Nice. Also, a big bar of chocolate to keep my strength up."

She pushed a cigar box out from behind the baby's box. I set it on my knee and opened it. Junk. A clump of short black hair with string wrapped around it. I held it up to Carlotta.

"That's virgin hair. Angelina's. We ate all the chocolate

already. I brought that box in here and put it up by my head. I almost slept. The squeezes weren't coming very often. Every ten minutes or so, maybe. And I'd just fade off and the squeeze would start and I'd wake up and then drift back when it was through. Aram was looking at this book he took from the library. Lots of gory pictures in it. He'd poke his head in and say, 'How are you?' and then go back out. But he didn't touch me. He didn't touch me once after I told him it had started."

Her eyes were accusing. Her face was set, satisfied with the evidence she'd delivered.

"I don't understand," I said. "Maybe a birthing belly is a fearful thing. But what are you trying to say?"

She rolled her eyes. "I'm trying to tell you that he ran away when the going got rough."

"Sam?"

"Aram."

She puffed at the dying cigarette before stubbing it out in the candle dish.

"It started to get strong after the sun came up. It was very bright because the sun comes in through this window. I couldn't rest at all then and I hit on this quick breathing with my belly that seemed to make the pains easier. I was getting excited again and sweating. I kept waiting to push. Jean said just when the baby is ready to come you get a tremendous urge to push. I thought it would be pretty soon. I called Aram and it took a long time for him to answer. He put his head in and I said, 'Hello!' and I smiled at him. I said, 'Soon now,' and asked him to put the new sheet under me. I had my legs up in the air most of the time. It felt like my belly would rip if I didn't. I lifted up a little between pains and he slid this clean folded sheet under me. It was for the baby to come out on. He only looked at my face. He wouldn't look at the rest of me. I said, 'How are you doing?' and he said he didn't know. He was sweaty again. He had his pants on and his shoes. I asked him to put the record on so the baby would hear something beautiful first thing."

"What were you wearing?"

"Nothing. The top sheet till the last. When he came back I wanted to sit up. It seemed easier sitting up. I saw this picture of an African woman once. She was squatting with two women holding her arms to keep her up. It seemed easier. As though gravity helps or something. I wanted Aram to help me sit up. He went to put his arm under my shoulders just as one of the pains came. I was breathing very fast and sweating and he jerked his arm away and stood up. When the pain was over I pushed myself up, sat leaning on my arms. I kicked the sheet off. I thought it was going to be very soon. He was staring at me with a horrible expression. Maybe there was blood by then, I don't know. Right up till then I was all right. I was getting a little tired. Once in a while I'd think to myself that I'd like to put the rest off till tomorrow when I'd had some sleep. But I wasn't afraid. The pains weren't as bad as I'd expected. But when he was looking at me like that it really scared me. I'd never seen that look on his face, or anything like it. I thought something had gone wrong without my noticing. I said, or maybe screamed, 'Aram! What's wrong?' and he jumped. He actually jumped a little away from the bed. I thought the baby was dead and I was dying. The pains were getting very strong then. Anyway, I tried to reach him with my hand, but he just ran outside. He didn't say anything or look at me, he just ran. I heard the door bang shut. I got too busy to think about it after that."

She was quiet for a minute, looking into the box. My hands were damp. My cigarette seemed to have fallen apart. I brushed the shreds of paper and tobacco off the mattress onto the floor.

She didn't seem upset, talking about it. A little nostalgic already. She looked tired, lying limp against the wall. The dress she was wearing was one I had never seen.

"I was still sitting up when the baby came. Kind of propped up against the wall with my legs bent. I could see him coming out. Once I started pushing they weren't really pains anymore. Just big pushes. A big shit. I'd close my eyes and grunt and then open them. After one of the pushes I saw his little head waving around on a long skinny neck. He looked like a blind turtle. His neck looked so long. There was all this ick on him. I could see he was alive. He was moving his head like he was trying to see. But his eyes were closed. Just a few more pushes and he was lying there between my legs. I could feel him between my thighs with all the slime dripping. All this blood around. I started to cry. I was so happy I reached down and picked him up and laid him on my belly. He opened his mouth and waved his fists and squalled a little and then went to sleep. I just sat there for a few minutes looking at him and then I began to push again. I thought for a second it was twins, but it was just this slimy sack of crap. Blood and stuff. It came out on the sheet. Awful feeling. The baby's cord was connected to it. All this time I thought the baby's cord was connected to the inside of my belly button, and when you cut it my half came back up inside me. I don't know where I got that idea."

"So, how did you get the cord cut and all that? Did Sam come back?"

"No. I put him down on the bed and tucked a pillowcase between my legs and went rustling around. I tied it off with dental floss and cut it with a boiled butcher knife. I just used clear water and a cloth to wash him. I'm not sure that was right. But I wanted to see him and get him covered. It wasn't so warm yesterday. He doesn't have any eyebrows, or any lashes

on his lower lids. There are just these invisible hairs on his upper lids. You can only see them against the light."

"Has he eaten yet?"

"A little, about three this morning. That was the first time
he woke up. I didn't have much milk, but I think there's more
now. He also took a shit. I can't figure out what he'd have to
shit. But it was this amazing dark green, and a lot of it."

"Maybe it's stuffing so his innards wouldn't collapse till he
could eat. Does it stink?"

"Not bad."

The small thing in the box seemed more like a baby as I
stared at it. Carlotta's eyes fixed on it and then moved again
over the red flesh that was too small to be open to the air.
Beasts of this size were fun, in my experience.

"So what happened with Sam?"

"Oh, he was just down by the river throwing sticks for
Angelina. I got us cleaned up and we went down and found
him. I wanted him to hold the baby while we drove over to
Dr. Bump. I was still wearing half a dozen sanitary napkins. It's
hard to reach the foot pedals when you're sitting on a lump like
that. I feel a little sprung, anyway."

She stretched. She arched her back and neck until they
cracked faintly. She spread her legs so that her pale feet poked
out of the blanket.

"Are you glad Sam panicked, or what?"

She broke off the stretch abruptly. "Not glad. But this way
I did do it all alone, from beginning to end. That's something.
The thing that irks me the most is that there was no one to re-
new the record so it was just spinning out there by the time he
came. He didn't hear the beautiful music, first thing."

"That's silly."

"I don't think so." The shawl had fallen behind her head.

The fabric of the blue dress began to darken at the left breast. She saw me notice, and she plucked at the wet fabric.

"I'm leaking milk. Will you get me some toilet paper?"

I climbed off the mattress and padded barefoot to the silent living room. The sunlight came through the small windows in a blinding band. An overpowering sour smell hit me when I opened the bathroom door. The rug draped over the toilet seat was damp. There were towels on hooks. A pair of women's tights hung limply from the shower rod. There was a row of colored glass bottles with exotic names on the labels. There were wrapped packages of toilet paper on the tank. I took one and backed out, closed the door tight.

When I entered, Carlotta had pulled down the collar of her dress beneath her left breast and the baby was sucking. Her shoulders were broad, freckled, and her collarbone stuck out sharply, a thick pale bar. She held her breast to the child's lips with one hand and hugged his small body against her. The child curled against her, already comfortable at the breast. His red arms hung down, and his red flesh was creased as if it were pickled. He lifted his fists to his chest. His mouth moved, his jaw clenching and relaxing. Carlotta let go of her breast and the baby's mouth closed more tightly around her nipple.

"Got some tissue?"

I tore at the package and yanked some loose for her. She folded it calmly, dabbed at the baby's mouth and her own breast.

There was a stack of diapers to the side of the box of baby clothes. I took one and laid it beside Carlotta. Stood itching for a moment, nervous, till I saw the tea bowls. I took them out to the kitchen.

"I wish you'd come for me yesterday. I do believe mineral oil is best for cleaning them at first."

Jean's voice drifted into the kitchen from outside. Footsteps in the gravel. They must have left the car near the road so as not to disturb the baby.

"My son! Oiled like a pasha!" Sam exclaimed.

"The whole principle of soap is to make the skin so slippery that dirt can't stick to it." This from Rennel.

The kitchen door opened and the three of them entered. Jean brought in the scent of lotion and cinnamon. A mother smell. Her round arms were golden in a blue-checked dress. We greeted each other with a grin. Sam and Rennel gawked at the doorway.

"The baby's eating," I said.

Jean's face lit up. She went directly to the bedroom and disappeared behind the door. Sam leaned stiffly against the sink, rubbing his hands.

"I have a stomachache. I've had it since night before last."

I waved my hand. "Just sympathy pangs."

"Did she tell you I got scared?"

"She doesn't seem too worried about it."

"I thought she was dying. I didn't want to see it. I just sat down by the river waiting until it was time to come and discover the body."

"Bodies."

Sam's face softened and he flushed pink. "What do you think of him?"

Rennel snorted from the doorway. "Yes. What does this famous kid look like?"

"He doesn't look like anything I ever saw. Maybe he's unique," I said.

Jean poked her head in, smiling. "He's absolutely beautiful. Will somebody run down to the car for the tub and my bag?"

She retreated into the bedroom. Sam and I both looked at Rennel. He shrugged and stepped out.

Sam winked. "You see, I had decided this whole thing was a joke. I didn't think there was really going to be a baby."

"That'll learn you."

"It gave me quite a jolt. All this time I should have been getting my head ready for it, I thought it was just for fun."

"You thought that Carlotta was just getting fat oddly."

"I thought she had a particularly lively tumor. Elizabeth the First's big sister had a lot of trouble like that. This history major was telling me. Everybody would humor her and pretend she was actually pregnant even though she was seventy or something. Then after nine months she'd go to bed and moan and they'd give her something to make her sleep and tell her, when she woke up, that her son had died. Then she'd start the rigamarole all over again. I think she finally died of puerperal fever."

The color was back in his face. He leaned back against the sink with his feet crossed. A thin stubble shadowed his cheeks. Rennel entered with a blue plastic laundry tub. It was lined with white cloths and balls of cotton. A bottle of clean liquid rocked heavily in the corner.

"Listen, Rennel. I've just been explaining to Sally that this whole thing has taken place in Carlotta's imagination and we'll all have to humor her until she takes an interest in something else. Maybe we can get her into pottery making."

Rennel dropped the tub with a bang and made a contorted expression. He propped his fists on his hips and groaned at the ceiling.

"You mean there isn't even a goddamn baby?"

"Oh, you must never let on to Carlotta. It would destroy her. It was a false pregnancy. These things sometimes happen. Now, practice with me."

Sam snatched a towel from the tub, draped it over his head

like a shawl, and strolled languidly toward us with downcast eyes and his arms cradling an invisible baby.

"You may look at him, but please don't breathe in his face."

I stepped up and grinned and tickled the air near Sam's left armpit.

"What a sweetie. He looks like you, Carlotta."

Rennel shook his head.

"Come on! Don't gawk. If you can't play it right you won't be able to come out here as long as she's got this delusion."

Rennel reached out and wiggled a sullen finger at the air.

"That's his feet. Remember, she'll always carry the figment with his head on her left side, so she can wipe up his puke with her right hand."

"A puking figment?"

"Is that tub ready?"

Jean's low heels clicked cleanly across the dusty linoleum. She bent and hoisted the tub up to the sink, flicked the tap on expertly. She gazed distractedly at the painted Madonna. Her fingers hung out in the rushing water as she waited for some secret temperature. Finally she slid the lip of the tub under the stream and watched it fill.

We watched her silently, embarrassed.

Jean turned. "Carlotta shouldn't be doing any work at all for a while. Can you cook for the both of you, Aram? And keep things neat? She shouldn't lift anything heavy for at least six weeks."

Rennel chortled. "He'll poison them both."

"No. I can cook. Sure. Don't worry about it. I'll take care of her."

Jean switched off the water and swung the tub onto the small kitchen table. She laid out a clean white towel, soap, the bottle of oil, and a box of cotton. As she left the room, a flash of white lace showed beneath her skirt. Her legs gleamed with some smooth sheen. Stockings. I'd forgotten what they looked like. Rennel watched the neat legs till they disappeared.

"Doesn't she know?" He leered and winked.

"Sssh!" I hissed.

Rennel frowned. "How come you were telling me all that shit before if there isn't really a baby?"

Carlotta was in the doorway with the child in her left arm. Her eyes flashed darkly beneath the gray shawl.

"The only thing there really is in this house is the baby."

She eyed Sam and the towel over his head. He snatched it off. She approached the tub as Jean came in with a diaper and shirt, folded neatly.

"I don't want my baby bathed in plastic."

Jean's brows crimped a little. "Well, it's handy and light. He won't hurt himself if he slips on it. But I've got an old enamel tub you can use when you're stronger."

Carlotta shrugged, unfolded the blanket, let it drop. The child was naked. The tiny limbs drooped awkwardly from his wide, swollen belly. His face was small and purple, his eyes closed. The belly rose and fell as he breathed. The umbilical cord was a black finger of flesh that rose abruptly from his abdomen, tied off in a neat white knot. Jean held the child firmly and easily on one arm. With her free hand, she smoothed water over his skin with a piece of cotton. Then a dab of oil. She wiped the ugly skin around his eyes, over his hair and ears, around the thick wrinkles at his neck.

Carlotta leaned forward, watched as Jean wiped the baby's groin.

Rennel whispered hoarsely, "He's got wrinkles in his ass!"

I watched Sam's face, inscrutable and pale, as he stared

from the dim corner of the kitchen. The baby's small face puckered, his obscene lips parted over his pink-ridged gums, and the sound that emerged between them lifted all the small hairs on my spine. My ears shrank back against my skull. Carlotta leaned farther forward, her lips set into a thin line. The baby took a breath and screamed again.

"There, there, little one, soon over." Jean smiled, her warm eyes admired the swell of the tiny rib cage. She set him onto the towel and patted him dry. Quickly, she applied more oil, dressed him, and swaddled him in a blanket. The screaming stopped. The baby's mouth closed. Peace. The child slept. My small hairs gradually relaxed. I could feel muscles loosening all over the room. Carlotta wiped the sweat from her face and neck. Jean handed the child to her. Carlotta clutched him, wrapped the tails of the shawl around him. Jean swept the towel and cotton into a wad, neatly dumped the water into the sink, wiped out the tub, and propped it in the corner.

"Just remember to wash his face before you wash his ass. Don't get his navel wet before the string drops off. And don't soap the hand you're holding him with. He's slippery enough as it is."

We all stood, silent. My knees felt wobbly. All of our faces bore a weak expression. Jean didn't seem to notice; she looked around for a towel and finally wiped her hands on the damp bundle from the bath. Sam lifted the towel he'd been holding, but it was too late.

"Would you like a cup of tea?" he asked.

"No, thanks. I've got to get back. My brood hasn't had lunch yet. They'll be having too much fun in the refrigerator."

Rennel stirred heavily. He shifted the crotch of his leathers down and cleared his throat. "I'll drive you."

"Thanks. That'll be fine." Jean looked around the room.

She picked up the bundle of laundry and stepped up to Carlotta. She lifted the edge of the shawl and peered in at the lump.

"He's lovely. He'll be fine. But you have to take care of yourself. He's still eating what you eat. If you want to make up a shopping list, I'll stop by later for it on my way to the market."

Carlotta nodded. Jean looked around at us again. Something puzzled her, like maybe she wondered why we weren't acting happy. She gave me a curious look and a wave as she followed Rennel outside.

The smell of her lotion lingered on for a while, but as soon as she left, the room felt grubby. I wanted to scratch.

Sam put water on the stove. Carlotta stood still, wrapped inside the shawl with the child. The light of the window fell on her in a showy way. It irritated me the way she stood there in the light, the shawl folded so that it would drape in that particular way. She assumed a familiar pose, and she bent low over the strange flesh huddling in her shoulder. I could see that a woman must stand this way with a child on her arm, and yet it seemed deliberate and sly.

She lifted her head gracefully. I would have been so grateful for an ungainly jerk. "She handled him like a potato."

"You mean Jean?" I asked.

Carlotta nodded. "She has no reverence."

Sam worried the air with a spoon and furrowed his brows. "She has a different philosophy of life."

Carlotta cast her gaze away from him and out the window. She frowned, breathed deeply. "I know her type. She thinks all a kid needs is a clean neck, hamburgers, and a warm lap to sit in for ten minutes each day. She doesn't recognize a soul."

"A soul! Ah!" Sam flourished the spoon again. The handle was stained dark with tea. "Do you think a child is born with a full-fledged soul? Or does it develop, like a personality? Is it affected by environment?"

He was smiling, but Carlotta's eyes slid over him in disgust. She pulled the shawl tight across her shoulders and shifted the little bundle slightly. "I'm going to walk under the trees with him."

"Don't you want some tea?"

The way she glided out the door into the sunlight seemed calculated to perfectly display the depth of gray in the shawl and the blue of her dress. The light leapt off her body as she disappeared.

Sam gave up on the tea. We couldn't talk. He went in and put on a record. I sat on the kitchen steps to wait for Rennel. He was a long time. He was smug when he returned. Said he'd had a picnic in the backyard with my nieces and nephews. On the way back to town I asked him why we were all nincompoops, but he didn't know what I was talking about. He asked me why I didn't smell like my sister-in-law.

᪣ ᪣ ᪣

It was an awkward time. I'd told Sam to call if there was anything I could do. He didn't call. That grated, I suppose, but I was glad. The skylight tired me out. The scratched phone outside my door rang constantly for a girl who'd just moved into the room at the end of the hall. Finally, for a little excitement, I spent a morning sitting in Mr. Greenyas's shop with my stocking feet on a bench. He told me about his boring professional hockey career while he put new soles and heels on my black suede boots. I came out a quarter of an inch taller and full of ideas of my educational grandeur. I decided to give myself a treat and walked by Rose's, the only delicatessen in town. It was a very lush place. Shiny chrome everywhere, in contrast to the matte upholstery booths. I stood in front of the window admiring the cake wagon and the roast beef and the scrawny lady in the black uniform on the other side of the window, her arms loaded with plates. They made a five-layer club sandwich there, and if you were a friend of the Roses you could order a genuine bagel flown out, frozen, from New York. During the lunch hour the more worldly members of the Junior Chamber could be seen at Rose's. In their dark suits showing their young paunches, they tilted toward each other with friendship, and for plates of knockwurst and sauerkraut. The gleam of their thick-framed spectacles and the occasional flash of a bright white sock cuff peeking out of a polished leather shoe gave the place an intensely stately feeling. There were never many women; the food was too fattening. I stood outside and watched the dark heads of men deciding between marble fudge cake and apple crumble, while they discussed the sale of a mountain of silent fir trees.

Toward the back of Rose's, the room widened and there were tables in the center of the floor as well as the booths lining the walls. I could see a tall, dark figure stand and pull out a chair. A smaller figure, a woman, got up from it and moved toward the counter; it was Moira Clancy. With her legs shaved. She wore a severe white silk blouse with long sleeves, a thick leather belt, and a flared skirt. She carried a bag of pink plastic that matched her high heels. Her hair was styled, fluffy and neat. Even her glasses looked clean. She walked into a door next to the counter marked LADIES. After a minute I removed my nose from the glass and entered the restaurant. Marched boldly past the counter to the restroom, and slid through the door. There was a carpet in front of the mirror, and Clancy stood on it, admiring herself. Tucked the tail of her silk shirt smoothly under her belt. She saw me in the mirror and smiled, grabbed my hand.

"Oh, Sally! How wonderful to see you! Please tell me how you all are. Sam and that girl and Rennel, too. I never get to see them anymore!"

I could feel myself frowning. Her face looked soft and vague beneath the powder she'd applied. She smelled good. I looked quickly at her hands, but her knuckles were clean and the yellow stains were gone.

"What the hell are you all got up for? What are you doing in this place?" I asked.

"Don't you know? I'm a secretary now. I come here with my employer. He's a wonderful man. A lawyer. So intelligent. He's like a father to me. I have to take notes when he has a business lunch. Isn't it a lovely place?"

"How did you get to be a secretary? I thought you were a piss ladler."

"But I made enough money on that job to take a course in typing and shorthand. I have a beautiful apartment with another patient of my psychiatrist. She's very nice. We became friends in the waiting room. My psychiatrist is proud of both of us. Let me give you my address!"

She pulled out a steno pad and wrote it out quickly.

"You must come to see me. How is Sam?"

"He and Carlotta had a baby."

She stopped and lifted her head, the paper clasped between her two clean fingers. Her eyes were wide, and then she flashed her teeth. "How wonderful! How wonderful. Is it a boy? Sam always wanted a boy. Are they all right? Do you think I could take them something?"

"They're okay, I guess. It's a boy. They haven't named him yet. How come you don't know this yet? Don't you see Rennel anymore?"

"No, not really. Not since that party out in the country. He came once to ask me to go to California with him, but I had just been hired and couldn't do it. It's terrible to feel that you're losing all your friends, but this job makes me feel good, it adds some meaning to my life. I've been practicing very hard on the violin. Next weekend, I am making a tape to send to my father. He is a fine musician, but I don't think he will be unhappy with the progress I have made. I have to go back now. Will you promise to come and see me?"

She pushed the slip of paper into my hand and grabbed up her purse. She smiled at me all the way to the door. I smiled and nodded back. I still thought she was ugly.

I stood for a minute making faces into the pink-tinted mirror. Walked out across the carpet, through nets of other people's conversations and the smell of their food. On the trip home, I stopped at Karafotia's for my cookies and grape soda. Also bought a can of stew. I hacked it open and put it on the hot plate in my room. Sat under the skylight spooning it up and sipping at the purple soda. Propped a broken copy of *Swann's Way* in front of me. A little entertainment. Read the first page a few times and then put it down. Told myself I'd perused enough of Proust for the time being and went to lie down and moan over my tacky mind. Nobody came to relieve me. After a while, I slept.

The house almost atop the hill

Now I think of myself in general terms rather than specific. All through the agony of my youth, cruel, raised voices informed me that everyone else felt the way I did, experienced the same things I went through. That I was not unique and original was unbearable. I felt a distinct need to prove at once my individual character; the awareness that others were like me was scalding. Were they also all crouched, hiding, alone, their minds electrified but their grotesque bodies helpless and still? My impulse was to cover my eyes and scream, to trample those voices with matched violence.

So many of the desperate things I did in my youth were to combat belonging to that mass identity. I felt that unless I could establish some particularity I would suffer great pain and die in self-disgust. All that cultivation of fantasy, the wooing of freight trains, the manufacturing of intricate motives for every word or movement, the curiosity for what I called the "phenomenology of the others," all the pain and the hatred—it kept me afloat.

Some years ago, when I lived in Boston, there was an old man in a hat who always sat on the same bench in the park as I walked by on my way to work, his hands clenched on the head of his cane. The blue, wingspread birds tattooed on the back of each of his hands complemented his erect posture, his ancient, sharply creased trousers, and the martial tilt of his fedora. He sat still, never spoke. I disliked him on sight. He was so obviously a military buzzard, puffed up with love for his country and the lust to obliterate all other countries.

One day as I passed, a platoon of policemen in heavy blue uniforms was drilling in the nearby street. I was not at all surprised to see a smile on the old man's face as he watched them. He saw me coming and nodded for the first time in all the weeks I had walked by him.

"They look like soldiers, don't they?" he croaked. I agreed, delighted that my analysis of his character was substantiated.

"Yes." He grinned, watching the close-order turn and turn again of the blue mass. "They tried to catch me, but I was too quick. I ran away from the First World War and I ran away from the Second World War. Thank God by the time the Korean War came, I was old enough they left me alone. Spent all my young years avoiding this war and that, the Spanish war—somebody was always offering up a war, but I ran like a whitehead every time." And his face bunched into a grin, his mouth opened wide to let out a fat laugh.

There was also a woman in a flowing gown who stood in the lobby of the concert hall and said, softly, gently, to her companion, "If you look at her again I am going to lie down right here on the floor and writhe around biting as many ankles as I can before they get me."

Or the silver-haired schoolteacher in the wedge-heeled oxfords who declared to her nearsighted colleague, "I could never have married. After eight hours in public each day, I spend the whole evening farting."

There was the awkward couple on the banks of the River Charles, her skirt rucked up and his fly undone, the King James Bible (Red Letter) open on their communal lap.

And the old man and the young girl, each in silver lamé

shoes, tap-dancing together on the echoing tile floor of the ladies' room in the train station at two in the morning.

And the small pale boy who calmly told the bus driver that he wished everyone in the world were dead so he could cross the streets by himself. "There wouldn't be anyone to drive," he said.

To all these things I feel myself respond, some rising bubble of recognition, an excitement that these mysteries exist. I despise them less now, or not at all—the humans. They are intriguing. They keep secrets for years and then announce them suddenly, if only to strangers. Now this "everybody," far from being a threat, is a perpetual consolation. And if I yearn for a banquet in my honor, or hate my neighbor because she embodies every virtue that I lack, or hold the direst grudge against those who have helped me in my most desperate time of need, I will announce it to the mailman. And if I choose to dine on ice cream and mysteries for the fifteenth day in a row, and glory to feel my last two teeth wobbling in their sockets, and find my patchy hair coming out in wads on the brush, I will mention it with pleasure to my brother when he calls. The mailman will give me a dirty look, my brother will lecture me and go out for a bag of oranges, but later, alone, I know they will feel some echo in their chest of the truth I have offered them, they will feel some enjoyment of their own oddities in recalling mine.

⁂

The summer session was over at the college. There was no one there but the janitors and the lady on the switchboard. The fat Russian cook was in charge of the snack bar. I stood for half an hour watching her make sandwiches for the men who were wiring the new wing of the library. She'd been promoted from the big potato masher in the main cafeteria. She was very proud and she spread tuna salad onto slices of bread carefully and quickly.

"It's the first bite that's important," she explained to me. "I spread thick at the corners so the first bites will all be nice. It can be a little thin in the middle."

She had *The Brothers Karamazov* propped open in the steam tray. A tangerine held her page. I stood peering blankly at the strange print, the peculiar forms of ink on paper. She shook her head at the book a little sadly.

"He's my last lover. He doesn't care that I'm dry and sagging. But he's very self-indulgent. It's like being loved by a boy. Only his madness is ravishing. I think it was real. Too many people pretend to be mad. They think it hides their dullness and allows them to be self-indulgent."

She gave me a tuna sandwich and sent me away.

"The men will be coming. They don't like to see a girl in the kitchen with long hair and no net. I don't mind, myself, but if they saw you here they'd be opening their sandwiches looking for hairs. It would be an insult to me."

I walked over to the municipal golf course and sat by the pond to eat my sandwich. The corner bites were very good.

My room was empty when I got back. The stench of the summer's cigarettes sat on the walls. There wasn't much comfort in the blankness of the skylight that day. I felt like being nice and having people like me.

I plugged a dime into the phone in the hall and called Jean, my brother's wife. She said don't be silly, of course I could come out for the weekend. She was making jam.

I took a bath and washed my hair, put on clean clothes. Sat under the skylight to dry, waited for my brother to stop by for me on his way home from work.

He howled, "Sally!" up the stairs; he'd never climb them all with his bad knee. And he was probably afraid of what he'd find at the top. I thundered down fast. He stood on the porch with a steel helmet tipped back on his head. A red mark from the sweat band had formed on his freckled forehead. I could smell his sweat. He wore scarred, steel-tipped boots. There was a red triangle at his throat, where his open collar let in the heat of his welding.

"This dump is just kindling. Can't you get a room lower down? You'd be cooked up there if it ever caught fire."

There were boards and pipes and tools in the back of the pickup. Sitting high in the cab, I looked down on the cars streaking past. Spike was thinking of buying land in Canada. His oldest boy would be eligible for the draft soon.

"Remember how Ma jerked us onto the farm when she thought I'd get drafted during the Korean War?"

"There were other ways to get out of it. I think Sam claimed he was psycho or wore pink underpants to the physical or something."

"He's still planning to move out into the woods. He worries me."

"I haven't seen them in a while."

"Jean goes over pretty often. She's trying to get his wife to bring their laundry over to our place. See, the thing that bothers me is it's not impossible to live like Aram wants to. My friend Little George has a place in the woods and grows his own food and just goes out logging a couple of months a year for the cash he needs. But I don't know if Aram can do that. He's a city boy. Seems to think if he can read a book about something and talk about it, it's as good as done. I don't see why he wants to be a trapper, anyway. He wasn't raised to it, and it's a hard life."

Spike turned the truck off the highway, through the one intersection of the little town, and up the steep hill. Toward the top, their house perched on the slope. Rooms and wings had been added as the children came, and windows peered out of unexpected places.

Three bicycles lay in the gravel of the drive. Spike pulled the truck up short, stuck his head out the window, and whistled. The boys appeared and scuttled off with their bicycles.

"Sorry, Dad."

"I'll sorry your ass!" He pulled the truck up to the garage and climbed out.

"Send me down a beer. I've got to finish a trailer I'm building for the guy who wired the basement. You know him. Old Brodigan."

Inside, Jean stood over a pot of sweet-looking purple goo. Her face was pink.

"How are you? Taste this. I've been smelling it all day and can't taste it anymore. Does it need sugar?"

I licked the spoon of grape jam she offered and smacked my lips.

"You can go with the kids for blackberries in a little while. Does he need beer?"

She emptied the jam into small, shining jars, and topped each jar with wax from a smaller pot. The hot jam sizzled and popped as it was poured, and began to thicken as soon as it was silent. The wax formed a scum atop the jam. The hot kitchen excited me.

Jean wiped her face with a cloth and retrieved a beer from the refrigerator, snapped it open, and poured it against the side of a glass.

"Want me to take it to him?"

"No. I haven't seen him all day. You can wash the pot. Did

he tell you we're going back to high school?" She chuckled at the glass of beer in her hand.

"What?"

"He wants to get his equivalency. The union's cracking down. Even with fifteen years seniority he can't get the best jobs without a diploma. It's a night course."

"What about you?"

"Oh, I just thought it'd be nice. The damn kids are getting snooty about how well-educated they are. Keep calling me a dropout."

She laughed her way down the steps to the basement. Listening, I heard the smack of his palm flat on her ass.

The sun was low when we set out for the blackberries. The kids wrestled in the back seat. Buckets bounced in the trunk. Jean pulled the car off into the grass and the crowd tumbled out.

"This is Mrs. Wright's place. I make her bread every week and we get all our fruit here in return. Her old man died a few years ago and she's letting the place go. She's too old to keep it up."

We walked through an apple orchard. The fruit lay soft and putrid on the ground. There was the steady glum sound of bees. They flew heavily and moved out of our way reluctantly as we walked. At the edge of the trees the brambles had taken over. They had mounted the fence and formed a solid tower, six feet high. The berries were thick and sweet and crushed each other in our buckets. "I don't care how much you eat as long as I get at least two quarts from each of you."

"Mama! I'm afraid of the bees."

The children's voices were soft in the air. They wedged their small bodies deeply in the crevices of the huge bush. I worked away from their voices. The thorns clung and scratched my skin. I walked along the edge of the patch and picked the low, easy bunches. The pail's wire handle dug into my arm as I filled it.

A line of gray trees marked the edge of the river. They were dead here, like at Sam's, so I figured it was the same stretch of trees. The blackberries thinned out and I climbed down the shore, balancing the pail on my arm. I moved a little farther on, a few steps more through the tangled brush. I could see the clearing across the river, and a small gray figure was hunched at the edge of the water. It was not far. Ninety feet. Eighty feet. The gray water looked thick and moved slowly. The figure rocked back and forth, and little splashes rose from her hands in the water. Her shawl slipped back and I could see the faint white of the part in her hair. Carlotta. There was a pile of white beside her on the bank. She lifted a white rag out of the water, shook it, wrung it in her hands, and dropped it on the pile.

"Did you see that?"

Jean stood behind and above me, her bucket sagging against her shoulder. She squinted at the figure across the river.

"What's she doing?"

"Laundry."

Jean climbed down and stood beside me.

"I don't know where she got those rocks. It's all mud along the bank there."

"What rocks?"

"Those. She puts one just under the water, puts the diaper on it, and then beats it with another rock. I keep trying to get her to bring them over and put them through my machine but she won't. That water's filthy. At least she promised to boil them after she's done them in the river, but I don't know if she does or not. The baby seems okay. I don't understand why she couldn't do them in the kitchen sink."

"It's against her religion or something," I volunteered.

"She'll think about religion when her kid's screeching with a rash."

Jean set her bucket down. She slid the last few feet down the bank into the water and grabbed a naked stick to steady herself.

"Carlotta!"

Her shout rolled out over the water. Somewhere farther up it echoed slightly. The little figure on the far bank uncurled. Carlotta stood, secured the loosened shawl, and said, "Hi," in a conversational tone that carried easily between the banks. Jean giggled, embarrassed. The sun was low, tipped strangely in the sky.

"Come on over and get some of these blackberries!" Jean called.

Carlotta shook drops of water off her arms. "Can't hear you. From that side you have to yell. The wind's wrong or something."

"Come get blackberries!"

Carlotta still moved as though she was pregnant. The shawl and the long dress ballooned around her as she stepped to the bush where the tired boat was tied. She pulled it up, stepped in gingerly. She knelt in the center of the boat and tipped an oar out, caught it just before it fell out completely. She pulled on it, and the slow current carried her a few feet from us. Carlotta stuck the oar in the mud on the downriver side to hold the boat. There was a sheen of sweat on her face. I nodded at Carlotta. She nodded back. Jean examined her bucket and mine.

"I'll give you this bucket. Sally's smashed all hers. They're only good for jam now." She swung her pail to Carlotta, who set it on the bottom of the boat.

"Thanks very much."

"Don't eat too many in one day. I suspect too much fresh fruit gives a nursing baby colic. They make great pies when you're sick of eating them with cream. How's your little boy?"

Carlotta smiled and lifted the shawl. Beneath, strapped below her breasts, was a sling. Carlotta bent forward and the bundle swung out from her body like a hammock. She lifted the cloth away from the child's face. We crouched to look. He slept. Eyelashes. A faint beginning of dark brows. The newborn lumps and wrinkles had smoothed; now the face was fat, the skin clear. The child's pouted lips were swollen, and a white blister ran the length of each.

"How come his lips are blistered?" I asked.

Carlotta flicked the cloth back over the little face and leaned back. The shawl fell over her breasts, and she covered the sling.

Jean tapped my shoulder. "That, spinster, is from the sucking. All babies get that. It doesn't bother them. He looks really good. He's gained a lot of weight. Have you named him yet?"

Carlotta nodded. "Yes. Ishi."

"Ishi Rommel. Well, I've heard worse." Jean flicked dust from her hem. "When are you coming over? How about tomorrow? Bring Aram and come for lunch. We'll have barbecue."

"That's nice. Maybe. I'm not sure we can." Carlotta smiled.

I took a step closer. "How is Sam taking everything?"

Her eyebrows raised slightly. She looked vaguely at the other bank. "He's with Lichtenstein in the cabin. They're planning something."

"Mama! Let's go!" A sharp shout from the slope behind us.

"Go get in the car!" Jean called. "We're coming!"

"Carlotta! Can we see your baaaaby?" The smaller ones started down the hill. Jean hoisted her skirts and ran, climbing, jumping, to head them off.

TOAD

Carlotta shifted the oar. The boat began to move sideways down the stream.

"Where's the other oar?"

"Lost."

"Can you make it?"

She nodded. Her arms and shoulders struggled with the long heavy oar. The sling rocked gently back and forth with her movements. Eventually the boat moved backward into the stream. Once she was near the opposite shore, Carlotta turned to wave.

"Goodbye!" I screamed.

And her soft voice calmly answered, "Goodbye." She climbed out of the boat and carried the pail. With her other arm, she scooped up the dripping diapers. She walked slowly up the bank through the gray trees.

There was black mush in my pail, a lot of juice slopping around the berries. I grabbed the handle and ran up the hill to where Jean and the children waited in the car.

Sam and Carlotta didn't come to the barbecue. Spike went over in the evening to see if they were all right. He took cream to eat with the berries. I didn't go along. I watched Jean place the lucid jam in the kitchen cupboard.

Spike came back with a friend he'd found on the way. He said Sam and Carlotta had been having supper when he arrived. They seemed fine. He went down to the basement to mend a drill the friend had brought. I fell asleep on the sofa watching an old movie. They didn't wake me when they went to bed.

Rennel

No man has ever pretended to pine for love of me, or sweat in fear of me. I believe in all my life the only sleepless nights I've caused have been my mother's. And it wasn't my goodness that prevented me from occupying men's thoughts. It was not my sweet consideration or spreading love. There are times when I indulge in wild self-flattery: "Ah, how I wounded So-and-so when I said such-and-such," "Oh, poor Whatsit, when I left him he must nearly have died," "How cruel I was to flaunt that in Thingama's face." But the truth is that I was the bloodied and scourged and deserted one. I chose that role deliberately, rather than be ignored entirely. My pride was late in developing. I am a little ashamed, now, to think of who I've pursued and how. It occasionally occurred to me that there were alternatives, but they always seemed vague and impracticable. And I should specify that this retreat of mine, this very comfort and solitude, had involuntary origins. Precisely this life was always one of the horrifying thoughts that ripped me when I had recently been mislaid by one of my beauties. "I'll become a hard-faced old maid," I would moan, "and never feel or be touched again. I'll keep a cat and take a vow of silence." And finally it happened, without the cat. And now I seem to talk to myself incessantly.

No, I have never been a type to inspire love. No passions

have burnt themselves out, only substantial flesh. Only a number of undirected lusts. And it's just as well; I would have despised anyone who purported to love me. I felt confidence only in those who needed me for something in particular.

The goldfish are suitable companions for me now—and even they antagonize me. They're livelier when their bowl is clean, but that's the only gratitude they express. I demand more from them than I would of any human. I've been daydreaming about their being dead. Not about killing them, but simply about carrying their corpses on a dustpan out to the compost heap and tossing them onto it. I can see them the next day with their eyes sunken and grayed, the color fading from their scales, and the flies busy over them. The trick is that in my fantasy the toad catches all the flies. He is sitting on a rock near their bodies, and as the flies lift, glutted from the rot, he flicks out that negligent tongue. His eyes disappear into his head as though to look quickly inside to see what he's got, and then reappear. This is not an exhilarating fantasy, nor is it depressing. It is just a recurring picture, as though I passed it ten times each day for years, like the snapshot of my aunt Erma wiping ice cream from the mouth of an unidentified boy in front of the roller coaster at the 19— World's Fair. That photograph is browning now. It is stuck in the corner of the hall mirror and I note, each time I see it, the fragile angle of her arm and the tidiness of her waist. I have never wondered who the boy may be. Perhaps the goldfish do not even wonder about me.

Only Rennel still wonders about me. And finally, to do him honor and to comfort myself, I have broken all my rules and invited him to spend the night. He knows too much about fish and complains about the jug environment I've provided. He knows too much about plants and snorts at the condition of my shrubs. But in all this month I have spoken to no one, and no one who knows me has spoken to me. Today Rennel came, as he always arrives on the last Saturday of the month and prevails upon me for tea.

I enjoy taking tea with Rennel. Everyone else drinks coffee these days.

He's quite fat now. He dresses well. He doesn't pull at his crotch anymore since his suits are cut for him. He's rich. It seems he deals in fabrics of the lusher variety, a wholesale source of the finest silk and brocade, the heaviest satin, the thickest velvet, the softest wools that a designer can ask for. But he still wonders about me, even though he's discovered over the years all the lies I've told him. He knows now that I was not suckled by a she-panda nor raised by pirates off the coast of China, and do not speak eleven Asian languages or commune with the spirits of Genghis and Attila during my morning meditations, but he still finds, in the pure lunacy of his innocence, room to wonder and hypothesize, to postulate and criticize, to renounce and encourage me.

Every last Friday of every month he flies out from New York and spends the afternoon and the following morning nosing into the activities of his branch hirelings, and every last Saturday afternoon he pulls up in front of my house with the characteristic squeal of rented brakes and comes up the path with the same look of curiosity on his patented mug.

For years I have given him tea and hermits at the kitchen table. He is a hermit addict, that heavy flat cake loaded with dark fruits. He eats them unconsciously, with a deep physical relish, and I have known him to go through two batches between lunch and dinner.

He is very odd now, I think. He lives alone in four white rooms near the top of a high building. His walls, so he tells me, are hung with climbing vines and tropical scrubs. A potted palm, so I understand, arches over each side of his bed, and he ministers to all these greens with what I imagine to be rude affection.

He swims daily at a local gymnasium in the company of a divorced male cousin. It's true, too, that his bulk is sleek and functional, not at all soft. He is still too conscious of his ass, but I have grown more tolerant since he lost his Greek proportions. He spends a piece of each day at an expensive office, lunches for business, and dines in the zealous investigation of, I do not doubt, attractive women. He takes a great interest in his friends and has several. Why do I think all that odd?

On our Saturdays he always leaves at suppertime. I announce that it's 6:00 p.m. and he must have a date. He bridles politely and then leaves. I watch him down the walk and listen to his car take off. He spends that night in his usual hotel, visits other friends on Sunday, and flies back Sunday night in his third impeccable suit of the weekend.

But this day, today, I have done something. Because of the length of the month, because of the scratch of my unused throat, and the ache of the shine that no one has seen on the fish jug and the fire irons and the floor, I am a failed recluse. Today I ask for company.

I have uttered at the doorknobs, "Thou shalt have no audience before me. I thy audience am a jealous audience." I chuckle into the recesses of the linen closet. But it is a lie, of course, and my clean house is only good if there are other eyes and dirtier houses. The depth of my tub and the heat of the water are luscious to me because of the shallower, chillier baths of other times. Rennel would not comment on the gleam of things. Would not notice. But he sniffs my soap and lotions as I pass his chair and doesn't scratch as much in this house as he has in some others.

Besides all that, I made the sauce for the periwinkles in front of him today. He sat over the hermits explaining an intricate exchange of prestige involving a bolt of antique lace and I nodded and laughed and minced garlic and sautéed tomatoes in front of him.

"What are you cooking?"

"Sauce for the periwinkles. Do you always eat in restaurants?"

"Not always. Did you get those in the village?"

"I took them off the rocks."

"You do yourself well."

"I was thinking I would like you to stay and have dinner with me."

He stops chewing, his cheek swollen with hermit. He lowers his brows suspiciously.

"I was thinking if you didn't have a date you could stay and read what I've been writing."

His brows hike up and he begins chewing again, methodically. He swallows and gives me one of his flirtatious leers. "I thought you'd decided I was too dense to read your stuff."

I grin into the reeking steam from my skillet. Once a year or so he says something that breaks me, that shows he's not the fool I think of him.

"That's only because you never like it. But I want you to eat a big meal and have peaches and tea afterward and then sit there in front of the fire and read this thing. That's what I was thinking. You can sleep on the sofa if you want."

I am older than he is. Have probably always been old to him. He swallows the last morsel of hermit.

"Do you really have peaches?"

"You can pick them yourself."

"It'd save me the hotel bill."

"You could stay tomorrow night, too, if you wanted to."

"It must be a real ordeal, this stuff you want me to read."

"I had a fight with Jean. She and Spike don't come here anymore."

"How long has that been going on?"

So we talked about that. Then he went to check out of his hotel and came back with a tidy, expensive suitcase. I sweated in the kitchen. How many years since there were two plates on that table when dark fell? Not since it belonged to someone else. Through the kitchen window, I watched him pick the peaches from the tree in the yard and put them in a bowl. The grass reached the knees of his well-cut trousers, and his wool jacket pulled up in rich folds beneath his shoulders as he reached for the flushed fruit.

I set the table around the fish jug. The salt and the dressings and the bread, still hot. I had to look for the good napkins. The three I use in cycle seemed suddenly faded. I found the bright ones in the back of the linen closet.

The Rennel who faces me across a table is someone it seems I've always known. Once when I was ensconced with a man in an old gray house that shared its leeward wall with a church, Rennel came to visit. In those days I thought myself ended, culminated, that my future would be a continuation of that present. I baked apple pies with baroque crusts and was the only female in the house. I ruled a supper table of soft faces, and Rennel's was often among them, with his childish, almost sideways grip on his fork, crumbs always caught in the corners of his mouth, his jaw contriving somehow to chew and talk at the same time. The inclination to wave the fork all around the conversation, the too-long pauses before answering a stranger's question, designed to lead a stranger to think he's forgotten their question. When I was groveling and begging Rennel offered me money, and when I thought I'd got myself another soft billet I invited Rennel to come and admire me. When I first came to this house and didn't yet enjoy being alone I called Rennel long distance and told him I was afraid a murderer waited outside my windows at night. And all this time I've been comfy here I have distributed austere teas to him on the last Saturday afternoon of the month, and imagined myself somehow superior to him, even though any elevating quality I once possessed has become vague and nameless, even to me.

Rennel knows me. He sits tonight and shakes his head over his fork while I dramatize my tantrum with Jean. He tells me about his prostate infection and I ask him whether he thinks premenstrual rages are a likely forerunner of anile psychosis.

He eats the periwinkles and I dip my bread in the sauce. We split the peaches and sit, two large, gray creatures, both of us grown heavy in our arms and torsos. The peach juice drips into the creases around our mouths.

"Do you think I'm getting too fat?" he asks.

"No. I like you much better fat. You were always too vain before. Women like a man who isn't aware of his looks. I'll bet you do a lot better with women now."

"If you'd been more vain you'd have had a better time. Always clumping around in baggy shirts with smelly pits and scraggy hair. For years I considered you a failed lesbian."

"I know. I was always afraid people would think that. But I looked like a muffin in anything that fit. Oh, well. Too late."

"Too late," he agrees, and we pour another cup of tea and each eat another peach.

He doesn't ask what the thing is about. He pokes up the fire and I do the dishes. My hands hang in the gray water for minutes while I think about what I am doing. Why do I think he has to read it? So he can praise me? Exonerate me? Can he say, "Yes, you took them food. You said what you knew to say. You did what you knew to do," and will that make it right?

He is sitting in there now. The house is full of him. I can hear the hiss of the coal and the rasp of his throat clearings. The pages turning. He'll read it. He won't skip or scan. He'll read it dutifully.

But I can't sleep with his noises and the fact that he is reading my story of Sam and Carlotta. Maybe after all he'll tiptoe in and make a pass at me. The dugong and the manatee, coupling in the briny sea, ta ra, ta ra, ta ra, ta reee . . .

This place is hard to find

It was an awkward time. Painful. New freshmen started arriving at the school, clean from home in clothes their mothers had helped them shop for. They were all busy shrugging into their new attitudes of being brighter, more poetic, or crazier than thou. I could feel the school sucking them in and encouraging their disguises.

The returning hordes bustled about, setting up houses together. They stalked around, trying out new images for the year or reestablishing old used ones. I bought gold hoop earrings and a short, thick cigarette holder. Sat with my high boots crossed in the snack bar and blew smoke down my nose at them all. It didn't seem to help.

The day before classes started I almost went to visit Clancy. I found the slip of paper on which she'd written her address, walked a dozen blocks in an unfamiliar direction, asked an old lady and a dirty boy about the number. I was only saved from knocking when I saw Rennel's car parked out front. There was no mistaking the Rambler with its dents and the psychology texts on the back seat.

I went back and moaned and bitched under the skylight all night. I took a bath the next morning. Washed my hair. Put on the gold hoops and a gaudy splash of cheap cologne. Thought I'd play hard-nosed madam of the fun house for a fresh string of teachers. Rennel was smoking a new pipe in my first class when I swayed in.

It took the wind out, as they say. I slouched over and dumped myself into a chair beside him. He was playing mature, sophisticated, man of the world. He took his pipe out of his mouth, exhaled smoke gracefully, and sniffed at me with raised eyebrows.

"It's called Tiger Piss."

"Pretty accurate. Have you heard anything about Sam?"

"No. What's he up to now?"

"Don't you know they left?"

"For where?"

"The cabin in Montana with Lichtenstein."

"Shit."

I broke a cigarette jamming it into the stupid holder.

"They came by my place to say goodbye. They said they were on their way over to you. They must have missed you and gone on."

"When was this?"

"A week or so ago. Thursday, maybe. Pretty early in the morning. I was still in bed."

"Where could I have been?"

"Out buying soda pop? Maybe they decided there wasn't time to wait."

"Who was driving?"

"Sam. Carlotta was holding the kid on the passenger side and Lichtenstein was straddling the gear shift. I think that bus of theirs needs a valve job. I'm going to do one on the Rambler. Spike's showing me how."

"When's your last class? Will you drive me out to their place?"

"You mean in the country? There's nothing left out there. I went out to get their old car. It was in the brush at the end of the driveway. Had to get a tow truck, which cost me ten dollars even with my Automobile Club card. Then the scrap metal place only gave me ten bucks for it."

"Mr. Jones."

"All I got out of that car was a red candle they had stuck up on the dashboard. The lights never did work on that thing. What a piece of junk."

"What about the animals?"

"They took them all. You should have seen the bus! They took out the rest of the seats. The goat was roped at the back, and they had three chickens, two dogs, and all their clothes and pans and stuff piled in the middle."

"Two dogs?"

"Some friend of Angelina's." Rennel smirked around his pipe, remembering. The highly advertised small class had assembled. The professor entered.

*, *, *,

I didn't look in my mailbox very often. Sometimes there was a mimeographed note from the school faculty. Usually there were just candy bar wrappers slipped through the slot by anti-litter people. It was nice to get a letter, but I had no idea how long it had been sitting in the box. The postmark was blurred. The envelope was a piece of folded lined paper sealed with long pink splotches of candle wax. The wax was broken and flaking. The flap hung over, showing the ring holes in the paper.

I'd never got a letter from Sam before, but I'd seen his unfinished essays and his calligraphy practices. The familiar pencil italic made my name glamorous and the box number romantic. The letter was a sheet of the same lined notebook.

It was night. A light rain falling. I stood on the concrete floor of the college mailroom and felt the cold coming up through the thinning soles of last year's fancy boots.

TOAD

Sally,

A pair of hawks live down the hill from us. We see them starting out in the morning. Do you understand? We watch their backs as they fly out over the valley. I wouldn't have known they were hawks, but Lichtenstein has good eyes and knows things like that.

What things I'm learning! Do you know how to tell a fir from a pine? Do you know how to burn ticks off with a cigarette? Could you recognize a muskrat? Well, you just better come up here as soon as you can and start finding things out!

The air here has vitamins. It's funny. I'd read about "air like wine" but never realized what that meant.

I sit here in front of the cabin every afternoon. I've written some haiku that I'd like very much to have you read. But I'm not going to send them to you. I want you to come and sit in this spot. You have to read it while seeing what I saw when I wrote it.

It's true, you know, that society is destroying us all. In this simple place with the wind booming through the chinks at night, I've found a sweet stillness of the world that I've never believed in. My concept of enlightenment was a state of pain compared to this. Please come. I need to share this happiness. Get Rennel to drive you. Write and we'll meet you in St. Ignatius. This place is hard to find.

Peace,
Han Shan Rommel
PO Box 24
St. Ignatius
Montana

I folded the letter carefully into my pocket. Walked out into the rain. It was too cold and dark and far to go home. I walked under blinking crosswalk signs and streetlights fuzzed purple by the wind.

There were lights all over Rennel's house. I opened the door and edged past the dismantled motorcycle. Voices were singing in the kitchen, pots banged around, and there was a suspicious smell of boiling vegetation. Up the loud stairs, the bathroom door was open. There were half-woven baskets soaking in the tub. The upright reeds bent in the light. Rennel's door was closed. I heard no sound from the other side. Knocked.

Rennel came to the door in a judo kimono. His chest was bare, and his legs stuck out above the executive socks. The electric typewriter buzzed lazily on the desk. He nodded, let me in, shut the door behind him, and crossed over to switch off the typewriter. He picked up a pipe and watched himself in the big mirror while he filled it. I sat down on the end of his mattress and leaned my head back against the wall. He sat down at the desk, turning, crossed his legs, continued with his long, elaborate pipe-lighting ritual. His kimono draped open suggestively, the yellow-stained front seams of his underpants bulged. I closed my eyes and sighed. He was still playing man of the world. Getting ready to set up a therapeutic practice someplace.

"I got a letter from Sam." I wormed the letter out of my pocket and tossed it to him.

He puffed his pipe while he read. He nodded and puffed more. He held up the letter and pointed to the tail of the "g" in "things."

"He must really have been feeling good when he made that. I'm taking calligraphy this year. I think Aram's getting some place, at least."

"Han Shan, you mean."

"Yeah." Rennel tapped the letter with his pipe stem. He worked up a reverent, serious expression. "It's interesting that he should choose that name. Kind of indicative that he's reaching something. It means 'cold mountain.' Did you know they named the kid 'Ishi' after that book I gave them?"

I lay down on the mattress. Gently cradled my head in my arms. Lovingly, painfully, curled my legs. I hugged myself and wanted to sleep.

"I'm tired, Rennel. I think I'm sick. Can I sleep here tonight?"

His mouth twitched nastily around his pipe.

"Sure."

He waved his pipe and turned back busily to the typewriter. It started humming again. He set the pipe down beside it and poised his hands over the keys. I watched him out of the corner of my eye.

"Do you want to run up to Montana this weekend?" he called over his kimonoed shoulder. "I think it's only about six hundred miles."

"No. Take Clancy."

He flicked nervously at the yielding keys. I woke up a while later. He was in front of the mirror in his underpants. He stretched and grunted and flexed his arms, watching himself constantly. I went back to sleep.

*, *, *,

December. The trees had given up the pretense and admitted death, but everybody else was still at it. There was some kind of masquerade at the school. A party. I was going as Popeye. I had a GI sailor suit left over from the last time the fleet had hit town. I tucked a can of spinach under my arm and a ten-cent

corn cob pipe into my mouth. I found I could stick a lit cigarette into the bowl and smoke a little, strenuously.

I was sitting in Jane's room in the dormitory. She was beyond my understanding, so I liked her. I suppose we would
have been friends if either one of us had been capable of it at
the time. She was going as a nun and arranged her wimple
at the mirror. There was a gallon of horrible red wine on her
desk. We were drinking elegantly from stemmed and only
slightly greasy glasses.

The guy came in who was taking her to the party. A nice guy,
silly-looking, with his bushy hair frizzing out of a white paper
cook's cap. He wore white gloves, a white shirt, white trousers.
His tennis shoes shed white dust on the floor. He said he hadn't
had time to wash them so he rubbed them with white chalk. He
said he was a tampon. Jane sprinkled red wine over his chest
and back for effect.

The door was open. We laughed and gulped at the wine.
When I saw Lichtenstein go by in the hall I jumped and dropped
my glass and ran out of the room, calling after him. It was his
shoulders I'd recognized. He'd shaved his head. He turned
around and although his forehead held the same sullen tension,
he'd plucked his brows completely off. His lashes were pale. He
still wasn't wearing a shirt. There was a red dot in the middle of
his forehead.

"Hi! That dot means you're a married woman, right?" I
asked.

He stared at me as if waiting for me to evaporate.

"Where are Carlotta and Sam? Aram. Whatever. Did they
come down off the cold mountain with you?"

His expression changed, his eyes went dark. I smiled, waiting, not expecting his voice to drop to a guttural whisper.

"You know—their baby died."

It was theatrical and practiced. His eyes bored into me, watching the effect of his words. My first reaction was to refuse him an equally dramatic response. I stared back and stubbornly continued to smile. He shrugged and turned away before I lost it. He banged out through the fire doors at the end of the hall.

I thought I would go home. I walked down to the end of the hall and exited through the same fire doors. The stairs down were lit, but not heated, and I felt suddenly cold. Rennel's white Rambler was in the parking lot next to the dormitory. It was raining. I thought I would sit in the car and wait till he came and then I would ask him to drive me home. I wanted to get back to the skylight. Inside, the Rambler was warm. The keys were in the ignition. I turned them and the car muttered and shook under me. I flicked the lever on the steering post and the car moved back a ways, slowly. The bumper came to rest against one wall of the dorm. I sat and looked at the thin lights of the dashboard. There were those stupid pedals to fool with, too. I flicked the lever again. The car jigged forward and started to climb somebody's Volkswagen. Fresh, I thought.

I left things alone for a while. Sat looking calmly at the dark trees against the dark sky. I breathed carefully.

A little man tapped at my window. I rolled it down and smiled at him.

"Hi."

"Are you a student here?"

It was Mr. Galvin. Two big men in dark uniforms with shining buttons stood behind him talking to each other.

"Yes. You're the men's counselor, aren't you?"

"Are you on drugs? You're bumping into a lot of things tonight."

His hoarse voice was comforting.

"I've been drinking some wine. Maybe that's it."

"Well, move over and I'll see if I can get this car untangled. I'll park it and then you'd better find some place to sleep it off. You can't drive like this."

"Actually, when you come right down to it, I can't drive at all."

I slid over in the seat and leaned back. He brought in a lot of cold air. He slammed the door and fooled around with the steering wheel. Something he did made a loud thump and we were suddenly several yards from the Volkswagen.

"Are those cops that were with you?"

"Yes. There's a report of somebody from the town out here selling drugs. That's why it isn't a good night for you to be bashing around."

The car came to a stop between white lines. The little man looked at me sharply.

"Have you got someplace to sleep?"

"Sure. Thanks. You really rescued me."

"Leave a note on that Volkswagen so the owner can contact you about the damages."

"Right."

He was still in the car when I got out and walked away.

There was a couch in the ladies' restroom of the main building. I went up through the bright empty halls and sat on it. It was an old couch with black flowers. For fainting fits and period cramps. During the day there was nearly always somebody moaning on it, for twisted love or academic foul-ups, whatever. I stretched out. Examined the cigarette burns in the slipcover. Listened to the casual grunting and gurglings of the toilets in the next room.

There was a phone on the wall. After a while I got up and put in a dime. Dialed the infirmary.

"I haven't slept for three nights," I said. "If I come over there, will you give me something to make me sleep?"

They said all they could give me was aspirin. I hung up and went back to the sofa. Curled up and went to sleep. I woke up when people started coming in on their way to classes the next morning. Went over to the cafeteria to wait for the coffee machine to finish perking. My dark wool sailor's outfit was rumpled and covered with gray fuzz. The pants were too tight, anyway. They rode up my crack and cut into my hip joints. I sat in the corner with a cup of coffee and picked at the lint.

A steely determination to die

Many times I have attended my own suicide, burial, and mourning. For those who I hope would be wounded by my loss, I have dealt out a ream of eulogies they might recite, pumped their tears, counted the meals they might leave uneaten on my account. I have listened to them quote my quips as well as my dissertations with the awed, too-late understanding of what was possessed in my company, now that they were forever robbed of it.

I love all that and have played it over in many variations for every crisis of my days.

"Go ahead! Do it! I'd be the last to interfere!" Carush snorted. He was another one of my beauties. I had fallen low enough by then to talk about it to him, bragging in soapy melancholy about my plans for my demise in the basement of the student boardinghouse. But all the time I slept with him I never went beyond talk and night walking and lurid fantasies of enacting my own death. He made me happy enough, in his dour and ridiculous way.

No, it was the next year, when I was nineteen, that my ambitions culminated, albeit incompletely. I had become a beastly creature, shredded by vanity, horrified by mediocrity in myself. "I wouldn't care if it was yo-yo throwing or tiddlywinks as long as I was the best there was." I thought that, and said it.

Carush, my serious paramour, the future CPA and reader of

Freud, Jung, Skinner, and Bettelheim, believed in me. His faith was devastating. I had only to open my notorious yap and wag it with sufficient solemnity for him to bow down with the weight of my nattering. His legs were tapered, finely boned, an elegant and restrained bit of work. He liked me, but had a wide eye for pretty girls. Jealousy burned in me terribly, that ghastly disease.

At a birthday party that I had arranged for Carush—a successful surprise, to the degree that he wandered around the crowd for twenty minutes before he realized that it was all in his honor—he enjoyed himself too much. I had invited all his favorites among my female acquaintance. Emma was my favorite, too. Small she was, and fluffy. She scratched her incredible poems on the tapes from the cash register at the grocery store or threw them out as a counterfeit of conversation in her perpetual confusion at parties. I suppose we could have been friends but we were too prickly for each other. But there she was, her tiny hand elevating her glass like a lucid bite of Christ, her head poised oddly above her shoulders, and he leaning toward her, leering, rapt to her every move.

I went into the bathroom and sliced my wrists with his razor. It was crass of me to do it at the party, especially a party where there is only one toilet. I sat on the side of the old chipped tub and sawed away, first at the left and then at the right. It hurt. I didn't go very deep. The blood seemed thinner than I had expected, but it moved in a satisfying way, sheeting out of the long cuts and filling my palms with warmth. I ran hot water into the sink and rested my hands deep in it, covering the cuts so that the blood curled out into the water and clouded it red.

A knock at the door. Somebody waiting to puke or pee.

"Sorry, it's busy!" I called.

The cuts didn't hurt, really; there was only a precise sting at their edges.

"It's urgent!" a voice cried.

"Esta ocupado! Go outdoors!" I yelled.

A new knock came right away.

"Busy!" I said.

"Sally?" It was a girl whose whisper I recognized from my humanities survey class. Clara something.

"Couldn't I just come in for a minute? I'm flowing all down both legs. I've got to insert a tampon."

"Clara, I really can't let you in. Go out in the backyard to do it!"

"Sally! For Christ's sake! My dress is gory already!"

"I'm sorry."

Tears dripped to my protuberant lower lip and slid off my jaw, making minuscule plips in the bloody sink. I put my forehead down on the edge of the sink to cool it and sat down on the lip of the bathtub. Another knock.

"Busy!" I yelled, tears gushing hot in frustration. Outside the door came the sound of horrendous retching, splattering. A thin, pink line of vomit crept under the door and pooled on the bald linoleum.

"I couldn't help it," came a small voice beyond the door.

Carush would be leaning over Emma still, his thickening penis filling the top of his left trouser leg. She had told me several times how revolting she found him.

The water was cooling around my hands, the pump of blood had slowed distinctly. I lifted a hand to turn on the hot water tap. The edges of the cuts were white and puffy, pink slits. The Romans, I began to suspect, may have opened the veins inside their elbows rather than at their wrists. I frowned, racking my brain to remember Tacitus. They certainly sat submerged in deep tubs of hot water continually renewed by weeping and solicitous slaves. The edge of the tub was pressing into the backs of my thighs, numbing both legs. I pulled the plug in the sink and let the red water whirl down the drain as the new heat poured in.

A loud rap at the door.

"Sally!" It was Carush. "Are you not letting anyone in?"

"I am having," I said calmly, "massive diarrhea, and I would like to be left alone."

"Mrs. Jorgenson has to go, Sally!" Mrs. J. was Carush's psychotherapist. An attractive woman.

"Tell her goodbye for me," I said.

"I mean she has to go to the toilet, Sally. Come on, for Christ's sake."

Mrs. J. was very pregnant.

The bleeding had definitely stopped. A few small red bubbles seeped out of the cracks in my wrists as I stared at them.

"Just a moment, please," I said.

I deliberately stood up, wiggling my toes to bring my reluctant legs back to life. There was Mercurochrome in the cabinet over the sink. I carefully dabbed it on the slices and pulled my long sleeves down. I rinsed the razor and put it on a shelf. The faint pink smears in the sink rinsed away with one gush of water from the tap. I finally looked into the mirror: A boiled potato. Basic tuber. A swipe of the cold cloth. A quick sketch of coal-black pencil all around my peeled eyes. I opened the door. There was no one there. The voices from the living room chuckled on. A vicious stench crept up from my feet. The pink vomit was thick under my shoes; chunks of the minced salami from the buffet I had assembled were discernible in the fluid. I carefully stepped out of my shoes, stranding them in the muck, and padded away from the bad smell. All through that night I did not speak to Carush, but there were so many people around that he didn't notice.

It was soon after that, when I got my first paycheck from the shirt factory, that I threw him out, before supper, after he had done his daily exercise and run around the block twenty times to excuse his appetite, because with that much money in my hand I was ashamed to go on living with him. His mother had sent checks every month before that, sufficient to feed us both. He liked me then. He wouldn't like me now.

The second time, years later, was similar. Joe had been living with me for nearly a year, but at least I had my own money. Then, one night he stayed out late with Leda Van Hoerderbroeck, that regal blonde. He had walked to the library and hadn't returned. It was midnight when I heard a motor in the street. I looked out the bedroom window. Leda's car was parked directly below my window. One sliver of the light of the streetlamp cut through the windshield so that I could see the peculiar plaid of his jacket inside her car, a white Jaguar, the only one I had ever seen at the time. No question about it. He had raved about her guttural, toneless singing at the local intellectuals' bar. She always came onstage dressed for secretarial school, with white gloves, pearl button earrings, and a small round collar. Of course, she was the color of clover honey from stem to stern and carried herself like a yacht. But I didn't find those qualities endearing at the time.

It was my pride still, and fear. Flesh was the only comfort that could get me through each night. Joe was the reflex from a previous attempt at solitude, at a maidenly hermitage. I had tried coming home each night to Latin grammar and a series of breathing exercises reputed to aid concentration. My rooms

TOAD

were always grubby. I never had more than two, and a shared bathroom, in old wood houses filled with students and vagrants and artists and the unloved old. The old people had the most power in those places. Their smells controlled the air. Sometimes I thought I would be able to work if only I had a Queen Anne desk and walls covered with gray damask, but that was nonsense. It would have ended always in the same frenzied prowling of cafés.

When I found Joe, I moved in with him before he really noticed what I had in mind. His skin was smooth. Lying with him, pressed against his back, was like sheltering against mother-of-pearl. At night I could feel the faint, reassuring pump of his blood along my whole body as I slept. I polished his little saws and dusted his workbench and brought him thick, luscious sandwiches while he rasped and glued. He made guitars in the living room of his house. He read Spinoza and Pascal and he went out every Saturday evening from 7:00 to 1:00 a.m. to drink red wine and listen to the singers at the Theorem Café. Sometimes he would take me there and we would sit, listening, watching, not speaking unless some friend came up to us. I would slip my hand inside the back of his shirt and let it stay flat against the long muscle next to his spine. He would keep my knee gripped in one big hand. It was peaceful, his soothing flesh, the bottomless wineglasses, the odd faces and movements in the dim, warm room.

That touch of flesh to flesh is the only ease I've ever known, the only antidote to fear. The mental conjurings, the mechanical exorcisms, the cranial hocus-pocus was always a temporary and not wholly satisfactory expedient. "Thinking of someone else" was in the same category as the stoked campfire in the tundra. It kept the wolves from pouncing, but it didn't drive them away. And their eyes glowed brighter with its reflection.

So Joe was all I needed at the time. He even had a good laugh. He was altogether too intent on protecting his hands; he refused to wash dishes or reach into dark places in the attic or handle rough lumber for fear of nicks and cuts. He had a fear of getting an infection that would require a hand to be amputated. He also talked continually of going to Seville to study the unique technique of guitar-making there. He never mentioned the possibility of my accompanying him.

He attended history lectures at the local college. He lettered placards in crayon at home and took them with him to class. He'd crouch on the floor with his tongue halfway out to scrawl, "Richard III—Teapot Dome—Chapultepec???" in vivid blue on a hunk of yellow cardboard four feet square.

"What is it for?" I asked, the first time, and he grimaced as he answered, slowly, laboriously, "A kind of comment."

He made various signs. Whatever they said, the question marks were always there at the end.

He was never good at talking. I imagined him sitting in a large classroom somewhere near the back, silently and obstinately holding up his gaudy card, at arm's length above his head, throughout the hour's discourse on the vagaries of Tudor economics or the evidence of Italian influence on the architecture of Byelorussia.

But these peculiarities were mild and amusing. I basked in the sensation of his skin. A refuge, it was, from my self. The light came in through the window where he worked in such a way that it made his skin look precisely the way it felt. I could watch him for hours. In the heat of the summer he liked to fling his shirt onto a bench, moving, lifting, showing his broad pollen-colored back to me. The sawdust, flour fine, lay in ridges at the top of his trousers, sifted inside the waistband until I grew anxious that it would rub and give him a rash.

But there he was outside my window in Leda Van Hoerder-broeck's Jaguar. When I first saw it, was sure finally that he was there with her, I sat very still, trembling in every limb. I would have to be angry when he came in. There was no way in which I could speak or move without conveying the sickness that was in me. I would make it worse. But it was still possible that he could explain it all away, and I would be well again, and I would sleep with my skin against his skin that very night. There could be some reason: she was designating specifications for a guitar for her accompanist; he had discovered she was a long lost sister-cousin-aunt; she had found him unconscious on the street, the victim of a brutal robbery, and was trying to bring him home when he passed out again and she was trying to wake him up so she could help him to the door . . . I was willing to accept anything, any pretense, any feeble attempt to placate me. The most absurd excuse or blatant invention would be at least an indication that I still had some value, that he might not throw me out, relegate me again to the groaning black at the back of my head. I would accept anything.

But a half hour passed. No movement or sound came up to me from the white car in the darkness. I could no longer see the section of Joe's jacket that had been revealed by the light in the glass.

I was sitting on a trunk beside the window. The room was lit only by the streetlight down the block. There was a small clock by the bed, and his big bed with the army blanket neatly spread. When I finally grasped that I had been sitting on the trunk peering over the edge of the windowsill for a full hour, I understood. There would be no opportunity for me to redeem my place by sheer sweetness of temper or inattentive cheer. It had gone too far.

Shame—that is, an inverted, self-devouring pride—began

to rise in me. It was right and necessary that any man, given the opportunity, should trade me in. A distant and lucid view of myself emerged: my plump casing, the curdled flaccidity of my flesh, the coarseness of the cut of my hair, the bludgeoned untidiness of my face, the thick lumpiness of my wrists and ankles, the mammoth, suffocating gawkiness of my thighs and buttocks.

"Why," asked the Fuller Brush man one day years later, over tea and cinnamon rolls, as I regaled him with tales from my youth, "why did you call it pride? The cause of that first wrist-slashing at the party. Why not jealousy?" And because his long, sad bones were set in sympathetic angles and his deep ravaged eyes repeated the question with a pure curiosity, I seemed to know the answer, if only for a moment.

"Because," I said, flourishing a spoon, "I always felt like a dirty toilet. It never seemed conceivable to me that a man, any man, could lust after me, could be roused to desire by my person. I assumed that I was a convenient, but not desirable, receptacle. When the need was great enough and the light dim enough I could provide friction that facilitated the discharge, but I was never its object or its cause. Many times I have known very surely that my partner was actively substituting some other face and body in his imagination even as he worked over me. And sometimes, I know, there was no image at all, only the sensation. I have been a second-rate masturbatory implement for years on end, and I have always known it and seen precisely why it was so." Satisfied with myself, I leaned back and grinned. But his puzzlement struck me immediately.

"How does that account for your pride? You're not usually so sloppy with the language."

I stared at him. He lifted a roll onto his plate and began to cut it methodically into gooey bits with his wrists arched high over the knife and fork. He finally began to eat, still watching me while his lean jaw moved rhythmically. When an answer finally came to me I felt hesitant, shy about it.

"It is grotesque for anyone like me to love. People trying to envision me engaged in copulation with anyone would be either disgusted or driven to laughing. And I do have a yearning for dignity. All the pompous dogmatics are my embarrassing attempts at dignity, decency. Still, I was perpetually in love and unable to restrain myself from chasing and flirting and the broadest intimations. The only way to halt the degradation seemed to be by obliterating myself."

"And did it really never occur to you," he asked, with the loaded fork poised in front of his mouth, "that it is nearly impossible to commit suicide without doing yourself some grievous injury?"

I was silent.

"Still," he said as he swallowed, "I believe I know what you mean. In a way it alarms me. It makes me wonder if the women I have used in that way knew it as well." His face was incredibly long, scored vertically by age and weather. A simple concern, uncomplicated by guilt, warmed and softened his creases.

"Don't say 'I have used' as though they were victims," I said. "Those approximations of love are all a lot of us have to look forward to."

"No. But before I met my wife there was a girl. I had to close my eyes and forget before I could touch her. But she was clever and funny. God, how she made me laugh. She worked in the telegraph office in Sidney and came home every night with some new tale to make me laugh. I didn't care to walk down the street with her, she was very fat and her skin was bad. You understand."

I had seen him smile, briefly, doing honor to some laughter

of mine, but a laugh? He put his hands into his lap and stared at the plate with its chunks of pastry and the fork dissecting its pattern. The folds of skin deepened above his eyes.

"When I met my wife I didn't give that girl another thought. Just after we married I began to wonder about her. I never think about her at night. It's always when I'm alone during the day, out on the route, between houses. Sometimes something she said will come back to me and I'll laugh to myself all over again."

He made me feel warm that day. I could feel the blood rush unaccustomed in my face at the idea that some one of those whose flesh I had attached myself to over the years might remember me with pleasure. Even for a small thing—the ingredients of my tuna salad, or the fact that my feet were never cold. I would be grateful if only the image that came to mind when thinking of me was only partially embarrassing. Not painful.

Joe, at that time, had the only words or voice that made me feel safe. He was, this must be said, though in the next page it becomes a lie, the only one I knew. But he was in the car beneath the window stroking or being touched, in a place of pleasure foreign to me, alien, because I did not share it. The time crawled over me, the seconds were like ants, gouging minutely, and a terrible anger welled up in me, revealing itself gradually. My anger became hatred: for his nodding over books, his visiting other lives, his brisk and hygienic fornication. In my rage, I raked over every detail of his existence, but above all else, I hated his stupidity, effrontery. What else could it be that parked him directly beneath my window, his own window? He knew I sat there at night. I pictured her sucking him skillfully in the front seat, beneath the steering wheel.

The hours piled onto one another.

"If you can't do it in twenty minutes, you can't do it." He said that once.

If they had been merely screwing, they would have been finished long ago. If they were talking all this time, I was finished. If he could find words for her, if he could tell her the silent strains of his thought, if he could listen to her speaking of herself there in the cold, then they were on ground I had never touched.

As I sat by the window, I entered a swirling despair, apocalyptic desolation. I felt a distinct cramp in my diaphragm; at times it was difficult to breathe; I felt a blow to my cranium, a rhythmic hacking, as if by a chisel, at the left side of my head directly above the ear. I cried.

I was still young, I still had fresh nightmares of Carlotta then. Youth in itself is what condemned me then, the complete faith in immortality that is natural to the young. The immortality of that moment, feeling a pain so intense that it seemed permanent, a condition from which I could imagine no freedom. The prospect was devastating.

A steely determination to die and escape the pain grew in me. It gave me something else to think about. The shame and loss receded slightly. Amid this ebbing, I busied myself, clinging to the mechanics necessary to accomplish the task.

I dressed quickly, pulled my three-piece wardrobe from under the bed, put on trousers, blouse, and shoes by feel. I grunted coarsely as I bent and tucked and tied. I slipped out of the bedroom, found my purse hanging on a doorknob in the kitchen, and rifled in it methodically. There was exactly one dollar. Not enough to die on, not enough to commit a comfortable suicide. I slumped in a chair, temporarily defeated. A seep of fetid tears oozed out of my eyes again. My nose began to run. I grabbed a handkerchief from the corner of the table. It stank of glue and wood dust—it was his blue bandanna. He used it to wipe his hands at the workbench. I shrieked and tossed the blue cloth beyond the table, out of sight.

The whole kitchen was suddenly toxic: his indentation in the chair cushion; his cup, the best in the house; a single brown hair coiled on the edge of the stained porcelain sink where he had washed his hair the previous afternoon; the skillet his mother had given him; the ragged dish towel left by some former lover; a refrigerator full of the food that made me fat.

The downstairs clock hummed smugly on the end of its electrical cord. Three o'clock in the morning. Three hours had run over me and he was still outside in the white car with Leda Van Hoerderbroeck. As I stood, it felt as if every cell inside me was leaking fluids through jagged holes in my body. I cannot explain the physical agony of a purely emotional injury. I needed, quite desperately, to die.

"I'll borrow money!" I grabbed the purse and collided with the front door as I went out. The steps led into a pile of refuse, old lumber, the evicted and ruptured seats of lost automobiles, but nothing seemed to be in my way. I was going to see Raymond.

Ray lived in austere dignity in two rooms at the top of an old house. He had a sort of odd affection for me, and I knew he would give me what I asked. He always had money. He was never down to his last dollar. I churned blindly, not screaming, down the black streets with their thin splashes of greenish light. The time was taken up in promises: "There, there, body, lungs, eyes, soon over, all gone soon," and I came upon his street swiftly, while the sky was still drowned in dark. There were no lights on inside the old house.

"Ray!" I shouted from the middle of the street. "Ray!" My voice was broken. Fallen out of control, plummeted to the knobby recesses of my lungs, the larynx so defeated by the soaking of the saline tears that it wobbled leathery and flaccid in my throat. "Ray!" I called in my deep, sad voice, and it began to rain.

The cool wet slid lightly over me. I lifted my hot face to it. "Ray!" A window slid open in a house across the street. "Ah, shaddup!" someone barked. I tiptoed up the steps of Ray's house and banged on the door. Ray opened the door in a formal dressing gown, only ever so slightly the worse for wear.

"Come in. Be quiet." Ray behaved with aplomb at nearly four o'clock in the morning. I followed him up the stairs. He flicked a switch as he entered the room. Books came to life on the wall, bright, standing beside each other. There was an imposing desk, a door on two trestles, its space organized with the things I always envied him: slide rule, letter knife, stamp box.

"Sorry to . . ." I waved my hands.

"Have a . . ." He held the cigarette box open for me. As I had suspected, his hair was not disordered by sleep.

"I want to borrow some money. I've been sick and I need to go home to recuperate."

"You really look it."

"About five dollars. Could you do that?"

His long pale face was swimming; his clear eyes, the color of water, searched mine. He did not believe I was sick, perhaps. Ray was not foolish, even before dawn. He moved purposefully. Hot water had appeared, strong tea, an orange sliced in many sections. He spoke calmly about the odd circumstances of his latest love affair. She had tried to stab him.

Did he think I was bent on murder?

"I'm sorry. I can't eat," I said. Beads of golden juice sat on the open flesh of the orange, their surfaces contained, globular.

He had the money in his hand. The gray-green paper was limp and soft. It made no sound as I took it. His clear eyes were shrewd, he wanted my story. He trusted me to be interesting.

"I'll tell you about it later," I said as I found my way to his door. But it seems to me now that I never paid him back, and though I have told a thousand versions of that day and the next, I never told one to Ray.

I spent some of the money in an all-night grocery, some in a never-closed bar, and the rest on the half-hour bus ride to my mother's house. It was not a house that I had ever lived in, but she kept rooms for her children in case some mother-blessed catastrophe should drive them back to her. She kept antihistamine in the bathroom, still, in case I should be stung by a bee in her vicinity, and she kept a jar of phenobarbital in case my epileptic brother should come home.

I walked stealthily around her hedge and behind the tool-shed in the yard. An old cherry tree bloomed there. I sat beneath it in the gray coming of the light. Now that I sat on the damp earth, packed from some old garden, the fatigue caught up to me. There was too much busyness in my head to sleep. My hands and belly and feet buzzed with the rush of my blood. It would be warm inside when my mother left. The comfort I looked forward to, tidiness, the humane order enforced by generations. A small caterpillar dropped onto my foot. It lay still for a moment and then coiled, twisting until its many feet had their purchase. Then its whole forward section lifted, stuck itself to my shoe with six or eight feet. Its tiny body reached, feeling the air. A toad began to sing.

Actually there were caterpillars everywhere. Inch-long, pale bodies, dots on each segment, flexing and paddling their feet in tandem. It seemed the earth was suddenly moving, creeping, boiling in the partial light. Another caterpillar dropped as I watched. Following its trajectory, I came to the lower branches of the flowering tree and there, securely knitted onto twigs and limbs, hung a large gray tent: the sheer web of the caterpillars' shelter. It was silken and sticky, weighted heavily by the life moving solidly inside and over it. Streams of the creatures swung by the extreme tips of their feet from minute scabs of bark in preparation for the long fall. These thousands of inching raveners were sending out explorer parties, colonizers of the unimaginable Vinlands and lush Floridas of the apple orchard, triumphant discoverers of the passage across the driveway to the maple tree on the other side.

The blooming cherry tree stood, resigned and still against the dawn. Its sad black skeleton was petrified, defenseless against this interior malignancy. The thick pink flowers, clouds caught in the twigs, were grossly twisted by the secret inhabitants. Their gaiety seemed frozen.

Once, in that childhood flux that reads allegory in each event, I watched a cardboard box burn. Its burning was secret at first, invisible from where I stood. I imagined the flames contorting, curving around the form of the box, seemingly repelled by the cool integrity of the cube. Then the color of the box began to change, brown became dull gray. The spot spread, but very slowly, and turned a luminescent black, nearly reflective, revealing a gradual growth of texture, a fine grain of truncated veins, shining.

When the first flame leapt up I was startled. Then the top of the box opened, quite suddenly, with an explosive sound, and lifted on all sides from the center like a flower to reveal a bright holocaust within. For whole moments, the corners held their clean shape, but the fire took them at last and they coiled and writhed. The black skeleton crumbled into flame, indistinguishable from its devourer.

When I saw the fate of the box, or rather the manner of that fate, how long the flame should be concealed while it glutted the inside, I thought of the heat of my own life: the fear and greed and the ghastly energy that consumed me. My placid exterior was soon to be ripped and the infection exposed. But now the flowering tree was posed quietly, too, still maintaining its courteous relations with the wind, and not seeming to notice the destructive pests.

The effort of getting to that spot had distracted me from my motive, but now I had empathized with the tree, conjured the image of our interiors invaded and destroyed by a secret gnawing. I gushed tears again as I replayed the tree's agony alongside my own.

A combined grief for the tree and myself and the necessity of fire completed my exhaustion. I lay down on the soft ground and relented to its coolness. My paper bag grew soggy. The bottoms of the bottles sank through. I wiped my eyes on the dry top of the bag and then crumpled it and blew my nose into it. The two bottles sat in the weeds beside me, the small bottle of aspirin and the big bottle of vodka. My nose kept running, and I crammed the wadded brown bag against it and sat looking at the infected tree.

The sun was well up by then, a hygienic gleam in an aluminum sky. The caterpillars were engaged in their innocent dances. Ten thousand bodies lifted forward to test the air with wonder.

I imagined that the house and all its neighbors were gone, and the tree was besieged in the hollow between wide, grassy hills. The grass was knee-high, waved in the wind. Crows came, and robins; a sheep trotted over the horizon and stopped to eat. If I were buried in the soil beneath the grass, my rot sinking into every blade, and the air above my body moved strange gases in the breeze at night—I wouldn't care. It seemed not such a bad ambition, to replace a couple hundred pounds of that fragile dust that collects on this spinning rock, to support its minute amazements.

This was what I felt. This was my only significance. All my hurts and ambitions and fears led only to this. But it was all right; I was crazy tired and had been jilted the night before, and my life's rhythmic end then seemed sweetly reasonable. The youthful caterpillars got my blessing, and the tree that nurtured its own death, and the soft earth that could hide me and keep me from the heated rock beneath.

A motor coughed directly behind me. I grabbed at the bottles guiltily and squashed the caterpillars that had found a footing on the glass. The automobile engine muttered steadily from the garage. A door slammed. My mother was on her way to work, warming her engine, creaming her face for the last time in the rearview mirror. The engine's sound changed, increased in volume, then drew away.

I crouched, listening until it was gone, and then stood up. Slowly, I moved around the house. A toad burped behind me.

She always left the key on top of the door frame. I felt for it, expecting grit and cobwebs, but my fingers slid smoothly until they touched the key. I smiled. Any place she touched so often would naturally be clean.

The kitchen smelled of coffee, warm, and was already bright with the metallic light pouring in. I went into the bathroom and washed my face and hands lingeringly. The antihistamine was there in its dark bottle, but there were only four capsules in the jar of phenobarbital. Had my brother been visiting? Had she been taking them to calm herself? Or to sleep? I took the bottles and went to my room. Civilization, of a kind.

She had given me every opportunity to be a lady. Only my physique stood in the way, and that odd heat generated by my brain by the incubating fat. I had never slept in the room, but she had made it with her own hands into a lady lair, dainty and seductive. Too much cloth in too large a print (she had not kept up with the fashion) hung stiffly from the room's pale surfaces. The small lamp was too far from the bed, set on a dressing table beside a mocking ceramic courtier who bowed and leered at the mirror. No one had slept in the room since she had dressed it so, but it reeked of sleep. The air was thick and still.

The lamp I moved to the bedside table, crawled under the bustling spread of the bed to plug it in. The bottles, once neatly arranged into a row beneath it, gave a soothing convalescent touch. I opened the window and a fresh chill came in. I trotted down to the drawer in the hall for a pen and pad of paper, then to the back closet for the flannel nightgown and robe that had been folded there for all the years since I left home. I got a large paper bag from the kitchen and a box of paper tissues for my nose. With all this I went back to the bedroom. It began to look dreamily pleasant, with a little wind stirring the voluminous flounces.

I dressed slowly, examining the cheese texture of my skin, the soft bulges around my knees, the Etruscan extensions of my buttocks, hips, and belly. A keg of soap, I thought, and the long svelte image of Leda Van Hoerderbroeck turned my very tits red with misery. I put on the soft robe, but it no longer buttoned closed in front. I went down to the bathroom and ran hot water in the tub.

After a long and detailed consideration of the various means of suicide I had realized fully that I had no desire to hurt myself. Leaping from high places was horrible. Guns, aside from being hard to get, were crass, messy, noisy, and mechanical. Knives, even razors, as my first experience revealed, were too dubious as tools. They required more strength of will than I could muster. No. I was seeking a termination of pain, a simple lack of sensations, since the only ones available ranged from discomfort to agony. The ideal was sleep, and the prospect of drugs was attractive because it was not direct. The relationship between the act of taking the pills and the final result was subtle, an interior process that allowed a discreet period of increasing languor before unconsciousness.

I got into the tub and scrubbed. This vanity was in deference to whoever had to lay me out. I scoured the tub afterward but left the damp towel on the rack in hopes that my mother would notice that I had cleaned up after myself and be brought to tears.

Back in the bedroom, the air was fresh. The sheets on the bed were so smooth and my few muscles so totally exhausted after the bath that I nearly wept again from the comfort of it. All this time a calm purpose controlled me. Only occasionally did some picture or phrase bring back the acute pain. The real motive by then was fatigue.

The bottles were easy to reach. I planned to wash the pills down with the vodka. I began with the antihistamine, fermented cherry flavor, and it went down easily. Then the smooth gelatin capsules, all four in one gulp with a swig of the vodka. The aspirin were the telling blow, and the disgusting part. The grit stung my throat as I swallowed, and clung all the way down. The hot wash of the vodka took the taste and feel away so I could shovel in another handful. The awful smell of the chalky aspirin crept up into my nose from the inside of my mouth. I began to gag, and clenched my gut fiercely to keep from vomiting up my supplies. When the aspirin bottle was still a third full, I quit. Enough of the damned stuff. There was still a lot of liquor left but I didn't want any more.

The soiled clothes I had folded into the large paper bag. I now tucked the bottles in among them and shoved it under the bed. This was to prevent my mother from guessing the true state of my affairs if I was not quite dead when she got home from work.

In theory there was nothing downstairs that would alert her to my presence in the house. Still I was afraid of being slotted with those unfortunates who intended to be discovered "in time!" In a society where suicide is frowned upon in principle—considered cowardly by the staunch, deranged by the wishy-washy, forbidden by law, and contemplated with varying degrees of lust by fifty percent of the population throughout twenty percent of their lives—in such a society nothing is judged more despicably self-seeking than failing in an attempt to do away with yourself. In this as in other endeavors, you can't argue with success.

The bandaged wrists and woeful eyes that were the aftermath of my previous experiment had proved totally useless as levers to buoy up the sagging interest of my lover. The few friends whom I had tried to intrigue with the tale were either bored, disbelieving, or openly scornful. But I didn't view the exercise as wholly wasted since it invested my culminating performance, extempore though it was, with more practical cunning than I might otherwise have managed.

With any luck I wouldn't be found until my mother's next dusting foray, and hopefully that would be before my rot was extensive enough to ruin this really marvelous mattress.

If, on the other tack, my mother's vaunted intuition should cause her to stick her nose in while I was only in a coma, she would notice no disarray, only her darling in a blue-flowered nightie sleeping deeply. Convinced that her maternal longings were to be satisfied and I was home from the wars to stay, she would tiptoe out, and flit down to the kitchen to roast some enormous hunk of meat and make a potato salad for a snack when I woke.

Lying on the fresh pillows and plotting thus, I waited to see if the reaction to my concoction would be drastic and immediate. Would the aspirin's acid devour the lining of my stomach and have me shrieking in agony? The discomfort in my gut was distinct but not really different from the whirring it had been suffering from nerves alone.

I decided there was time to write a farewell note. My pad and pen were beside me. I doubled up my knees and began to write in my tidy calligraphy.

This is just to say that I have had enough. No one is responsible for my death except myself.

I signed it, wrote the date and the hour, and then slid it under the pillow.

I lay and continued to wait for signs of inner turbulence. There were a great many birds singing outside. I wondered peacefully whether they were feasting on the caterpillars. In my most noble voice I proclaimed, "I wish you joy of the worm!" and chuckled softly. I felt fine. A little tired. My eyes and upper lip burned a little from overuse, but the sources of all my tribulations seemed swabbed away, forgotten already because I would not have to face them anymore. I began thinking tenderly of those who would grieve for me. I decided it would be kind to leave a note for my mother assuring her that my death in no way implied a failure on her part.

I sat up and wrote a long, loving letter to my mother in which I reminisced at length and ended by thanking her for what I swore had been a rich and vivid panoply of experience, despite the fact that I simply couldn't bear the thought of another day of it. The letter was six pages long, closely written in my most minute hand. I folded it and put it under the pillow.

Then I wrote a letter of loving encouragement to my epileptic younger brother, and a gush of fond reminiscence to my older brother. Soon after that I decided a friendly and philosophical farewell to Joe would be in keeping. That was only four pages. By this time I was sitting vigorously forward, scribbling with great industry. The bed was littered with inky paper. I wrote a very witty apology to Raymond for being unable to repay his kind loan, since my earning power would be sadly curtailed at any moment. This was followed by increasingly ribald final greetings to several friends.

Finally, in the middle of a sentimental effusion to a history professor whose eyebrows I had always found enchanting (I was claiming adamantly that if anything could have provided me with the courage to face the next day it would have been his annual lecture on the Quattrocento) I began to feel very tired. I lay down abruptly without bothering to order my letters. They crackled and slid off onto the floor when I stretched my legs out. My neck seemed to have no muscles. My head flopped to the side. I could see the curtains being lifted by the air that moved behind them. In this new position my belly suddenly found itself in distress. The thin, bitter taste crept up the back of my throat. A mean spasm twisted my gut. "Uh-oh," I muttered, afraid to lose any of my potion.

The flies will come in, I thought. I should have shut the window. As I closed my eyes to stanch the nausea, an old image displayed itself in my mind: a big aluminum tub full of white fat that had been trimmed from beef, my mother approaching with a good-intentioned smile. "I'm going to make all our soap from now on," she said, and reached into the tub. The next moment she was shrieking, her face dark and stretched around her mouth, grown enormous, her tongue wide and flat and vibrating in the din. I stared at her and then looked into the tub. The limbs and shards of pale tallow were streaked bloody, and contained the crawling havens of hundreds of plump, curling worms. They lay calmly in their hatching place. "Maggots!" my mother shrieked, and deftly vomited into the tub.

Next I endured the agony of unexplainable bouncing and banging. My whole body was shaken and hammered. My face was cold. Wind rushed over me at a terrible speed. I didn't bother to open my eyes. I was lying in the bed of a pickup truck; this was unmistakable. The grit, the corrugated metal beneath me, the sizzle of passing traffic. The wind and the bouncing slowed and then stopped. Something moved on my hands. I had been holding them in some soft grip, which was now released. I was rolled and lifted. A swooping sensation in my belly; I swallowed bile. Warmth, stillness. I opened my eyes. A young woman in a white uniform looked down at me. I smiled, the smile got away from me, kept growing until it leaked into my ears.

"This is not, I gather, the train to glory?"

I meant to say it, but I began chuckling instead, a bubbling in my chest. The young woman's face moved away and I lifted my head to see what she was doing. She had a hypodermic needle and was preparing to inject its contents into my thigh, just below my crotch. As the needle went in, I could not believe the severity of the pain. I stared at her, shocked. She punched a second needle into my other thigh. This one convinced me. I lay back and slept.

It was another day when I woke again. The incessant buzzing in my ears proved to be deafness. Then, too, my legs would not respond at all. I seemed paralyzed. I had wet the bed. The deafness, I learned later, was the natural due of the aspirin. The paralysis was the accidental result of the injections. The incontinence no one bothered to explain.

A faceless aide rolled me over and slid the sheet out from under me. I lay looking at the floor where it met the pale green walls. When she rolled me to the other side I saw a woman in the other bed. She was reading quietly, flat on her back, the book held with both hands above her nose. When I was in place on my back again I felt thin plastic crackling beneath the bedsheet.

At some point a man came in and stood at the foot of my bed. He stared at me for a moment and then spoke. The buzz in my ears had receded and I could hear him, but fuzzily. His voice had the effect of being overheard, just that blur of volume and clarity that would occur if he were speaking to someone else entirely. He introduced himself as Dr. Bump. He looked so fierce when he spoke the name that I grinned. He was annoyed.

"What made you do a stupid thing like that?"

I grinned blankly.

"Wouldn't your father let you use the car that night?"

His scorn was heavy. I thought of his daughter immediately and then it occurred to me that he must not have read my chart if he thought I was still a chubby teenager. He was lined and pale. His eyes seemed lidless, uncovered and angry.

"And like all of them, you did a fouled-up job. Aspirin in sufficient quantity acts as a stimulant, which, combined with the depressants you took, the alcohol and whatnot, was simply canceled out. You were nowhere near dying. Not for a minute. But I'll tell you what you damned near did. You came close enough to making yourself deaf for life! That's what aspirin can do!"

I felt myself blushing.

"I can't seem to move my legs," I said.

"Sure you can. It will just hurt for a few days."

"Have you got a daughter?" I asked in my friendliest tone.

"Yes. And do you know what I'd do to her if she ever pulled a stunt like yours?"

I smiled, anticipating.

"I'll tell you what I told your mother when she asked me if you should see a psychiatrist. I told her, 'If my daughter ever did what your daughter just did, I wouldn't send her to a psychiatrist, I'd bend her over and blister her bottom with a hairbrush.'"

I laughed delightedly. The only way to disarm the old clot. I looked forward to his coming again so I could impress him with my intelligent good humor, but I never saw him again.

Good humor had taken me over. I laughed at nothing and was impulsively courteous to the aides. An odd repose had penetrated my entrails and permeated my every system. I slept and ate and lay watching the walls and the window and listening to the activity in the corridor.

That first afternoon a man came to visit the woman in the other bed. It was her husband. He leaned over her, held her hands, sat near her head, and talked softly. I watched them surreptitiously. That night I slept alone without dreaming, easily.

After the morning oatmeal, I dozed again. When I woke, Joe was looking at me. The skin above and below his beard was white, lit from the window, and his eyes were set with dutifully worried creases, and also a blank puzzlement. I grinned at him.

"Ah, Sally, God," he said at once.

"How did you get here?" I asked.

"Your mother called me. She said . . ." He pulled his mouth into a crook at the corner.

"I haven't seen her. How did you find me?"

He sat down. There was no use trying to deal with my

relatives. I had no interest in them, and Joe was at his best as a low-key raconteur. He had unwillingly received the anxious blast of my mother's confidences and felt, it seemed, a certain relief in being able to pass them on to me in this comradely way. He had, I know, been anticipating being tasked with reclaiming me from my melancholia on his own, and so approached this alternative with gusto.

It was two worms. She had made an appointment with the tree surgeon and left work early to be at home when he arrived. He was actually sawing through the infected limb prior to spraying when my mother came out to watch. She turned to look at the rear of the house and saw the upstairs window open. With a nervous perspicacity wholly typical of her, she determined to investigate the window while the workman was still on the premises, just in case there should be a burglar huddled in some closet.

Joe hesitated at this point. His embarrassment was suddenly acute, we had encountered a part of the story he would rather not have heard. Or perhaps his shyness was not in knowing it but in telling it to me.

I had fouled the bed. My mother would have noticed the smell immediately. I casually shielded my eyes with one hand not to see his face. Convinced that I was very ill, she had called out the window for help and was in the process of rolling me out of my own loose dung when she came across the bag beneath the bed. She reached into it, looking for a cloth of any kind to wipe me off, and encountered the bottles. A quick glance at the litter of papers would have provided the rest of the evidence.

She stripped off my nightgown, wrapped me in a blanket, and carried me by my feet. The tree surgeon took my shoulders. He drove us to the hospital in his pickup. She sat in the back holding my hands.

"Why hasn't she come to see me?" I asked suddenly.

Joe shrugged. "I thought she had. She called me early this morning."

I let him off lightly. I could have managed to harrow him, even in my peculiar jubilant state. Of course, it was myself I was sparing by not accusing him, not weeping in his presence.

"Your mother seemed to think that it must be my fault somehow," he said. His brows creased the skin of his forehead again.

"Ridiculous," I said, and let my face fall on the pillow. "I'm sleepy now. Thank you for coming."

I let my eyes close and waited, listening through the thin remote buzz that was all that remained of my deafness. His chair creaked, was still for a moment, and then creaked again as he rose from it. I worked to contain my self-congratulatory smile until he was outside the door. I felt clever for using my condition to relieve me of such dangerous company. I hadn't cried. I hadn't grabbed his hand and smeared it with snotty kisses. I had not begged him to lie to me or wail about my love—a triumph. I grinned.

I opened my eyes. Simultaneously, there was an unpremeditated movement in my legs; my thigh muscles were nearly audible, like the tearing of dry cardboard. I lifted my knees a fraction, however reluctantly. So the crass doctor was right: paralysis, too, was only fear.

*, *, *,

The buzz was faint and reassuring in my head, but some niggling interfered with my complete satisfaction. My hair had not been brushed in days and felt reptilian, but that did not account for the vague unease in my gut. I replayed the story Joe had told me. It was too bad about that wonderful mattress. I certainly knew that death, hanging in fact, caused the involuntary release of the anal sphincter. I could have given myself an enema, but I hadn't thought of it. But then I didn't die, did I? Was nowhere near it, the doctor said, was never anywhere near it. The chuckle started again in my chest.

Then it stopped, and I remembered what had bothered me about the story. I thought of my mother, opening the door and smelling fresh human feces. In her alarm she had thought first of cleaning me. My shame was still her own. And then the hands that held mine in the back of the truck. All those letters on the bed and under the pillows. Fine to write in that maudlin strain if you were dead, but . . . at least they were all kind letters, certainly the most loving I had ever written. But she must be very angry, she whose belly I had kicked in, who sadly wiped away my dirt. It seemed reasonable that the source of my life might not want to see how eager I was to discard it. She had not come to see me. She had not sat beside me in her most becoming coat with her purse balanced in her lap, as was her custom when visiting friends in the hospital. She had not visited me.

But two days later, when I was released, she was waiting for me. She was cheerful and matter-of-fact. She didn't mention why we were both there. I was still stiff in the legs and this made a convenient excuse to put me downstairs on a sofa rather than upstairs in the defiled room. The failed room. Her failure and mine.

I stayed for two weeks. She telephoned from work two or three times each day, casually, and I answered casually.

A random poppy bloomed on the edge of the garden. I brought it in and put it into a jar of water. It sat on the desk for days. I watched it relax, loosen its hold on its wine-colored petals until they lapsed open, sluttish, drunken, allowing the musty purple core to protrude. The dark dust of the center had fallen onto the base of each spreading petal. The opening was a revolution of color, dark maroon to a blind, flat black that seemed to suck light greedily.

All that time I slept innocently. The narrow sofa warmed my back, the reading lamp cast a soft light over my head whenever I woke. In the days, I cleaned and polished and cooked to prevent the anxiousness my mother displayed, no matter how tired she was, if a blur of dust declared itself when she returned from work. It began to take a toll on her. She was accustomed to command it all, to dance from dawn to dark in a military surveillance of the premises. My presence was an interference. With the best intentions I could not do the dishes to her satisfaction. I made her a stranger in her home.

I grinned to see it twisting her. She wanted me to lie down and be still where she could see me. She could not abide an idle healthy body. I was an interloper on her domain, yet she would have fumed over and scorched any meal she felt required to serve to a non-worker. She did want me, though she couldn't bear the necessary fact of my presence. She did not dare to quarrel with me.

We never mentioned the suicide. I moved back to town.

Still, the triviality of my death had impressed me. The horror I once had of my own death had disappeared. All I fear now is pain, my own and that of others. Being dead is not important at all. Being dead is the least important thing.

Siesta Time 24-Hour Laundromat

Something had to be done. It was one of those days. I wandered down to the basement of the house, where there was only one occupied room. Most of the space was waiting to be partitioned with cardboard into more rentable rooms. I found rags and brooms in a corner and took some upstairs.

I'd never cleaned the place or put up a picture. Not a poster or a cartoon. My four books were hidden in the cardboard box beneath the bed that also held my spare clothes. The two cups and two spoons took up a corner in the box, next to my tooth-brush. There was a small gas ring with its miniature tank beside it and a one-pound coffee tin rustling on top of it. The sight of it used to annoy me, but I sat and slept with my face turned away from it. That's all there was. Sometimes my boots and socks were strewn under the bed. Still, there was a crowded, dirty feel to the place.

With the first stroke of the broom under the bed I pulled out a used condom. It gave me a jolt. I went to the bathroom for a piece of tissue to pick it up with. It was dry, almost crack-ing between my fingers. I dumped it into the toilet and watched it flush. I went back to sweeping, coughing at the dust. There were hairpins in the corners.

I'd filled the coffee can with hot water and was standing on the chair to wipe at the skylight when Rennel poked his head in and groaned.

"I didn't hear you coming," I said.

His face was strange—he had a hurt, honest expression. "Aram and Carlotta are down there. They want to see you. I came to see if you were here first."

I stepped off the chair. Water jumped out of the coffee can and ran down my wrists.

"Did you know their baby died?"

"Yes. How are they?"

His face twisted. "I don't know, I don't know! Can I bring them up?"

I nodded. I heard him on the stairs as I threw the rags and broom out into the hall, rinsed out the coffee can, filled it with clean water, and put it on the gas ring to heat up. The room smelled like a wet dog. My stomach was flipping up and down. I carefully got out the cups, went to the bathroom for the tooth mug, measured out instant coffee. I could hear the long sad chorus of three sets of feet climbing the intricate stairs. I arranged myself on the bed. But then it seemed to me Rennel would probably sit on the bed, and I didn't want to be lined up with him. And Carlotta should definitely be the one to sit on the chaise. I stood up and waited just outside the range of the door until I heard their feet on my landing. Then I stepped out and saw them.

Carlotta was first. She moved fast. I thought for a second that she was going to hit me, but she grabbed my face in her two hands and looked at me. I tried to put some feeling into my eyes for her. She was pale and thin. Her hair had been cut roughly, ear-length, as though she'd sawed at each braid with a knife. At first I thought her cheeks were painted, but the lines were four thin scabs, two on each side. The cuts started under her eyes and ran down toward her jaws. It gave her a formal, symmetrical look.

Her eyes pored over my face, examining me, anxious. Like she was looking for something in particular. I tried to put warmth into my eyes. I could see Rennel beyond her face, and Sam. His face was hollow, sunken in around his eyes and cheeks.

Carlotta dropped her eyes and hands and turned away. Then Sam came up to me with the same searching look in his dark eyes. I put my arm around his neck and laid my face against his collarbone. The fuzz of his beard surprised me. He pulled away.

"Did you know?"

"Only that it's dead. Sit down."

Carlotta's weight hardly dented the chaise. She lay nearly flat, staring at the ceiling sloping close to her. Sam sat straight in the chair with his hands on his knees, not looking at her. Rennel looked uncomfortable on the bed and I cast about for a place, and ended up crouched against the wall. The water began to boil. I bustled with my back to them. Pulled my sweater sleeves down to act as pot holders, turned off the gas, tilted the can gingerly over the cups, watched the black water rise to the rims.

"So," I said as I passed out the cups. "What happened?"

Carlotta's eyes narrowed. Sam blinked and smiled softly.

"It's been strange."

He looked around, but nobody agreed or disagreed with him. We waited while he stared at the cracked cup steaming beside him. The gray light of the room aged us all and gave us a kind of dignity.

"It was nice up there." He curled his hands around the cup. "I wrote you a letter, I think. I was learning a lot. Lichtenstein was teaching me. But also just the air and the trees and the steepness of the hill had things to teach me. I was feeling good. Better all the time. I felt the best of my life about a half an hour before the baby died. But when that happened I half thought this one bad thing should negate all the good things I was learning. All the beauty there was."

Carlotta snorted loudly. She turned onto her side, facing away from us.

"Now, I don't know," Sam continued, watching her. "I wish you could have been there, but . . . It was just the best day. There'd been snow for a while, but we could see valleys from the stoop that were still bare. Then this day the sky cleared and it was almost warm. We took off our shirts and sat outside after supper. I was sitting on a stump with my shoes in snow and my shirt off, getting a tan. If it hadn't been so windy I'd have sweated, really!"

I slid down onto the floor.

"We were never there, Han Shan," Rennel said. "Was it really cold?"

Sam smiled. "I keep forgetting that you don't know anything about the place. That's at least partially because I thought so much about you both while we were up there. I really wanted you to come and I kept having imaginary conversations with you. I'd get very involved in explaining to you everything I was doing."

Sam giggled softly, shook his head. Carlotta wore a pair of Levi's and Sam's work shirt. Her hip bones poked sharply through the denim. Her pale feet were piled at the ends of her pant legs. Her thinness hurt to look at.

"This cabin belongs to Lichtenstein's uncle," Sam went on. "It's like a square teepee. It's one room with a fireplace in the middle. There's a hood over the fire to catch the smoke and a chimney going out through the roof. I guess the place was never finished. There was no glass in the windows and the door hadn't been hung. We nailed up blankets and draped a blanket over the door. We didn't really need windows because a lot of light came in through the cracks between the boards in the walls. Early in the morning when we woke up the room looked like it was underwater, these thin pieces of light floating around. At night, Lichtenstein would put his blanket down on one side of the fire and we'd put ours down on the other side. We had a kerosene lamp. They give a weird light. You can write by it, but it's very hard to read.

"Also it was a kind of revelation to me to be in real woods. That place is on the mountain, but below the timberline. Maybe you've been in real woods before, but I'd just piddled around on Long Island. And even the trees on our place by the river were more like park than wilderness. I hadn't realized . . ."

Sam patted at his clothes with his square hands. He pulled out a dark pipe and a pouch of tobacco.

"I'd go behind a bush to piss and take half an hour to find my way back. It was really something. Anyway, we ran into these crazy problems. Like we'd drive into town every few days or so to shop. But the place didn't have a butcher, much less a horsemeat butcher, so we kind of went vegetarian. But that meant we had to buy canned dog food for Angelina because she never developed a taste for rice. It was peculiar to sit on the front step watching squirrels and rabbits and hearing deer crashing around and still have to feed your dog canned whale meat. Also, we were short on money. Carlotta's parents had started writing to my parents, and they each found out that the others were sending us an allowance, so they both cut back pretty sharply. Lichtenstein didn't have any money at all. But then he was getting us the place rent-free, so . . ."

Sam thumbed around in the bowl of the pipe. I glanced at Carlotta with her bludgeoned hair and scabbed face. Did she look in a mirror when she did it? To make sure the scars would be lined up?

"How did you come to change your name?" I asked. "Why Han Shan?"

Sam puffed and his eyes sparked. "Oh, listen! He's this fantastic old Zen saint. He lived a million years ago in China. He studied in a monastery for a while, but then he disappeared into the mountains and nobody knew what had become of him. Then, years later, he came to the monastery gates with a skinny little man who was deaf and dumb. Han Shan himself was big and fat. Well, he knocked at the gate and they asked him what he wanted. He just laughed and tore the gate down. He roared in and picked up bags of rice and salt and clothes and sandals, piled some on his little friend, and they ran out laughing and disappeared into the hills again. The monks couldn't stop him. He was too strong. They're pacifists, anyway.

"After that, Han Shan would appear at the monastery, break in no matter what precautions were taken, and raid the place. He never answered, no matter what anybody said to him. He just laughed very loudly. Went around giggling all the time. The monks decided he was crazy. He never took much and he didn't hurt anybody, but I think it must have irritated them a lot. Still, they didn't do much about it. Maybe the Chinese think madmen are touched by God, like the Indians do. Anyway, this went on for twenty years.

"Han Shan grew fatter and stronger as he got older, but nobody knew where he and his friend lived. Nobody ever saw them between raids. Then one year he didn't come. The old master of the monastery sat waiting for the raid. Summer went, but still no Han Shan. The master waited two more years, but Han Shan never came again. The master got worried and sent all the monks and novices into the mountains to search. For months they found nothing. Then, one day, they came upon a tiny hut at the top of the tallest mountain in the whole country. The hut was falling apart. When the monks looked inside they found two skeletons seated, perfectly balanced in the lotus position, facing each other. One was the skeleton of a small frail man. The other was the skeleton of a huge man. On the walls were written hundreds of beautiful poems all signed by Han Shan. The monks carried the skeletons down to the monastery. They carefully dismantled the hut and carried it down. Even the roof beams had haiku carved on them. The old master studied the poems and discovered that Han Shan had been enlightened. From that day everyone knew that he had been a saint. Lichtenstein knew all about him. Lichtenstein knows a lot of things like that."

The momentum of the story died on Sam's lips.

"Well." He pushed his cup across the table. "We were sitting on stumps in front of the cabin. We'd stopped bathing when the snow started. I saw a movie once of an old king. He crawled out of his bed in the morning, naked with a fur wrapped around him, and broke the ice in the top of the water bucket so he could wash his face. I always wondered why he didn't have somebody heat water for him. Wouldn't you? If you were king?"

The question sank into the walls. I nodded and heard the bedsprings squeak as Rennel nodded.

"The sun was just getting fancy across the valley. There were chickens and the goat. I was waiting for the energy to get up and shoo them inside for the night. Lichtenstein was talking about a girlfriend he'd had once. A champion pool player. He was still kind of interested in her. It was very quiet. I don't know if you can quite understand how quiet it is in a place like that. I could hear the creek down the hill and Lichtenstein's voice was the same as the water. But the quiet beat on your ears. Then there was this sound from the cabin. A groan or something. Lotta stepped out of the doorway and stood there for a minute. She looked strange. I don't know how else to describe it. Her mouth was hanging open and her eyes were all white. Then she made the noise again."

Sam stared at the ceiling pitched low near his head. He turned stiffly to Carlotta, still facing away on the chaise.

"It wasn't a regular sort of noise." He paused again. "There was this little white dog that we had brought along, Pogo. A friend of Angelina's. The dogs were lying in front of the door. There was an ax Lotta used to cut wood. She'd gotten pretty good at it. This ax was leaning against the step. I wasn't really paying that much attention to her, I was just sitting in the last sunshine, you know? Then I saw Lichtenstein's mouth drop open, watching Carlotta. I looked up just as she brought the ax down. I saw all her muscles move through her dress. Angelina yelped and jumped away, but this little Pogo didn't move. He wasn't very sharp. The ax went through his neck. His head fell over, with the tongue hanging out. It didn't fall all the way off. It was just hanging over to the side, almost upside down. But he was white and the snow was white, and the blood sprayed out, like a water balloon breaking.

"Carlotta lifted the ax again, as though nothing had happened, and started walking over to Katie. I was just sitting there looking. I couldn't do anything. I guess I didn't want to do anything. It was the sort of thing you don't believe when you see it."

Sam wet his lips. I could feel my heart in my ears, in my throat and wrists, even a thick pulsing in my nostrils. Rennel's white hands were clenched in his lap.

"Well, she axed Katie. She was tied to a log. She hit her

across the back, but the blade had turned around so the blunt side struck first. Katie screamed and fell down. I got up then and started walking toward Lotta. I didn't have anything in mind to do. I didn't understand, you see? I had my hands up and I just walked toward her, but before I got there she'd got the blade turned around again and hit Katie's front leg. It was broken and bleeding everywhere. Katie's eyes were open and she was screaming. You wouldn't think a goat could scream like that.

"Lotta didn't notice me at all. She was standing there with the ax, looking at the chickens. They were making a lot of noise and running around. Angelina had run off into the woods. I grabbed the ax. She didn't try to stop me. It was hot. I suppose it was from sitting in the sun, even though there was snow on the ground. But at the time I thought it was blood that made the ax hot. It was just at that minute that I thought of the baby. I said, 'Where's the baby?'

"And then Lotta laughed. Very sarcastic, like. I went into the cabin. She hadn't killed him. I could tell right away. He slept in this wooden box. He was doubled up in a corner. I knew he was dead when I saw him. He looked stiff already. His eyes were closed. I guess he died in his sleep. He was a funny color."

Sam fumbled with the pipe. The cold ash stuck wetly to his fingers. I spent some time finding a cigarette and a book of matches. Cigarettes for Rennel and me, as well. Sam blew two full lungs of smoke at the skylight.

"After a while, when Lotta was calmed down, she wrapped the baby up in blankets and we got into the car. We left Lichtenstein there. He was just kind of standing around. The goat was still making noises. Angelina hadn't come back.

"We got into the car and drove to town. I didn't know what to do exactly, but I knew deaths have to be reported. It isn't a town, really. There's a store with a post office inside and a gas pump outside. The other building is the guy's house. But he's a real sheriff. It was dark by then. They'd closed up and were just getting ready for supper. We stood on the front porch and knocked. Carlotta was holding the baby. She still hadn't cried or anything. He was nice to us. His wife, too. They brought us in and tried to feed us. We sat at the table while they ate. They gave us tea. She was a big fat lady. The sheriff was fat, too. But Lotta wouldn't put the baby down anywhere, so she sat there at the table with the baby in her arms. It was dead, you know? But she kept sneaking little looks at the baby. She'd pretend not to be paying any attention to him, but every minute or so she'd take a quick hard look to see if maybe, after all, you know?

"Anyway, the sheriff said he didn't have any authority in this kind of business and we'd have to drive to Missoula and report it to the coroner. The sooner the better. There was no use waiting. We went out to the car. It was about eighty miles.

"Driving at night in the mountains is something very strange. The roads are tight, snakey. There are bits of cloud wandering around, your headlights hit them and they flash and disappear. I saw ghosts. I can tell you they were mist and reflections, but I believe they were ghosts. Carlotta wasn't talking. She just sat there holding the baby, making sure his head didn't touch anything, bump against anything. He had a lot of hair. Anyway, I don't ever want another ride like that. All the time I was wondering how long before he began to smell and if they'd put me in jail or something.

"It was late when we got there, eleven, around that. Everything was closed up. It's a pretty dead place, Missoula. Finally, a cop stopped us and we asked him directions. The coroner's office was in the basement of the municipal building. Everything else was dark. There was just one night clerk in this standard green room full of beat-up file cabinets and fat record books. There was a bad smell, and this high counter where we stood.

"This was just the recording office. There's a morgue some-place in town, I suppose. This guy was very cold. Carlotta was standing there holding the baby wrapped up in a blanket. I guess I was a little hysterical by that time. I kept joking with him, this clerk, but he kept handing me long forms to fill out and the pens he had didn't work. He kept asking these ques-tions as though we'd killed the baby. He wanted the coroner to come and look at him to make sure we hadn't strangled him or something. So he called the coroner and we were supposed to wait until he came. Then the clerk started talking about funeral arrangements. I think he and the coroner must run a funeral parlor together on the side. All this was carried on in this bu-reaucratic monotone except when I'd start to giggle. We started to bicker about the cost of funerals, and he went into this busi-ness about pauper's funerals, where the state or the country or somebody pays for it. Trying to shame me, see. In the middle of it Carlotta laid the baby out on the counter and opened up the blanket. He was stiffening up in this funny position, curled up. He always did look like a toad, but I think his belly was swelling or something. He looked very odd. Anyway, she just walked out and left him there. I ran out after her, and the clerk was saying, 'You can't leave that here! That goes to the funeral home.' But I went out and up the steps. We were parked right in front. Carlotta was sitting in the car. We didn't say anything. We just drove back to the cabin. Lichtenstein was gone. The damned chickens were eating Pogo. Katie wasn't dead yet. It was dark, but I could see it in the snow in front of the cabin. Her eyes were glowing. The car was acting funny. We were go-ing to just stop in Portland long enough to pick up some things we'd stored in the basement of Carlotta's old dormitory. We wanted to get to California. Carlotta wanted to see her psychiatrist, and we thought we could put up with her folks for a while. But the car kept acting funny. I pulled into a service station in the middle of nowhere and some old man came out and said he wasn't a mechanic. But it still kept clanking and going slower and slower. Rennel says it needs a valve job. I stopped about thirty miles outside of town here and then it wouldn't start again. We called a tow truck. While we were waiting Lotta went to the can and cut her hair and her face."

Sam stubbed out the cigarette he hadn't really smoked. Carlotta still lay with her back to all of us. It was getting dark outside, the room was dim.

"What are you going to do now?" Rennel asked, his voice harsh. Whether it was real pain or pain he thought he ought to feel, I didn't know. Didn't matter. It was none of my business anyway. None of it was my business, actually.

Sam drew on the pipe. "I don't know. We're staying with these people. A guy from the college and his girl. Sleeping in their living room. The tow truck wanted to know where to take us. I thought it was a nice quiet street so I said, 'Stop here!' That was funny. Our car was as big as the tow truck. We rode in our car all the way back, sitting in front, leaning far back, watching the hood bouncing past the tops of light poles. I suppose I could have had him take us over to the college parking lot, but it was costing a lot of money. We were going down a good street, so I had him stop and back us up to the curb.

"We sat there most of the evening. I walked down the street and brought back donuts and milk. I thought we could sleep in the car until we found out what to do. I was making up a bed when this guy came out onto his front porch. He came down to talk and ended up inviting us to stay in his living room for as long as we want. He's a strange guy. He's interested in computers. He thinks he can make a killing in horse races by feeding information into this massive computer in the basement of the psychology building. He's got it down to a couple hundred variables. What he comes up with is odds. Probabilities. He compares it to the odds the bookies are taking and lays down a bundle whenever his are more favorable. He just about breaks even."

Sam stopped again. His small eyes were wide and bright. "Well."

Carlotta rolled over before he could start again. Her scars shone in the twilight.

"I want to do some laundry." Her voice cracked with anger.

"That's an idea," I said. "I have some, too."

I went to the box beneath the bed and wadded my clothes under my arm. As I followed Carlotta out the door, I called over my shoulder, "You can make more coffee. There are cookies in the box."

Carlotta got her laundry from the car; it was a big T-shirt stuffed with other clothes. We stopped at Karafotia's for some cigarettes and a box of soap. Carlotta paused in front of a rack of apples and looked at them. After a while I realized she wasn't really looking at them. The little guy behind the cash register lifted his battered eyebrows and watched her. He sighed while he rang up my cigarettes.

"Is she sick? On drugs or something?"

"Sad, I guess."

"Why don't you take your grape soda from the cooler? Why should you torture yourself with lukewarm grape soda? Does she need anything? Tell me if she does."

I waited at the door until Carlotta came unstuck from the

apples. She looked around before she saw me and came out. We went down to the Siesta Time 24-Hour Laundromat.

Portland is one of those towns where a lot of the social life takes place in laundromats. Nearly everything else is black and cold by ten o'clock at night, but there is always a laundromat open somewhere. In the daytime I suppose they are full of the usual ladies popping in and out with their clothes separated carefully into whites and coloreds. These are the honest women whose men are out working. By five o'clock they've all gone home. After that, until eight, there are working girls and men, who, for whatever reason, do their own laundry. There are flirtations over the change machines. When the honest people go away there are long hours of empty brightness. In the long hours between nine at night and nine in the morning, there are peculiar goings-on in the laundromats. If you walk in at midnight there will be a lone body in shabby shoes propped on the bench frenziedly reading philosophy from a thick tattered book. Solitary figures ravage cigarettes beneath the harsh lights. In the winter, thin men sit out of sight of the door and cuddle the heat and movement of a washing machine to keep warm. Runaway children spend long hours here staring at their shoes. Runaway husbands pencil maudlin messages to half-forgotten women who may themselves be sitting in some nighttime laundromat. No laundromat is ever really empty in these hours. If you look carefully past the rows of metal, past the magazine scraps, into the corners where the day's spent matches and butts have drifted, there is always somebody miserable sitting there. The social life consists of knots of juvenile enthusiasm, which, deliberately or not, is calculated to drive the melancholy natives out into the cold. It's only natural that adolescents should resort to laundromats in a town where the street corners are dark and frequently wet. And the college students go there, of course, to make just such sociological observations.

So Carlotta and I went down to the Siesta Time 24-Hour Laundromat to do the wash. To have some privacy. To talk.

My armload of clothes smelled about the same as hers. We didn't hesitate to throw them into the same machine. I put quarters into the slot and jammed them home.

"I'll pay for the drying," she said. We sat on a dirty green bench to wait. A lone woman in a business suit and house slippers was shaking out blouses before putting them into the dryer. She put in money and went to a corner to do her nails.

It was dark outside. The light fell in long tubes from the ceiling. It pretended to be honest, but only managed to be cruel. It made the tidy scabs on her cheeks look fresh somehow. Her hands were clasped on her knees. Her bare feet were gray on the gritty floor.

I told myself it was important to be sympathetic. I stared at the floor to avoid the effort of looking at her face.

"How do you feel?"

"I don't feel anything."

"You seem angry."

"Oh."

Didn't seem to be anyone home at her house.

"Do you blame him for the baby dying?"

"Han Shan? No. He just disgusts me."

The machine groaned in front of us. The dryer at the end of the room tossed clothes aimlessly, lazily, while the lady in the corner intently filed her nails. It was raining again.

"I don't understand."

"He was disgusting up there. He and Lichtenstein together disgusted me."

We weren't whispering but we sat so close, our throats

tight, that our voices hissed and shuddered like we were sharing secrets.

"They didn't do anything. They talked. Han Shan talks about the ice in the bucket, but he doesn't mention how the bucket got up the hill. They cut down a tree the first day we were there for firewood. At first one of them, or both of them, would build the fire, but after a while they just sat and talked and strolled around under the trees. Lichtenstein always wanted his clothes washed."

There was poison in her eyes and in her clenched fist.

"How did you do the laundry, anyway?"

"In the stream on a rock. That was nice until it got so cold. Then my hands would hurt and nothing would dry. They complained if I put things near the fire. There'd be diapers hanging for days all over the room. I kept running out."

"It must have been cold."

"Han Shan didn't care about the baby."

"You mean, that it died?"

"That, too. He got sick of it. He didn't say anything, but when the baby cried, he'd get this mean look on his face."

"When did that start?"

"He was that way before we even went to the mountain. You know how he was supposed to cook and do the housework for a while after the baby was born? That lasted two days, exactly. He swept the house and made the rice and tea. The baby had to eat every three hours then, so I kept waking up all the time. All night and all day. Every three hours. And every time he ate, he shat. Eight times a day. It was green. At first, very dark green, then a chartreuse. After a few weeks it turned yellow. That was so beautiful. They weren't shit colors, they were deep and bright. The shit was so soft it was like oil paint, straight from the tube. And it didn't smell bad, really. Strange, but not bad.

"Anyway, the third day I was up in the morning feeding the baby. When I put him to sleep I made some tea and brought it to Han Shan. He'd been trying to be nice. He thought I was mad at him for running away when the baby was being born, so he kept asking if I wanted anything and then making a huge mess in the kitchen. I brought this bowl of tea for both of us to have in bed. He sat up and asked me how I felt. I said, 'Fine.' Starting from then he didn't do anything more. He left it all for me."

"Well, you always wanted to be a squaw."

I shouldn't have said it. It just came out. It took a second to hit her. Then I could feel her shrinking away from me. Her whole body shied from my touch.

"Carlotta, I'm sorry. I didn't mean that, the way it sounded. I meant that things were already set up that way between you and Sam. You'd always done the work."

Her black eyes pounded me with hate.

"I'd forgotten about you. The way you are. You never even came back after you saw the baby. All that fine advice before he was born, and then you just dropped out."

"I know. I know. I hide my head during the scary parts in the movies, too."

"I don't doubt it."

"Carlotta, I'm sorry. I'm sorry. I'd like to have been brave and smart. I wanted your baby to grow up. It never occurred to me that he wouldn't. I thought that he'd be peculiar, but that he wouldn't have the same things wrong with him as Sam and me. And maybe you."

The moving water in the machine changed speed. Carlotta cried quietly. The lady in the corner nibbled the end of her nail file and read the ads in a ragged section of a derelict magazine.

"His eyes were still dark. They were going to be dark brown. And the way he'd look at things. He was really looking at things."

"How did it happen?"

"I don't know. I'd just fed him. He was only getting up once in the night to eat by that time. He took a lot of milk. I changed him. It was hard there. There wasn't anyplace warm to undress him. I had to just unwrap his bottom half and be very quick. He had a bad rash, too. It had bumps and red scabs. I had some lard for it, but it didn't work. I couldn't bathe him after the snow came. I was afraid to. At first Han Shan would hold up a blanket near the fire when I had the water warm. To keep out the wind. I'd sit there with the baby and wash him all over. But then Han Shan started going for a walk whenever I told him I wanted to bathe the baby. Lichtenstein always went with him. Sometimes I thought they were homosexuals. Han Shan kept talking about putting mud in all the cracks in the walls, but then the ground froze. Then he said when it had snowed enough it would drift up all around the walls and keep the wind out. But it didn't drift up. The snow didn't pile up at all until it got into the trees. Cold like that is just like being cut. When it's deep enough it loses its name and it's just pain. The same as all pain, no matter what causes it.

"He was beginning to smile. Just beginning. It would happen as if by accident. When his belly was full and he was dry and his thick little lips would open, crooked. You could see his gums. He looked so silly . . . or something."

Her tears fell faster, but her face was still. I folded my hands around her cold hands and we sat crying quietly on the bench. The lady in the suit marched over to the dryer. She banged it open and pulled out armfuls of clean white blouses. She folded them up and put them in a plastic bag, then paused in the doorway. The clothes still must have been warm in her arms. It had started to rain. The woman ducked, leaned forward, and disappeared into the rain.

The machine cycle changed.

"It was like this: I carried him during the day. On my belly. You saw the sling I made. He ate around noon. He ate again at four thirty or so. We didn't have a clock, but around that time, anyway. Then I made supper. Rice. Sometimes I fried apples to put into it. It takes a long time over an open fire. I kept the fire going all day. It was hard to start. I had to lay him down when I cut wood. I was afraid a splinter would hit him, or the butt of the ax. I'd try to find someplace soft, but after the snow came . . . I asked Han Shan to get me a piece of rubber, something waterproof, but he couldn't find anything in that town. Lichtenstein had a slicker, but he was afraid the baby would piss on it. But I think he was warm when I was cooking. One side of him was against me and the fire must have warmed his other side. We ate early so I could have time to heat water for the dishes. When it was cleared up, the dishes, I gave the leftovers to the chickens and the goat. When that was all over, the baby would be hungry again. He only woke up once in the night after that treat.

"On that day, dinner was finished and those two had gone outside. I changed him and fed him. He was fine. There was nothing wrong with him. I put him down in his box and draped a blanket over so the wind wouldn't get at him. Then I went down with the bucket to get water for the morning. The stream was down the hill. There was a dirt road up to the cabin that cars could use. But you crossed that road and went straight down through the brush to the stream. It was steep. The water was dark, almost black. The edges were frozen. There was just a clear run in the middle. Coming back up was the worst. You had to grab branches and rocks to pull yourself up with one hand and try not to lose the water. The sun doesn't reach there even in the afternoon, so nothing thaws at all. They were sitting out front talking. They didn't pay any attention when I came past with the bucket. Do you know how that kind of anger eats at you? I hated them. I went in and put the bucket by the fire. I rubbed my hands and jumped up and down fast to get warm. There was some leftover rice on a piece of paper. I was going to throw it to the chickens. I took a bite and I went over and lifted the blanket, still chewing, you see. To look at the baby. He was dead. Just dead. That's all."

Our hands sweated together. The machine had finished. Silent now. Carlotta's eyes were dull and she continued to cry.

"What about the dog and the goat?"

"What about them? That was nothing. It should have been Han Shan and Lichtenstein. But I didn't have the guts. Even then."

I slid my hand wetly from Carlotta's. My legs were stiff. My back was cramped. I opened the machine and hauled out twisted clothes, piled them on my arm and moved carefully toward the dryer so they didn't fall to the filthy floor. Dimes in the slot, slammed the door. Air blew, the drum turned, and the little pile of clothes tossed roughly behind the glass window.

"Did this cabin have a dirt floor?"

"Wood."

Carlotta was hunched on the bench. Behind her on the wall there was a faded old mural. A big cartoon sombrero with the regulation legs and feet coming out from underneath. An imaginary cactus on a wavy blue horizon line. Maybe the owner's wife painted it. Or his oldest daughter who would have liked to go to art school, but then she got married. One day twenty years ago, slapping paint on the new green plaster wall and laughing at the trademark of what was supposed to be the first in a long chain of Siesta Times.

"The sheriff's wife. I should have killed her, too. She kept saying, 'Let me put him out in the hall. Was it a boy?' 'Put him on the sofa. There's no reason to hold him now.' And then she kept pouring tea and eating this meat. She was fat. Flaps hanging. All these doilies on the arms of the chairs. She kept saying, 'Drink your tea, dear. You must keep up your strength.' And she said, 'I know it's always terrible when it's your firstborn. We lost three of our seven, but the first boy was strong, thank God.'"

Carlotta snickered. It sounded dangerous somehow. The scratches on her cheeks twitched, then her face was expressionless again. Her eyes held mine, watching me. Triumphant Madonna sorrow. My hands were clammy and shook at my sides.

"What did you do with the shitty diapers? Did you have a diaper pail or something?"

She frowned. "I rinsed them in the stream. Why?"

"I don't know. I'm just trying to figure out what it was all like. Did he dirty a lot of them?"

"Yellow. He shat yellow. Three or four times a day, but never much at a time."

Her brows lifted, and for a moment she looked bewildered. She started to cry again. Some lost question in the angle of her eyebrows. When she spoke, her voice was low and broken, clogged with mucus.

"I loved his shit."

*, *, *,

We walked back in the rain with the hot clothes under our shirts to keep dry. I lifted my face up for the rain to wash off my sticky tears. They say the rain isn't clean anymore, either.

We stopped on the deep old porch to catch our breath for the stairs. Carlotta slumped against the wall.

"What are you going to do now?"

It was dark in the way of lighted towns. She looked to me like a figure in an old black-and-white photograph. I must have looked that way to her, too. Souvenirs of ourselves.

"I want to get to California. See my psychiatrist." The scratches on her face were nearly invisible in the light from the streetlamps. "Do you know anything about psychic readers?"

"There seems to be one on every block. I always figured half of them must be whores. Why?"

"I want to try to contact my baby. There was something in his eyes that makes me think it might be possible."

"What would he have to say? 'Goo'?"

She turned away from me sharply.

"Carlotta, I'm sorry."

"Are you going to open the door?"

"It's not locked."

She stepped inside. The vague yellow light in the hall colored her suddenly. She ran up the stairs. I followed her wet footprints. Arrived at the open door of my room with my laundry still bouncing under my shirt. Rennel's face was inquisitive. His coffee cup was empty and stained.

Sam watched Carlotta, anxiously. She stood over him, gripping the clothes and glaring.

"Do you really want to go right now?"

She didn't answer him, but turned and walked out the door without looking at my face. The stairs creaked beneath her.

Sam gave me a pained smile. "I thought you would be gentle with her."

"I'm too vain."

I threw my bundle of laundry into the cardboard box.

Plopped myself onto the floor and dealt angrily with a cigarette. Rennel cleared his throat.

"I've been telling Han Shan about the valve job I did on the Rambler. That's what his car needs. I'm going to get him started and then he is going to do it himself."

"Lovely."

Sam leaned forward with the light of another story on his face. "It might be interesting. I watched a man once who was a good mechanic. He was a simple guy. Wanted to make a good living for his kids. He kept stopping work to call his wife about her menstrual pains. The thing that struck me most was how much of the whole mechanic business was sheer superstition. He'd listen to the engine and run his hands over things. Then every once in a while he'd give some part of the contraption a slam with his wrench or jam a screwdriver into some hole and wriggle it around. All the time he'd talk to himself. He'd lean over the engine, staring at it with this bewildered look, saying, 'What the fuck is that?,' 'Ho, here's something,' going on like that constantly. He was like a high priest trying on different little rituals to bring on rain. Very interesting. He didn't really know why the things he did worked, but they did. Of course he didn't call it religion. He called it experience."

Rennel shook his head and waved away Sam's words.

"Believe it or not, some people really do know what they're doing."

I'd have been more interested if Rennel weren't thinking of himself when he said that. Instead I felt hollow, bleak. Darkness poured in through the skylight. My rain-soaked clothes chilled my skin.

"So what are you going to do, Sam?"

"Well! I'm going to get some new valves at an auto parts store, which has got to be one of the most mysterious premises open to lay visitors, it's like a reliquary or something. And I'm going to get grease all over my clothes and hands and lean over the engine with a cigarette hanging out of my mouth and burning my eyes. Whenever anybody on the street stops to ask me what I'm doing I'll wipe my hands on a red rag and talk about combustion and gaskets and pistons. I'll drink beer at lunch. Maybe I'll change my name to Gary and get a job in a service station." He smiled. "I think that's probably what I'll do."

He rose slowly out of the chair. Grains of tobacco fell to the floor from his lap. "I'd better go."

Rennel asked, "Do you want me to drive you?"

"No. I'd like to walk in the rain. I might catch Lotta."

Sam stopped in the doorway, looking for something more to say.

"Whatever happened to your six-guns, Sam?" I asked.

He smiled and straightened a little. "You know, I'd forgotten all about them. I think they're in a trunk somewhere."

He waved and left.

Rennel's eyes were half closed. He looked almost sick. Drifts of his smoke were visible in the dim light. Finally he turned to me and the hurt in his eyes hurt me.

"There was a baby, wasn't there?"

"I think so."

We sat looking at each other. Not a very comforting sight for either of us. Loneliness is hard and cold. A sick thing.

"Rennel, do you suppose we ought to live together for a while? You and me?"

His face hardened. His hips undulated briefly in his leather pants. "No. Actually, not." He sighed. "No," he repeated. "I don't think that would be very nice at all."

He got up then and went away. I climbed up onto the chaise. Carlotta's cup, full of dark coffee, was beside me. The smoke lay still on the air. The rain pecked at the skylight all that night.

The cat, the fish, and the toad

I might as well get a cat. Why not have the picture complete? Not having a cat may be an originality I can't afford anymore.

This is going to be one of my sluttish days. I will not get dressed. I will keep the lamps on all day. It's raining anyway. If it rains for a week, I'll have a sluttish week.

I think the most depressing thing about this past weekend was that Rennel slept. It would have been all right if he had dozed off with my pages fallen in his lap and happened to sleep till morning. But he stacked the papers in a neat pile on the desk. He went into the bathroom and brushed his teeth and put on his pajamas and then deposited himself tidily in the bed I had made for him on the sofa. His glasses folded neatly on the coffee table. His blue velvet robe on a chair above his slippers. I found him that way the next morning. He had even brushed and hung his suit. He lay flat on his back pouting softly at the ceiling. His eyelids swollen over their contents. It made me angry. I went straight through to the kitchen and made a lot of noise to wake him up.

His stomach seems to have settled with age. He's become a big breakfast feeder. I was thrown off by his ankles and feet. I had quite forgotten other people's unclad ankles and indiscreetly presented feet beneath breakfast tables. His manner was clinically cheerful. Nobody could ever complain that Rennel was unwilling to discuss.

"Tell me now," with his cheek full of half-mauled toast, "have you always felt such resentment for me? Do you still?"

"I'm too gray and fat now to resent anything."

"You're the same size now that you've always been."

"I've been pretty fond of you for years now, off and on."

"Yet you have insulted me, and Sam, and yourself. You've insulted us all."

"Do you think so? I thought it was the truth."

"Babies die."

"Yes."

"We all die."

"It's not the death, it's the pain."

"Pork fat."

"Have some toast."

"I'm going to send you down Greek honey."

"If you're finished with the bacon pass it over here."

"Why don't you do something about these poor damned fish?"

I've just been out to the kitchen for my day's supplies. I fed the fish. I have the cookie jar and a quart of milk. Two detective novels. The bed is still warm from my night's sleep. I shall have a rich sluttish day and tomorrow I'll clean house and ask at the pound about cats. Or there's that white brute at the butcher's. They always drown her litters anyway. If I took one of her next batch it wouldn't do any harm. We could play out a cartoon tableau, the cat and the fish and I. Still, I don't know if I'm ready for a warm-blooded creature yet. Would a cat eat a toad?

EDITOR'S NOTE

Naomi Huffman

For years I've kept multiple copies of Katherine Dunn's *Geek Love* around; right now three editions sit on my bookshelf, and one in the seat pocket of my car. Each time I read it, I am stunned by Dunn's singularly depraved imagination and her don't-give-a-fuck swagger, how her sentences strut across the page.

After her death from lung cancer in 2016, my interest in Dunn became insatiable. I read everything I could about her. I'd initially assumed *Geek Love* was her only book, the single pearl of a dark and brilliant imagination, but then I learned about *Attic* and *Truck*, the novels she published twenty years before *Geek Love*. I devoured them and still wanted more. In the online catalog of Dunn's archive, at the Aubrey R. Watzek Library at Lewis & Clark College in Portland, Oregon, where Dunn once taught creative writing, I found a list of several short stories I'd never read. Most of them were published in the 1990s in small, now-defunct journals, which explains why they'd eluded my initial search. Editions of these journals were nearly impossible to find online, so I wrote to the staff at Lewis & Clark College and crossed my fingers. Within a few days, I received an email from Zach Selley, the associate head of special collections at the Watzek Library. He sent me images of the original handwritten and typewritten pages. Reading them, I was reminded what it is like to sit in the magnetic field of Dunn's imagination, to be jolted by her voice.

Zach introduced me to Eli Dapolonia, Dunn's surviving son, who, at the time, still lived in Portland. We struck up a correspondence; he was generous with stories of his mother and patiently answered my questions. In September 2019, I flew to Portland to visit the archive in person. Eli and I met for breakfast at the Stepping Stone Café, where Dunn once waitressed. Over coffee and eggs, he told me about sitting at the chrome bar top after school while she finished her shifts. When I described the difficulty of locating her stories, he said it had been very important to his mother to see her work in small journals, even after the success of *Geek Love*. He also told me about *Toad*, his mother's completed but unpublished novel (Harper and Row, the publisher of *Attic* and *Truck*, declined the novel, even after a round of revisions). He thought I might like to read it, too.

␥ ␥ ␥

Sally Gunnar, the maligned and self-deprecatory central character of *Toad*, reminds me of myself in my twenties. She scuffs around in a pair of beat-up leather boots, smokes too much, spends a lot of time thinking about writing but never getting around to it. She toils at menial jobs and earns enough cash to make possible this lifestyle but not much else, which is fine by her—her desires are unconventional, if a little vague. When it all seems pointless, she sinks into her decaying pink velvet chaise (mine was green), the secondhand centerpiece of her shitty attic apartment, to drink purple soda, nurse her disappointments, and wait for something else to happen: "I lay there with the weight of unspecified darkness, contemplating suicide, and hoping for an interruption." I knew *Toad* would be as meaningful to other readers, that it was a significant contribution to the history of women's writing and feminist fiction.

Despite how deeply I connected with *Toad*, I was unprepared for the isolation of editing the work of a deceased writer. Up to that point, for me, editing had always been a conversation, a pleasing tension between two people. When I prepared to make even the smallest edits to *Toad*, I found I could not; the writer wasn't there. I held both ends of the rope, and the responsibility was stymying.

A deft procrastinator, I decided to read *Geek Love* yet again, in hopes that it might divine the way forward. In fact, the table of contents offered some advice. *Geek Love*'s chapters have brassy titles like "Popcorn Pimp" and "Blood, Stumps, and Other Changes." *Toad* initially lacked uniform section breaks as well as demarcated chapters and parts, so I imposed chapter titles composed from the text. It felt like a small thing, but afterward the novel possessed a discernible architecture upon which I made subsequent changes.

In *Toad*, there are two Sallys: one is a young woman who is plagued by self-hatred, maintains a string of relationships with unfaithful men, and is disappointed in her own unrealized dreams. The other Sally, having survived all this, relishes the life she's made: lonely and modest, but sweeter because all of it is her design. In the original draft, the alternating perspectives were sequenced haphazardly; I rearranged some for the sake of pacing, and others so that the Sallys more clearly mirror each other across time.

*, *, *

The months I spent reading Dunn's unpublished fiction are marked by a frustrated incredulity. Surely someone has been here before, I thought, again and again. Wouldn't someone else already have come looking for this? One afternoon, I printed it all out, everything that I had read in full: the manuscript for *Toad*, the transcribed stories, extant poems, and correspondence from the archive. I wanted to see it all together, feel the weight of it. All this work, all these words, all the hours, all this time, I thought, turning the pages, turning the pages. This writing, these words, this woman.

After *Toad* was announced, one journalist described it as a "lost" book, a term often applied to texts unearthed from archives or reissued after many years of being out of print. But it never seemed accurate. It overlooks the detailed work the archivists at the Watzek Library devoted to Dunn's papers to guarantee they *weren't* lost. And it suggests that one only had to read this book to see its value. I've come to consider "lost" a sinister fiction that elides the cascading failures of an industry that for centuries has heralded the work of white cis men and erected a canon that celebrates only a sliver of the spectrum of human experience. The consequences of this narrow-mindedness, this pitiful vision, are vast. It normalizes and maintains the belief that great literature is the province of certain men and infers that the women and other outsiders who rival them are unusual and rare. Their books aren't lost; they're forgotten, neglected, subjugated by a system that disincentivizes their existence. I'm glad *Toad* is no longer relegated to that fate. I hope it helps usher in a greater understanding of what we can learn from overlooked literary histories.

*, *, *,

I don't know that it would have occurred to me to search for more of Dunn's work if it weren't for small presses, journals, and magazines like And Other Stories, *Another Gaze*, Cita Press, Dalkey Archive Press, Deep Vellum, Dorothy, the Feminist Press, New Directions, New York Review Books, Persephone Books, the Second Shelf, Silver Press, Ugly Duckling Presse, Verso Books, Wendy's Subway, and many others. I am grateful for their inspired efforts, their differing visions of a more radical and inclusive publishing industry. I am thankful for the folks who read *Toad* alongside me: Mitzi Angel, Emily Bell, Jonathan Galassi, Sean McDonald, Jackson Howard, Julia Ringo, Patrick Ford-Matz, and especially Lydia Zoells and Daphne Durham.

And to Eli, for breakfast, and for your trust.

March 2022